❧ SHE KNEW SHE HAD HIM ❧

He was moving not just his arm but the weight of his whole body. Kori dropped the basket and pirouetted to face him. She glimpsed his startled eyes as she leaped into the air and kicked out. Her toe hit his wrist, hard. He gave a grunt of surprise as his hand opened, releasing the pole, letting it fly into the air.

Kori was already landing on her feet, dropping into a crouch. She fell backward, caught her weight on her hands, and kicked out with both legs, scissoring them around Werror's ankle. He flailed his arms, trying to keep his balance, but his forward rush had given him far too much momentum. He toppled like a great tree, struggling helplessly to pull his ankle free.

Kori released her hold as he hit the ground. She glanced up just in time to see the pole as it fell. She grabbed it out of the air and turned toward Werror as he rolled onto his back on the ground in front of her.

Kori angled the pole and stepped forward. She rested the end of the pole against the big man's chest. "I win the game, Werror," she said softly.

He turned to Kori, bowed his head, and held his hands out to her. "I acknowledge your strength as our chieftain. You have won my respect. . . . But one day," Werror went on, "we should play this again."

HarperChoice

THE OCEAN ❧ TRIBE ❧

CHARLOTTE PRENTISS

HarperPaperbacks
A Division of HarperCollins Publishers

HarperPaperbacks
A Division of HarperCollinsPublishers
10 East 53rd Street, New York, NY 10022-5299

This is a work of fiction. The characters, incidents, and dialogues are products of the author's imagination and are not to be construed as real. Any resemblance to actual events or persons, living or dead, is entirely coincidental.

ISBN 0-06-101011-1

Cover illustration © 1999 by Luis Royo

First printing: January 1999

Printed in the United States of America

Visit HarperPaperbacks on the World Wide Web at
http://www.harpercollins.com

❖ 10 9 8 7 6 5 4 3 2 1

THE OCEAN
❦ TRIBE ❦

PART 1

1

They were dangerously far from the shore when they lost their sail.

Kori had been daydreaming, lying in the bottom of the dugout canoe, staring up at the pale sky through half-closed eyes, enjoying the powerful rhythm of the ocean swell. There were few times like this in her life when she could find true peace and let her thoughts wander. She watched a gull as it circled high above, riding the wind, looking out across the world below. Kori wondered how it must feel to be so free. She had achieved a lot in her life—more than she had ever expected, and more than any woman could hope for. She was the founder of her tribe, the leader of her people; still, she felt constrained, frustrated by a great gulf between her vision of how things should be and—

Her thoughts were interrupted by a shouted command. Her daughter, Meiri, was holding the steering paddle while her son, Feroh, was sitting up by the mast.

"Turn to the south," Feroh called out, and a moment later the small craft heeled over sharply as it exposed its flank to the swell. With concern, Kori realized how much the wind must have risen. She heard the sail flapping noisily—and then, without warning, there was a terrible tearing sound.

For a moment she didn't move. Her mouth opened, but she didn't speak. She was frozen with disbelief. Then her strength returned and she dragged herself upright, her hand clenching painfully on the rough-hewn rim of the canoe as she stared at the terrible sight in front of her.

A short, sturdy hardwood mast was set in the center of the canoe, braced with cords of woven hemp. The mast was fitted with two horizontal spars that carried a sail stitched from sections of deer skin. Now the stitches had ripped completely apart, leaving the sail in two pieces that flapped uselessly in the wind.

Kori's shock turned to anger. "Feroh!" she screamed.

She saw her son's back stiffen, but he didn't look around. *Too proud*, she thought to herself. *And too ashamed.*

She turned to her daughter, kneeling behind her in the stern. "Meiri! What happened?"

Meiri was twelve, one year younger than Feroh. She had inherited Kori's kind, pleasant features, but she lacked her mother's strength. The girl's face was full of fear as she stared wide-eyed at Kori. "We were turning," she said.

"Yes," Kori said, trying to rein in her temper. "I know we were turning. What happened?"

Meiri glanced nervously at Feroh, then back at Kori. The girl's hands moved restlessly on the handle of the steering paddle. "He—" She paused, gathering her courage. "He dropped the rope."

"Liar!" Feroh shouted.

Kori looked toward him and found him glaring at her, his eyes full of righteous anger. Those eyes were so dark, so fierce, their intensity disturbed her. Her son was a handsome boy, with a proud jaw, a firm mouth, and dense, wavy black hair that hung free around his shoulders. He could be charming when he chose, but even when he smiled there was still something strange in his eyes, as if a part of him was never friendly, always looking out at the world with suspicion and hostility.

She saw that he was holding the ropes attached to the spars—but he'd had time to pick them up while her back was turned, and Kori knew instinctively that Meiri was telling the truth. Feroh had lost his grip on the ropes while the canoe was turning across the wind, causing the sail to flap wildly, which was when it had ripped in two.

"I'm not a liar." It was Meiri's voice, sounding plaintive. She turned to Kori. "Tell him it's not right to call me a liar."

Kori held up her hand. It no longer mattered who was at fault; other things were more important. Now that she was sitting up, she saw they were much farther from the shore than she'd realized. The canoe was equipped with paddles, but paddling all the way back would be an arduous task. They'd be lucky to make it before dark.

Also, the wind had picked up, and it had veered, moving to the south, so that it blew parallel with the shore. It would be no help to them now that their sail was gone.

Worse still, Kori saw that the weather was changing. In the early morning the clouds had been high and thin, a pale uniform haze promising calm weather for the rest of the day. But that promise had been broken. More clouds were blowing in, lower and darker, and in the far south Kori saw dark columns of rain.

She shivered. Her warm, languorous mood was just a memory as she found herself confronted with a real threat to their survival. She cursed herself for daydreaming instead of keeping watch over Feroh—yet he should have known better. She glared at him. "Why did you bring us out so far?"

"The fishing is better here." He spoke without a moment's hesitation, and she saw he'd expected the question.

Kori shook her head impatiently. "The ocean is always generous. There are more fish than we need, no matter where we cast the nets." She knew the real reason he had taken the canoe so far: he wanted to prove his prowess. He always wanted to go farther than he had gone before. "Cut the nets," she snapped at him.

Feroh looked shocked.

"There's a storm coming!" Kori said. "We have no sail, and we're so far from the shore, no one can see us. The wind has veered, and it may veer more. We must carry as little weight as possible."

She saw a flicker of self-doubt in Feroh's face as he understood, finally, the seriousness of what had happened.

Kori hated the idea of losing the nets. She had helped to weave them herself, sitting with the people of her tribe, painstakingly stripping, stranding, and knotting the precious hemp. But as she looked again to the south, a sudden gust of wind smote her in the face, so powerful that it almost tipped her backward. "Do as I tell you," she said, turning back to Feroh. She pulled a flint knife from her pouch, leaned forward, and started sawing through the nearest length of heavy twine where it was knotted around a peg in the side of the canoe. She felt almost as if she were amputating one of her limbs, but it had to be done.

Feroh reached across and cut the other cord, and the little craft leaped forward as the net sank behind it.

"Now," said Kori. "There's nothing to fear if we head directly for the shore. But it's a long journey, and we must save our strength. Do you both understand?"

Feroh nodded reluctantly, avoiding her eyes, and she realized he was angry with her for criticizing him and taking away his authority. He so wanted to be a man, and in fact, he almost was a man. Three days from now, he would have his coming-of-age ceremony. But at this moment he had to obey his mother, and she didn't care whether he liked it or not.

She turned and looked at Meiri. The girl's face was even more fearful than before. "We will be all right," Kori said, softening her tone. "Just do as I say. Trust me, Meiri."

The girl gave a quick nod. She looked down at her hands, still clutching the steering paddle.

"You come forward," Kori said. "I'll steer."

The girl pulled the paddle out of the water and stood up. Her nervousness made her clumsy. The canoe rocked, the outrigger on the left dipped down beneath the waves, and Meiri almost lost her balance. Quickly Kori reached out and caught her daughter's arm, steadying her.

For a moment Kori looked into Meiri's face and saw herself at that age, awkward and insecure, always afraid of making mistakes. "Be calm and take small steps," Kori said, squeezing Meiri's hand tightly. She stood up, and they changed places with elaborate caution while the canoe pitched under them on the heavy swell.

Kori kneeled in the stern on the square of soft hide that was placed there, and she picked up a spare paddle that had been stowed against the hull. Meiri squatted near the mast, while Feroh moved silently to the prow.

Kori turned toward the shore, and all three of them began dipping their paddles. They were traveling across the wind now, which meant that the waves were crossing their path, making the canoe roll more violently than before.

Kori looked at the outriggers, small hollowed sections of tree trunk on wooden spars that braced either side. Without them the canoe would capsize immediately. Of course, there was no reason why the spars should break, and Kori told herself not to think such terrible thoughts. Her husband, Uroh, had built this canoe with his own hands, and he was a meticulous craftsman. In fact, he was the one who had conceived of outriggers originally. Until that time, no one had ever dared to venture onto the open sea.

Kori felt a sudden deep pang of yearning. She wished more than anything that Uroh could be with her now. Yet, if he was so meticulous, why hadn't he checked the stitching of the sail? It must have grown rotten, soaked repeatedly with salt water and dried by the sun. He should have known that. He *would* have known it if he'd spent more time thinking about practical matters instead of retreating from her into his own strange, private world.

But this was no time to think of such things. Kori noticed Feroh leaning forward, putting all his weight into each stroke of his paddle. He was working too hard, and Meiri was trying to imitate him, which was exactly what Kori had feared they would do. At this rate they would exhaust themselves long before they could reach the shore.

Kori opened her mouth to admonish them, then realized there was a better way. She started singing one of her tribe's seafaring songs. "Across the water," she shouted out, "through the day, we trust the sun to guide our way. Across the water, through the night—"

Instinctively her children joined in, and instinctively they slowed their paddling to the rhythm of the familiar words.

Another seagull drifted by, and Kori saw its beak open as it gave a hoarse, rasping cry. The wind was blowing so fiercely now, the gull made no attempt to fly against it or even across it. Kori glimpsed the bird's black, gleaming eye gazing down at her. For a moment she felt as if the gull were chiding them for their foolishness in challenging the ocean with nothing more to protect them than a fragile wooden shell. Then the bird was gone, swept away by the wind.

As Kori and her children sang, the canoe made its way slowly among the heavy gray waves, heading for the distant line of cliffs that marked the shore. But the light was gradually dimming as heavier clouds blew in from the south, and soon the waves were wearing white crests that trailed tails of spray. The canoe lurched vio-

lently, throwing its crew from side to side, and it started
shipping water.

"Meiri!" Kori shouted. "Tie yourself to the mast,
then bail."

Meiri set aside her paddle, groped in the bottom of
the canoe, and found a long leather thong. She lashed it
around her waist, then around the mast. Her nervousness and her cold hands made her fumble with the
thong, but she finally finished the task and picked up
the leather bucket that was kept for bailing. She started
scooping water with it and throwing it over the side.

Kori looked to the south, hoping to see the end of
the storm clouds, but instead she saw that the weather
was still worsening. She told herself to be strong. The
canoe had been made by hollowing out a massive redwood tree; it would stay afloat even if it was filled to the
brim with water. Still, she could feel the cold wind, the
spray, and the water in the bottom of the canoe leeching
heat from her body, and as she peered ahead, trying to
see the shore beneath the dark clouds, she heard an
ominous hissing sound that grew swiftly louder.

She looked to her right and saw a curtain of rain
moving in. The hiss of droplets striking the ocean
became a roar, and the light dimmed till she could
barely see the mast in front of her. Rain smote her like a
weapon, sluicing across her face, coating her skin under
her clothes. She gasped. The visibility was so bad, she
could no longer tell which way the canoe was heading.
Worse, she found herself growing nauseated as the craft
pitched under her. If she couldn't see the horizon, it was
almost impossible to keep her sense of balance.

She pulled her paddle in and thrust it between her
knees. There was no point in paddling so long as she

didn't know which way they were heading. She shuddered, bending double and clutching herself. Surely, she thought, they could not die here. So many times in her life she had been bold, taking risks and exposing herself to danger. It would be absurd, humiliating, to lose her life out here in this storm.

"Meiri!" she cried out. "Feroh!"

She heard their answers faintly through the roar of the rain.

"There is nothing we can do till the rain stops. Protect yourselves as well as you can. Be patient, and be brave. It will pass."

Neither of them answered. Meiri was too scared, and Feroh was still too proud—or perhaps he heard the uncertainty in her voice, and he saw no point in sharing her pretense.

Kori was stricken with feelings of shame. Even if Feroh had been reckless, allowing them to venture so far from land—even if he had been careless, allowing the sail to tear—still, she carried the ultimate burden of responsibility. If her children drowned with her here, it would be her fault.

The sea surged, tipping the canoe till she feared she would be thrown out of it. She retrieved her paddle, dug it into the water, and fought to turn the craft into the fierce wind. This way, at least, they would be safe from capsizing.

Then she hunkered down again, trying to find strength inside herself among the towering waves as the rain smacked her shoulders and the wind tore at her clothes.

2

The rain lasted for longer than she thought possible. The wind blew stronger, and stronger still. From time to time she raised her head and squinted ahead, but all she could see were the hunched shapes of her children amid the storm.

Kori clung to the canoe as it careened from one wave to the next, and she tried to be patient. The storm would pass; it had to pass. But it was not in her nature to sit passively and endure such a punishment. She found herself weeping—not from fear but in sheer frustration.

As the rain and spray stole more heat from her body, she began to shiver violently. Her hands and feet were painful for a while, and then they turned numb. The coldness began to chill even her thoughts, and in the swirling grayness she glimpsed fleeting shadows at the edges of her vision. Some of her people believed that there were ocean spirits that helped or punished those who were foolish enough to stray into storms. Kori rejected such superstitions; still, she feared the shadows because they were like dream shapes, making her wonder if she was losing her grasp on reality. She slapped herself with her numb hands, trying to remain alert.

She forced herself to summon her strength. She breathed deeply and began to sing—but not one of the seafaring songs. "We are the people of the Ocean Tribe," she sang, shouting the words into the rain. "Upon the land or o'er the sea, we are forever proud, we are forever free. Friendship and peace are all we seek; but in our generosity, we are never weak. All are welcome in our domain—but those who turn against us shall be slain."

She had created the song herself, for her people. Again she sang it—and this time she heard her children joining her, reluctantly at first, then with more vigor, till they were shouting with the same defiance. And somehow the song warmed her. So long as she could sing like this, surely nothing could take her life away.

Suddenly—miraculously—the rain ended. Kori looked up and saw that the sky was a lighter gray. Yet her relief was short-lived. As she looked around, trying to see among the waves, she realized that they had not moved to the edge of the storm, but to its center.

The air was dry here, but the wind was wilder, blowing first from one direction, then another, in sudden, vicious gusts that tore at the mast and slapped the tattered remnants of the sail against the spars, creating a flurry of sharp, cracking sounds.

She felt a terrible foreboding. Sometimes in the spring, cold air and warm air would mix over the ocean to create a small hurricane that wandered across the waves, whipping them so fiercely that they turned to foam. Several times she had witnessed this from the safety of the shore, but no one had ever seen it from within.

Feroh turned to face her. His black hair was saturated and pasted to his glistening skin. His eyes were wide with wonder as he looked past her. His mouth opened with a shout that was swept away by the gusting air. He pointed.

Kori turned and saw the vortex at the center of the storm, a wide swirling column of froth that had been torn from the surface of the sea. For a moment she found herself hypnotized by the spectacle. Then she seized her paddle and tried to urge the canoe away from the thing that threatened to devour her.

All three of them paddled furiously—but they had already lost much of their strength, and the canoe was sluggish, weighed down with more water from the high seas and the torrential rain.

The wind veered again, and Kori realized there was no way to predict its direction. The sea hurled the canoe to one side, and she cried out as she felt herself almost being thrown free. She flailed her arm and seized the edge of the canoe to save herself. Then, just as suddenly, it plummeted into a deep trough and her body slammed painfully against the opposite side of the wooden shell.

Bruised and shaken, she clawed herself back into a kneeling position. Meiri was still there, and Feroh—but another great wave lifted them, making the canoe spin around.

The wind and the sea were too violent, too powerful for her to fight. Kori let out a shout of despair. Once more she dipped her paddle, still trying move away from the whirlwind. But it was wandering randomly, and her efforts were just as likely to take her toward it as away from it.

She saw Meiri staring at her. The little girl's face was blank with fear. Her cheeks were wet with tears amid the ocean spray. She reached out to Kori as if she just wanted to cling to her.

Kori wanted to comfort her daughter, but more than that, she wanted to save her. Again she dipped her paddle, just as Feroh voiced another warning shout.

At first Kori couldn't understand. He was no longer looking at the whirling center of the storm; he had seen something else. Then she saw it herself: a black, glistening, rounded form, like a huge boulder amid the waves. For a moment Kori wondered, incredulously, how they could have moved so close to the shore. Then the rounded shape rose up and a powerful jet of water blasted from a blowhole. A mouth slowly opened, revealing a curving row of conical teeth.

Orcas were a familiar sight up and down the coast. Kori knew that the great whales never attacked humans, but still, she was transfixed with shock by the sight of its mouth gaping so close, she could almost reach out and touch its teeth with the tip of her paddle. Then she saw the creature's tiny eye, down at the side of its great head, and she realized that it was watching her.

Another big wave came between them—and the whale disappeared. Kori wondered why it had materialized at the center of the storm, and why it had left just as suddenly. Then there was a scraping sound, and she felt the canoe shudder under her. It lurched upward, making her scream. There was a furious frothing as the ocean churned behind her, and she realized the whale was lashing its massive tail, butting against the canoe.

Kori dropped her paddle and braced herself as the canoe leaped forward. Within moments, it was skipping across the water like a stone. She squinted against the blast of wind, and with mounting horror she realized that the whale was pushing them almost directly toward the center of the whirlwind. The roaring vortex came closer, and she felt her sodden clothes flapping, tugging at her body, trying to lift her entirely into the air. Her braids unraveled and her hair streamed out, sucked by the terrible wind. Her body felt light, as light as a seagull. She imagined that if she let go of the canoe she would find herself flying up to join the birds above the clouds. She gasped, finding it hard to breathe. "Hold on!" she cried to her children. "Be strong! Hold on!"

For an instant the canoe seemed weightless. Kori looked up and glimpsed the core of the vortex lit by a pale, salmon colored, eerie glow from above. She saw strands of seaweed and streamers of water whirling into the air—and then the canoe moved on and plunged back into the dim gray fury of the rain.

Still the orca drove them forward, forcing a path through the storm. It paused for a moment, and she heard a great gushing sound as it raised its head behind her, blasted water from its blowhole, and took another huge breath. Then it sank back beneath the surface, and once again it thrashed its tail.

The canoe crested a wave and plunged down the other side, and its prow dug deep into the water, soaking Feroh where he squatted with his arms folded around his head. The canoe climbed another wave, plunged down, climbed again—

The speed of the violent pitching was terrifying. Kori found herself looking up at the dark clouds one moment, then down at water mottled with white, hurtling toward her so fast that it seemed certain to swallow them alive. Yet the canoe rebounded and rode to the crest of the next great wave, and the next, till Kori became numb, staring blankly, barely aware of the howling wind and the rain and spray that still lashed her face.

It seemed as if the pitching of the canoe would last forever. Finally though, the light grew slightly brighter and the rain eased a little, and Kori realized that the waves were no longer so frighteningly high.

More time passed, and the wind ceased its desperate howling. Kori peered ahead, and she dared to imagine that she saw a break in the weather. She told herself not to be seduced by a false hope; but she looked again, and truly they were emerging from the worst of the rain. The daylight was dim, but not because of the heavy gray clouds. The afternoon was almost over, and the sun was setting.

Then she heard a sound that roused her with a renewed stab of alarm. It was a rhythmic crash and roar—the sound of breakers pounding rocks on the shore.

She felt the canoe slowing its wild motion. She glanced behind her and saw the orca lagging back, then turning away. It paused for a moment, and she felt certain that it was watching her again. Then it sank beneath the waves, and she saw just its tail churning the sea as it swam away. She waited, but it didn't reappear.

She turned back to her children. "Meiri!" she cried out. "Feroh! Listen to me!"

Both of them were still hunkered down against the storm.

"Look ahead!" Kori cried. "Listen!"

Slowly they straightened up, and then they heard what she had heard. Feroh seized his paddle. He struggled onto his knees, turned, and squinted into the dim dusk light.

Now that they were close to the shore, the waves were rolling in, taking the canoe with them. The best that Kori and her children could do was try to steer a path among the great boulders just ahead.

But it was so hard to see! Kori strained her eyes—then cried out as a sheet of spray exploded in her face. She glimpsed a sheer stone surface looming in the dimness, and she flailed with her paddle. The tip of it met rock, and the paddled jerked in her grip, almost twisting out of her hands. The canoe lurched, and another wave thrust it forward with inhuman power. There was a terrible fracturing sound. The canoe jerked violently, then toppled to one side. With a stab of fear Kori realized that one of its outriggers had been torn off.

"Let go your paddles!" she shouted. "Get down!"

With the outrigger gone, she could only hope that the wooden hull would protect them like a turtle's shell. The canoe rolled over onto its side and started filling with water. Kori plunged beneath the surface, but she resisted the temptation to abandon the canoe and swim. Her unprotected body would be hopelessly vulnerable among the rocks.

Another wave lifted the canoe, and her face emerged long enough for her to take two desperate breaths. She glimpsed a thin strip of beach directly ahead, beyond the rocks. She didn't recognize it; her village must be far away. Then the canoe was carried forward, turning, spinning on the crest of the wave. Wet stone gleamed on either side of her. She heard the crash of the breakers, the hiss of the foam, and the sucking roar of the undertow.

She thought for a moment of Uroh and she shouted out to him silently inside her mind, because at this moment, she truly believed the ocean might kill her. A bone-jarring impact threw her against the bottom of the canoe. Her head slammed into the wood, stunning her. The canoe rolled across a flat rock, making tearing sounds. She tried to brace herself, but she didn't have enough strength left. She found herself flying out of the canoe, tumbling across the flat rock, then plunging down, splashing into the water. Instinctively she put out her hands to break her fall—and found her palms slapping against pebbles and stones just below the surface.

She rolled onto her back with the ocean surging around her. Another wave came in, engulfing her. With the last of her strength she sat up, fighting the fury of the sea as it threatened to drag her back. She reached out and gripped smooth stone crusted with barnacles and striped with seaweed. With a dim feeling of wonder at finding herself still alive, she struggled onto her feet.

Her legs almost buckled under her. She was so cold, so exhausted, so desperately tired—but she forced herself to stand. "Meiri!" she called out. "Feroh!"

There was a faint answering cry. She saw small, dark shapes up on the flat rock where the canoe had broken apart, and she realized that her children had managed to stop themselves from being thrown clear of it.

"Come to me!" she cried out. "Quickly!" She felt a great rush of emotion—excitement, relief, and gratitude—but still the emotion was tempered with caution. Even now her children could be swept back into the ocean.

Feroh scrambled toward her. Another wave broke around him and struck Kori in the face, but she hardly felt it. She seized Feroh's hand, and she exulted in the warmth, the life in his flesh.

"Meiri!" she called.

"I've hurt my arm." She sounded lost and scared.

"Come *here*!" Kori screamed at her.

Meiri crawled forward. Kori reached for her and dragged her off the rock, down into the water.

"No!" Meiri cried, as she felt the sea surging around her.

"You're safe," Kori told her, giving her a little shake. "We're on the beach. Do you hear me?"

The girl said nothing. Kori turned back to Feroh— and found him letting go of her, half running, half stumbling out of the sea onto a steep beach of rough sand.

Kori followed him, pulling Meiri after her. The girl had been so viciously pummeled by the storm, she still didn't seem to understand where she was. Well, she'd be able to rest soon enough.

Kori felt sand under the soles of her feet, and she realized that she had lost her moccasins. It didn't matter. Nothing mattered compared with the glorious, ecstatic feeling that came from being here on the land.

She moved farther up the beach, instinctively wanting to put as much space as possible between herself and the ocean. Then she found herself staggering.

The world turned, and the land tilted under her.

She fell on her hands and knees. The rough sand rasped against her skin. Her clothes were a sodden mass, weighing her down.

"Take your clothes off," she called to her children, knowing that even now they were still in some danger. The air was warmer, and there was no rain. Still, they had been deeply chilled by the ocean.

Kori struggled out of her clothes and kicked them away. The sand was dry; the storm hadn't touched the beach. It must have followed the line of the coast instead of pursuing them ashore.

"Dry yourselves on the sand," Kori called to her children. "So long as the water is on our skin, it will chill us." She rolled over, using the beach as a sponge to take the moisture from her body. She waited while Meiri did the same, then hugged the girl close.

"Here!" Kori called to Feroh. She dragged him to her, to conserve their warmth as much as possible. "We will rest a moment," she said. "We are safe now."

As she heard herself speak the words, the last of her strength ebbed from her. She slumped down with her children, still gasping and shivering from the storm. She closed her eyes, and she passed out.

3

Suddenly she was awake. She lay blinking, confused for a moment by fragments of a dream. Sunset had faded to a dim red line at the horizon. The sky was dark but clear, strewn with stars.

She was still lying on the beach. She was alive. Meiri was curled up against her, and Feroh was there too, all three of them huddling together, their skin coated with sand.

Kori told herself that there was nothing to fear. Yet something had woken her. A footstep? She sat up and looked around, and suddenly her breath caught in her throat as she saw a shadowy figure in the darkness.

Kori gave a little cry of surprise. The dark shape facing her was a man dressed in a bulky robe that rustled in a gentle breath of wind.

"Who are you?" she shouted at him.

He hesitated. She heard him breathing, and it made a rasping sound, as if he had a sickness. Then he turned his face so that it caught the last light of the sunset, and Kori felt revulsion mingling with her fear. His skin was so deeply furrowed and scarred, his face looked like old driftwood that had been eroded by the seasons and scored with a knife. Worse still, only one eye gleamed in the dimness. In place of the other was a dark, empty socket.

Kori was weak from her ordeal in the storm, but still she would do whatever she could to defend herself and her children. She looked around and saw her robe several paces away, lying where she had thrown it aside. She had a knife in her pouch, but her pouch was with her robe, and there was no way to reach it quickly enough.

She struggled up onto her feet and balanced her weight carefully, eyeing the stranger. She took note of the stranger's weak points—his throat, his stomach, his groin—so that she could kick him or strike him with her fist if he ran at her. He wasn't carrying a spear, but he might easily have some other weapon under his robe.

For a long moment they stared at each other.

"Who are you?" Kori shouted at him again.

Feroh stirred beside her, and then Meiri made a sleepy sound. Kori ignored them. She tensed as she saw the man gathering his robe up, as if he were freeing himself to run at her. But he turned away. He started fleeing from her up the beach, stumbling in the sand, flailing his arms to keep his balance. She heard the wheeze of his breathing as he climbed the slope and disappeared among dry scrub and stunted trees that grew where the sand ended.

Feroh was on his feet. He had seen the man and

was staring after him, ready to pursue him. Kori seized the boy's shoulder and held him back. "Don't be foolish," she whispered. "He may not be alone."

Feroh's face was a pale shape in the darkness as he gave her a doubting look. "If he had friends," said Feroh, "he would have called them down here."

Kori grunted with irritation. "Never attack unless you know the strength of your enemy."

Feroh jerked his shoulder free, but he remained beside her, glowering at the dark line of trees where the man had gone.

Kori tried to calm herself. Feroh was probably right: if the stranger was hostile, and he had friends, he would have called for their help. Still, she should leave this place immediately. Her tribe had no enemies among the other people who lived along the coast, but she didn't know how far her canoe had taken her. She could be in an unknown part of the land.

"Mother?" It was Meiri, sounding sleepy and confused. "What's happening? Where are we?"

"I don't know where we are," said Kori. "But our clothes should be drier now. Dust the sand off yourself and get dressed. We must head south."

"I'm tired," Meiri complained. "I hurt all over."

"You will do as I say," Kori said. "We're lucky to be alive, Meiri. But we may still be in danger."

"The stranger didn't attack us," Feroh said.

"No," said Kori, "but he didn't answer my challenge. He ran as if he feared us—which means he expected conflict between us. And there was evil in his face. I sensed it."

He gave her a doubting look. "Our tribe has no enemies."

"None that we know of," she snapped back at him. She squatted down, found her clothes, and opened up her pouch. It was wet inside, as she'd expected, so the tinder and fire sticks were useless. The little packets of medicinal herbs were still intact, though, and she found her bone needle and thread, leather thongs, strands of hemp, and flint knife.

She glanced at her children and saw them pulling on their leggings and robes. Both of them still had their moccasins. Kori wished she knew what had happened to hers. She hesitated for a moment, looking toward the ocean. She thought she saw a jagged silhouette atop a big flat rock, where the canoe had been smashed by the surf. Possibly, she might find her moccasins if she went there. There was a spear in the canoe, too—at least there had been. It could have been lost in the violence of the storm, or it could have been thrown clear, as Kori herself had been.

She made her decision. She wouldn't waste precious time hunting around in the dark. The most important thing was to move away from this place.

She seized her clothes and put them on. "Quickly now," she said, touching Meiri and Feroh on their shoulders and urging them forward.

She led them down to the edge of the sea. The surf was still heavy, even though the wind had died down. The white-crested breakers were phosphorescent in the night.

"Why must we walk down here?" Meiri said.

"The sea will hide our footprints," Kori told her. "I don't want anyone to follow us."

"You mean the man back there?"

"Yes, or perhaps other people from his tribe."

"Do you really think he wanted to harm us?" Meiri asked.

Instinctively Kori glanced behind her. But the beach lay empty. "I don't know," she said.

For a while the three of them walked without speaking, breathing heavily with the effort of hurrying across the soft, wet sand.

"I'm hungry," Meiri said.

"Stop complaining," Feroh snapped at her.

"We're all hungry, Meiri," Kori said, trying to be patient. "When it gets light I'll see where we are, and then we can go to the nearest tribe and ask them for food."

They walked for a while longer—and as the beach remained empty behind them, she began to feel more secure. When they reached a stony ridge that cut across the sand, Kori led Feroh and Meiri up onto it and followed it inland, away from the sea.

Meiri was stumbling, and Feroh was probably more exhausted than he would admit. Still, they had to find a safe resting place. Kori led them into a thin forest of pines. She moved slowly here, testing the ground with every step. Her feet were protected by a heavy layer of calluses, but she could still injure herself if she was careless.

They moved deeper into the forest, ducking low branches and detouring around brambles that they could barely see in the faint starlight that filtered down to the forest floor. Kori strained her ears, but all she could hear was the soft sound of footsteps on pine needles, and the roar of waves growing fainter behind them.

Finally they came to a thicket that she judged was

dense enough to hide them. "We will sleep here till morning," she said.

"Can we make a fire?" Meiri asked.

"Do you want that one-eyed man to find us?" Feroh snapped at her.

"There are dry leaves and pine needles for us to lie on," Kori said, kneeling and feeling the ground. "If we keep close together and cover ourselves with our robes, we should be warm."

"You don't know where we are, do you?" Feroh said, as the three of them hunkered down among the bushes, covering themselves as well as they could.

"No," said Kori. "Do you?" Feroh often roamed alone, just like Uroh. Kori, on the other hand, spent most of her time among the people of the tribe.

"I can't be sure of anything in the darkness," Feroh said.

"So, we will wait till dawn," she told him.

He grunted, barely acknowledging the sense of what she said. Kori suddenly found herself feeling angry with him for his surly nature and his lack of respect. She felt angry, too, with Meiri for complaining and asking for help. She had saved them, hadn't she? Despite everything, they were alive.

Then she realized she was feeling short-tempered because she was still angry with herself. Once again she cursed her own carelessness. Never again would she give Feroh so much responsibility without watching over him.

With difficulty, she stopped her chattering thoughts. Still, it was not easy to sleep. Her stomach was cramping painfully—but food wasn't their greatest worry. They could go without eating for days if they had to. They couldn't go without water, though, and she had no idea where they would find a stream.

She told herself not to worry about that now. She had to rest, otherwise she would be of no use in the morning. She wrapped her arm around Meiri, finding some comfort in her closeness. Already the little girl had fallen asleep.

Once again, Kori wished that Uroh was with her. She wondered what he was doing. He would have seen the storm, and he might think that she had died in it. Maybe he was searching the ocean for her now— although he was a cautious mariner, and he might not be reckless enough to go out onto the sea at night. No, he was probably lying on the straw mattress in the hut that they shared, wondering and worrying about her. She tried to call out to him with her mind, to tell him that she was alive. She imagined his face turning toward her, with his calm eyes and his friendly smile—and that was the last thing she thought of before she fell asleep.

4

Kori woke at dawn feeling so deeply, overwhelmingly tired, she couldn't understand how her eyes possessed the foolish strength to open. Her body felt so heavy and stiff, it pained her when she merely raised her arm to rub her face. For a moment she felt old, too old to be living like this, fighting storms at sea and confronting a sinister stranger on a dark beach. She had lived for thirty-four years; surely, she needed some rest.

But the emptiness of her stomach didn't allow her that option. That was why she had woken. She knew she must act to protect herself and her children.

She sat up, grunting with pain from the sore muscles in her back. Her feet were cold, and she saw they had been scratched by brambles during her short walk through the forest. She must replace her moccasins; that was her first priority.

Meiri and Feroh were still asleep. She decided not to disturb them yet. She reached for her pouch, pulled out her knife, and cut two long strips from her deer-skin robe. She wrapped the strips around her feet and up around her ankles and used her bone needle to punch holes in the leather. Finally she threaded thongs through the holes and tied them carefully, not too loose but not too tight.

Early-morning sun was striking between the trees, and there was a dawn chorus of shrill birdsong. Kori saw a thin film of dew glistening on the bushes around her, and she smelled pine sap and springtime vegetation. All around her she saw new, pale shoots among the darker green.

She looked down at Meiri. There was a large bruise on her forehead. One of her arms was stretched out from under her robe, and it, too, was mottled with purple bruises. The palm of her small hand was blistered and had been rubbed raw from the handle of the paddle.

Kori felt a pang of guilt for speaking harshly to the girl the previous night, but just as quickly she realized there had been no other choice. She turned and looked at Feroh—and gave a little start as she realized that he had woken and was watching her silently with his dark, intense eyes.

She smiled at him. "Did you sleep soundly?" she asked.

He nodded. He stood up, moving slowly, and she guessed that his muscles must be just as sore as hers. Still, he didn't utter even the tiniest sound of protest. Over the past few years, she had watched him learning to control all of his emotions, as if his most important goal in life was to conceal any hint of weakness. Perhaps, Kori thought to herself, after his coming-of-age ceremony he would feel less need to prove himself.

Feroh turned and stepped into the bushes, and she heard him urinating. Then he came back to her. "We must find water and food," he said.

"Yes," she agreed. She urged Meiri awake, ignoring the girl's little complaining noises. Then she led the two of them through the forest, heading toward the south.

For a long while they walked without speaking. Kori's improvised moccasins were clumsy on her feet, making it hard for her to walk as quietly as she liked. All her muscles still hurt, and the pain in her back was intense when she had to duck under low branches. Still, she forced herself to ignore it. She was constantly alert, watching for any sign of human life—and searching for any familiar landmark.

Meiri tugged at her robe. Kori turned and found the girl standing with her head tilted back and her lips slightly parted. Her expression was intent. "I smell something," she whispered.

Kori drew a slow breath, tasting the air. She frowned. "I don't think—"

"I smell it, too," Feroh interrupted. "Deer meat. Someone is cooking deer meat."

Kori looked from one of her children to the other. It was hard for her to accept that her sense of smell was not as sharp as it used to be, but she shouldn't be surprised. Young people were always better at picking up faint scents in the forest.

She licked her palm and held it up, turning it first one way, then the other. The wind was barely perceptible, but it was coming from the south. "They are ahead of us," she murmured.

Normally, she would have hurried forward, eager

to find the strangers and beg a portion of their game; but after her encounter with the one-eyed man she was determined to be cautious, and she saw her caution reflected in the faces of Meiri and Feroh. She didn't need to tell them to move quietly as she started creeping forward.

She paused often, but she saw no sign of human life. There were no broken blades of grass, no crushed leaves on the forest floor, and the carpet of pine needles was undisturbed.

Finally she smelled the odor of cooking meat herself, and it was undeniable. Her mouth started watering reflexively.

Directly ahead, the underbrush was thicker. With great care, she started threading her way among bushes and brambles, bending each slender branch aside. She glanced back at Meiri and Feroh—and froze, sensing something that she couldn't name. A prickling sensation started at the back of her neck and spread down across her shoulders.

She realized then, there had been a subtle change in the steady sound of birdsong. It came more from behind her now than ahead of her. Directly opposite her, a thrush burst out of its nest high in a tree, screeching with alarm.

Kori tensed as she saw a tiny movement among the leaves. Something caught a stray ray of sun. A spear shaft? She chided herself for letting her imagination color her judgment; but no, it *was* a spear shaft. She opened her mouth to shout to Meiri and Feroh, but at that instant a man came out from his hiding place, making a huge amount of noise as he swung down from branch to branch, finally leaping to the ground. She glimpsed his tanned skin, his robe flapping around him as he reached for the spear that had been strapped behind his shoulders. He raised it high in one swift movement.

Kori's first thought was to protect her children. She gave a shrill cry, hoping it would sound fearful, and she plunged into the thick bushes to draw the hunter after her. She took four steps, then hurled herself down as if she had fallen. Thorns raked her face and hands; she ignored them. She landed hard on the ground and rolled as she fell, groping in her pouch for her knife. The touch of its cold stone renewed her strength and courage. She drew up her legs and sprang into a squatting position. Through the tangle of twigs and leaves she saw the man standing with his spear, hesitating to dive after her into the thicket.

Kori focused on him and summoned her strength, directing it to her muscles. She threw herself out from the dense bushes, venting a wild scream.

She glimpsed the man's startled face. This was the last thing he had expected, but it was the wisest thing for Kori to do, because the man's spear would be useless at close quarters. He would be unable to maneuver the long shaft.

She hurled herself at him and butted her head into his stomach. A moment later she brought up her leg and kicked out. Her foot hit the warrior's wrist, and he yelped with surprise. His hand opened, and his weapon fell.

"Get the spear!" Kori shouted to Feroh.

The man was still standing, staring at her with astonishment that quickly turned to anger. His anger would make him more dangerous—but it would also make him clumsy. He reached for Kori, but she dropped down, seized his ankle, and dragged it forward. He fell hard on his back, and she heard him grunt with pain. A moment later Feroh was beside her with the man's spear—and then Meiri was running forward, stepping onto the man's long, braided hair so that he was pinned to the ground.

Kori found herself breathing hard. Her skin was hot and her mouth was dry. "Give me the spear," she snapped at Feroh.

He didn't move, and she saw his look of resentment. She made an impatient sound, seized the spear from him, and turned the point till it almost touched the throat of the man stretched out before her. "Who are you?" she shouted at him.

But even as she spoke, she knew the answer. She saw the distinctive stitching in his robe and the zigzag patterns etched along its edges. They were embarrassingly familiar.

She saw his eyes move. She turned quickly—and found herself facing half a dozen men moving toward her through the underbrush, all of them armed with spears.

For a long moment there was silence, broken only by the cries of startled birds and the flurry of their wings as they fled from the confrontation.

Kori eyed the six men. She tossed her spear aside, stowed her knife in her pouch, then spread her hands to show that they were empty.

"Kori?" The oldest of the men spoke the word as if it tasted strange to him.

"Yes, Baryor, I am Kori, and this is my daughter Meiri, and my son Feroh." She inclined her head respectfully. Then she turned to Meiri. "Let him go," she said, gesturing to the warrior on the ground. "These men are not our enemies."

A little later Kori sat on the forest floor with Meiri on her left and Feroh on her right, in a clearing where a deer carcass roasted over the embers of a fire. The man named Baryor sat opposite her, with a score of hunters ranged silently around him.

"I apologize," Kori said respectfully, "for embarrassing your hunter. He surprised us, Baryor, and he brandished his spear. I didn't realize that he was from your tribe. I feared he was going to kill us."

Baryor was almost the same age as Kori, but he had the mannerisms and the elaborate dignity of an older man, and his face had been marked by winter winds and summer sun. "There is no blame, Kori," he said, waving his hand as if he had the exclusive right to determine such things. He turned his head. "Weyar, come here." He beckoned to the man that Kori had confronted.

The hunter stepped forward. He carefully avoided looking at her, and Kori knew she must have damaged his pride by taking his weapon from him and throwing him down. He stared straight ahead and said nothing.

"You should accept this apology from Kori," Baryor said. "She is a friend of our tribe. She meant no harm."

Weyar nodded, though he still refused to meet Kori's eyes.

Baryor smiled faintly. "Do not be embarrassed, Weyar. Kori is no ordinary woman. She is the chieftain of the Ocean Tribe."

Weyar paused, and his face showed slow understanding. Finally he looked at Kori, showing new respect. "I didn't realize—" he began.

"You were doing your duty," Kori said. "You were guarding your people." Privately she thought that he had made a poor job of it. A lookout became useless if he exposed himself. Weyar should have stayed in his tree instead of confronting her. He should have used a signal to alert the rest of his party. Still, he was a young man, barely of age, and she judged that he had not been properly trained. Despite Baryor's proud manners, he was not a strong leader.

She turned back to him, wondering why he had bothered to post a lookout. "Are you hunting here in the forest?"

"Yes, we are on a hunt." He gestured to the roasting carcass. "Are you hungry?"

It had been difficult for Kori to sit so near to the food and ignore it. She glanced at Feroh and Meiri and saw them staring at the meat with unconcealed yearning. "We are very hungry," she said. Briefly she told Baryor about their journey through the storm.

A few moments later she found tall, strong men serving her and her children huge portions of meat and fresh water from leather bags. Politeness and self-restraint were no longer necessary. She gorged herself shamelessly while Baryor and his people watched, smiling.

Afterward, when she was sated, she reclined beside the fire. It had been many months since she had last seen Baryor, and even though she wanted to return as quickly as possible to her tribe, she was eager for news. He was the chieftain of the Green Valley Tribe, one of the biggest along the coast, numbering almost two hundred men, women, and children. They lived in a cluster of great houses in a fertile valley where they cultivated corn and other grains to supplement the game that they hunted.

Once a year, in the autumn, the Green Valley Tribe sent emissaries to Kori's Ocean Tribe, bringing corn and smoked venison which they traded for smoked fish, dried fish, dried seaweed, and handicrafts that Kori's people made.

Baryor had inherited his position as chieftain when his father died ten years ago. He was a decent man, and he treated Kori with respect even though she was a woman, but his people thrived because they had mastered the art of cultivating crops and were willing to work hard through the year. They had little need for a chieftain to tell them what to do, and if they were concerned about their safety, Baryor certainly wasn't the right man to protect them.

"So tell me," Kori asked him, "where are we along the coast? It was so dark last night—"

"Our village is half a day to the northeast," Baryor said, gesturing. "Yours lies one day to the south."

Kori felt a wave of relief. Still, she remained haunted by her strange encounter the previous night. Briefly she described it to Baryor.

"Did this man attack you?" His voice showed disbelief.

Kori shook her head. "He refused to speak, he offered us no help, and when I confronted him, he ran."

"So, he was just a wanderer."

Kori felt irritated by his dismissive tone—and yet, she realized, her words couldn't convey the air of evil she had sensed around the figure. "Well, I would still like to know if you have seen a one-eyed man like that," she said.

Baryor shook his head. "I don't believe so. Certainly, there's no one in my tribe."

Kori watched him carefully. She decided he was telling the truth. He was a decent man, and most of his people were simple farmers. There had never been conflict among them.

"Still," Baryor went on, "there are rumors of strangers away to the east."

"There are always strangers," Kori said. "Most of the adults in my tribe were wanderers who chose to stay with us."

"No," said Baryor, "the strangers I'm talking about are not wanderers. I've heard that they are warriors. That's why I posted lookouts around our camp here."

Kori felt a chill—but she wondered if she should believe Baryor. She studied his lined face. His father had been renowned as a great hunter, but she doubted that Baryor himself had ever faced danger. He was more a crop grower than a hunter, and like most crop growers he was superstitious, always performing sacrifices and rituals, praying to the Sun God or the Rain God and worrying about the changing seasons. He'd be no better at judging rumors about warriors than he was at posting a lookout.

So, there was no way for her to know what to believe. And in the pure light of day she found herself wondering if she might be mistaken. She had been dreaming just before she woke on the beach, and she had been exhausted . . .

She stopped her train of thought, realizing it was

pointless to speculate. "I thank you for your hospitality," she said. "May there always be peace and friendship between our people."

"Of course!" he said, spreading his arms. "Always! You will visit us soon, Kori. Come to us at the winter solstice, and we will celebrate with fermented corn." He winked at her. "I remember how you enjoyed it last time."

"Thank you," said Kori. "But we must journey back to my tribe now. My people will be thinking that I died out there on the ocean." She stood up. "Hunt safely, Baryor."

He gave a short, sharp laugh. "We shall be safe enough. Far safer than if we ventured out there on the water."

Even now, after more than a decade, other tribes still thought Kori and her people were reckless and foolish to fish the ocean. Of course, it was true that the ocean would always be more dangerous than the land, but when she and Uroh had established their tribe, the best land had been occupied already by others.

She turned to Meiri and Feroh. Since neither of them had come of age, they'd remained silent while she spoke to Baryor. "Come," she told them. "If we leave now, we can be home by nightfall."

5

The village stood atop a high rounded hill that ended abruptly in cliffs at the edge of the ocean. The sixty people who dwelled here in stone-walled, wooden-roofed huts could look out across the sea to the west, and across a wide expanse of forested land to the north, east, and south. The village was in a commanding location—which was why Kori had chosen this place for it. She was determined that her people should be secure.

The sun was almost setting when she started along the well-worn path that zigzagged up the eastern slope of the hill.

She heard the cry of a lookout. Then there were more distant cries, and she saw figures gathering at the summit. By the time she reached them, with Meiri and Feroh close behind her, everyone in the village was there. They greeted her with joy in their faces and their voices, and Kori felt so touched by their affection, for a moment she thought she might cry. Little children wormed their way through the crowd and clung to her, women pushed forward and hugged her, men hailed her, and elders at the back of the crowd waved to her, nodding and smiling.

The people were an odd assortment. Some wore deer skins; others were dressed in clothes woven from hemp; some were bare-chested; some wore their hair in braids, while others let it hang loose and free. The tribe had grown by accepting nomads and wanderers, and Kori had never suggested that any of them should change their customs. Only a few of them chose to fashion their robes like hers, with rippling patterns symbolizing the river that had brought her and Uroh to the coast originally.

Everyone was talking at once. They wanted to know what had happened to her canoe, and why she was arriving now from inland, and how had she survived the terrible storm, and why was Meiri so badly bruised, and where were Kori's moccasins? Kori held up both her hands, and gradually the chatter of voices subsided. "I will tell you everything," she said. She paused a moment, looking from one face to the next. "But where is Uroh?"

Suddenly there was no sound except for the murmuring of the wind, and the pleasure on people's faces was replaced by looks of embarrassment.

Kori felt a wave of concern. "Is he out on the ocean searching for me?"

"I think he is waiting for you in your hut," someone said—a plump-faced, motherly woman named Raia.

Kori suddenly felt foolish—then angry.

"You know how he is," Raia went on, with a brave attempt at humor. "He likes to sleep late."

There was some uneasy laughter. Kori forced herself to smile. She turned to Feroh. "Go with everyone to the Meeting Place," she told him. "Meiri, go with him. Answer people's questions." She looked back to the crowd. "I'll join you all in a little while."

Once again they shouted their good wishes to her, but their voices were more subdued than before, and her anger churned in her as she strode among the little houses.

The home she shared with Uroh was at the far end of the village, perched at the edge of the cliffs. Kori barely noticed the sunset painting a swath of coppery light across the waves as she jerked aside the strip of bear hide that hung over the entrance to the hut.

It took a moment for her eyes to adjust to the dim interior. Then she saw him sitting on their bed, leaning against the wall, with his hands clasped across his chest. "Kori," he said, and his teeth gleamed in the dimness as he smiled. "When I heard the people shouting, I knew you must have returned. Welcome!"

He was the most important person in her life; there was never any doubt of that. She had never felt interested in any other man. But again and again, he hurt her and he maddened her. "If you wanted to welcome me," she said, "why didn't you get up off the bed? Why didn't you join everyone else who came to greet me?"

His smile faded. He looked puzzled. "Well, I knew you would come here. This is your home, after all."

She stared at his friendly face. The years had been kind to him; he was her age, yet he looked five years younger. He still had the eyes of a child—or a dreamer.

Her anger rose inside her again, and she found it hard to speak. "I was humiliated," she said, "to find everyone in the village running out to greet me—and my husband not among them. Don't you see that?"

He got up off the bed in a fluid movement and gripped her arms in his big, gentle hands. "Kori, I'm happy you're back. Why does it matter where I show you my happiness—here or at the other side of the village?"

She pulled free from him and picked up a shallow dish of sun-baked clay that contained a small puddle of oil and a hemp wick. She took it to the fire that glowed in the corner of the hut. If she hadn't come back here, she guessed that Uroh wouldn't have bothered to light the lamp. He'd have been happy just to sit in the dark, lost in his own strange thoughts, whatever they were.

The hemp sputtered, and the hut was lit with a weak glow from the little yellow flame. Kori glanced quickly around. Uroh had left a fishing net casually bundled in one corner, and his favorite spear was lying on the floor beside the bed where someone could easily trip over it. Generally, though, the hut was neat enough, no different from the way she'd left it.

She looked at the children's bed at the other end of the small space, with all the toys and charms that Uroh had made over the years dangling from the roof on thongs. There were dozens of beautiful little carvings of animals and fish fashioned from wood, shells, and bone.

Nearby, Kori saw her clothes hanging over wooden pegs embedded between the stones in the walls. Uroh had built that wall, and he had cut and shaped the pegs, and he had decorated her clothes with an artistic skill that she could never match.

She glanced up at the smoke-blackened beams

supporting the roof of packed earth, which Uroh had constructed with such elaborate care thirteen years ago. Some of her anger drained out of her, and she sighed. "I suppose I shouldn't be ill-tempered," she said. "I know you care for me." But then she was gripped by another little spasm of irritation. "Still, I almost lost my life out on the ocean, and so did our children! Weren't you even worried about us?"

He smiled. "I knew you would come back."

His calm certainty irritated her even more. "You *knew*? How could you know?"

He sat back on the bed. "I—felt that you were fated to return. It's hard to explain, Kori."

"Why is it hard to explain? Am I too foolish to understand?"

He clasped his hands around one knee and stared at them, avoiding her eyes. "You only believe what you can touch and see," he said, speaking so quietly, she could barely hear him. "I think there may be more in life than that."

She hated it when he talked this way. He made her feel if she were blind to things that were as clear to him as the sunlight on the ocean. "What else is there in the world?" she demanded. "Are you talking of spirits?"

"No." His eyes strayed, and he seemed to be looking beyond the hut. "But when I am alone on the ocean, I feel the presence of all living things. And I think they feel my presence as I feel theirs."

Kori sighed. "So the fish in the sea told you that I was still alive?" She didn't try to keep the scorn out of her voice.

"Maybe so." Unexpectedly, he laughed. "Or maybe it was just my imagination."

It was hopeless. He was a dreamer, and he always had been.

Then she remembered how the orca had rescued her from the storm, and suddenly she felt unsure of herself. That had been so sudden, so strange, and inexplicable to her. Uroh was right when he said that she only believed what she could touch and see. Of course, she believed there was a human spirit that was set free when a person died; but that was very different from strange ideas about sharing one's thoughts with sea creatures.

Kori moved restlessly. "Listen," she said, retreating to a topic where she felt more sure of herself, "there are things you should know. The sail of our canoe was torn in two by the wind. The stitching had rotted. You must check all the sails."

"But that should never have happened," Uroh said. His face changed; he looked deeply concerned.

Well, Kori thought, this was something that he took seriously.

"I'll repair it tomorrow," he went on.

She laughed without humor. "You can't repair it. The canoe is gone. It was smashed on the rocks, more than a day north of here."

Now he stared at her in dismay. "The canoe was destroyed?"

"Yes, all your precious handiwork." Sometimes he seemed to care more for the things he made than for her or his children or the tribe. She turned away abruptly. "I must go to the Meeting Place. Our people are waiting."

Uroh got to his feet. "And I should go down to the beach. I must check the sails on all the canoes. We can't afford to lose another."

She looked at him in disbelief. "The sun is setting."

"It doesn't matter. I can still test each sail. If it tears, I'll leave it torn to warn people not to use that canoe tomorrow. In the morning, we can make repairs." He started for the door, moving purposefully.

"But people will expect you to be with me in the Meeting Place!" she protested.

"This is more important." He walked out of the hut.

Kori went after him—and she found Meiri hurrying toward her through the grayness of the evening. "Mother, people want you!" Meiri called.

Kori hesitated, seeing Uroh striding toward the tiny path that led down the cliff to the beach. She realized there was no point in trying to call him back. She could never change his mind.

She turned back to Meiri as the girl reached for her hand and started tugging at it. "All right," Kori said. "All right, Meiri. I'm coming."

A few moments later she entered the circle of firelight, joining Feroh where he stood facing the tribe. Big portions of roasted fish were being passed from one person to the next on pieces of birch bark, with smaller helpings of corn, venison, and precious dried berries. The fire was crackling, the flames were leaping, and Kori saw faces flushed with good food and good cheer. Still, she sensed an undercurrent of concern.

Before Kori could speak, one of the elders—a man named Taran—slowly rose to his feet. He was more than sixty years old, and the tribe respected his great age. His teeth and his hair had gone, and his face was so dry and red from the sun and wind, so heavily mapped with wrinkles, it looked as if it would crack into pieces if he smiled.

Well, there was no risk of that; Kori had never seen

him even begin to smile. He was a sour man, always the first to scorn an achievement or criticize an idea. Kori preferred not to deal with him, but clearly, now she had no choice.

Taran didn't bother with polite preliminaries. He seemed to feel that his age exempted him from that obligation. "Where's your husband?" he said.

Kori didn't like his manner, but she warned herself to keep her irritation hidden. "He's gone down to the beach," she said calmly, "to check the stitching of the sails. Did Feroh tell you, our sail ripped in two?"

Taran grunted. "Your son told us a lot more than that." He eyed the boy skeptically. "He told a tale that is hard to believe."

Kori glanced quickly around the circle of faces. Now she understood why they seemed concerned— and she realized why Meiri had been sent to fetch her.

"Your son says you were attacked by a stranger," Taran went on. "A one-eyed man—"

"He did not attack us," Kori said without raising her voice, knowing that she would be more persuasive if she remained calm. "I woke during the night and found him near us on the beach—"

"You slept on the beach?" Taran eyed her as if even this was hard to believe.

"We were exhausted," Kori said, still forcing herself to speak politely, though she wanted to stride over, grab the old man by his shoulders, give him a shake, and tell him to sit down and be quiet. "We had been through a terrible ordeal."

There was a murmur of sympathy from the crowd.

"And when I woke," Kori went on, "the sun had set. A man in a dark robe was standing over me. One of his eyes was missing, and his face was deeply scarred. I called out to him, but he backed away, and when Feroh stood up beside me, the stranger ran into the forest above the beach."

Taran grunted. "So, he was just a wanderer.".

"Perhaps," said Kori. "All of us here were wanderers once—except for the children who have been born into this tribe. But when we were wanderers, did we creep up on people while they slept? If someone called out to us and asked us our names, did we refuse to speak? If someone needed help, did we turn and run away?" She paused, looking slowly around.

Taran still held his ground. "Still," he said, "you have no reason—"

"This morning," Kori said, "we encountered Baryor, the chieftain of the Green Valley Tribe, with a score of his hunters. There are rumors of strangers to the east. He claims the strangers are warriors, and they are hostile."

Taran grunted. "That's just idle talk."

"Of course it is," said Kori. "But since I did encounter a man who acted suspiciously, we should be cautious, don't you think? Our lookouts must stay alert, especially at night."

There was a murmur of agreement.

Taran scowled. For a moment, at least, he had run out of things to say.

"Tell us about the orca," a woman called out. It was Raia, the same woman who had told Kori that Uroh was waiting for her in her hut.

"This was an amazing thing," said Kori. "It came to us when we were helpless in the hurricane, and it pushed us to safety." She spread her hands. "I cannot explain why this happened, but it did happen."

"An orca led me out of a rainstorm once," someone said.

"The whales always know where the fish are," someone else put in. "Sometimes they lead us there."

Suddenly every fisherman around the fire seemed to have a story to tell about the great whales. Kori couldn't help smiling. Her people were reluctant to believe in a hostile, one-eyed man, but they had no trouble believing she had been rescued by an orca. In fact, this probably made them respect her more. She had been saved by the sea creature that they revered the most.

"This is all very well," Taran protested, shouting above the babble of voices. "But what I want to know—" He paused and glared at people until the talk died down. "What I want to know is, what you were doing so far from shore in the first place."

Kori had been hoping that he wouldn't raise this question publicly. She glanced at Feroh and found him looking straight ahead, calm and unconcerned, as if nothing she could say would hurt him.

Did he really feel that way? She couldn't tell. But his coming-of-age ceremony was now just two days away, and he was almost a man. Perhaps she shouldn't feel so protective.

"I gave Feroh command of the canoe," Kori said. "Perhaps I should have watched over him more carefully. But Feroh is almost a man, and he chose to explore the waters farther from the shore. I was lying in the canoe, resting. By the time I realized where we were, it was too late." She forced a smile. "It's in the nature of young men to want to explore."

She glanced again at Feroh. His posture had changed subtly. His back was stiff and straight, and the muscles in his neck were rigid with tension. He was angry again, she realized—furious with her for blaming him publicly.

Well, she could never lie to her people. She had made a vow once that she would always place the truth first, and she had honored that vow.

There was an uneasy silence around the fire. All of the villagers were seafarers, men and women alike. They respected the great power of the wind and the water, and none of them took unnecessary risks. They had little respect for reckless mariners, because such people could endanger other people's lives. Young people in the Ocean Tribe admired Feroh as a brave young hunter—but Kori saw looks of disapproval among the older men.

"Well," she said, clapping her hands to drive away the looming silence. "The main thing is that we are back among you, and we are safe again."

There was a murmur of agreement that grew gradually louder. "Welcome back!" shouted Raia.

"Welcome!" other voices echoed her.

Within moments the somber mood was gone and Kori found herself surrounded again by warmth and friendship. It was a mysterious thing, this love that her people showed. It always surprised her, because she had never expected to lead a tribe, and she never felt she deserved any great respect.

Their love warmed her—yet there was sadness in her, because the love of her people could never replace the love of her husband. And Uroh wasn't by her side, where she wanted and expected him to be. He had chosen to do what he had done so often before: he had gone away on his own.

6

South of the village, where the bare, stony hilltop sloped down into woodland, a glade lay hidden among the trees. The grass grew tall here, and there were sun-yellow and sky-blue wildflowers. Insects hummed, crickets sang, and the air always seemed a little warmer, a little calmer than anywhere else. This was Kori's favorite place when she needed time to be alone, or to speak with someone privately.

Today was a bright day, a warm afternoon that gave a foretaste of summer. At sunset Feroh's ceremony would take place, but Kori had already done all her duties to prepare for that. The food had been chosen, the Meeting Place had been swept, timber had been fetched for a big fire, and it was Uroh's task now to prepare his son. As the sun entered the last quarter of its arc across the sky, Kori came to the glade.

With her, she brought Meiri. Two days had passed since their return to the village, and Kori had been waiting for an opportunity to speak to her daughter alone. On this special day, there were things that desperately needed to be said; things that should have been said months or years ago.

First, though, they had time to practice some of their skills together.

Kori broke a long branch from a tree, then walked to the center of the glade and kneeled so that Meiri could blindfold her with a strip of deer skin. Meiri made sure that the blindfold was secure, then backed away.

Kori stood up, and she waited. Slowly she turned her head from side to side, listening for the tiniest sounds. In the far distance, away at the foot of the cliffs, she heard the ocean washing the shore. Above her she heard the cry of a bird. All around her was the waft of the wind, the rustle of leaves, and the singing of crickets.

She stood motionless, breathing slowly and softly. Even though she was a restless, impulsive woman, she had trained herself to be patient, because she had learned that patience is one of the greatest assets a hunter can possess.

She knew that Meiri, too, was waiting somewhere in the glade—waiting for Kori to become restless and inattentive. But Meiri was too young to be truly patient. She started creeping forward, circling slowly around Kori, placing her feet cautiously in the grass.

Kori heard a faint sound to her right. Was that a footfall? No; it was too loud. Meiri had thrown a stone. Kori turned toward the sound anyway, knowing that Meiri was watching her.

Now Kori heard a real footstep—the faintest sound of a moccasin slipping between tall, dry stems, and an even fainter sound of leather pressing into loose earth. Kori visualized the space around her. She felt as if she were looking down from above. She saw herself, and she saw Meiri. She heard another tiny sound, nearer to her—and she whirled around, sweeping the tree branch in a semicircle. It thwacked against Meiri's thighs just as the girl was about to leap forward.

Kori whipped off the blindfold as Meiri squealed, annoyed that she had been caught so easily. For a moment both of them stood looking at each other.

"I'll never catch you," Meiri said. "You always hear me. Always!"

Kori shook her head. "There will come a time. Remember when you were young? You never even came close. Now you're just an arm's length away." She held out the blindfold and the tree branch. "Your turn."

Meiri never liked to trade places. She kneeled reluctantly to let Kori blindfold her.

Kori made sure that her daughter couldn't peek around the strip of deer skin. Then she backed away—far away, right to the edge of the glade. She squatted down in the grass, then decided to make herself more comfortable. She lay back and looked up at the sky.

There were thin streaks of high, white cloud running from west to east across the bowl of blue. Kori recognized the pattern; it almost always meant that another change of weather was on the way. Once again she found herself remembering everything that had happened in the storm—and she had to stop herself, consciously and deliberately. There was nothing to be gained from blaming herself further.

Kori sat up and looked at Meiri standing alone in

the center of the glade, waiting and listening. Kori threw a stone, and then another, and another.

"You don't fool me, Mother!" Meiri shouted.

"Listen, don't speak," Kori said, holding her hand diagonally across her mouth to make it seem as if her voice came from elsewhere. "So long as you hear yourself, you will never hear me." She stood as she spoke, and she started running lightly around the edge of the clearing.

Meiri turned, listening more intently now. Without much trouble, she followed the sound of Kori's footsteps.

Kori squatted down again, and she waited. The time dragged by, and Meiri became visibly restless. Still, the girl didn't complain; she had long since learned that it would do her no good.

Kori plucked a tall dandelion and crushed its stem between her palms. She rolled it into a ball, then started creeping directly toward her daughter. She walked in slow motion, barely disturbing the grass as she moved. She kept her arms rigid so that they wouldn't cause her robe to rustle, and she breathed lightly through her open mouth so that even the air passing in and out of her body would make no sound.

Finally, when she was just a couple of paces away, she flicked her wrist, tossing the crushed dandelion stem over Meiri's head.

It landed on the other side of the girl. The noise it made was almost imperceptible, but Meiri whirled around.

Kori leaped forward. She threw herself onto the grass at Meiri's feet, reached up, and wrenched the branch free from the girl's hands.

With a quick, irritable gesture, Meiri pulled off the blindfold. "You always win!" she cried.

"One day," said Kori, "a year from now, or two years from now, it will be different. Already, your senses are sharper than mine. You smelled the venison in the forest before I did, remember? All you need is practice and experience."

Meiri tossed the branch aside. "It's too hard."

Kori gave her a stern look. "You know I never want to hear that." Her tone was sharp. "You seem to forget, I was once like you, unsure of myself and insecure."

"I know, I know!" Meiri complained. She looked afraid of Kori, yet determined to speak. "You grew up in a tribe far away, and the people were foolish and superstitious, and when their village caught fire, they chanted prayers instead of trying to save themselves. You and Uroh were the only ones who escaped, and you came here to start a new tribe where people wouldn't make the same mistakes they made before."

Kori stared at her daughter in amazement. She felt deeply shaken. She had never heard Meiri speak like this, blurting the words out, mocking the story that was the foundation of Kori's life.

Meiri saw her mother's expression. Her defiance was fragile; she looked suddenly ashamed. "I'm sorry," she said. She looked down at the ground. "But I've heard it so often. I couldn't stand to hear it again."

"I see," said Kori. Perhaps, she thought, Meiri was starting to change as she, too, approached her adulthood. "I hope you understand," Kori said carefully, "every word of that story is true."

Meiri nodded. She said nothing.

Kori stood up. She reached out, pulled her daughter close, and hugged her. "I'm sorry, Meiri, if you think I nag you and scold you too much. I just want you to be strong, so nothing can hurt you. One day, you will be the leader of this tribe—"

"I know!" The girl's voice sounded shrill again.

"Yes, of course you know." Kori blinked, feeling confused. Had she been wrong to force Meiri to listen to the same lessons too many times? The lessons were important. They were more important than anything else in Kori's life. "It's only because I care about you so much, Meiri," she said.

The girl relaxed a little, but she didn't speak.

Kori forced a smile. "Come, now. Let's practice our other skills."

Meiri turned away. She was no longer openly rebellious, but she was still sullen.

Kori took the branch that Meiri had been holding. She broke off two twigs, kept one, and handed the other to her daughter. Then she stepped back four paces. "You move first."

Reluctantly the girl took the fighting stance that Kori had taught her, standing at an angle so that her body presented the smallest possible target. She bent her knees and balanced herself carefully, focusing all her attention on Kori. She waited for a long moment, completely motionless under the steady sunlight. She took a slow breath, held it—then gave a wild cry and ran forward, dancing as she ran, holding the twig as if it were a knife. She feinted, ducked, and made a sudden thrust.

Kori sprang to one side, but still she felt the twig brush across her robe. "Good!" she called out as she fell, rolled, and sprang back up onto her feet.

Meiri paused, breathing hard. "I was close," she said.

"Very close! Try again, now!"

Meiri took another slow, deep breath, and her face became expressionless. She positioned herself and focused on Kori. For another long moment, she didn't move.

Kori watched her daughter with wide, unblinking eyes. The moment dragged on, and Kori felt her leg muscles starting to cramp. Still, she waited.

Finally Meiri gave her attacking cry and leaped forward—then jammed her heels down and stopped herself as Kori jumped back, avoiding the thrust that never came. Meiri switched the twig to her other hand. She ran again, threw herself to one side at the last moment, and pirouetted so that she avoided the twig that Kori was holding. Kori found herself lunging into empty air; she was off balance as Meiri fell into a crouch, then sprang like a young mountain lion.

Kori attempted a back-flip, but her muscles were still stiff from her desperate efforts to save the canoe in the storm, and her legs failed her. With astonishment she found herself falling on her back. Meiri stopped and stared at her. Then she regained her initiative, and with a wild look, she started forward.

"Wait!" Kori cried, holding up her hand.

Meiri hesitated. "Why?" she said.

Kori squirmed around. She seized Meiri's leg and dragged it, toppling the girl. Then she rolled onto her and thrust her own twig against Meiri's chest.

"But that's not fair!" Meiri cried out. Angrily she struggled free. "You told me to stop!"

"Of course," Kori said. "If these were real knives in

our hands, wouldn't you cheat to save your life?" She smiled at her daughter. "Next time, you won't make that mistake."

Meiri threw her twig aside. "I still say you cheated!"

"Maybe so," said Kori. "But you would have caught me this time if I hadn't fooled you. Doesn't that make it feel better?"

Meiri clenched her small fists. "I think—" She hesitated, summoning her courage. "I think this is a stupid game."

"No." The sharpness returned to Kori's voice. "There are evil people in the world. The man on the beach—"

"I hardly saw him!" Meiri protested. "By the time I woke up, he was running away."

"But he was there," said Kori, "and I saw him."

Meiri said nothing.

"You find it hard to believe," said Kori, "because you have lived all your life in this place where we have no enemies."

"Yes, we have no enemies!" Meiri cried out. "So why must we always pretend? Maybe—maybe things aren't the same anymore as they were when you were a girl."

Kori opened her mouth to reply—then realized she was nagging Meiri again, and this was no longer the time. It was getting late, and there were other words that had to be spoken before the end of the afternoon.

Kori moved forward. She embraced Meiri. "I'm sorry," she said. "I promise I'll stop scolding you. Your brother will have his ceremony soon, and we must be there for that. But there is one other thing I have to say. It's the real reason I brought you here this afternoon."

Meiri looked up warily. "Did I do something wrong?"

Kori laughed. Gently she tugged one of Meiri's braids. "No, you did nothing wrong. But listen now. This is another story about the time when I was young—but it's a story you have never heard before. In fact, it's a story that I have never told anyone. And you must promise not to speak of it to anyone. Do you understand?"

Meiri wasn't angry anymore. Kori had roused her curiosity. "I'm not even allowed to tell Uroh?"

Kori thought about that. "He already knows," she said, thinking carefully. "So I suppose you could speak to him about it—although he might prefer not to be reminded about it. But no one else knows, Meiri. No one in the whole world. And no one else must ever know."

Meiri heard the seriousness in Kori's voice. She looked appropriately solemn. "All right. I promise to keep it a secret."

Kori sat in the grass, making herself comfortable. "You know I've spoken to you about an evil man, long ago, in the village where I grew up. A man named Yainar."

Meiri gave a curt nod. "He didn't want you to leave with Uroh. And—you had to kill him so that you could escape. And there was another man who tried to help him, named Derneren. And Uroh killed him, too."

"That's right," said Kori. "Yainar and Derneren. They were both evil, the most evil men I have ever known." She paused, summoning her mental strength. She had tried to make herself talk about this with Meiri many times, because she believed with all her heart that nothing was more important than truth. Yet each year she backed away from the subject, because the time wasn't right, or it was too painful to think about, or Meiri was still too young.

Now that Feroh was coming of age, there could be no more excuses. The story had to be told.

"Listen now," Kori said. Her stomach clenched as she remembered her childhood, when she had felt so unsure of her future and had been so naive. At first she had been impressed by Yainar's handsome face and his hunting skills, and had imagined being his mate. After all, he was the strongest young hunter in the tribe.

Gradually, though, she had discovered his true, cruel nature. She remembered his hut full of animal trophies, and she recalled the way he had trapped her, tied her, and forced himself on her with cruel pleasure.

"This is the way it truly was," Kori went on. "Yainar—took me. As my lover. Do you understand?"

"You mean he was your mate?" Meiri said, staring at Kori in amazement.

"No." Kori shook her head. "He wanted to be, but we were never paired. I despised him. But—he still forced me. Twice."

Meiri looked deeply shocked. "You weren't paired, but he put his seed in you?"

Kori nodded, feeling sickened by the memory, and so ashamed, it was hard to look her daughter in the eye. "I tried to stop him. But yes, he put his seed in me, the way I've told you a man may make a woman pregnant. I didn't know how to defend myself then, as I do now."

Meiri's eyes were wide. The girl just sat and stared, and she said nothing.

Once more, Kori summoned her strength, because

the hardest part was still to come. "When it happened," she went on, "I thought I had pulled free before—before his seed had a chance to enter me and grow. But two months later, after I killed Yainar and I was with Uroh, and we had left my tribe and we were traveling down the river that led here to the sea—I found I was pregnant. I thought that Uroh was the father of my child, but when the child was born, he looked so much like Yainar, I feared the worst. And as he grew older, the resemblance was impossible to deny."

Meiri's mouth opened, but it took her a moment to form the words. "You mean—Feroh isn't my brother." Her voice was loud in the stillness.

"Hush!" Kori cried. She reached forward and pressed her finger to Meiri's lips.

Meiri jerked away from her. "You never told me!" she cried. She stared in horror at Kori, and her whole body trembled. "You tricked me!"

This was worse than Kori had feared. "Hush," she said again, dragging Meiri close, even though the girl struggled to be set free. "Meiri, listen to me! Listen! I couldn't tell you till you were old enough to understand, and old enough to keep it a secret. I couldn't take the chance, don't you see? I had to wait."

Gradually Meiri's struggles subsided.

"I'm sorry," Kori whispered to her. "This is such a terrible thing. It was far too terrible for a young girl to know."

Meiri suddenly started crying. "But I could have kept it a secret," she complained. "You could have told me. You could!"

Maybe there was some truth to that—or was there? "I couldn't take the risk," Kori insisted. "You could have told Feroh in a moment of anger. And Feroh must never know, Meiri. He would feel ashamed. And—he would turn against Uroh. And—he would hate me, because I killed Yainar. I speared him in the river. I watched him die." She drew a shaky breath. "I killed Feroh's true father, Meiri, don't you see how terrible that is?"

Meiri sniffed back her tears and fell silent. Kori released her hold on the girl, and Meiri slumped down in the grass.

Kori sighed. "It has been so hard to mother my son, knowing his father was the man I despised more than anyone in the world. You must see that."

"Did you really have to kill him?" Meiri said.

Kori nodded. "He was so full of hate, so determined to possess me, he tried to kill Uroh. So long as Yainar lived, Uroh was not safe, and I could never be free."

Meiri pressed her hands to the sides of her face. She sat motionless for a long time, saying nothing. Finally she shivered. "This is a very bad secret," she said.

"Feroh must never know," Kori said. "You understand that now, don't you?"

"But you always say we should tell the truth," Meiri objected.

"Yes, and I am telling you the truth now. And if Feroh ever asks me, I will have to tell the truth to him, too. I won't lie, Meiri. But I will keep a secret to prevent someone from being hurt. And you promised to keep that secret with me."

"All right," Meiri whispered. "I'll say nothing."

"You'll say nothing to *anyone*," Kori persisted. "If you break your promise, I will never forgive you."

The girl nodded silently.

Kori trusted her daughter; yet she felt anxious. "What are you thinking?"

Meiri looked away, and her eyes reflected the sky. "I'm thinking—that Feroh has always been mean to me. I wonder if he senses, somehow, that Uroh isn't his real father."

"I wonder, too," said Kori. "But both of us have tried to love him as if he's our own. Always, we've given him as much love as you."

The sun was nearing the horizon, and the sky was changing color, from yellow over the ocean to purple above. Kori reached out and stroked her daughter's face, erasing the tears. "We must get back to the village," she said softly. "And you will act as if nothing is different. I know you can do that for me, Meiri."

The girl gave a curt nod.

"Good," said Kori. She stood up. "Come. Be strong, now. As strong as I am."

Meiri made a little despairing sound. "I can never be—"

"Yes you can." Kori's tone left no room for argument. "You *can*. Quickly now; we're late."

Without looking back, she led the way out of the glade.

7

As Kori followed the familiar path back to the village, she heard the distant sound of chanting. For a moment she felt confused, as a wave of memories swept through her, releasing a cascade of emotions. She remembered all the times in her childhood when the people of her tribe had chanted—and she had chanted with them, praying to the Old Ones, the deities that her people had believed in.

Kori had to stop for a moment to calm herself. Meiri paused beside her, looking up at her curiously. "Is something wrong?"

Kori took a slow breath of the cool evening air. "I wish they would stop," she said, forcing herself to speak lightly.

"Well, you could *tell* them to stop," said Meiri.

"Yes, I could." She shook her head. "But the people of my tribe must always be free to follow their customs. Many of them believe that chanting is a way to seek favors—from the Sun God, the Moon God, and other gods. If I refuse to allow it, they'll be fearful and unhappy. They'll resent me."

"Don't you believe in *any* gods?" Meiri asked.

Kori suddenly felt impatient with her daughter's questions. "It does no good to think about such things," she said. She frowned, looking up at a high outcropping of rock that stood beside the path. "Kireah!" she shouted.

She waited, but there was no reply.

"He's probably gone to join the ceremony," said Meiri.

Kori strode ahead. "He has no right to do that. It was his turn to stand guard. He should be up on that rock until the sun has set."

"But Mother," Meiri said, hurrying to keep up with Kori, "it's a special time."

"Do our enemies know that?" Kori asked. "Will they be kind to us and leave us in peace when we have a celebration?"

"We have no enemies," Meiri muttered, almost too quietly for Kori to hear.

As they entered the village, Kori found it was alive with sound and light. While a score of people in the Meeting Place sat chanting and beating drums of deer skin stretched across hoops of birch wood, others were carrying torches and lamps soaked in oil, setting them high up on every little stone hut to spread a warm, flickering radiance through the twilight.

Villagers gave joyous shouts of greeting as they saw Kori. They bowed and called upon the spirits to favor her. After her conversation with Meiri, she felt in no mood to talk to them, but still she greeted each person by name, and she clasped their hands and thanked them, till finally she reached her own home.

Inside, she found Feroh sitting cross-legged on the simple bed that he normally shared with Meiri. His back was straight, his head was tilted high, and he stared straight ahead, ignoring Kori and Meiri as they entered the hut. Two lamps sputtered, resting in niches in the wall on either side of him. Uroh was bending over the boy, painstakingly painting his face with powdered charcoal soaked in oil.

The task was almost done. Feroh's forehead and the upper halves of his cheeks were completely black, while his jaw and neck had been whitened with chalk, in the same pattern as the head of an orca. His hair had been pulled back tightly and wetted so that it gleamed in the yellow light. He was dressed in a heavy robe of whale skin, and he was wearing whale-skin boots.

The people of the Ocean Tribe revered the orcas, and would never think of killing one, even if they were able to. But every year or two, one of the great whales would die of natural causes and its body would be found along the shore. The Ocean Tribe would plunder it—not for its meat, which was sacred, but for its bones, its skin, and its oil.

Kori glanced at Meiri and found the girl staring at Feroh with a strange, brooding expression. For a moment Kori regretted telling Meiri the truth about Feroh's father. Just as quickly, though, she knew there had been no other way. In fact, she wished that Feroh himself could know the truth, if only there was a way for it not to harm him.

"Is he ready?" Kori asked softly.

Uroh paused for a long moment, carefully inspecting his work. He nodded slowly. "Yes, he is ready."

Kori looked at Feroh one last time. No matter who his father was, Feroh was still her son. But now he would be a man like any other man in her tribe, and her only authority would be as his chieftain—not as his mother.

She felt a pang of loss, and then a sense of relief. It had been so difficult raising Feroh, especially with Uroh missing for so much of the time.

"Well," Kori said, "I should dress myself." She went to her clothes where they hung from a peg on the wall, slipped out of the simple robe she was wearing, and put on her ceremonial bear skin ornamented with shells and feathers. The bear skin symbolized strength, the shells denoted her tribe's link with the ocean, and the feathers symbolized the freedom that she had won for herself and her people. The robe covered her from her neck to her ankles, and the shells had been painstakingly drilled and stitched among the black fur in a rippling pattern that imitated the river that had brought her here. White and gray gull feathers were ranged around the collar of the robe like the crest of a great bird. Uroh had made the robe for her, and it was her most treasured possession.

She turned and saw Meiri looking at her with brooding eyes. "Yes," Kori said softly, laying her hand on the girl's shoulder. "One day it will be yours."

Meiri blinked. She took a step backward, quickly shaking her head. "That wasn't what I was thinking," she said. "I was thinking—I can never be as beautiful as you."

"Oh, but you already are," said Kori, stroking the girl's braided hair. Once again she found herself thinking back to her own childhood, when she had felt so different from the rest of her people. She'd been certain that she must be the ugliest girl in the village. And when Uroh had first told her she was beautiful, she'd thought he must be lying, or mad.

She shook her head, trying again to drive away the memories. She pulled down a smaller robe of black wolf pelts. "Put this on," she said to Meiri, "and we will go outside."

Kori waited while the girl changed her clothes. Feroh was still sitting absolutely motionless, still acting as if the women didn't exist. Well, Kori thought, he would probably prefer her not to be there. In many tribes a boy was surrounded only by men on the day of his ceremony, and he would undergo tests of courage and strength to prove his bravery. In fact, several men in the Ocean Tribe had told Kori that this kind of ritual was necessary for a man to feel pride and self-respect.

She rejected that idea. In her tribe, there were no painful initiations. She wanted her people to live for happiness, not pain, and she feared the trait in men that made them want to hurt each other.

She heard voices outside. "Come," she said softly to Meiri, taking her hand. She led the girl out through the door flap and found more than a dozen people waiting, all of them dressed in colorful costumes—patchwork robes of animal skins that had been bleached, etched with patterns, and colored with berry juice; necklaces of bear teeth and whale bones; porcupine quills stitched together to form ribbons; headdresses of feathers and woven grasses; and boots of whale skin and beaver hide. The people called out their greetings and good wishes as she and Meiri joined them—and they raised their voices in a great cheer as Uroh and Feroh emerged a moment later.

Spontaneously the villagers started singing a song of praise for the boy who would soon become a man. Some of them were carrying drums, while others blew through dry, hollow reeds. Feroh moved forward, stepping slowly with Uroh beside him. The villagers started whooping and leaping, clapping their hands and shaking clusters of sea shells strung on thongs, making so much noise that it was painful in Kori's ears.

The procession reached the Meeting Place, and now everyone in the village was there, with mothers carrying their babies and young children running around screaming excitedly, everyone shouting and chanting and banging drums, while Feroh moved with dignity to a flat-topped stone at one side of the fire that burned in the center. He stepped up onto the stone and stood with his hands by his sides, staring out over the heads of the people gathering around.

The singing and shouting lasted a long time. The Ocean Tribe loved any excuse for a celebration, and since Kori was their chieftain, and Feroh was her only son, this was the best excuse there could ever be—at least until such a time as Feroh was paired with a wife.

Finally, though, the people settled themselves around the fire. Food was passed around and the feasting began, although Feroh was not invited to step down for his share. One at a time, people went to the stone where he stood, and they began paying public tribute to him.

The young hunters made the longest, most generous speeches, praising Feroh's strength and skill with a spear, and telling anecdotes about his bravery. Kori watched her son's face, wondering if he was gaining some pleasure from the praise. He still showed no flicker of emotion as he stood rigid, as still as the stone under his feet. Kori frowned, wondering why it should be such a matter of pride for him to behave this way.

The elders of the tribe took their turns, testifying that he was a fine, brave boy who would make a good, wise, honorable man. Some children stepped up and gave short, shy little speeches. And then it was time for Meiri to speak.

Kori watched her daughter standing in front of the tribe. Meiri was still small for her age; she looked thin and frail despite all the time that Kori had spent training the girl in fighting skills. There was an expectant silence—and the silence deepened as Meiri stood with her hands clasped, her eyes moving restlessly in the flickering firelight.

"Feroh is my brother," Meiri said finally, and Kori felt a wave of relief. For a moment she had wondered if Meiri was going to speak at all. "I have known him all my life," Meiri went on. She paused, and there was another long silence as she searched for words. "This is his birthday," Meiri said—and Kori sensed the villagers becoming a little restless, wondering why the girl was telling them such simple facts. "He has been wanting to become a man," Meiri said, looking increasingly unhappy as she faced the tribe. "And now, today, he has what he has always wanted. So I am happy for him."

She spread her hands and gave a strained, unhappy smile. Then she turned and hurried back to Uroh and Kori where they sat by the fire. She squatted down between them, hugging herself, staring down at the ground.

Uroh stood up quickly. "Thank you, Meiri," he said, with warmth and appreciation, as if his daughter had just given the most generous testimonial of all. He turned, smiling at everyone, and the simple warmth of his personality was infectious. Suddenly the awkward silence was erased. He reached out to Kori, and she took his hand. He pulled her up beside him, and together they walked to the stone where Feroh stood.

Kori felt contradictory emotions fighting inside her. It was good to be standing with Uroh like this, in front of the tribe they had built together. It was good to be testifying that Feroh was now a man. Yet, when she looked at his solemn face, she couldn't help seeing his true father's features in the shape of his jaw and the set of his mouth. No matter how hard she tried to avoid the memories, she saw Yainar as she had known him four-teen years ago—and she also saw his body bleeding after she had driven her spear into him.

She hardly heard Uroh as he began talking, prais-ing Feroh's strong muscles and sharp mind. Uroh could be eloquent when he chose to be, and he had obviously taken care to prepare for this moment. He told anecdotes about Feroh's first clumsy attempts with a spear, when the boy had been just six years old, and soon all the villagers were smiling and applauding. Uroh went on, describing how he had taught Feroh to sail an outrigger canoe, and the times they had traveled up and down the coast. He spoke with love for the boy—although Kori noticed that he never actually referred to Feroh as his son.

By the time Uroh was done, people were standing up, shouting their approval. Kori looked at their faces, then looked at Uroh beside her, and she saw that there was no way she could add to his speech. Anything she said now would be an anticlimax.

"My husband has told you everything," she said helplessly, when the villagers were quiet again and it was her turn to speak. "Really, there is nothing left for me to say. Feroh is my boy-child, my only son. I love him, as we all love him. I'm proud of him, as we are all proud of him. So now, let everyone know: Feroh is a boy no more. He is a man, and we invite him to sit with us as a man, and share in our feast here by the fire. This is what I say, as the chieftain of our tribe. And it is so."

There was another great shout of approval. The people banged their drums and shook their noise-makers, and Feroh stepped down from the stone, still moving slowly, blinking as if he had just woken from a trance. Everyone pressed forward, gathering around him, slapping his shoulders and cheering him.

Finally he allowed himself to smile. Kori felt glad—but then he glanced in her direction, and even though he was grinning, showing his young, white teeth, his eyes were just as dark and brooding as before.

Well, she told herself, that was just his way. There was always this strangeness about him, and there always would be. And really, he did seem happy enough, seizing his share of the food, thanking the people who had praised him, and trading jokes with the other young men.

Kori felt a small hand clutching hers, and she

found Meiri beside her, looking pale and worried. "I'm sorry—" the girl began.

"It's my fault," Kori interrupted her. "I shouldn't have told you—the thing I told you—so soon before this ceremony. But no one even remembers now that you found it difficult to speak. They probably thought you were just shy."

The girl gave a quick nod. She said nothing.

Kori led her over to Uroh and they sat together by the fire. Soon there were songs to sing, and as the night grew colder, some of the women took their babies and infants away to bed. The older men started telling stories, as they always did, trying to outdo each other with their tales of fantastic adventures, danger, and bravery.

Suddenly Kori noticed that Feroh had gone.

"Where is he?" she murmured to Uroh, peering into the shadows at the edges of the Meeting Place.

Uroh gave her a puzzled look. "You mean Feroh?"

"Yes. He was there a moment ago. And now he's missing."

Uroh shrugged. "He never stays late by the fire."

"But tonight is his night," Kori said, standing up. "After all the generous things that people said, he has an obligation to be here."

Uroh gave her a quizzical look. "If tonight is his night, he has no obligation at all. He should be able to do whatever pleases him."

"No," Kori said, feeling a moment of irritation. She turned and walked away from the fire, into the darkness.

A few moments later she reached her hut. There was no light inside, but when she stepped in and stood for a moment, looking and listening, she sensed his brooding presence. "Feroh," she said, deliberately keeping her voice level so that it wouldn't sound as if she were scolding him. "Feroh, why are you here?"

There was a faint rustling sound, and she realized he was lying on the bed of straw at the far end of the hut. "I felt like being alone," he said.

Kori sighed. "Didn't the ceremony please you? This should be a joyful day, Feroh. What did we do to disappoint you?"

He made a scornful sound, but he said nothing.

Kori moved slowly forward, feeling her way in the darkness. She squatted down beside the simple bed. "I'm trying to understand, Feroh," she said, now showing just a faint edge of impatience in her voice. "We did everything we could—"

He made the sound again, louder than before. "You said nothing."

Kori paused. "You mean, before I pronounced you a man? Uroh had already said everything there was to say."

"He made jokes about me. He humiliated me."

Kori wrestled with her impatience. "He spoke lovingly, Feroh. And when people laughed, they weren't laughing at you. They were sharing his love for you, remembering how they knew you as a boy, before you learned to be a man."

He rolled over, and suddenly she felt the warmth of him. His face, she realized, was just a hand's breadth from hers. "None of them knows me," he said. There was a new sound in his voice, sharp and dismissive. "None of them knows anything. They're fishermen. I have no respect for any of them."

Kori felt shocked. She had often seen him angry, but she had never heard him speak quite this way. "There are some hunters among them," she said, "and it takes courage to sail the ocean—"

He rolled off the bed, pushed past her, and strode to the door. He didn't leave the hut; he just stood there with his back to her. She heard him breathing heavily.

"Feroh," she said, "what is the matter with you?"

"I'm not happy here." The answer was immediate.

Kori sighed. "I know. I often sense that you aren't happy. Yet I never know why."

She heard him turn around quickly in his heavy ceremonial robe. "What is there for me here?" he said. "Look at this tribe, a crowd of wanderers and nomads ruled by a woman. And you've made it clear, Meiri will take your place, not me."

"Ah," Kori said. "So that's the source of your discontent." She stood up. "But I've explained to you, Feroh. There is a spirit in men that rises up and urges them to hunt and kill and fight. I've seen what this spirit can do. I've seen two tribes spilling each other's blood. And so long as I live, I will never allow that spirit to rule this tribe."

"Then maybe there's no place for me here," he said. The anger was gone from his voice. He sounded indifferent.

"We love you, Feroh," Kori told him.

He grunted. "Meiri hates me. She envies my strength and she always wants to cut me down. Uroh has no interest; he only cares about sailing alone. And you care for Meiri far more than you care for me."

"No!" Kori cried, feeling overwhelmed with the

unfairness of what he said. She had tried so hard, so very hard, for so many years, to prevent him from feeling this way. She felt as if she were trapped in a pattern, a mesh as tight and unyielding as a fishing net, forcing her to be here and listen to her son say these terrible things.

"Feroh," she said, summoning her strength to make a last effort to placate him. "There can be many pleasures for you here. You can hunt, if you wish—"

"The best lands belong to other tribes," he snapped at her.

"And you will pair with a woman," she went on, ignoring his interruption. "You will father children—"

"There are no women for me to pair with here."

Kori sighed. "You were born when Uroh and I came here, before others joined us. Naturally, other people's children are younger than you. But if you wait two years, there will be choices for you then."

"I don't want to wait."

Kori had wanted this day to be the most joyous day of his life. She had pledged that she would do everything she could to make it so. But now, finally, she lost her patience. "Is there anything that would satisfy you?" she demanded.

"To be the leader of this tribe." He said it without hesitation. "I'm strong, I'm brave, and people respect me. Meiri is weak and small and scared of her own shadow. It's wrong, it's *stupid*, that she should inherit your power."

For just a moment Kori contemplated the idea. She saw why it made sense to Feroh, and why he felt it was so unjust for him to be rejected.

Yes, he could be a fearless leader—but that was the

very reason why he should never have the chance. "The man who seeks power," Kori said softly, "is the last man who should be allowed to possess it." She moved to the door, brushing past him in the darkness. "I realize this is hard for you to understand," she told him. "But I can never change my mind about this. And you have to accept it. Otherwise, Feroh, I fear that you will *never* be happy among us."

8

That night, when the celebration was over and everyone was sleeping, Kori woke to the sound of a scream.

She found herself lying beside Uroh on their simple bed, with her pulse racing and all her senses suddenly alert.

"Stop it!" It was Meiri's voice. "Feroh, you're hurting me!" And then another scream.

Kori scrambled off her bed—and bumped into Uroh as he, too, stood in the darkness. "What's happening?" he asked, as if somehow she would know the answer.

She ducked around him, searching for the red glow of the fire, but it had burned out. "Meiri, come here!" she called. A moment later the girl fell into her arms.

Meiri's head pressed against Kori's shoulder. The girl's skin was wet, and Kori realized with shock that the wetness was blood. She circled her arms around Meiri's waist, picked her up, and dragged her quickly out of the hut.

Night was almost over. The huts of the village were barely visible as black silhouettes against dim gray light in the eastern sky. Still, there was no moon, and not enough dawn light yet for Kori to see what had happened. While Meiri made protesting sounds, Kori carried the girl to the Meeting Place.

She sat Meiri on the flat stone where Feroh had stood during his ceremony. Then she turned to the glowing embers of the fire, lit a length of dry wood, and held it close to Meiri's face.

The girl blinked and squinted in the sudden light. She reached up to touch her forehead where blood was running freely from a deep cut.

"Press your palm against it," Kori told her. "Press hard." She frowned. "We need to stop it bleeding. How did this happen?"

"He banged my head against the wall." Meiri was able to speak calmly now, but her face still showed her anger and hurt.

"Why did he do that?" Kori asked.

"Because—he said he's a man, and he should have the bed to himself. He told me to sleep on the floor."

"And you refused?"

"He hit me, so I hit back at him. That was when he grabbed me."

Meiri grunted with impatience. "Wait here," she said.

She walked to the side of the Meeting Place where torches were kept: lengths of wood with hemp wound around the ends, soaked in whale oil. She chose one, lit it, then strode back to her home.

Inside, in the light from the torch, she found Uroh sitting facing Feroh. "Soon enough you will have a hut of your own," Uroh was saying. "The tribe will help you to build it. You know this. Until then, we must all share our home together."

Feroh was sitting on his bed with his arms folded, staring fixedly at the opposite wall, saying nothing.

Kori was in no mood to be tolerant anymore. "Show some respect, Feroh," she warned him. "What Uroh says is true."

Feroh gave her a look of disgust. "Respect must be earned," he said. His voice was higher pitched than normal; she could tell that he was nervous about the way he was confronting her. But he maintained a defiant stare.

Kori realized she had been foolish, imagining that he would be easier to deal with after he became a man, because he wouldn't feel such a need to prove himself. Just the opposite: his new status had given him the courage to expose all the anger he had been afraid to reveal before.

Uroh smiled—and that smile made Kori even more apprehensive, because she had seen Uroh like this only a few times in her life, when he faced an adversary. He squatted down in front of Feroh, reached out, and gently patted the boy's cheek.

Feroh jerked back, looking angry and suspicious, but Uroh was still relaxed, still smiling. "You're so fierce," he said. "You want to fight the world, Feroh. But anger makes people stupid, and fighting wastes the strength of a man. Haven't I told you that?"

"Yes," said Feroh. His lip curled. "You've told me that."

Kori found herself gripping the wooden torch so tightly, the rough branch dug painfully into her palm. "Uroh," she called out. "Don't." She didn't know what he was going to do, but she knew beyond a doubt that something bad was going to happen.

Uroh ignored her. He was staring intently into Feroh's face. "Perhaps there is really only one answer," he said, half to himself. "If I must *earn* your respect, and you only respect men who are strong, perhaps you have to fight me." His smile widened as he spoke, as if he found the idea amusing.

A tic pulled at Feroh's face. "You lack the courage to fight," he said.

"Then why not hit me?" said Uroh. He tilted his head, examining Feroh's face. "Perhaps you are afraid. Yes, I can see that now."

"No!" Feroh's voice was a sudden shout. He swung his arm wildly.

Uroh raised his hand, moving casually, as if he had merely intended to scratch his nose. With no trouble at all, he seized Feroh's wrist and held it.

Feroh stared at him in surprise. He made a wild, inarticulate sound, swung his other arm—and Uroh caught that one, too. Uroh was far stronger than he looked; he kept his grip on both of Feroh's wrists while the young man struggled helplessly.

"Perhaps you have something to learn from me after all," Uroh said, still smiling. "Perhaps I could teach you to hold your temper."

Feroh screamed between clenched teeth. He drew a deep breath, then jerked his right wrist with all his strength. It wrenched free from Uroh's grip—although

Kori saw that Uroh had expected this, and maybe even wanted it to happen.

Feroh wrenched his other wrist free and paused for a moment, breathing heavily. His face was flushed scarlet, and his wrists were red where Uroh had held them. His hands were trembling and his eyes were wild. Suddenly he reached out and seized a spear that stood in the corner of the hut.

"Stop!" Kori shouted.

"He cannot hurt me," said Uroh, still speaking softly, still smiling.

"Stop!" Kori repeated, screaming the word. Her voice was so loud, both men flinched from it. Feroh gave her a startled look, as if his rage against Uroh had made him forget that she was in the hut.

Kori stepped over and swept her arm, seizing the spear out of his hands. "No man shall ever raise a spear against another man," Kori shouted at Feroh. "Do you understand? Never in this tribe. Never!"

It was her most sacred rule. For a moment Feroh looked unsure of himself.

"Go to the Meeting Place," Kori told him. "Go there! *Now!*"

Reluctantly Feroh stood up. "But this was not my fault. Uroh said—"

"Go to the Meeting Place, or I will tell my people to take you there. Which will it be, Feroh?"

A terrible mixture of emotions showed in his face: confusion, anger, and hurt. He was still a boy, she realized, despite all his posturing. He was a boy who wanted to be a man, wanted to be so strong that nothing could hurt him.

Feroh glared at her for a long, silent moment.

Finally, without a word, he left the hut.

Kori tried to calm herself. She closed her eyes for a moment, taking slow breaths.

"You are upset," said Uroh. He stood and went to her, taking her in his arms.

"I don't think he has ever made me so angry," said Kori. She felt some of the tension draining out of her. "And you, you should never, ever—"

"I think I could have helped him," Uroh said softly.

Kori opened her eyes and looked at his wide, friendly face. "How could it possibly help him, to provoke him so that he would try to stab you with a spear?"

Uroh turned away. "He has so much emotion in him—I think it has to come out. Until it comes out, he will be unhappy, and so long as he is unhappy, he will be dangerous."

Kori felt confused. Uroh sounded so sure of himself, but once again she couldn't understand him. "He could have hurt you," she said, clinging to the most obvious fact that she was sure of.

Uroh shrugged. "He's not as dangerous as his father was."

Kori shuddered. She stepped close to her husband and embraced him. "It's a rule in this tribe, no person shall *ever* point a weapon at another person. If I allow the rule to be broken, here in my own home—"

"Yes, people would lose their respect for the rule," Uroh agreed. "So, I see what you are saying now: I took a risk not just for myself, but for the tribe." He lapsed into thought for a moment. "Perhaps I was unwise."

She turned away from him and seized her pouch of herbs and salves. "Either way, we must settle this quickly. Our daughter is waiting for me in the Meeting

Place, and Feroh has gone there, and I'm sure the noise has woken people."

"I'll come with you," said Uroh.

She blinked, feeling slightly surprised. "You will?"

He nodded. "I am involved in this. So it's my duty, don't you think?"

"Thank you," she said.

Outside, dawn was breaking. "Kori!" a voice called to her.

Kori peered in the dim light and recognized Geren, one of the elder women of the tribe.

"Did I hear shouting?" Geren asked.

"Yes," said Kori. She looked at Geren's face for a moment, wondering how the woman would react when she learned what had happened. Geren was a kind person, but she could be just as impatient as Kori, and just as severe, and she had no patience with anyone who broke the rules of the tribe. "Come with us," Kori said. "There's something that requires your attention."

When they reached the Meeting Place they found Feroh standing to one side with his arms folded, refusing to look at anyone, while half a dozen villagers stood around Meiri where she sat clutching her injured forehead. "Let me through," Kori called out, till the people stepped aside and she reached her daughter. "Someone bring water, and hot stones from the fire."

Meiri looked embarrassed now by the attention. "It doesn't hurt so much," she said.

Kori pulled the girl's hand away from the wound. "But it's still bleeding, and it must be cleaned." She looked down as a boy brought a leather bucket and placed it beside her. She reached in her healer's pouch and pulled out some thin, soft mole skin. She wetted it and wiped the cut, then took out some dried barberries, placed them in the mole skin, squeezed them to add their essence to the water, and wiped the cut again.

"Shall I add these stones?" a voice asked.

Kori saw Geren beside her, gingerly holding a couple of big, round stones on a pair of sticks. The stones were so hot, the sticks were starting to smolder.

"Yes, Geren," said Kori. "Thank you."

There was a splash and a hiss as the stones fell into the water. Moments later the water was boiling. Kori pulled little bags of herbs from her pouch and sprinkled into the water a mixture of barberry root and white powder that came from the underside of lodgepole pine bark. She waited for the powder to infuse the water with its healing power, then soaked her mole skin again and gave it to Meiri. "Keep this on the cut. It will soon stop bleeding."

Meiri nodded.

Kori repacked her healer's pouch, trying to ignore the murmur of excited conversation behind her. She hated having to share her family's private affairs with the rest of the tribe, but this time there was no choice.

She stood up and turned toward her people. "I brought Meiri out here because I wanted to see what had happened, and the fire in our home had burned out," she explained. "Meiri cut her head. I believe she had a fight with Feroh. I'm sorry if some of you were woken by the noise."

"I heard your voice, Kori," someone said. "You were shouting."

"This is true," said Kori. She reached a decision. "I should talk about this with the elder women of the tribe. After we talk, we will come to you and explain

what happened, and what must be done." She beckoned to Geren. "Come to the elders' hut. Someone find
Raia and Shoeni, and tell them to join us there."

There were some more shouted questions as she
turned away from the crowd, but most people seemed
too sleepy and confused to pester her for an explana-
tion. Clearly, it wasn't a crisis for the tribe; family argu-
ments happened often enough. On the other hand, it
must be a serious matter for Kori to need to discuss it
with the elder women.

A little later she sat in the tiny hut that was reserved
exclusively for the elders. Geren had started a fire and
was heating some fish left over from the feast the previous night. Raia joined them, settling her plump body
onto the woven matting that covered the floor. Then
Shoeni arrived, a sharp-faced, sharp-witted woman
who was as tall and thin as Raia was short and fat.

"I'm sorry I had to call you here," said Kori, looking
at each of the three women in turn. "But our most
sacred rule has been broken."

"By Feroh?" Shoeni asked quickly.

"Yes," said Kori. She looked down, feeling
ashamed.

"Tell us about it," said Raia. She gave Kori a friendly
smile. "I'm sure it isn't so bad. You always take things so
seriously, Kori."

Kori sighed. "This is a serious matter. He hit Meiri's
head against the wall, and later he took a spear and
turned it against Uroh."

Raia's smile faded. She shifted uneasily.

"Was he provoked?" Shoeni asked.

Kori told the story as well as she could. The other women listened closely, nibbling from time to time from the helpings of fish, but Kori felt she couldn't stomach any food. Whenever she had to talk publicly about Feroh, she felt haunted by the terrible truth about his father, which she could never reveal.

There was a thoughtful silence when she finished speaking.

"Your Feroh," said Raia. She forced a laugh and shook her head. "Always so difficult, and so fierce. And Uroh! Kori, your husband's such a gentle man. Who would have thought he would act like that?"

"He can be braver than any man I know," Kori said. "He just chooses not to show it."

"He did provoke Feroh," said Geren.

"Yes," said Shoeni, "but that is no excuse. Feroh seems to think that, now he is a man, he can do as he pleases. He attacked his sister, and he raised a spear against his father."

Geren nodded. "He must be punished," she said in her firm, strict voice—just as Kori had known she would.

There was another thoughtful silence.

"The trouble is," said Kori, "if Feroh is punished, and if it happens in public, it may make him even angrier, even harder to control than he is now."

"But if he tries to inflict pain on others, he should feel pain himself," said Geren. "Otherwise, why should he ever stop?"

"What do you think, Raia?" Kori asked.

The big woman looked unhappy. She glanced at the other women as if she wished there was some way they could relieve her from the responsibility of speaking. "I don't like punishments," she said. "I like everyone to get along. I think it works better to be kind than cruel."

Geren and Shoeni started to object, but Raia held up her hand. "I haven't finished," she said. She fidgeted for a moment. "It seems to me, in this case—I don't know, Feroh is such a wild one. Maybe he needs to be tamed a bit. Maybe Uroh's been a bit too easy on him."

"Well, Kori?" Geren said, sounding a little impatient now. "The three of us all seem to agree."

Kori forced a smile. "Thank you," she said softly, "for your advice. It's hard for me to punish anyone, because my own mother was so strict and cruel. But in this case, I accept your wisdom."

"He should be made to stand in front of his people," Geren said.

Kori nodded. "All right."

"If you wish," said Shoeni, speaking gently, "I will announce the decision."

"No," Kori said, gathering her strength. "It's my responsibility."

She stood up quickly and walked out of the elders' hut.

9

A dead oak tree stood at the north side of the village atop a bare, rocky mound. The tree had been shattered by lightning long ago, leaving its thick trunk standing alone, terminating in splintered fingers that poked into the sky.

Two men of the tribe led Feroh to the tree and stood him with his back against it. He wore only a pair of leggings, leaving his chest and feet bare.

The men tied his wrists behind him, then looped a length of hemp around his neck and knotted it carefully so that it wouldn't tighten. The free end of the hemp was tied around the tree trunk, pinning him to it.

Kori felt such intense waves of emotion, it was hard for her to speak. She hated this ritual, and she took pride in the fact that it was seldom necessary. For the most part, her people were gentle and easygoing. They respected each other and avoided fighting with each other. To see her own son singled out for this humiliation was almost more than she could bear.

Still, the elders had advised her, and she knew she should accept their advice. She turned to the rest of the tribe. Everyone had gathered in a ragged group, looking deeply uneasy, forced to face this punishment ceremony so soon after honoring Feroh the previous night.

"Feroh is here because he broke the most important rule of our tribe," Kori told them. "This is hard for me to speak about, because I am not just his chieftain, I am his mother. And this should still be a time of celebration, now that he is a man. But——" She forced herself to continue. "He injured Meiri, and he raised a spear against Uroh." She turned to Feroh. "Do you deny this?"

He said nothing. He ignored her as if she didn't exist.

The villagers talked nervously among themselves, and several of them shouted questions.

"I will not answer your questions now," she told them, feeling suddenly overwhelmed with weariness and wanting to end this business as quickly as possible. "You can ask the elder women later, if you wish. Just know that what I say is true."

She breathed deeply, knowing what must happen, and dreading it. "It is the way of our tribe," she went on, "when someone breaks a taboo, for all of us to show our disapproval, in whatever way we wish. And it is the way of our tribe for the person who is being punished to face each person who punishes him." She turned her head. "The elders shall go first. Geren, Shoeni, Raia."

The women moved forward. They climbed the mound where the tree stood, till Shoeni stood in front of Feroh. She stood for a long moment, eyeing Feroh coldly. She slapped his face, paused a moment longer, then gave a curt nod and moved on.

Geren came next. She picked up a short, dead branch and swung it from the left and from the right, thwacking it across Feroh's thighs and shins, hard enough to make him flinch.

Raia ambled up. She avoided looking at Feroh as she bent down, scooped some mud, and rubbed it quickly into his hair. She turned away, shaking her head sadly.

The rest of the villagers followed. Some of them hit Feroh with their fists. Some kicked him, some threw small stones, and some merely scolded him. He was lashed with brambles and with nettles, and more mud was daubed across his face and body.

Through it all, he said nothing.

Finally Uroh took his turn. He stood in front of Feroh for a long time, frowning, as if he simply couldn't decide how to deal with the situation that he found himself in. Then, unexpectedly, he took Feroh's face between his hands and kissed him lightly on the forehead. "Perhaps that is your greatest punishment, Feroh," he said. "To know that we care for you—and to fear that one day, we may stop."

Uroh moved away and walked back toward the village, ignoring the other people who were still standing and watching the spectacle. Kori felt an impulse to run after him, just to be with him and feel soothed by his company. But clearly, her duty compelled her to stay here.

She turned to her daughter. "Meiri, now," Kori said. "It is your turn. And then it will be mine. And then we shall forgive Feroh and welcome him back among us."

Meiri hardly seemed to hear what Kori said. The girl was standing with her fists clenched, her mouth compressed to a tiny thin shape, her eyes watching Feroh with awful intensity. Her head was bandaged with a strip of deer skin where he had injured her. She took a slow breath, then marched up to Feroh. She raised her hand, then swung it, hitting the side of his arm.

It seemed an innocent blow, but Kori knew better. She had taught Meiri how to use her hands as weapons, slicing or stabbing to inflict severe pain. She'd never imagined, though, that she'd see Meiri using this knowledge against Feroh.

Meiri drew back her hand and struck again, in the same spot as before. Feroh jerked in his bonds, and he gasped.

Kori frowned. "Meiri," she called softly. "Not too hard."

The girl paid no attention. She eyed Feroh carefully, then spun around, adding the force of her body to the power of her hand as she struck Feroh a third time on the side of his arm.

This time, Feroh was unable to maintain his self-discipline. He let out a cry.

"Meiri!" Kori shouted.

The girl still paid no attention. She was breathing heavily, and her cheeks were flushed. All her attention was focused on Feroh. She screamed as she hit Feroh hard in the stomach.

"That's enough!" Kori said, stepping forward.

Meiri still ignored her. She threw herself at Feroh in a frenzy, raking him with her nails and drawing blood. She seized him by the hair and started banging his head against the tree trunk.

Kori grabbed Meiri by her upper arms and dragged her back. "Enough!"

Meiri struggled wildly, still staring at Feroh, who had slumped in his bonds and was making choking noises, trying to recover from the savage blow to his stomach. Suddenly Meiri pulled free from Kori and threw herself at him again, pounding him with her fists.

"Meiri!" Kori cried. She wrestled with her daughter and shook her. "Meiri, stop! He's your brother!"

The girl turned. "No!" she cried.

For a moment mother and daughter stared at each other. Then Meiri blinked. The haunted expression left her face. She looked suddenly ashamed. "I'm sorry," she said, raising her hands and pressing them to her cheeks. She shook her head as if trying to clear it. "I don't know—I'm sorry."

"Say that to Feroh now," Kori told her fiercely. She turned Meiri around by her shoulders, hoping and praying that Feroh hadn't understood Meiri's outburst.

"I'm sorry, Feroh," Meiri said, forcing the words out with difficulty. She hesitated, and Kori felt the girl tremble with emotion. "But you shouldn't have picked on me all those times!" Meiri shouted. "You shouldn't have been so mean to me. All the times when no one was looking, and you hit me or hurt me—" She broke off. She turned and ran, pushing between the villagers, ignoring their looks of concern.

Kori found herself alone with Feroh, feeling overwhelmed with sadness. She reached to untie the knots in his bonds. "I'm sorry," she said. "This was not a wise idea. I did it because the elders said it should be so, and I didn't trust my own judgment, because you're my son." She plucked at the rope and saw that her hands were shaking. She was almost in tears, and it was unthinkable to show such weakness in front of her people.

She forced herself to be calm as she finally freed Feroh, and he stumbled forward, away from the tree. He was a pathetic figure, smeared with mud, crisscrossed with bramble scratches, and bleeding where Meiri had gouged his chest with her nails.

"Go down to the place where the river meets the ocean, Feroh," Kori called after him. "Bathe and clean yourself, and then come back to us, and we will welcome you."

Feroh didn't answer. The villagers opened a path for him, and he walked between them, limping slightly, clutching his arm where Meiri had hit him so savagely.

"We care for you, Feroh," Kori shouted. She spread her hands, appealing to her people. "Isn't this so?"

There was a growing murmur of assent. But Feroh ignored them all as he went toward the village and finally disappeared among the huts.

Kori sighed. "It can be hard," she said, "to know what's best." She looked at the people facing her. "The punishment is over."

She stood, waiting, and one by one the villagers turned away. She tried to reassure herself that most of them probably didn't take the situation as seriously as she did. Most of them didn't even know exactly what had happened. Still, she felt overwhelmed with shame, to see such terrible displays of uncontrolled anger from both her children, and to feel so helpless, knowing she must be partly to blame, but not understanding how or why.

As her people left the punishment place she

noticed a face in the crowd—a boy named Raor, who was one year younger than Feroh. He was skinny and shy, but he was always practicing with a spear, holding himself proudly, trying to move with the poise of a hunter. He seemed to idolize Feroh.

"Raor," Kori called to him. "Wait. I must talk to you."

The boy looked uneasy as he held back from the rest of the people and waited for her.

"You are Feroh's friend," Kori said, placing her hand on Raor's shoulder. "Isn't that so?"

Raor hesitated. "I hope so," he said. "Maybe I am." He tried to deepen his voice as he spoke, but really, it was the voice of a child.

"He's spoken of you with respect," Kori said.

Raor gave her a cautious look. "Really?"

"In any case, he certainly needs a friend now," Kori went on. "I want you to go to him, Raor, down at the beach, where he's washing himself. Just go and be near him. But don't say that I sent you. In fact, you don't need to say anything at all. Sometimes that's what a person needs most from a friend."

"All right." Raor drew himself up. He looked proud that she'd chosen him for this task. "I'll do it."

"Good, Raor," Kori said, patting his shoulder.

She turned back to the village. People would be talking, trying to understand. She would need to move among them, explaining herself and reassuring them. Some of the villagers, such as Taran, would be critical of her. Others would be sympathetic. Either way, she had to let them speak with her.

First, though, she must see Meiri.

Kori went to her hut, hoping she would find the

girl there. Sure enough, Meiri was lying on her side on her bed, hugging herself, facing the wall, staring at it dully.

Kori stepped softly across the floor of natural stone. It was so strange to think that just a short while ago she had been sleeping here with Uroh, completely unaware of all the wild anger and emotion that was about to be released among her family.

And where was Uroh now? Sailing, she guessed. Anytime something worried him or puzzled him, he tended to seek solitude; and he could feel more alone on the ocean than anywhere else.

Kori lowered herself gently onto the edge of the bed where Meiri lay. She placed her hand on the girl's shoulder. "I know you felt bad," she said. "But I have to say, Meiri, it hurts me that you acted that way."

The girl closed her eyes. "I'm sorry," she said. She shivered, dragging her robe tightly around herself. "Once I started hitting him, I couldn't stop." Her voice was very small. "I just wanted to hurt him more, and more, and more."

"But why?" Kori asked.

Meiri shook her head. "You don't know all the times he's tormented me. He always managed to hide it from you—till last night, when I think he didn't care anymore. He's hurt me so many times."

"So you should have defended yourself," Kori said. "I've taught you how."

"No!" Meiri cried. She looked up at Kori. "You still don't understand. He scared me. He's so full of hate—he told me he'd kill me if I ever did anything against him."

"Why?" Kori asked, feeling lost, as if she could no longer believe in any of the things she had always assumed were true. "Why is he so full of hate?"

Meiri was silent for a long time. "I don't know," she said finally. "But when I saw him tied to the tree, and I knew he couldn't hurt me, I just kept thinking of the things he's done to me, and how his father raped you, and I wanted—I wanted just to destroy him." Suddenly Meiri started crying. Her small body shook with great sobs.

Kori sighed; she lay down and wrapped her arms around Meiri, hugging her close. "You're right," she whispered. "I didn't realize how bad it's been for you."

"I really believed him when he said he would kill me," Meiri sobbed. "He has such a temper, he doesn't even know what he's doing sometimes."

Kori closed her eyes, feeling weary. It was good to know the truth, she told herself. The truth was always good. Yet this truth was so hard to bear—and now that she knew it, it was just another burden, because she saw no way to resolve the problem.

"We will find a separate place for him to live," she said. "Clearly, he can't stay with us here anymore."

Meiri didn't answer. She turned away. Kori told herself she should leave the girl now, and get up and go among her people—yet it was good to lie here with her daughter like this, just for a little while.

She closed her eyes and rested a moment. Some time passed, and still she put off the moment when she would get up and go to the Meeting Place.

Then she heard a high voice shouting.

Gradually she realized it was someone calling her name. She heard small footsteps running closer, then the door flap was pushed aside, and suddenly Raor was standing there, gasping for breath, barely able to speak.

Kori sat up and looked at him in dismay, wondering what new catastrophe could have made the boy so distraught. "Calm yourself!" she told him. "Sit. Sit there." She gestured to her bed.

He stumbled over to it and slumped down. "Feroh," he said, still taking huge gulps of air. "Feroh, he's gone."

Kori frowned. She wondered if she'd misheard him. "What are you talking about?"

"He said to tell you. He's gone. He won't come back."

Kori stared at him in silence. She felt numb. Then she looked quickly around the hut. She saw now what she should have seen before: that Feroh's spear was missing, and his travel pack, and his moccasins. He'd had just enough time to seize some food from the Meeting Place and pick up his belongings from the hut before he ran down the cliff path to wash himself.

"Do you want me to go after him?" Raor asked, looking at her anxiously. "He took the north path. He told me not to follow him, and I didn't know if I should. But I will, if you want me to. Maybe I can get him to come back."

"No." The word escaped from her before she even had time to think. She stood up swiftly. She felt confused, and there was a strange, painful feeling of loss—a feeling that she guessed would grow worse in the days ahead. But there was also a feeling of—rightness, somehow. "Feroh has become a man," she said. "He is free to make his own decisions. He is just as free as any man or woman in our tribe. If he chooses to leave, we cannot stop him."

"But where will he go?" Raor said.

Kori paused for a moment, thinking. "He's a good hunter, it's springtime, he can live off the land for a while at least. Before the winter he should be able to find a home in one of the other tribes."

"I don't think that's how it will be," said Meiri.

Kori turned to face the girl. "What do you mean?"

Meiri looked at Kori, then at Raor. "You still don't understand Feroh, either of you. He won't just run away from a place where people have humiliated him."

"He brought it upon himself," Kori objected. "He knows the customs of our tribe, and he knows the penalties."

Meiri violently shook her head. "No. No, he doesn't respect your customs. He's too proud. You know how proud he is. He thinks he's better than you, better than everybody."

Kori frowned at Meiri. "So you think he will return?"

"Yes," said Meiri. She fretted with the edges of her robe. "I think he is angrier now than he has ever been. I think he will wait until he is stronger, and he will bide his time and plan what he wants to do, until he feels sure that he cannot fail. And then, perhaps in the summer—he will return, because he will want revenge."

PART 2

10

On a hot afternoon, Kori worked with her people in a grove of tall redwoods at the bottom of the hill where the village stood. Five days had passed since Feroh had left, and Kori still found herself spending much of each day thinking about him, remembering all the times she had tried so hard to understand him and care for him—and had failed.

Her people saw that she was unhappy, and they tried to show sympathy, even though she saw now that Feroh had never been very well liked. They were not especially concerned by his sudden departure, and they didn't miss him. Even Uroh seemed ready to accept what had happened, and Meiri was actually happier without him.

Still, Kori felt melancholy and haunted by guilt, forever wondering whether she could have changed the path that Feroh had followed, if only she had been more sympathetic, or stronger, or gentler, or—

"Tired?" It was Uroh's voice, close beside her.

Kori looked up with a start. "No," she said, "I'm not tired." She forced a smile and picked up her stone ax. A massive tree lay on its side where the villagers had felled it two days ago. They had separated one section of the trunk from the rest, and now they were stripping away its bark. Almost everyone from the tribe was here, half-naked in the warm air, working to build a new canoe. Their axes swung with a steady rhythm, and the noise of stone against wood merged with the sound of singing. "Across the water," they sang, "through the day, we trust the sun to guide our way. Across the water, through the night—"

"You're still blaming yourself," Uroh said. He spoke so softly, so close to Kori, no one else could hear him.

"Of course." Kori gave a little shrug. "I think now I should have gone after him, or sent someone after him. I don't like it to be this way, never knowing what he's thinking or feeling. If Meiri is right, or even half-right—"

Uroh put his arm around her shoulders. "You cannot always force the pattern of things," he said. "Sometimes you must accept fate. This was fated to happen, Kori, and there was nothing you could do to stop it, and there's nothing you can do to change it now."

"You know I don't believe that." He was trying to comfort her, but when he spoke like this, he irritated her. "We all have a duty to shape our lives."

Uroh looked at her with his calm, kind eyes. "The only thing we should be shaping now is this tree." He turned away suddenly. "Jebal!" he called to a boy of ten working just a few paces away, wielding an ax with wild, ambitious strokes. "Not like that. You waste your strength that way. First understand the shape of the tree. If you don't understand it, how can you make it do what you want?"

Kori watched as Uroh strode over, closed his hands around the boy's hands, and showed him how to swing the ax, cutting almost parallel with the wood in order to split the bark away. Kori found herself remembering another day, five years ago, when her people had been working on another tree here in the redwood grove, and Uroh had tried to show Feroh the best way to use his ax. "Let me do it the way I want to," Feroh had said, with a resentful look. Kori could still hear the boy's defiant voice.

Kori sighed. She raised her own ax, swung it, sliced the flint blade into the bark, and levered a section away from the tree. She smelled the rich odor of moist, fresh-cut wood, and heard the bark creak as it yielded to her. She swung the ax again while dragging the bark back with her free hand.

Soon the whole section of the tree would be stripped, and then the real work would begin, cutting away the upper side of the trunk and hollowing out the remainder. Finally they would drag the shell around the northern path to the beach, where they would waterproof it with whale oil and fit it with a mast and outriggers. The whole task would take months to complete, and it was grueling work. Still, she enjoyed it as a way to bring her people together, and a way for her to be with Uroh, and a way to take her mind off the things that she needed to forget.

She swung the ax. Her people had sung the last

verse of their song, and the only sound now was of their
tools. That, and the faint screeching of an owl in the distance.

Kori looked up suddenly. It was late afternoon, and
the sun was still bright. No owl should be crying at this
time of day.

She turned away from her work and strode
among the trees till she reached the edge of the grove.
She shaded her eyes, peering up at the hill where the
village stood. Yes, there was a tiny figure silhouetted
against the sky, screeching out the owl cry and waving
his arms. Kori saw another figure running down the
path—a child on his way to deliver a message.

Kori cursed herself for being so preoccupied. She
should always be alert. She strode back to her people.
"Stop!" she called to them. "Listen!"

They paused in their work. Now they heard it
too—the cry that was used only if there was an emer-
gency on the ocean.

"But no one is fishing today," Uroh said, quickly
checking the twenty people around the felled redwood.
"All of us are here."

"Well, I saw the lookout waving," said Kori.

They set down their tools and followed her, pulling
clothes over hot, flushed skin as they strode through the
forest. When they emerged into open sun, the boy
whom Kori had seen came running toward them
through the tall grass. "Someone on the sea!" he cried,
pointing behind him as if he needed to tell them where
the ocean was. "They were shouting. Need help." He
was so out of breath from running, he could manage
only a few words at a time.

"Who?" Uroh asked him sharply.

"Don't know." He looked from one face to the next. "Joro on lookout. Told me—"

"Good," said Kori, patting the boy's shoulder. "You have delivered your message. Thank you." She glanced back at her people. "Quickly!"

They ran across the grassland, taking the northern path that curved around the hill, allowing easier access to the beach than the cliff path that led down from the village itself. Kori felt her legs sweeping through the tall, dry grass and the sun on her face, but she was barely aware of these things. Most of all she felt anxious. She hated mysteries and surprises, and there had been too many in the past days.

She crested a low ridge and squinted ahead against the glare of the sun on the waves. Yes, someone was out there, a black speck against the silver and blue. But when Kori looked down at the beach, she saw that no canoes were missing. This made her feel even more alarmed—and confused. Her tribe was the only one that had braved the challenge of the ocean. It was theirs alone; they had never had to share it—or the fish they took from it.

She ran down to the beach. She wanted to know, immediately, who the strangers were and where they came from. On the other hand, if they needed help, she would help them, because that was the way of her people. And she could hear a man's voice now, calling faintly above the roar of the surf.

"They are not in a canoe." It was Uroh speaking, close behind her.

She glanced at him, then looked out again across the waves. His eyes were sharper than hers. "You mean they're swimming?" she asked him.

"No. On a raft, I think."

That made her feel relieved, because it meant that the skill of building canoes must still be unique to her tribe. But why would anyone try to sail the sea on a raft?

"You should tell our people what to do," she said to Uroh, as the rest of the tribe gathered around them.

He nodded briefly, then shouted instructions, quickly assigning fifteen of the best, strongest mariners among four of the canoes. "The rest of you wait here," he shouted.

Kori was aware of her limitations. She was far better than Uroh at setting goals for her tribe, resolving disputes, and organizing everyday tasks, but Uroh was more skilled as a mariner than she could ever be. Whenever she ventured out onto the water with him, she always yielded to his authority. Even though he was a shy, gentle man, people obeyed him without question—because they, too, observed his skill.

Soon four canoes were being pushed out into the surf. Kori joined Uroh and two other men named Lamiar and Perner as they strode into the cold water. The sea surged around them, and the canoe rocked and twisted under their hands like a living thing, eager to plunge into its watery world. Kori kept a tight grip on it as she strode ahead, feeling seaweed twining around her legs and hard ripples in the sand under her moccasins.

"In!" Uroh shouted when there was a gap between waves.

Lamiar and Kori hoisted themselves from opposite sides, balancing the canoe with their weight. Uroh and Perner joined them a moment later. The other three canoes were close behind, their sails flapping in the wind.

Uroh seized the steering paddle and kneeled in the stern. "Lamiar, Perner, go forward," he shouted. "Kori, take the sail."

She moved swiftly, instinctively, squatting down, making herself secure, then seizing the ropes that harnessed the spars. The wind out here on the water was from the north. It felt cool—and suddenly she was overwhelmed by a burst of vivid, frightening memories. Once again she was back in the storm, struggling and fighting through the towering waves and the cruel winds and rain. She shuddered.

"Can you manage the task?" Uroh's voice was abrupt, but when she looked back at him she saw kindness in his face. He understood what she was feeling, and he knew exactly what to say.

She felt her back straightening, felt herself becoming indignant at the idea that she might not be able to cope. "Of course I can manage," she called to him. She seized the ropes and hauled on them, turning the sail across the wind.

The canoe heeled over and veered to one side as the wind filled the sail. Uroh corrected it with his paddle, and the heavy wooden shell righted itself slowly. It pitched up as a wave rolled in, then rode the crest and moved forward, gradually gaining speed, urged on by Lamiar and Perner, who were paddling hard near the prow.

Kori turned her face from side to side to judge the exact direction of the wind. She trimmed the sail slightly, then wrapped the ropes around pegs in the hull. The wind was steady; it shouldn't be necessary to adjust the sail any further, at least till they changed course.

She squinted ahead, shading her eyes from the sun. As the canoe crested each wave, she glimpsed the raft ahead. Two people were on it, one much larger than the other. A man and a child? The man was waving and calling excitedly, and she wondered where they could have come from. Perhaps from much farther up the coast, or—the thought made her shiver. Could there be some other piece of land far away to the west, on the other side of the stretch of ocean that her people knew?

She had talked about this with Uroh. She still remembered the way her childhood tribe imagined that no other tribes existed anywhere, because they lived in such a remote location, no one had ever visited them. Then, one day, warriors appeared from beyond the mountains that her people had always thought of as the edge of the world.

In reality the world was so huge, there was no way to be sure where its limits lay. But Uroh had spent years sailing up and down the coast, and he had never seen any sign of a distant shore, nor any strangers out on the ocean.

These thoughts chattered in Kori's head as the canoe brought her closer to the raft. She leaned forward, trying to see the people's faces. Did they seem hostile? Did they have spears?

"Loose the sail," Uroh shouted.

Kori fumbled with the ropes. She was excited and impatient, which made her fingers clumsy. Finally she freed the ropes and turned the sail's edge to the wind. The deer-skin panels flapped wildly, and she felt a pang of concern as she remembered what had happened when she was out with Feroh and Meiri. But Uroh had already replaced the stitching in this sail. In any case, they weren't far out from the shore, and there were other canoes nearby. She tried to push aside her anxieties.

Now that the sail was no longer cupping the wind, the canoe was more maneuverable. Uroh steered a course that circled around the raft and approached it from the far side. Meiri could see the people on it clearly now. One was a strong, tall man with long unbraided hair that blew around him in the wind; the other was a frail girl who looked no older than ten. She was lying on her stomach, clutching the timbers of the raft as it rode the swell, while the man stood, steadying himself by holding hemp ropes attached to opposite sides of the crude wooden platform. Kori looked carefully, but the strangers had no food, no weapons, and no paddles—nothing but the clothes that they were wearing, which were patterned like the robes of the Green Valley Tribe.

Uroh was shouting instructions, guiding the other canoes. He watched and waited while they arranged themselves around the raft, pointing toward it from three sides. "Cast ropes!" Uroh shouted out.

Men hurled long, braided cords. The man on the raft squatted down, using one hand to balance himself, and grabbed the ropes as they fell across the raft. "Tie it!" Uroh shouted to him. "Do you understand?"

"Yes," the man called back. He had a deep, powerful voice; it resonated within his broad chest.

Soon the ropes were stretched tight, holding the raft firmly between the three canoes, so that it could no longer drift and turn randomly with the wind and currents. "Forward now," Uroh called to Lamiar and Perner. "Slowly."

Kori kept the sail slack as their canoe edged toward

the raft. She realized that Uroh must have planned this approach before he even left the beach. He had known immediately how he wanted to hold the raft stable, to eliminate any chance of it hitting one of the canoes and causing damage. In everyday life he seemed vague, uninterested in any practicalities. She marveled that he could be so different when he was out on the ocean.

The canoe closed on the raft. "Stop!" Uroh shouted when they were still an arm's length away. "Hold steady!"

Kori saw the young girl staring at her with wide eyes. The girl looked terrified. The man reached down for her as if he planned to lift her and pass her across.

"No," Uroh called. "Lamiar, throw a rope. You, there—tie it around her waist."

They did as he said. Even though the raft was tethered, it was still rocking wildly on the swell, and Uroh's canoe was moving out of step with it. The child could easily slip and fall, and from the look on her face, Kori felt sure that she didn't know how to swim.

"Now," said Uroh. "Pass her to us, then you come aboard."

The big man kneeled on the raft, spreading his thighs to keep his balance. He took hold of the girl under her arms and stood her up.

She wailed in fear and tried to cling to him. He muttered something to her, then lifted her into the air. She panicked and started kicking and waving her arms. She gave a high, thin scream that was stolen away by the wind. The man ignored her struggles as well as he could, waiting for the right moment. When the raft and the canoe were aligned with one another, he thrust the girl forward.

She screamed again, louder than before. Then Lamiar grabbed her forearms, took her weight, and swung her down into the canoe. There was a thud as her feet hit the wood, and she fell, limp and wide-eyed, her fear gradually giving way to gratitude.

Lamiar untied the rope around her waist. He turned, ready to throw it to the man who was still kneeling on the raft—but the man was already edging forward, trying to reach across the gap between the raft and the canoe. He seized the canoe and Kori felt it dip under his additional weight. At the same time, it tilted as a wave passed under it. The stranger gave a startled cry as his feet lost their grip, and suddenly he was dangling with his legs thrashing in the water.

Kori glimpsed his face and saw his bravery yielding to fear. Lamiar swore. He seized one of the man's wrists and Perner seized the other. Kori reached forward, grabbed the little girl's arm and pulled her from under the men's feet. With a huge effort they dragged the stranger up. He managed to get one knee over the side of the canoe, and then he tumbled into it with a comical expression of surprise.

His face was red from the sun, and his lips were dry and cracked. Still, he was a big, handsome man, with a strong neck and powerful shoulders.

"Don't try to stand," Uroh called to him. "We don't want to have to pull you out of the water a second time."

For a moment the stranger looked angry—but then he checked himself. He threw his head back and gave a great laugh. "You're right, friend," he said. "You tell me what to do. You know the ocean. I'm a stranger to it."

"Good," said Uroh. "Then we understand each

other. So long as you are in my canoe, you must follow my instructions."

The stranger nodded. He reached for the little girl, pulled her to him, and hugged her against his chest. "I am Werror," he said in his deep voice. "And this is my daughter Jalin." He looked from Uroh to Kori, and she saw his eyes narrow as he took in her face. Then he grinned again, showing fine white teeth. "I thank you," he said. "Thank you for rescuing us. For saving our lives."

11

Uroh shouted commands and the canoes headed back to the shore, abandoning the raft behind them. Lamiar gave Werror a skin full of fresh water, and the man grabbed it. He hesitated, restraining himself and passing it to his daughter. She drank from it urgently. Then he took it from her and drained the rest of it in a few big gulps. He lay back for a moment and closed his eyes, breathing deeply.

There were a dozen questions that Kori wanted to ask him, but she saw she would have to be patient. This was not yet the time.

When they reached the shore and beached the canoes, Werror seemed to regain his energy. He leaped out onto the sand, threw back his head, and gave a great happy shout. The villagers clustered around him, admiring his strength, chattering among themselves, and shouting questions. Werror ignored them for a moment. He reached for his daughter and hugged her, relishing the feel of solid land under his feet.

Finally he faced the crowd. "Greetings," he said. "I am Werror; this is my daughter, Jalin." He turned to Uroh, who was dragging the last of the canoes up above the tide line. "What is the name of your tribe?"

Uroh paused. He smiled faintly. "This is not my tribe. My wife is our chieftain."

Werror looked disconcerted. "While we were out on the ocean—"

"The ocean is the only place where I tell anyone what to do," Uroh said, dusting sand off his hands. "On the land, my wife leads us."

Werror turned and looked at Kori. "This is your tribe?" He still sounded skeptical.

She studied his face and clothes. Now that he was standing in front of her, the style of his robe was unmistakable. "You're from the Green Valley Tribe," she said.

"That's true," said Werror.

"Well, then," said Kori, "you must have heard of me."

He frowned. "What is your name?"

"Kori."

He slapped his palm to his forehead. "Then this is the Ocean Tribe. We drifted for so long out there, I imagined we were much farther south. I saw your husband giving orders, and I thought I had met some other tribe that had mastered the art of sailing on the sea." He stretched out his hands and inclined his head toward her. "Forgive me, Kori. I meant no offense."

She clasped his hands. Their backs were raw with sunburn, and the palms were dry. She held them gently. "There is no offense, Werror. We welcome you."

"How long were you drifting?" one of the villagers called out.

Werror turned to the man. "Through the night, this morning, and this afternoon."

"Wind's from the north," someone said. "Not strong, though. Without a sail, this is about as far as it could have carried him."

People nodded, seeing that it was so.

Werror gestured at the water. "I know nothing about traveling on the ocean. I'm a hunter, not a mariner."

"We realize that," Kori said. "And this makes us wonder why you should try to build a raft."

Everyone fell silent. The cheerfulness gradually faded from Werror's face. His eyes became somber. "There has been a terrible conflict," he said. "Many people have died."

Kori felt a chill. Instinctively she clutched her arms around herself. And yet—she wasn't surprised. Somehow she had been expecting something like this, ever since she had been trapped in the storm.

Werror set Jalin down on the sand but kept her close to him, cupping his hands around her thin shoulders. "The Green Valley Tribe was attacked at dawn yesterday," he said. "The warriors were from the east—strangers, nomads, I don't know who they were. They massacred my people."

Kori watched his face, and she saw his strength falter. He turned and looked out over the ocean for a moment. When he turned back again, he had regained his self-control. "I ran with Jalin into the forest, with a handful of others. But the attackers came after us. They hunted us like deer. I had no spear; I couldn't defend myself. My friends were killed. I hid and waited till the attackers went past me—but I knew they would return, and I was desperate. The beach was close by, and there was a lot of driftwood. I lashed it together as well as I could, with thongs and vines, and then we pushed it onto the water. I knew your people had mastered the ocean. I was desperate enough to try it myself."

For a while the only sound was the roaring of the surf. Kori saw her people eyeing him with deep concern, not wanting to believe that such a thing could have happened.

"Well," she said finally, "we always knew that warriors might invade our lands one day. And when I spoke with Baryor several days ago, he warned me—"

"Baryor is dead," Werror interrupted her. "I saw him die."

Kori stopped short. She'd known that the Green Valley Tribe was poorly led and barely defended. Still, it shocked her to realize that the man who'd talked with her and fed her in the forest had had his life stolen from him.

Suddenly she felt anger welling up in her. "I warned him," she said, clenching her fists, feeling helpless. She turned suddenly to her people. "I warned him just as I have warned you all, so many times. Perhaps now you understand why we should learn to defend ourselves and our village—"

She felt a hand on her shoulder. She turned quickly and found Uroh standing there. "There's no need to scold them," he murmured. "They've done their best. You know that."

Kori blinked, feeling disoriented. He was right, she realized. Her shoulders slumped. "I'm sorry," she said.

"Werror," Uroh said, turning to the big man. "Where is your wife? Was she killed by the warriors, too?"

Werror shook his head. "She died two years ago, from the coughing sickness."

There was a sigh of sympathy from the villagers.

"Well, you are welcome here, Werror," Kori said. "All wanderers who come in peace are welcome in our tribe. Stay with us as long as you wish. And you can help us if you tell us more about the men who killed your people. We need to know all we can, so that we can make ourselves more secure in case the warriors come south."

Werror gestured disparagingly. "They have no reason to come here. They have good homes now, and good land. As much as they could possibly want." He paused, and an expression of pain crossed his face. Then he reasserted his will, and his big, friendly grin returned. "But thank you, I would like to stay with your people." He looked down at his daughter, who had remained completely silent, staring up at everyone with large, fearful eyes. "What about you, Jalin? Do you want to stay here?" He gave her shoulders a squeeze.

The little girl nodded.

"Then it is decided," said Werror. "For now, at least."

The villagers cheered him, and they closed around him, slapping his broad back and welcoming him. Their voices were subdued, though, and Kori saw anxiety in their faces. Finally they realized what she had always known: that there were enemies in the world, and if the people of the tribe didn't protect themselves, no one else would do it for them.

*   *   *

The villagers took Werror up the steep path etched into the cliff face. He carried Jalin on his back and didn't complain about the climb, even though he couldn't have eaten in almost two days. Walking behind him, Kori watched the muscles under the smooth brown skin of his powerful legs. She thought he must be the strongest man she had ever seen—and she realized she was studying his body with more than casual interest.

She felt her cheeks reddening, and she was glad that people were scattered ahead of her and behind her along the narrow path, so that no one could see her face. She felt shocked and confused. She loved Uroh with a deep, pure, lasting passion. She never eyed other men.

Yet something in this giant had touched her, and she realized what it was: despite his great strength, he was a gentle man. She remembered seeing him offer the skin of water to his daughter before he drank from it himself. Of course, this was what any man should have done. Still, his concern for the girl moved her.

When they reached the village there was a fresh round of questions from the elder women and young children who had remained there while everyone else was down by the ocean. Raia took a liking to Werror, and insisted that he and Jalin should stay with her in her hut. "I'm an old woman," she said, grinning at him, "but seeing as the young women here have husbands already, you may as well stay with me." She winked at him.

He roared with laughter and hugged her. "Be careful, Raia," he said, wagging his finger. "If you tempt me too much, I may surprise you."

Raia blushed, and there was a lot more laughter.

"I must say, though," Werror went on, "since you mention food, this is something that's on my mind. Jalin here is terribly hungry."

There was a chorus of cries as villagers offered to share their food with him. They clustered around, dragging Werror and Jalin to the Meeting Place. They threw fresh wood on the fire, sat him down, and placed a feast in front of him.

Kori stood with Uroh to one side, watching quietly. "I've never seen them take such a liking to a stranger," she murmured.

"He has a generous spirit," said Uroh. He glanced at Kori. "Like you."

She looked at him, wondering what was behind his words. "You mean I am similar to Werror?" She felt embarrassed. Uroh could be frighteningly perceptive in his strange way. Had he sensed already that Kori found the big man physically attractive?

"I just mean that when people feel that someone cares for them, they care for him in return," Uroh said.

"Oh," said Kori, feeling foolish.

"There are two things that worry me, though," Uroh went on.

Again she felt a chill. The last thing she needed now was something new to concern her. She felt her muscles clenching reflexively. "Not big worries, I hope," she said, with a tightness in her throat.

"Perhaps not. But it occurs to me, someone who rouses your people so easily might be a danger to you, if there ever comes a time when he advocates one choice, and you advocate another, and your people must decide which person to follow."

Kori felt her tension flowing away as quickly as it had gathered inside her. She laughed. "If that ever happens," she said, "that will be their decision, and I'll wish them well."

He gave her a knowing look, narrowing his eyes, as if there was something he wanted to say. Then he shrugged, letting it pass.

"And the other thing that worries you?" she pressed him.

Uroh looked again at the big man and his daughter beside him. "Well, see there. Werror is so generous with his spirit, so quick to laugh and reach out to people around him. Isn't it unusual that such a friendly man should have a daughter who doesn't speak at all, and looks afraid of everything she sees?"

Kori paused a moment. She realized that Uroh was right. "Why could this be?" she asked slowly.

"I don't know," said Uroh. "All I know is that it seems strange to me."

Later, as the sun set, the Ocean Tribe sang songs around the fire. Werror knew none of them, but he learned the words quickly, and his great voice was soon booming out while Jalin curled up against him, falling asleep with her head against his shoulder despite all the noise.

"You've given me a fine welcome," Werror said during a break in the singing. He slapped his stomach. "And fine food. I never knew there are so many animals in the sea. I've seen many tribes in my life—"

"You've traveled beyond Green Valley?" someone asked. Stories from travelers were always popular in the Ocean Tribe, since so many of its people had been wanderers originally.

"I grew up in the north," said Werror. "My family moved south in search of warmer weather and an easier life. We saw many tribes before we settled in Green Valley, when I was fifteen years old."

"I thought you had a bit of a northern accent," someone else put in.

Werror acknowledged it with a nod. "But you are the friendliest people I have ever met," he went on. He looked slowly around him—and his eyes met Kori's. "You are also the only tribe I've ever seen that has a woman leading it."

She met his gaze steadily. There was nothing hostile in the way he looked at her. She saw instead he had a simple curiosity. "I created this tribe," she said. "But I don't lead my people. I serve them."

"Ah," said Werror. His eyes were alert now. "A woman who is not just strong and beautiful, but wise."

Kori felt her cheeks reddening as she heard people laughing. She struggled with her emotions. It was disrespectful of Werror to praise her beauty like this, with Uroh sitting on one side of her and Meiri on the other. Yet he seemed to mean no harm by it. And even though it annoyed her, she felt flattered.

"You are very kind," she said stiffly.

He shrugged. "I speak only the truth, and the truth is obvious enough. But since I am speaking truly—I have said you are a strong person, but in most tribes, the chieftain is strongest of all. He needs to be, doesn't he, to win respect from men and lead them when they hunt or fight?"

Kori felt her people turning to her, watching her, waiting for her to respond. She felt her embarrassment disappearing and her confidence returning. A challenge like this was much easier for her to deal with than a compliment. "Sooner or later," she said, "anyone who visits this tribe asks this kind of question, Werror. They all wonder how a woman can be strong enough to serve as a chieftain."

Werror nodded slowly. "And what is your answer?"

"I've learned that it's pointless to answer, because words alone are useless."

The villagers glanced at each other knowingly, because this was a scene they had witnessed many times, and it never failed to entertain them. Werror sensed the change in their mood, and he frowned. "Your people understand you, but I do not," he said. "Tell me what you mean."

"I mean that some things must be demonstrated, not spoken," said Kori. "But perhaps this isn't the time. You must be exhausted after your ordeal. It wouldn't be fair to demand anything from you."

There was more laughter from the people around the fire. The laughter was friendly—but still, Werror looked annoyed by it. He smacked his fist against his shoulder. "Your food has restored my strength," he said, tossing his long hair back behind his massive shoulders. "I'm the equal of any man." He gave her a thin smile. "Or any woman."

Kori rose smoothly to her feet. She stretched, testing her muscles. "Are you sure?" she asked. She spoke lightly, but the implication was clear enough.

Werror heard the challenge in her voice. He turned to a woman sitting beside him. "Take Jalin for me," he said, handing her his sleeping daughter. Quickly then, he jumped up. "I respect you, Kori," he said, "and I am thankful to you for saving my life. But I must warn you, I am a proud man, and if you challenge me, I must respond."

Kori quickly shook her head. "I do not challenge you, Werror. That would be foolish. I just suggest that we should have an opportunity to compare our strength."

Werror glanced again at the people gathered around, and once again he saw their knowing smiles. His eyes moved uneasily. "If that is all you want," he said, "it should be simple and quick enough. Clearly, I am stronger than you."

Kori turned to Meiri. "Bring the basket and the pole," she said.

The girl nodded. She ran into the shadows, then returned a moment later. She went to Werror and gave him a long, smooth, straight piece of wood, the same length as a spear. Then she gave Kori a deep basket, the size of a man's head, with two handles woven onto its sides.

"It is a rule in our tribe," Kori said, "that none of us shall ever raise a weapon against another."

Werror hefted the wooden pole. "That is a good rule," he said.

"Still," Kori said, stepping forward, "we may play from time to time." She gestured to the wooden pole. "So, we will pretend that it's your spear, Werror. I will hold this basket so that its mouth faces you, and you will try to stab the pole into the basket. The game can only end in one of two ways. If you succeed, you win.

If I take the pole away from you, you lose."

He looked at her cautiously, suspecting a trap. "Where is your weapon?"

She shook her head. "I need no weapon."

He looked at her incredulously. "And no one to help you?"

She laughed. "Of course not."

He rubbed his jaw, still wondering how the game could be so easy. "Is there a reward for me if I succeed?"

"If you succeed," said Kori, "I will serve you as if you are the chieftain of this tribe instead of me."

He looked offended. "Now you are trying to make fun of me."

"No, Werror, I am quite serious." She tossed the basket lightly into the air, spun around, kicked the air in front of him, landed lightly, and caught the basket without even bothering to look at it.

He stood still for a long moment. For the first time, his face showed respect. "Suppose I lose this game," he said cautiously. "Is there a penalty?"

Kori shrugged. "You acknowledge me as your chieftain, nothing more."

Werror shrugged. "Well, your rules seem fair."

"Then you will play this game with me?" She smiled at him, feeling a tingle of anticipation. She didn't doubt that she could win, because no matter how strong he was, a big man could never be as agile as a smaller woman. The sheer weight of his body would hamper his movements. Still, Werror's size was impressive. She had never faced such a giant, and she couldn't help feeling excited by the idea of proving herself against him.

He tossed his hair back again. "Of course I'll play."

Kori saw that he was wary of her. He had seen how quick and confident she was, and her confidence unnerved him. Also, he must be realizing how humiliating it would be to lose to her.

"Clear a space for us," Kori called to her people.

Quickly they made a wide circle near the fire. Kori glanced behind her and saw Uroh and Meiri in the crowd. Uroh was unworried, but Meiri wore a nervous, doubting look. Kori winked at her.

She turned then to Werror. "Begin," she said simply.

He wriggled his shoulders and weighed the pole in his hand, holding it by its center, ready to cast it. He took a couple of slow steps, circling around her. "And the only way I can lose is if you take my weapon from me," he said.

Kori opened her mouth to speak—but Werror was already moving, feinting, lunging at her. He had spoken merely to distract her. He didn't need her to repeat the rules. She saw him coming at her, faster than she'd expected. She'd been overconfident. She was off balance. She tried to turn, and she lost her footing. She felt her moccasin slip on the stony ground. Her arm moved up reflexively, raising the basket, making it an easy target. She glimpsed Werror's face, grinning as he saw his chance. She saw the faces of her people around her, some of them gasping with dismay.

Kori flicked her wrist, tossing the basket away as she fell. Werror tried to turn the pole to follow it. The shaft brushed the side of the basket, knocking it to one side.

Kori fell on her palms. She bent her arms, feeling a wave of anger at her own carelessness. The anger gave her a burst of new strength, and the strength flowed into her biceps. She sprang up off the ground, crouched, reached up, and seized the basket before it could hit the ground. She tossed the basket up again, did a back-flip, and caught it as she landed, standing upright.

She paused, eyeing Werror carefully. "You won't take me by surprise a second time," she told him.

He watched her carefully. "What if I tell you that there's a bear behind you, eh? Or what if I say the moon has turned green, wouldn't you want to take a look to make sure, eh?"

She laughed, watching his eyes, knowing that they would betray him more quickly than his hands or feet. "You won't distract me, Werror."

He looked from her face to her body. "Even if I tell you that your robe is hanging open?"

Once again he moved as he spoke. And once again, despite herself, Kori was caught by surprise. She knew her body wasn't exposed to him, and she wouldn't care if it was, because this contest was all that mattered. Still, the sudden intimacy in the way he spoke made her slow to react as he lunged with the pole. She moved her arm—but he anticipated her. She saw the pole thrusting toward her, and she saw no way to evade him.

She dropped the basket. His pole jabbed into empty air; the basket bounced; she kicked it high, then turned a cartwheel and caught the basket once again as it fell.

She turned to face Werror, feeling new respect for him. He was far more cunning than she'd expected. Still, she saw him taking deep breaths. No matter what he claimed, he was tired from his ordeal on the raft.

"Here," Kori said, stepping forward, holding the

basket out to him. "I see this game is too hard for you, Werror. I should make it easier."

He straightened his arm, letting the pole hang below his hip. "I need no favors," he said. At the same time, he brought his arm up to stab the pole into the basket that hung like a gift in front of him.

This time, Kori was ready. She tossed the basket to her other hand and laughed happily, feeling some of her confidence returning. "Come, Werror, tell me how I can make this easier for you."

He grunted with irritation. "This is a foolish game," he said, pretending to turn away—then whirled around. His judgment was fine; he stabbed the pole into the precise place where Kori held the basket. But the basket wasn't there anymore; she tossed it up, did a handspring, landed lightly, caught it, and once again she held it out to him.

"Should I grasp it in two hands, instead of one?" she asked. She stepped forward. "Here, I can see you're getting tired."

Werror tried to smile, but she saw he wasn't amused anymore. He was finally realizing just how difficult and exhausting this game could be. He stood absolutely still for a moment, measuring her carefully with his eyes, as she held the basket out to him, cupping it between her palms, within easy reach.

He moved without warning, as swiftly as a snake. Still, he was too slow. Kori dropped her arms, and the pole missed its target.

Werror made a sudden flurry of thrusts. Once the pole brushed the side of the basket, but Kori had no real trouble evading him, even though she still held it between both her hands. She ducked, sprang from side to side, crouched down, then jumped up, dancing like a mosquito in front of the big man.

He paused a moment, and she saw perspiration gleaming on his forehead in the firelight. Now, she thought, the time was right. "Perhaps I should turn my back to you," she said. "Would that make it easier?" She took a step back from him, then another step. She looked at him carefully, absorbing every detail of his position, his posture, and the way he held the pole. Calmly, then, she turned away. She transferred the basket to her left hand and extended her arm horizontally from her body, with the mouth of the basket pointing directly back at Werror.

She waited, listening intently. She heard the hissing and crackling of the fire, and she heard faint shifting sounds from the crowd gathered around as people jostled for position, trying to get a better view. But Kori also heard Werror: his heavy breathing, and then the sound of a footstep as he moved cautiously toward her. His robe rustled; yes, he was raising the pole. She saw him clearly in her imagination. He was trying to move quietly, but he was too tired and too heavy, and too annoyed with her. She heard another footstep. Then he drew in a sharp breath, and she knew he was gathering his strength. An instant later his robe rustled sharply as he rushed forward.

Now she knew she had him. He was moving not just his arm but the weight of his whole body. Kori dropped the basket and pirouetted to face him. She glimpsed his startled eyes as she leaped into the air and kicked out. Her toe hit his wrist, hard. He gave a grunt of surprise as his hand opened, releasing the pole, letting it fly into the air.

Kori was already landing on her feet, dropping into a crouch. She fell backward, caught her weight on her hands, and kicked out with both legs, scissoring them around Werror's ankle. He flailed his arms, trying to keep his balance, but his forward rush had given him far too much momentum. He toppled like a great tree, struggling helplessly to pull his ankle free.

Kori released her hold as he hit the ground. She glanced up just in time to see the pole as it fell. She grabbed it out of the air, and turned toward Werror as he rolled onto his back on the ground in front of her.

Kori angled the pole and stepped forward. She rested the end of the pole against the big man's chest. "I win the game, Werror," she said softly.

The crowd shouted with delight. People started chanting her name.

Kori stepped back from Werror, watching him carefully. Sometimes when she played this game, men would be so angry at losing to her, their rage would cause them to act foolishly. For a moment she feared that Werror might actually jump up and try to hurt her. But then, slowly, he grinned. He shook his head ruefully, picked himself off the ground, and turned away, slapping dust out of his robes.

"People!" Kori shouted out, holding up both arms. "People! Hear me!"

Gradually their cheers died down.

"Werror fought cleverly," Kori shouted. "He almost won. Each of you here has tried this game with me. You know how hard it is. You saw how well Werror played it."

There was a murmur of agreement.

"Show him your appreciation," Kori said, clapping her hands together.

The crowd applauded and Kori saw Werror's shoulders relaxing, losing their tension. He waved to the crowd and waited for them to be silent again. "By the time the game began," Werror said, "I realized it must be a trap. But by then, it was too late. So—" He turned to Kori, bowed his head, and held his hands out to her. "I acknowledge your strength as our chieftain. You have won my respect."

There were more cheers and applause.

"But one day," Werror went on, speaking so that only Kori could hear him amid all the noise, "we should play this again."

12

Soon after dawn the next day, Kori took Werror on a tour of the village. This was her custom with any new member of the tribe, but she had a special reason in his case. Few of her people were skilled fighters; most had been outcasts of one kind or another, or nomads who preferred to wander alone. Werror had impressed her the previous night with his strength, his swiftness, and his cunning. If he could be trusted, he would be a fine asset to the tribe.

She took him first along the cliff edge, past her own home, along a narrow trail through grass that was lush and dense, nourished by the moisture that blew in from the sea. In the autumn season blackberries grew here.

"Where does your tribe find its fresh water?" Werror asked, pausing and looking out across the ocean.

"There is a spring that rises not far from the Meeting Place," she told him.

"And it is sufficient?" The wind buffeted his hair across his handsome face and made his robe flap like a flag. "What if more people join your tribe? Will there still be enough then?"

Kori shrugged. "Sometimes in the summer we have to fetch water in skins from a river at the bottom of the south slope. I suppose if more people join us here, we'll need to do that more often."

Werror nodded to himself. "Perhaps you should keep stores of water, just as you keep stores of food," he said. "Then you would be better able to survive if another tribe ever surrounds you."

He was right, Kori realized, and she felt annoyed with herself for not thinking of this herself. "But do you think it's likely that people would ever lay siege to us?"

"Probably not." He looked away from her, and his face was suddenly somber. "But after the massacre that I witnessed in Green Valley—I see a need for every tribe to defend itself."

Kori touched his arm. "Step carefully here. There are rabbit holes."

Werror looked down quickly. He gave a short, sharp laugh. "So many ways to die, eh? If I trip in a rabbit hole, and I fall over that cliff, then I have no need to worry about enemy tribes anymore." He grinned at her.

She let go of his arm, drawing back her hand as if she had been burned. She found herself suddenly thinking of Feroh, and all his dignity and pride. Werror was the kind of man that Feroh had always wanted to be, strong and confident, handsome and charming. Yet Werror seemed to feel no need to flaunt his pride or impose his will as Feroh had, and Kori saw why: Werror felt secure inside himself. He knew how strong he was. He had no need to prove it.

They walked on, past the cliff path that led down to the beach. A lookout was sitting there—an old man named Buria. He waved his spear cheerfully as Kori and Werror walked past.

"Are his eyes sharp enough?" Werror asked quietly when they had passed him.

"Probably not," she admitted. "But it's not likely anyone would ever try to attack us from the cliffs. Not in daylight. And he only takes that post every five or six days. We have a younger man who is normally here. He was the one who saw you out on your raft yesterday."

Werror grunted. "Lucky for me that Buria wasn't on duty then." He glanced around at the landscape, and the huts of the village nestling together on the hilltop. "I feel fortunate to be here, Kori." His eyes met hers and he looked at her with frank appreciation.

"We are fortunate to have you here," she said. She gave him a shy smile—then moved quickly ahead, feeling shocked by herself. Was she flirting with him? It certainly felt as if she was. How could she do such a thing? Was it just because she found him so physically attractive? Were the simple needs of her body so strong, they could take complete control of her mind?

She walked briskly, leading Werror around the north edge of the hilltop where it sloped down steeply amid a tumble of loose rocks. "It would be hard for a group of strangers to find their way up this slope without making noise," she said. "A small misstep would send many stones tumbling."

Werror nodded. "True enough." He looked out

across the vista of rolling hills mottled with forest and scrub. "We can almost see Green Valley from here." He pointed northeast.

"Yes, it's just a little more than one day's quick march," Kori said. She pulled her robe tighter around herself. The land looked so peaceful under the morning sun: a soothing blend of dark green, purple, and brown. But not so far away, that same land had been soaked in blood.

She led Werror on around the hilltop, till they came to the eastern side where the main path zigzagged down to the valley. Faint sounds of stone axes against wood came from the forest at the bottom of the hill.

"They are working on a new canoe down there," Kori said, as she saw Werror cocking his head to listen. "I wondered if I should tell everyone to stay up here at the village. But we will need that canoe, and I doubt that the warriors who attacked Green Valley will have any reason to come here—not yet, at least. From what you say, they have everything they need."

"That's true," Werror said.

"But I keep a lookout here anyway," said Kori. She pointed to a high boulder where a small figure was silhouetted against the sky. It was Raor, the youngster who had wanted to befriend Feroh. Kori called to him, and he scrambled down.

"Raor, meet Werror," Kori said.

Raor stole a glance at Werror's face, then looked down in embarrassment. "Saw you last night," the boy said, blurting out the words.

Werror grinned. "You saw me outwitted by your chieftain and forced to admit defeat."

Raor grinned nervously. He scuffed his moccasin in

the dirt. "But you're a great fighter," he said. "You're strong. You almost won! I mean, you could have, if you'd practiced the game before."

Werror reached out and ruffled the boy's hair. "You mean you wanted me to win? Against your chieftain?"

Raor glanced anxiously at Kori. "No!" he blurted. "I mean—I'm sorry." He lapsed into a confused silence, realizing that whatever he said now would be disrespectful to one of the adults in front of him.

"It's all right, Raor," Kori told him, patting his shoulder. "It was only a game."

Raor nodded vigorously. "Of course."

"You'll be a fine hunter one day," said Werror. "I can see that. Then maybe you'll be the one who wins the game."

Raor's pale young face turned up toward Werror. The boy looked doubtful—yet clearly, he wanted to believe the big man.

Werror nodded solemnly. "But now you should be doing your duty, isn't that so?"

"Of course." Raor turned back toward the high rock, and Werror boosted him up onto it.

Kori moved on, and Werror strode beside her. "I sometimes wonder why it is," he said quietly, "that boys are so eager to be men. If they really understood the world, they might want to remain young."

Kori thought again of Feroh, and she felt a pang of regret, wishing he was still here at the village. Surely, Feroh would have respected Werror, and Werror would have been able to speak sense to the boy as she and Uroh never could.

"You have lookouts posted here at all times?"

Werror went on, gesturing back toward the rock where Raor stood. "At night, every night?"

Kori dragged her thoughts away from what might have been. "Of course," she said. She wondered if she should mention that sometimes, when she crept out to check, she found the person sleeping. No; she was too embarrassed to admit that. In any case, she liked to think that her people would be more alert after what had happened at Green Valley.

"And your people," Werror went on, "are they trained to fight?"

"Yes," said Kori, with more confidence than she really felt.

"Yet they seem to be peace-loving people," Werror said. "And most of them would rather fish than hunt, isn't that so?"

"There is some truth to that," Kori admitted. She felt uncomfortable, being forced to admit their weaknesses. "But this hilltop is a secure place for any tribe to be, where no one can take us by surprise. And my people are more courageous than you might think. They have to be brave in order to sail the ocean."

Werror eyed her for a moment. It was a shrewd, evaluating look. "I see that this is so," he said. "I've seldom been so scared as I was on that raft."

"Still," Kori went on, "I'm sure that many of the men could use more practice with their spears. If you have skills yourself—"

"I'll be happy to show anyone what I know," he said.

Kori smiled awkwardly. "Thank you." She felt odd, asking his help. This was her tribe, after all, and normally she felt confident of her ability to lead it. She

wondered what it was about Werror's presence that
made her feel unsure of herself, willing to trust his judgment more than her own. Maybe it was the way he
walked with such confidence and surveyed the land as
if he ruled it. Or maybe it was his sheer strength, the
same strength that made her want to watch his body as
he moved.

"What lies this way, to the south?" Werror asked
her.

They had circled farther around the village. They
were walking through small trees, emerging into a
secluded grassy space—the glade where Kori practiced
her skills with Meiri.

"The hill slopes gently toward the south," Kori said.
"There are eucalyptus trees, and pines, and scrub."

Werror narrowed his eyes. "So this would be the
safest way for a hostile tribe to approach your village."

Kori gestured to the northern end of the glade.
"There are boulders there, and only one easy path
among them. I keep another lookout posted at that
point."

"Ah," said Werror. "Good." He smiled at her. "You
protect your people well."

The way he spoke was flattering—but it made her
uneasy. Why was he choosing to flatter her? What did
he want from her? There was something strange about
the way he looked at her. He had clear, penetrating eyes.
He glanced down, and she had the sudden suspicion
that he was looking at her body, imagining her without
her robe. The thought made her furious. But was anger
the only emotion rising inside her? Her skin felt suddenly hot.

"Tell me," he said softly, still staring at her. "How

did a woman like you learn those skills you showed me last night in the Meeting Place?"

Kori hesitated. Maybe she was deluding herself. Maybe he was looking at her body just because he wanted to know how she had managed to beat him so easily at the game with the pole and basket.

She gestured awkwardly. "My husband, Uroh, prefers not to hunt and never to fight. But he came from a fierce tribe of warriors, and he learned their skills as a child. He is the one who taught me most of what I know."

Werror nodded slowly. "That's very interesting." He was still studying her intently.

"So," Kori said, making her voice brusque. "Have you seen all that you need to see?"

He smiled faintly. "Not yet."

Did he know the effect he was having on her? Was this just another game to him?

"I would like to learn from you," he went on. "Last night, when your back was turned—and then you faced me—you knew exactly where you would find me. That is a skill I would like to have."

She wished she could see inside his mind. She still couldn't tell if there was anything behind his words. "Surely," she said, "you have spent so much time traveling and hunting, you already know—"

He shook his head. "A hunter uses his eyes, even at night. I have never learned to trust my ears alone."

Maybe, Kori thought, she should stop tormenting herself like this and simply take him at his word. "All right," she said, "I can teach you that skill."

"Now?" he asked, gesturing to the glade where they stood.

She felt taken aback. Surely, there were things she should attend to. And yet—really there was nothing urgent. She could stay here with Werror for a little while at least, even though the prospect made her nervous.

"If you wish," she said, trying to sound casual. She walked to the center of the glade, searched for a moment, and found the leather blindfold where Meiri had stripped it off and cast it aside on the day of Feroh's coming-of-age ceremony. "Come here," Kori said.

Werror strode over. When he stood close to her, he blotted out the sky.

"Cover your eyes with this," she said. It felt odd to be giving him instructions, but she tried not to show that it bothered her. She stooped and picked up the same long stick that she had used with Meiri. "When you're blindfolded, you hold this and wait. I will creep up to you. If you can touch me with the stick, you win. If I take the stick away from you, you lose."

"So, it's another game," he said, smiling slowly.

"An easier one," she said.

"All right." He knotted the strip around his head, covering his eyes. He held out his hand and Kori placed the stick in it.

She backed away. "Pretend you are a hawk, staring down," she called to him. "Create a picture in your mind. Turn your head slowly and listen to every tiny sound."

She started circling around him. She stooped, picked up a twig, and snapped it. "There! Do you see where I am, now, inside your mind?"

He turned toward her. "Yes."

Kori retreated to the edge of the glade. "I will stop

making noise," she said. "You'll have to strain your ears to hear me, Werror."

He nodded slowly. She watched him as he parted his lips and breathed slowly through his mouth, tasting the air, trying to catch her scent. Kori moved quickly to the opposite side of the glade, where she would be downwind from him. Then she squatted in the grass.

She waited. Werror stood listening intently. He was absolutely, completely motionless, and Kori realized there would be no point in trying to exhaust his patience. He was a skilled hunter; his patience would be greater than hers. She picked up a stone and threw it; and then another.

He grinned, still saying nothing. He didn't bother to turn toward the sounds.

Kori lingered a moment longer, watching him. He was such a fine, powerful figure, standing with his legs slightly parted, his shoulders thrown back, his head tilted up. She couldn't help looking at the bare skin of his arms where the sun gleamed on the rounded shape of his muscles. She couldn't help wondering how it might feel to touch those arms—

Angrily she cleared the thoughts from her mind. She stood and started moving diagonally across the glade, placing her feet with utmost care.

A bird suddenly flew across the open space. Werror turned quickly—then realized the source of the sound. Still, it gave Kori an opportunity. She took three quick strides, till she was almost within reach of him. Then she froze.

He realized she had changed her position. He turned his head slowly, but he had lost track of her. Kori eyed the remaining distance, trying to decide whether to take another step. If she did, he might hear her. She made her decision: she should trust her ability to move faster than he could, just as she had last night.

She crouched, tensing her muscles. Then she threw herself forward.

Everything happened in an instant. As Werror heard her and turned toward her, Kori reached for the stick that he held—but just as quickly he swept his arm, throwing the stick aside, and Kori found herself clutching the air. She stumbled and collided with him.

He took a step backward but didn't fall. He stripped off the blindfold and grabbed her by her upper arms. Kori stared up at him in astonishment. She felt her body pressing against his, and she saw his face just a hand's breadth from hers. Her breath caught in her throat.

He looked at her for a long moment, grinning. Kori regained her footing. She tried to pull away from him— but still he held her. "You fooled me at first," he said softly. "But this time, you didn't seize your prize. This game is a tie."

She groped for words. "You can let me go now," she said finally.

His grip didn't slacken. "The lookout that you mentioned," he said, still speaking softly. "The one who stands between us and the village. Can he see us?"

Kori tried to swallow. Her throat was tight. "He will hear me if I shout," she said.

"Will you shout, Kori?" He lowered his face toward hers.

Kori jerked in his grip. This was wrong; it was outrageous; it was unthinkable. She tried to wrench herself free. She felt furious—at herself, and at him.

His lips brushed the side of her neck. Kori felt as if she had been stung. Her skin flushed and burned. She gasped. "Stop this," she cried, except that it was not a cry, it was a whisper.

"Will you shout?" he asked her again. He kissed her neck, then her shoulder, and still he kept his grip on her.

Kori tossed her head from side to side. "Let me go. This must not happen."

"But I saw how you looked at me," Werror said. "You desire me, Kori. Isn't that so?" He gave her a little shake. "Isn't it? Speak truly!"

She grimaced. Even now, her code would not allow her to lie. "Yes," she said, "but—"

He released her without warning, and she found herself falling. In an instant he was on the ground beside her, forcing her backward, covering her with his body in the tall grass.

She raised her hands and pushed at his chest, but it was as futile as pushing a boulder. He ripped open his robe, then hers, and his smooth, golden-skinned chest pressed hard against her. She felt the heat of his body, and she felt the strength flowing out of her muscles.

Kori moaned involuntarily. Her whole body was trembling. She couldn't remember when she had last felt this way. The lust was so deep, so intense, there was no way she could suppress it. She wanted Werror, wanted him inside her, and it was impossible now to stop herself.

He took her face between his big hands and kissed her on the mouth. This wasn't like the gentle kisses she received from Uroh; she felt as if Werror was trying to devour her. He circled one arm around her shoulders and dragged her body up against his, and she gasped at the feeling of overwhelming power. With his other hand he reached down and touched her thigh, sending shivers that traveled from her belly to her toes.

Then he thrust his fingers inside her, and she cried out.

"Hush," he said, kissing her cheek, her neck, and then her ear. "I don't want anyone to find us, Kori. And neither do you."

Even in her state of wild arousal she understood the truth of that. She couldn't begin to imagine what would happen if her people knew, or Uroh knew, or Meiri knew what she was doing.

As she realized that she was deceiving the people closest to her, Kori felt deep shame. But her desire was greater, and it forced the shame aside. She closed her eyes, yielded to the desire, and she refused to think about what was happening.

Werror moved his head lower and kissed her breasts. He caressed them until the skin throbbed, and then he turned Kori on her side and lay behind her. His big hands roved down the front of her body, and he buried his face in the side of her neck. He reached down, opened her thighs, and put himself inside her.

He took her that way, lying behind her in the grass. Kori cried out, then found her cries smothered as he closed one of his hands across her mouth. His other arm circled her hips, dragging her against him so that she couldn't resist as he forced himself deep.

Kori felt totally possessed. She no longer owned or controlled her body. She shook with his thrusts and moaned behind his hand.

Quickly he climaxed. She felt his body stiffen, she

heard him gasp, and then he slowly relaxed behind her.

His hand left her mouth and she lay for a while, taking deep breaths, trying to calm herself. She felt dizzy and confused. She wasn't satisfied; she wanted more. She found herself suddenly remembering her early days with Uroh, when he hadn't really known how to make love to a woman. She'd had to teach him how to satisfy her.

Werror excited her wildly—but the excitement came from the look of him, the way he moved and smiled, not from the way he had just taken her. With a sense of wonder, Kori realized that even though he seemed so capable and wise, he had never learned how to please a woman. Perhaps no woman had ever dared to tell him.

She squirmed around to face him. He was lying with his eyes closed, breathing gently. She reached out tentatively and ran her fingers lightly across his face, tracing his features. Then she touched his chest. Her fingers crept across his tight, flat belly, down to his genitals.

Kori felt surprised. Here he was no bigger than any other man.

He opened his eyes. "What are you doing?" he said, frowning at her.

"Learning your body." She tried to look at him boldly, but something in his eyes made her pull her hand back.

"You surrendered to me," he murmured, "and I have taken you. But now you touch me as if you own me." He shook his head, looking at her as if she were a species of animal he had never seen before. "How can that be?"

"Perhaps I'm unlike other women," she said, feeling

more confident now. He was not so godlike, after all. He was a man with weaknesses, like any man. "You said last night," she went on, "I'm strong, beautiful, and wise. Isn't that what you told me, in front of my tribe, and my daughter, and my own husband?"

She saw tiny movements in the muscles of his face as different emotions stirred in him. Clearly, he had never been challenged like this by a woman. But he suddenly threw his head back and laughed.

"I'm glad I amuse you," said Kori. She sat up and covered herself.

"You surprise me," he said, turning serious again. "You seemed to yield—yet now I see that you didn't."

"I gave you my body," she said. "Not my mind."

He nodded slowly. "But you won't tell anyone about this," he warned her.

"Neither will you," she said.

"Obviously not." He straightened his robe and tossed his hair back. Then he hesitated. "There is one thing I would like to know from you. When a new man joins your tribe, you always play the game with him that you played with me last night, isn't that so?"

"Almost always," Kori agreed.

"So, I am wondering if this here is another game that you always play."

She looked at him in shock. "This is no game, Werror." She drew herself up, glaring at him fiercely. "I have never touched another man. Never!"

He raised his eyebrows. "Your husband has always satisfied you?"

She felt a wave of wild, inarticulate anger. "Don't ever speak of Uroh like that." Her voice was as sharp and dangerous as a spear thrust.

He held up his hand. "I meant no offense." He watched her face, waiting for her to relax a little. "Every tribe has its own customs. You are an unusual woman. How could I know what to think?"

Gradually she regained control over her emotions. She thought for a moment, deciding exactly what she wanted to say. "I will tell you what to think," she said finally. "I am older than you, Werror, perhaps ten years older. I'm flattered by the way you look at me and speak to me. I'm excited by you. I have yielded to temptation. But I am loyal to Uroh. No matter if he is a dreamer, if he spends time away from me, if he ignores me sometimes. I have such loyalty to him, you cannot comprehend it. It is absolute. I would make any sacrifice for him." She waited a moment. "Now do you see?"

Werror grunted. "Yes," he said. "Now I see." He looked down at her body. "Perhaps I should have understood this before. My seed is in you now. If you should conceive—"

She shook her head quickly. "That will not happen. When I birthed Meiri, it was bloody and painful, and I think—I hurt myself inside. I have not conceived since then. And that was a dozen years ago."

He hesitated for a moment. "Very well," he said.

Kori rose to her feet. "I think we should return to the village. I don't want people to wonder about us. Uroh is down with the people in the forest, working on the canoe; but the elder women are still up here, and they have sharp eyes."

Werror stood up. Kori looked at him, and even though she still desired him, she no longer felt overpowered by his presence. His face and body were beautiful, but he looked less sure of himself now. Probably he had thought she was dissatisfied with her husband; he had assumed he could overwhelm her with his charm and his strength. Well, he had been half-right, but only half-right.

She brushed dry grass off his robe, then waited while he did the same for her. She looked down at the flattened area where she had coupled with him. The furtiveness of the act dismayed her. It had become a secret that she would have to keep, and she hated secrets.

Still, she had made her choice, she had yielded to her passion, and there was no point in regretting the past. She had to admit, despite her guilt, Werror's lust for her had made her feel desirable—powerful, even— in a way that she'd begun to think she would never feel again.

"Tell me about your wife," she said, as they started back toward the village. "What was she like?"

Werror shrugged. "She was a quiet woman."

"Like your daughter Jalin?"

"Like Jalin, yes."

There was a reserve in his voice that she hadn't heard before. She hoped her fierce spirit hadn't insulted his pride too much. She still needed his help, and she still respected him. "Your wife must have been beautiful," she told him, "to birth such a beautiful daughter. Although—she does seem strangely quiet. Did you warn her not to speak to strangers?"

For a moment Werror looked angry. "She's frightened," he said, and his voice was harsh. "She saw many people murdered. It will be a long time before she trusts strangers."

Kori felt foolish. She grabbed Werror's arm and

turned him to face her. She stood for a moment, feeling awkward. "I'm sorry," she said. "I spoke foolishly. You are a good man, Werror. You seem so sure of yourself, and so strong, it's hard to remember what you've suffered."

He inclined his head, accepting her apology. "There's much pain in the world, Kori." His voice was gruff. "But there is pleasure, too. No matter what happens, there's always pleasure if we look for it. Isn't that so?"

She smiled at him. Tentatively she touched his cheek. "That is so," she said. "And I should thank you for reminding me of that. Perhaps I spoke a little harshly. You gave me pleasure today. You made me feel younger than I am." Impulsively she embraced him.

Then she turned and led the way back to the village.

13

Later, Kori went to her people down in the forest as they labored to strip the rest of the bark from the felled tree. After Werror made sure that his daughter felt secure with the elder women of the village, he joined the cutting party, too. He turned out to be a willing worker, but he had never tackled this particular task, and he needed guidance. Uroh had to show him the best way to use an ax.

Kori tried not to look at the two men. She could still feel where Werror had clutched her skin; her mouth was still bruised from his kisses; and she still felt where he had forced himself inside her. When she allowed herself to think of these things, she felt confused and distraught, incredulous that she should have wanted it and allowed it to happen.

She tried to focus all her attention on the ax in her hand and the tree in front of her. Still, she heard Uroh talking to Werror, sometimes demonstrating, sometimes guiding the big man's movements. Uroh was patient, as always, giving advice in his diffident way. A couple of times Kori stole a glance at him, and she saw Werror smiling—but it wasn't the same warm, friendly smile he had shown to the tribe the previous night. There was something patronizing about it, and Kori realized he was smiling at Uroh in the way a man might smile at a child who took himself too seriously. Werror no longer respected Uroh, because he had coupled with Uroh's wife.

Kori felt a twist of anger; but clearly, there was nothing she could say or do. The situation was her fault, and she would have to live with it as well as she could. Of course, in a way Uroh was partly to blame, because he had ignored her so often over the years and had left her feeling hungry for someone who would excite her and make her feel desirable. But it was her fault that she had chosen to deceive him— hadn't she? There was no way she could blame him for that.

Late in the day, when the blue sky started to darken above the forest canopy, the people set down their tools and walked out from among the trees. That was when they saw a solitary figure moving across the land toward them, making his way toward their village in a weary, shuffling run that suggested he had been traveling all day.

Kori and her people paused, watching the figure as he came toward them. Once again she felt apprehensive, as if fate itself was shifting the world around her, disturbing the calmness of her life, forcing her to follow a path that struck out in a direction totally different from the one she felt she had been following for so many years. She was not a superstitious person, but still, she sensed ominous portents.

Then, as the running figure came closer, she recognized him. "Pettrar," she murmured to herself.

"From the White River Tribe," said Uroh, moving close to her.

"Yes," said Kori. "I remember, he was one of the traders who visited us last summer." Instinctively she reached for Uroh's arm. "Do you think something has happened to *them*, now? Surely—"

"They are a tribe of hunters," said Uroh. "Not farmers, like the Green Valley Tribe. They know how to defend themselves."

Kori realized that he was right. The White River Tribe's village lay to the southeast among steep mountains, and it was well defended. "So why is he here?" Kori asked.

Pettrar stopped six paces from them. His chest was bare. His moccasins were caked with mud, his leggings were marred by bramble scratches, and his face was filmed with grime and sweat. Still, he stood tall and proud as he faced them. For a moment he was silent, breathing heavily and resting on his spear. Then he cast the spear down into the grass and bowed toward Kori. "Peace between our peoples," he called out.

"Peace between our peoples," Kori responded, knowing that the White River Tribe was always concerned with formality, and would never speak with her until their rituals had been satisfied.

"May I come among you?" Pettrar asked.

"You may come among us," said Kori, feeling impatient. "There has always been friendship between our tribes, Pettrar. You know this to be so."

He stooped and picked up his spear. He held it out, resting it on his open palms. "I offer my weapon," he said.

Kori had learned long ago that she should never accept this offer. "You may keep your weapon," she said, "because you come among us as a friend." She waited as Pettrar nodded solemnly and rested the end of the spear on the ground. "Now," said Kori, "please tell us why you are here."

Pettrar stepped forward till he stood two paces from her. "I have news," he said.

Kori paused, looking at the man's face. His formalities had been even stiffer than usual, and he still wasn't smiling. She couldn't imagine what could have caused Pettrar to run from his village to hers; but she was sure now, the news wasn't good.

She glanced quickly at her people gathered around and saw that they shared her foreboding—all except for Werror, who seemed unconcerned. "Tell us your news," she said.

He averted his eyes. "It would be best to speak to all your people."

Instinctively Kori wanted to argue with him—but she knew from experience that a hunter from the White River Tribe would never yield in an argument, least of all with a woman.

"Very well," she said. "Come to our village. We will give you food and water, and then you can say what you have come here to say."

A little later, after he had refreshed himself, Pettrar stood before the tribe. The villagers had barely spoken; all of them were eyeing him apprehensively.

He stood without smiling, and his eyes were somber in the dim evening light. "I have come here," he said, "with news of Feroh, son of Kori, leader of the Ocean Tribe."

Kori felt her stomach clench, but she said nothing. She heard a murmur from the people around her, but she stood in silence, watching Pettrar, and waiting. She felt Meiri beside her, clutching her hand; but she ignored the girl.

"Yesterday," said Pettrar, "Feroh came to our people. He told us that he had been cast out from your tribe."

Kori felt her anxiety turning to anger. "That is not so!" she called out. "Feroh chose to leave us. He turned away from us without warning, without apology, without even bidding us farewell."

Pettrar looked at Kori for a long moment. His face was still impassive. He showed as little interest in her as if he were looking at a stone. "I am sure you speak truly," he said. "But the way in which Feroh left this tribe does not concern me here. He came to our people—and he asked to be accepted among us."

There was another murmur of surprise and concern from the villagers gathered around.

"He was told," Pettrar went on, "that it is not a simple matter for a man to be accepted among us. He must prove himself, and while he proves himself he must be treated as we would treat a boy-child. Also, we told him that we could not accept him until Biffrar, our chieftain, had spoken with you, perhaps during the summer, when our tribes meet to trade."

Kori couldn't restrain her impatience any longer. She had no time for formalities, and Pettrar's manner was beginning to annoy her. "I'm glad you bring us this news," she called out. "But I'm sure you have something more important to tell us. Please explain what that might be."

Pettrar's angular face tightened as he looked at her. "We allowed Feroh to stay as a guest in our tribe last night," he said, "because there has always been friendship between our people." His lip curled as he spoke the word "friendship."

"And where is he now?" Kori asked.

"This morning he had disappeared," said Pettrar. "And Tithea, our chieftain's daughter, had gone with him." He drew himself up and his eyes flashed with anger. "We do not believe she went freely. We are sure she was taken by force."

Finally Kori understood. She strode forward, realizing that there was only one way she could hope to repair the damage that had been done. She stopped in front of Pettrar, and then, slowly, she bowed to him. "My son has brought shame on our people," she said. "I beg your forgiveness. If you wish to look for Feroh among us, I urge you to do so. Every one of our houses is open to you, Pettrar. I give you my solemn word, we have not seen Feroh."

She straightened her back, and looked at the man in front of her.

Pettrar still stood motionless, and his face was still impassive. Finally he inclined his head to her. "Thank you," he said, in a softer tone. "I will walk among your houses, as you suggest—because if I return to Biffrar, my chieftain, without searching for Feroh here, he will be very angry."

Kori allowed herself to smile. She didn't know what Biffrar might choose to do, but she was sure that his anger would be unpleasant. For a moment she almost felt sorry for Pettrar.

"One last thing," said Pettrar. "Hunters from my tribe have gone out searching for Feroh in case he is hiding near our tribe." Stiffly he returned Kori's smile— but there was no humor in his eyes. "If they find him," he went on, "and if Tithea has been violated by him, they will torture him, and then they will kill him." He spread his hands. "I hope you understand, our chieftain's pride allows us no choice."

Meiri seemed fearful, confused, and worried by all the upheavals in her life, so Kori took the girl back to their home while Uroh accepted the wearying task of showing Pettrar each person's home in the village.

Kori brought a burning brand from the Meeting Place and started a fire in the corner of the little stone-walled hut. Then she lay on the bed that she normally shared with Uroh, and she told Meiri to join her. For a long time the girl lay beside her in silence, hugging her.

"Will the White River Tribe attack us?" Meiri finally asked. "Will they kill us, the way the people in the Green Valley Tribe were killed?"

Kori stroked the girl's head. "No, Meiri. They are angry with Feroh, not us."

"Then what will happen to Feroh?" Meiri asked, her voice rising in pitch. "Will they torture him, and kill him, the way that Pettrar said?"

Kori felt a wave of despair. "Yes," she whispered, for she couldn't lie to her daughter. "They will, if they find him. But Feroh must know that. He will hide from them, and I think he will probably escape."

"Then will he come back here?" Meiri sounded plaintive. She looked up at Kori. "I don't want him to come back here. If he comes back here, the White River Tribe will torture and kill us too."

Kori wished she could deny that—but there was some truth to it. The White River Tribe were proud people. They chose to live in peace with the Ocean Tribe because Kori had always been careful not to trespass on their land, and they benefited from trading with the Ocean Tribe. Still, they would go to extremes to defend their honor. If Kori ever tried to conceal Feroh from them, there would be warfare without a doubt.

Was that her choice now? To abandon Feroh and allow him to die a horrible death, or search for him and try to protect him, and risk the lives of everyone around her? Then another thought struck her: was this what Feroh *wanted*? She suddenly felt sure that he must have known what the consequences of his wild action would be. He wanted to embarrass her and endanger her people.

The door flap was pushed aside, and Uroh ducked into the hut. Kori sat up quickly as she saw Werror following him, then Pettrar.

Kori looked from one face to the next. It disturbed her to see Werror and her husband standing together like this, and she wished suddenly that Werror had never come to the tribe, tempting her to violate a pact that had always remained unbroken. Still, she could not allow herself to reveal any trace of her feelings. She kept her expression carefully neutral as she looked at the men.

Pettrar glanced around the hut, then nodded to Kori. "Your son does not seem to be here," he said. "And all your people tell the same story about the way in which he left you. I apologize if I may have seemed to doubt your word. But you understand, this is a serious matter. Our chieftain has no son. Tithea is his eldest daughter. She has come of age, but has not been paired. If she becomes pregnant, and if *her* child is a son—" The thought seemed to make him feel physically sick.

"I understand, Pettrar," Kori said.

"You will want to protect your son," he went on. "But if you do so, the peace between our tribes will end."

His words were like a weight bearing down on her. Suddenly she just wanted him to leave her alone. "I understand," she said again. "It is very clear to me, Pettrar. My son has done a terrible thing, and I cannot protect him from your justice, because he has violated your deepest taboos." She stared at him, willing him to listen to her and believe what she said.

He nodded doubtfully. "I will take your words back to my people," he said.

"You can stay with us in here tonight, if you wish," she told him, gesturing to her hut.

"No." He drew himself up. Evidently, it was against his code to accept such an invitation. "I will sleep by your fire in the Meeting Place. I cannot accept your hospitality until this matter is settled." He nodded to Uroh, and to Werror. Then he left the hut.

Kori lay down again and hugged Meiri, while Uroh crossed the room and squatted by the fire. Werror stood by the door.

"Is there something you want?" Kori said, looking up at him. Immediately she regretted the words. She was lying on her bed in front of him, and she knew from the way that he looked at her, he was thinking about coupling with her in the glade. There was still something he wanted, and it was the same as before; she had no doubt of that.

"Werror has news for us," Uroh said, still squatting by the fire.

Werror nodded. "The boy," he said, speaking very softly. "The one who was serving as your lookout today, up on the rock."

"You mean Raor?" Kori asked.

"Yes." Werror edged a little closer, then kneeled down beside the bed. His body was so large, he seemed to fill the hut. "Raor came to me a little while ago. He thinks he knows where Feroh has gone. There is a place that Feroh showed him once, a secret place that only Feroh knows about. It lies somewhere between here and the White River Tribe."

For a moment Kori felt relieved. No matter what Feroh had done, and no matter who his father had been, he was still her son, and she wanted him to be safe.

But then, just as quickly, she felt a wave of dismay. If Raor was right, what should she do? Finding Feroh would place her in an intolerable dilemma.

"Werror has a plan," Uroh said, as if he had read Kori's thoughts.

The big man shifted uneasily. "I'm a stranger among you," he said. "It may seem wrong for me to offer advice. But I have traveled among many tribes—"

"You are a shrewd man," Kori said. "And I listen to advice from anyone. Tell me what you have in mind."

"We should find Feroh," Werror said, lowering his voice still further. "We should hold him—not here, but in a secret place. Then we can negotiate with the White River Tribe. As time passes, they will lose some of their anger—especially if Tithea is returned to them, and a month passes, and they find that she is not pregnant."

Kori thought about that, and decided he was probably correct. "But what if Feroh *has* made her pregnant?" she whispered.

Werror shrugged. "You can offer to punish Feroh yourself. He is your son, after all. But at least, this way, you may be able to save his life."

Kori sighed. Once again she felt a great weight of despair. "I have never had to decide anything like this," she said. "None of us has. We have always lived a quiet life. A simple life. And suddenly nothing is the same anymore."

"I think we should follow Werror's plan," Uroh said.

"But the risk!" Kori exclaimed. "If we find Feroh, and we keep him in a secret place, and we tell the White River Tribe that we have him—surely, they'll be angry. They'll attack our tribe, they'll take hostages of their own. Anything could happen."

"I think not," said Werror. "I think I understand them. I believe they respect people who are honest with them, and strong. If you are not strong, they will not respect you, and then you will be vulnerable to them."

"Werror wants to go out to look for Feroh with Raor," Uroh said. He turned to look at Kori, and his face wore a brooding expression in the firelight. She had never seen him look at her quite like that before. "And Werror wants you to go with him," Uroh went on. He grabbed a piece of wood and threw it abruptly onto the fire. There was a sharp cracking sound, and a flurry of sparks.

Kori flinched from the suddenness of his movement. She looked at Uroh in confusion. "Why me?" she asked.

"Because Feroh listens to you, and to no one else," said Uroh. "Even now, I think you have some influence over his will, while Werror is strong enough to control him physically. And Raor can lead you to him." He stood up. "I will stay here and look after Meiri till you return."

Kori looked from Uroh to Werror, and back again. She had the uneasy sense that something very different lay behind Uroh's words. But he was still looking at her in that same brooding way, and she couldn't imagine what it meant. Surely, he didn't guess that she had coupled with Werror; if he did, he wouldn't be urging her to go out with Werror on this journey.

"I suppose this can do no harm," Kori said slowly. "It certainly can't make things any worse for Feroh."

"Precisely," said Uroh. He moved around the hut and lay down on the bed, close beside Kori, but not quite touching her. He looked steadily at Werror, who was still kneeling opposite them.

"It's decided, then?" said Werror.

Instinctively Kori wanted to refuse—at least until she had time to think, to understand what was happening around her. But there was no time. The White River Tribe was already looking for Feroh. It was even possible that they had found him.

She looked down at Meiri. The girl had somehow managed to go to sleep. It should all be as simple as

THE OCEAN TRIBE 163

this, Kori thought to herself. A mother and her sleeping child, lying peacefully in their home together.

But Feroh had done something which made that impossible. Kori sighed. "Very well," she said. "I agree."

"Good," said Werror. He gave her a lingering look that Kori couldn't begin to interpet. Then he stood and left the hut.

For a long time, there was silence. Kori stared up at patterns cast by the flickering firelight on the wooden roof. She tried to imagine what was going on in Feroh's mind now. Was he enjoying the idea of tormenting her this way? She felt sure that he was. And he was so arrogant, he probably believed that nothing would happen to him.

She turned to look at Uroh—and found him staring at her. Uneasily Kori smiled. "It's good to have you here beside me," she said.

He said nothing.

She felt a sudden overwhelming need to tell him the truth. No matter how much he had ignored her and made her feel unloved, she should not be deceiving him. But if she told him that she had coupled with Werror, it would make everything even more difficult and complicated. Or was that just an excuse, a way to spare herself the penalties that came from speaking truly?

"Uroh," she said tentatively, "you know I have often felt lonely in the last few years. Sometimes I've felt you care more for the ocean than for me."

Still he said nothing. He just lay there, watching her.

"I've—never looked at another man," she went on,

forcing the words out of herself. She glanced quickly down at Meiri, but Meiri was still asleep.

"I know these things," Uroh said. "But I also see that Werror is strong, and handsome too, and there is a gentleness in him that I think you must like, and he flatters you with his attention."

Kori felt as if time had frozen around her. She stared at Uroh, speechless.

"I saw how you looked at him last night," Uroh went on. "I don't think you even realized it yourself." He turned on his back and clasped his hands behind his head. His face was serene now; it had lost its brooding look.

Kori wondered for an instant if Werror had confided in Uroh. No, she realized; Uroh still didn't know how far she had already gone, and what she had done that morning. He just knew that it could happen. He knew her better than she knew herself.

"Why," Kori whispered, "do you want me to go on this journey with Werror tomorrow?"

Uroh shrugged. "If something is fated between you and this man, it will happen, and there is nothing I can do to prevent it."

"But Uroh," she said, feeling tears suddenly starting at the corners of her eyes. "Uroh, my loyalty is to you, don't you see that? You are the one I want to be with—"

"Then you will return to me," he said. "Isn't that so? You'll return, just as you returned from the storm that almost took your life."

She looked at his face. Tentatively she reached out to touch his cheek.

Calmly, deliberately, he turned his back to her.

"Are you testing me?" she whispered to him.

He was silent, and the moment dragged on for so long, she wondered if he had heard her.

Finally he spoke. "You would speak of it that way," he said. "I prefer to speak of it like this. I believe you will come back to me, Kori. But you have shaken my faith a little. So, I must be sure—and this is the only way I know."

14

Kori's heart was heavy as she set out from the village the next morning. Pettrar had already left at dawn, heading back to his tribe. Kori had watched him go, and waited till he was safely out of sight. Now she followed a trail that led east through the forest, with Raor ahead of her, Werror's heavy footsteps behind her—and Jalin following along behind him. Werror had insisted that his daughter should come with them, because she was afraid to stay in the village without him. Kori worried that the girl was too weak and timid, but Werror claimed he would carry her on his back if she became tired. Kori could see that the big man wouldn't listen to her, so she yielded to him.

Raor was excited by the importance of his role, serving as a guide on this journey. He strode purposefully among the trees, holding his spear as if he was ready to strike down any enemy or predator. At any other time Kori would have been amused by his show of bravado, but not today. She felt sickened by the prospect of having to stalk and capture her own son. She dreaded having to negotiate with the White River Tribe, knowing that even if they were lenient, they would still demand some awful punishment. And she still felt haunted by the brooding look she had seen on her husband's face, not only last night but again this morning, when she had left him. He had refused to stir from his bed, and he had said nothing. He hadn't even watched her leave.

Well, she told herself, there had been more than a dozen years of peace and happiness in her home and her tribe. She had always known it was a fragile state, no matter what her people chose to think. Now she must confront her problems with the kind of bravery she had urged upon her people and her children. If she was brave enough, she would prevail.

She carried her own spear, plus two more slung under a pack that she had filled with food and other necessities, including her healer's pouch, several knives, and a long coil of hemp rope. Raor said that the place they were going to was up in the eastern mountains, where a rope might be useful. But that wasn't the only reason she was carrying it. If they found Feroh, and if he resisted them, they might need to take him back as their captive.

Shortly after noontime they emerged from the forest and started up a rocky slope. Raor moved with less authority now, pausing often to check his surroundings.

"Are you sure this is the way?" Kori asked him when they reached a flat table of gray rock. An even steeper slope lay directly ahead, leading into a V-shaped canyon where a stream tumbled across boulders that were green with lichen. Coarse, wiry bushes grew in crevices in the rock, and there were thousands of tiny yellow wildflowers.

"I'm sure," Raor said, pitching his voice low.

Werror moved to the other side of the boy. "How far?" he asked. Beside him, Jalin squatted on the rock, looking tired but saying nothing.

"This canyon turns twice," said Raor. "You can see the first turn there." He pointed up ahead. "The second turn leads through a narrow gap to a place where there are cliffs all around, on three sides, like walls."

"That's where you think he'll be?" said Werror.

Raor nodded, looking uneasy. He shifted his grip on his spear. "There's a pool that feeds this stream, and there's space for a small camp, and bushes and small trees for firewood."

"Is there any other way into this hiding place?" Werror asked.

Raor hesitated. Finally, reluctantly, he shook his head.

"Then there's no way we can take him by surprise," said Werror. He scowled at the boy.

Raor gestured with his spear. "If I go up ahead of you, I can talk to him."

Werror made a sound of disgust. "He may kill you before he has a chance to recognize you. He knows the White River Tribe are out looking for him. Don't you see?"

Raor blinked, saying nothing. He wouldn't meet Werror's eyes.

Werror looked at Kori. "This boy is no help."

Kori returned his stare. "Raor will certainly be no help if you frighten him."

For a moment she and Werror glared at each other. Then Werror's face changed; suddenly his smile reappeared. "You're right," he said. His voice was calm again. He turned to Raor. "Forgive me for being impatient," Werror said, ruffling the youngster's hair. "This isn't your fault."

Kori frowned at Werror for a moment. Then she, too, turned back to Raor. "Is there some way we can climb to the top of the cliffs, above where Feroh may be hiding?" she asked.

Raor still looked unsure of himself. "Maybe," he said.

"Have you ever tried?" she prompted him gently.

He nodded. His eyes moved from her to Werror, then back again.

"You're afraid you may not remember the way?" Kori asked him.

Once again he nodded.

She put her arm around his shoulders. "You must try to find it, Raor. If you can't, there'll be no blame. We'll just try something else instead."

His shoulders straightened. "All right," he said. "This way."

Kori followed him into the canyon. There was just enough space to find footholds alongside the gushing stream, but the rocks were slick and treacherous with its spray. Kori heard Werror breathing heavily behind her, and she sensed him struggling with the climb. When she glanced back, she saw why: he was carrying Jalin, just as he'd said he would.

"Why not leave your daughter here?" Kori said to him. "This is the only way up, so we'll be coming down the same way."

He quickly shook his head. "Can't do that," he said.

Kori thought that if he was really so devoted to the girl, he wouldn't want to expose her to danger. Still, she saw in his eyes that this was another matter where he wouldn't yield. She turned and continued following Raor.

They reached the point where the canyon turned—and Raor gestured straight ahead. "Up that slope," he whispered.

It was so steep, it was almost a cliff face. Still, the rock was crossed with deep fissures, allowing numerous footholds.

"We'll follow you," Kori whispered. Her words were almost lost in the hissing of the water beside her.

Raor looked even more nervous than before. He seemed to have realized, finally, that this was not a game; that Feroh might turn against them, even though he was Kori's son. Still, Raor started up the rock face.

Kori followed. Werror was right behind her, with Jalin clinging to him with her arms around his neck. The girl's mouth was a thin, tight line and her eyes were clamped shut. She looked terrified.

But the climb was less arduous than Kori had feared. When they reached the top of the rock face they found a ridge that sloped up more gently. They crept up it, moving very carefully so as not to dislodge any small stones that would reveal their presence.

Finally they reached the summit. There was a rough plateau with dry little bushes and clumps of grass growing in crevices in the rock.

Kori breathed in and smelled wood smoke. She looked at Raor, then at Werror, and saw that they had noticed it too. Raor pointed ahead wordlessly. Kori nodded to him, then got down on her hands and knees and crawled slowly, silently to the edge.

She found herself looking down a vertical face of rock, into a hiding place that was just as Raor had described it. Water flowed out of a deep fissure, filling a pool. There was a flat area beside it, where a fire was smoldering. Kori felt her breath catch in her throat. A figure was crouching beside the fire, but that wasn't what caught her attention. Another figure was lying stretched out on the ground. She was a girl, barely of age, lying with her ankles tied to stakes that had been driven into cracks in the rock. Her body was naked, and there was a strip of deer skin wrapped around her mouth.

Kori turned her attention to the figure beside the fire. It was Feroh; there was no doubt of that. Feelings welled up inside her, and she found herself becoming so distraught, she was almost on the point of tears. Until this moment she hadn't quite believed that he had really taken Biffrar's daughter. It was unthinkable that he had done this thing. The sight of it made her feel sick.

She heard a tiny noise beside her and found Werror lying close by, peering down.

"What shall we do?" Kori whispered. Her emotions were so powerful, she didn't trust herself to make a decision.

"You have that rope in your pack?"

Kori nodded.

"Is it strong enough to hold me?"

She nodded again. "It's strong enough for several men."

"All right." He gestured to her to move back from the cliff edge.

Kori noticed Raor watching her uneasily, with Jalin sitting close by, silent and solemn as ever. "He's there," Kori whispered to Raor. "And Tithea is with him. But she didn't come with him freely. He has her tied."

Raor blinked, absorbing this news. "Why would he do that?"

"Because he wanted her, and he wanted to make trouble between our tribes," Kori said. "Feroh is not the person you imagined him to be, Raor. He has a lot of anger—toward me, and all of our people." She took off her pack and fumbled with it. She saw that her hands were shaking as she dragged out the rope and passed it to Werror.

"I still don't understand," said Raor.

"I don't understand either," Kori said. "I have told you all I know."

She watched as Werror searched around, found a stone the size of his two fists, and tied one end of the rope around it. There was a crevice in the rock close by; he jammed the stone deep into it. Then he wrapped the rope once around his body, under his arms. He glanced at Kori, then at Raor. "You two have your spears ready," he whispered. "Feroh will look up if he hears me. Shout to him, Kori. Show your spears and warn him not to kill me." He grinned, but it wasn't the friendly, amiable expression she'd come to know. There was something else in his face: a wild spirit. She realized that in some strange way, he was enjoying this.

"There must be a safer way," she whispered.

He looked at her and waited, saying nothing.

She tried to think. "He'll need more food. He must leave this place to go hunting. We can lie in wait for him—"

"The girl needs help," said Werror. "And each time he couples with her, his seed has another chance to grow."

There was grim truth in that, Kori realized; still, she thought there must be a better, safer method to capture her son.

Werror turned back toward the cliff. Evidently, he had made up his mind, and she saw there was nothing she could do to stop him.

"Spears," Werror reminded her.

Kori reached quickly for her pack. She slid a spear out of it, then motioned Raor forward. Together they crawled to the edge of the drop. Werror waited for them to get into place, and then he stood up. He tugged hard on the rope, testing it. Then he moved to the edge, turned his back to it, and paid out some of the rope till he was leaning out over the drop. Quickly he started walking backward down the sheer rock, with the rope sliding around him, supporting his weight.

At the bottom, the water made a steady rushing sound as it flowed into the pool, masking the noise of Werror's descent. Kori watched Feroh, but he didn't look up. He was roasting a rabbit over the fire, Kori realized, staring at the flames, oblivious to everything—until Werror's foot dislodged a loose fragment.

Stones and dirt suddenly rattled down. Feroh jumped to his feet. Kori saw his face turning upward, and she saw his mouth open in shock and surprise. An instant later he turned and seized a spear lying close beside him.

"Feroh!" Kori cried. "Feroh, stop!" Her voice echoed around the walls of the canyon.

Werror kicked himself away from the rock face.

The rope hissed against his robe as he fell free, landed heavily, rolled over, and leaped to his feet. Feroh stared at him in confusion. He started to raise his spear, but Werror stepped forward, seized him by the neck, and threw him down. Feroh cried out in pain as he hit the ground. Werror landed on top of him and dragged the spear out of Feroh's hands. Slowly, then, Werror picked himself up. He turned the spear till its point was just a hand's breadth from Feroh's throat.

"Kori," Werror shouted, without looking up. "You and Raor bring Jalin down to me. Not down the rope—go back around, and up the canyon. And take your time. Feroh, here, will wait for us."

15

By the time Kori reached the little camp that Feroh had made, Werror had untied Tithea. He used the same thongs to bind Feroh's wrists, and he sat Feroh down with his back to the cliff. Feroh's face was pale with rage, and his dark eyes were wild as he glared at Kori.

Tithea was struggling into her clothes, making slow, tentative movements and wincing from the stiffness in her limbs. "Are you all right?" Kori asked her. "Are you injured? I am a healer, I can help—"

"You are Kori of the Ocean Tribe," said Tithea. Her tone wasn't friendly, and she stared at Kori without respect. She was shivering in her clothes, and Kori saw bruises on the girl's face where she had been beaten. Still, she held herself defiantly.

"Yes," said Kori, "I am the chieftain of the Ocean Tribe. And Feroh is my son." She felt a savage mixture of sadness, anger, and despair. "But I haven't come here to defend him. He has brought shame upon my tribe, and he has committed a crime against your people." She paused, waiting to see if the girl would respond.

Tithea said nothing. She still eyed Kori suspiciously.

"Pettrar came to us yesterday," Kori went on. "He told us what Feroh had done. I knew then that I had to find him and save you from him."

Tithea considered this. Kori saw that the girl was not as brave as she wanted to seem. She was exhausted, and she had been terrified.

"You should have told my people where Feroh was keeping me," she said finally. "They are the ones who should have come here to find him." She turned and gave him a hateful stare. "They are the ones who must punish him for what he's done."

"That may be so," said Kori, feeling the heaviness in her heart. "But we weren't sure if we would find him here, and it was quicker for us to come here than go back to your tribe with Pettrar and then lead your people back here. That would have taken at least an extra day. Anything could have happened to you in that time."

Tithea blinked. "I see," she said. She was no longer defiant. Suddenly she just looked like a scared little girl. Kori felt sorry for her—and relieved. She desperately needed Tithea as an ally, not an enemy.

She stepped forward and took Tithea's hands. They were terribly cold. "Sit," she urged the girl. "Try to warm yourself. We'll heat some water. I have fresh valerian root, which will help." She turned to Raor. "Put hot stones from the fire in that bag of water there, and bring me my pack."

The boy quickly obeyed. Jalin, meanwhile, was sit-

ting on the ground while Werror stood over Feroh,
watching as Kori dealt with Tithea.

"Tell us what happened," Kori said, as she sat
Tithea by the fire, then seized a bear skin that Feroh had
been using as his bed and draped it around the girl's
shoulders.

Tithea huddled under it, shivering more violently
as she gave way to the fear that she had been trying to
deny. "He seized me during the night, from my own
home, where my father and my mother and my sisters
were sleeping." She sounded incredulous that such a
thing should be possible. "He stuffed something in my
mouth, dragged me from the village, and told me he
would kill me if I disobeyed him." She closed her eyes.
"I thought he was a handsome young man when he first
came to our village. We talked, and he was respectful
toward me." She shook her head quickly. "But now I see
that he is no better than an animal. I know he is your
son, but still—"

Kori put her arm around the girl. "Did he hurt
you?"

She nodded. "He tied me here, and he told me I
must pledge myself to him, because that would give
him the right to take me in any way he wanted. I
refused—so he started to torment me. He placed hot
embers on my skin. He hit me and beat me. He left me
out to shiver in the night air, and he refused to give me
food. He told me he would give me two days to pledge
myself, and if I still refused—he would kill me."

Kori stared at Feroh, wondering yet again if she
would ever understand him. He had recovered his
usual self-control, and he stared away from her, ignoring everyone around him.

Kori felt a wave of anger. She stood suddenly and strode to her son. Before she knew what she was doing, she swung her arm, hitting his face, knocking him over on his side. "You are evil," she cried, standing over him with her fists clenched. "I owe you nothing, Feroh, do you understand me? I cannot defend you. I cannot abide you." She felt down onto her knees, seized him, and shook him violently. "Listen to me!" she cried.

He turned his face toward her, but still he remained silent.

Kori had never felt so desperate, so filled with frustration. She wanted to punish him, to make him apologize for everything he had done—

She felt Werror's hands on her shoulders. "This will not help you," he said quietly. "And it will not help your people. We must know whether he forced himself on the girl."

Slowly Kori regained control of herself. Werror was right, she realized. She turned away from Feroh, forcing him out of her mind. She moved back to Tithea. "I'm sorry," she said. "This is very difficult for me."

Tithea nodded. She looked at Kori differently now, with trust instead of suspicion. "I see that," she whispered.

"You must tell me," said Kori. "I know that this is a shameful thing, but I must know. Did Feroh couple with you?"

"No!" She shouted the word.

"All right." Kori patted Tithea's shoulder, trying to calm her. She glanced at Werror and saw that he, too, was heartened by the news. "So," Kori went on, "Feroh stole you from your people, and he hurt you, but he didn't take your virginity. He will be punished, of course. Your people and my people will decide how that should be done. But you can return to your tribe, and some time in the future, you may still find a mate without shame."

"Yes," said Tithea, more quietly now.

"Here's the hot water," said Raor, holding out the bag.

Kori thanked him and took it from him. She opened her pack, found the packet she was looking for, poured some powder into her cupped palm, and dissolved it slowly in the water. Then she gave it to Tithea. "This will make you feel better."

"Thank you." The girl sipped it. She grimaced at the taste, but it seemed to be familiar to her. She gulped the rest of it quickly.

"She should leave soon," said Werror, glancing up at the sky. "Only half of the afternoon is left."

Kori nodded. The sooner the White River Tribe saw that Tithea had not been defiled, the easier it would be for Kori to make peace with them.

"You should all come with me to my people," said Tithea.

"I think not," said Werror. He squatted down opposite her. "It'll take time to explain to them what happened, and what didn't happen. Do you understand? If they see Feroh, they're likely to kill him before they hear your story."

She glanced at Feroh, then back at the big man. "But—he *should* be killed," Tithea said.

"He must be punished," Werror said. "But only for things he did, not for the things he didn't do. And this is for your chieftain to decide, with Kori. It is not for you to decide."

Tithea looked down at the fire in front of her.

"You go back to your people," Werror went on. "Tell them everything. Tell them that we risked our lives to rescue you. And we saved your life, because Feroh was planning to kill you tomorrow if you didn't surrender to him. Isn't that so?"

"That is so." Her back straightened, and Kori saw that the valerian was having its effect, revitalizing her.

"All right," said Werror. "Your people can talk and decide what they want. Kori here can decide what she wants. You see she is too emotional now to know what's best. After a day or two, she can meet with your chieftain, and they can reach an agreement."

"All right," Tithea said. She looked up at Werror. "You speak wisely," she said. "And—I do thank you, for saving me."

Werror grunted. "I don't want to see more tribes turning against each other."

"I have a question."

Kori jumped; the voice came from her left. She realized it was Feroh speaking.

Feroh stared at Werror. "Who are you?"

Werror turned to assess him. "From the Green Valley Tribe," Werror said. "My people have been attacked by warriors from the east. Your mother's people took me in, with my daughter there." He nodded to Jalin.

Feroh absorbed this news for a moment. His mouth twisted with disgust. "So now you have the right to speak for my tribe? You have the right to discuss how I should be punished?"

Kori touched Werror's arm, warning him not to speak. She stood and moved in front of Feroh. "Werror is a decent man. I trust him and respect him, Feroh. You are my son, but you are an evil man, a foolish man, and a liar. I cannot trust you, and I cannot respect you." The words were like knives in her throat, but her outrage forced her to speak them. Half of her still wanted to strike him, hurt him, inflict the things that he had inflicted on Tithea. At the same time, she was still his mother, and she wished somehow she could save him from himself. She stared at him and her face twisted with emotion. "Why!" she suddenly shouted at him.

He was silent for a long time, staring up at her. "I have nothing to say to you," he said finally. The words were quiet and calm. He spoke them as if their truth should have been obvious. He looked away from her to the other people gathered around him. "I have nothing to say to any of you. I despise you all."

Kori turned away. She was trembling, overwhelmed with her own failure.

"All right," said Werror. "We should leave. We'll move down out of the canyon, and then Tithea can go back to her people." He hesitated. "Raor, maybe you should go with her, to show we're concerned about her welfare. Do you think you can do that?"

The boy stood up quickly. "Yes, of course."

"Kori and I will take Feroh back to the Ocean Tribe," Werror went on. "When your people are ready, Tithea, they can speak with us."

The girl nodded. "It shall be so."

Kori was so distraught, she was finding it hard to think clearly. Werror's plan sounded sensible enough—yet it was different from what he'd suggested before. Hadn't he said that they should keep Feroh in a secret place? Maybe he was deceiving Tithea. She couldn't tell, and she hated this business of negotiating for the life of a son she despised.

Well, certainly, they should leave this place. There was no doubt of that. She helped to gather Feroh's possessions, and then she followed Werror as he marched Feroh in front of him at spearpoint, down through the canyon.

When they reached the flat table of rock at the bottom of the canyon, Kori saw that the day was brighter than it had seemed while they were surrounded by the cliffs. "How far is your tribe from here?" she asked Tithea. "Can you reach it before dark?"

"I don't think so." The girl was calmer now that she had emerged from the place that had been her prison. She squinted up at the sky, then at the forest that lay to the south. "There's a place not far from here where my people camp sometimes, while they are out hunting. I'm sure we can reach that. Then we can travel the rest of the way to my tribe tomorrow morning."

"Good," Werror said. He slapped Raor's shoulder. "Are you ready to go with her, young man?"

"Yes," said Raor, trying to sound brave and confident.

"Take this." Werror handed him Feroh's pack. "There's food inside, and a warm bear skin, and a couple of knives. And you have your own spear."

"Yes," Raor said again.

"Go," said Werror. He gave Tithea a stern look. "Remember what you must tell your people."

"I will." She gave him a shy smile, and Kori saw that the girl had been touched by Werror's mixture of gentleness and strength, just as she had been herself. "Thank you, Werror," Tithea said. She turned to Kori. "And thank you, also." Quickly, then, she started down the slope to the forest, with Raor beside her.

Kori watched them with mixed feelings. She saw nothing wrong with what Werror had decided—yet it bothered her that she had allowed him to speak for her. Since she first established her tribe, she had never deferred so much to another person's judgment.

"I hope they will be all right," she said, half to herself.

"Raor's not come of age yet, has he?" Werror asked her.

"No. Not yet."

The big man shrugged. "So, even if he was tempted by Tithea, he's not able to couple with her."

Kori looked at him in shock. "I trust Raor. I trust him completely."

"Did you trust him, too?" Werror said, nodding to Feroh.

Kori shook her head, feeling more confused than ever. Behind Werror's friendly smile was a hardness, a callousness that disturbed her. "I'm just concerned that Raor will be safe when he takes Tithea back to the White River Tribe," Kori said. "If they are angry enough with my people, they may punish him instead. If they want Feroh badly enough, they could keep Raor hostage."

Werror shrugged. "If they want to hold him while they negotiate, that could be helpful. It could make them feel the matter is being dealt with fairly."

Kori shook her head, feeling a deep wrongness in his words. "But Werror, Raor is just a boy. I know his mother; she's a dear, good woman. How can I tell her—"

"Kori!" His voice was sharp. His eyes were hard and fierce—and then he reined in his anger, just as he had before. His smile reappeared, erasing the stern lines she had seen in his face. He stepped closer and rested his heavy arm around her shoulders, and she smelled his thick, musky odor. "I apologize," he said, "I didn't mean to speak so sharply. We're concerned with stopping a war between two tribes, don't you see? We must do whatever we need to do. The lives of all your people are at stake, not just Raor."

"This is true," she said cautiously.

He touched her cheek, then let his arm slide down till his hand rested on her waist. She resented the sudden intimacy, and she saw Feroh staring at her strangely. Kori felt herself wanting to pull away from Werror; yet at the same time, the nearness of him still aroused her. She even found herself wondering if he would try to couple with her while they were out here in this wilderness, far from the rest of the tribe.

She banished the thought instantly. She stepped away from him. "I'm not sure that there's enough daylight for us to reach our village," she said, suppressing all emotion from her voice. "And it might not be wise to travel through the forest at night, with hunters from the White River Tribe looking for Feroh."

"Agreed," said Werror. "We should camp here, then move at dawn."

He was still talking as if the decisions were his, not hers. She frowned at him. "I'm glad you agree with me," she said.

He grinned at her. "Always best to agree with my

chieftain." He turned to his daughter. "Jalin! Lay out our bedrolls here. Let's start a fire and heat some food. We won't want to keep it burning after nightfall." He glanced around, checking the terrain. "I think we should be safe enough here." He went over to Feroh, turned him, and checked the thongs binding his wrists. "Are your hands numb?"

"No," said Feroh. His voice was barely audible.

"Good. Sit there." Werror placed him against a boulder. "Kori? Can I have the rope?"

She passed him the rope that he had used to lower himself earlier. He tied one end around Feroh's ankles, the other end around a massive outcropping of rock. "Now he can't wander off."

Werror went over to Jalin then, where the girl was starting a fire. He gathered dry wood, busily organizing their camp for the night, while Kori stood watching, wondering why she allowed him to take control like this, and why she had found him so desirable, and why she had given herself to him.

She thought of Uroh; and she felt a wave of yearning.

No one spoke while they ate their meal. Feroh refused to speak to anyone, Jalin was as silent as ever, and Kori was in no mood to talk. Werror seemed lost in his own thoughts, and long before sunset he smothered the fire, opened his bedroll, stretched out on it, and closed his eyes. Kori saw that he was careful to rest his body across the rope that tethered Feroh. His free hand lay on Jalin's shoulder where she made herself as comfortable as she could beside him.

Well, Kori thought, it would be good to rest. She had barely slept the previous night, because she'd felt so tormented with guilt toward Uroh.

She lay down a little way away, and she tried to sleep—but her mind was filled with anxiety. She imagined Raor being attacked by the White River Tribe, and tortured as they vented their anger upon him. She imagined warriors from Green Valley exploring the land, moving toward her village, planning to kill and conquer. She thought she heard faint noises in the forest as hunters from the White River Tribe came near, ready to seize Feroh and tear him apart.

Time passed, and still she couldn't sleep. The sun set, and she lay with her eyes half-closed, looking at Feroh where he sat with his hands still tied behind him. Even now, his face was impassive, and he said nothing. He hadn't complained about the cold night air. He hadn't asked for food, and when Werror had offered him water, he had accepted it grudgingly. Kori wondered what he was thinking, but she knew now his mind would always be closed to her.

She slipped into a half sleep haunted by looming nightmare figures, men with spears, women screaming—and then she woke suddenly, hearing a faint sound.

It was a moonless night but the sky was clear, and she saw a bulky silhouette against the stars. For a moment she panicked, still dazed from her dreams. She jerked back from the figure.

"It's just me." It was Werror's voice, a low, soft whisper. He squatted down beside her. "I was checking Feroh, nothing more."

Gradually she quietened her panicky breathing.

But there was still something about Werror that made her nervous, though she couldn't say what it was. Her spear lay beside her. For no special reason, she found herself groping for it, closing her hands around the wooden shaft.

"Are you all right?" He peered at her in the starlight.

"Yes." She gripped the spear tightly. What did he want? Was he hoping to couple with her out here? Squatting beside her in the darkness, as big as a bear, he scared her. "Why are you staring at me?" she whispered to him.

He paused for a long moment. She wondered if he could sense her hostility.

"No reason," he said. He turned away without another word, and she saw him go back to his bedroll.

It took her a long time to go back to sleep after that. She kept imagining that she heard more noises in the night, and no matter how many times she sat up and looked around, she couldn't calm herself.

In the end, though, she simply had no choice. She was so tired—so deeply exhausted by everything that had happened—she yielded to her need for sleep.

When she woke, the new day was already bright.

She sat up slowly, feeling stiff and chilled, wondering why Werror hadn't woken her. Surely, he was the type of man who would always want to set out early.

She blinked in the brightness, shaded her eyes, and looked across at his bedroll. Her breath caught in her throat, and she scrambled up onto her knees. What she saw made no sense.

The bedroll was gone. She turned quickly to look at Feroh—and he, too, had gone. Everything had disappeared, except for her own spear and her pack tucked between her and the rock face.

Kori stood up. She strode to the spot where Werror had slept. She saw where his body had scuffed a scattering of pine needles out here on the flat rock. She felt the rock itself, but it was cold.

She went to the place where Feroh had sat, and she looked for any sign that he had escaped. But there were no fragments of shredded rope, and she saw no indication that there had been any kind of fight.

Kori stared around at the forest that stretched away below the table of rock. The trees stood silent, telling her nothing.

Werror had simply abandoned her. He had freed Feroh and had taken him and Jalin away with him. The knowledge made Kori feel dizzy. It made no possible sense to her.

Now she felt concerned. When she couldn't understand a man's motives—a man who was almost a stranger to her—she distrusted him. All her uneasiness about Werror suddenly coalesced into a deep foreboding.

She shouldered her pack and seized her spear. There was no time for breakfast; she ran down the rocky slope into the forest, determined to return to her people as quickly as possible.

16

She heard them working in the forest, hacking the tree with their axes. She came running through the underbrush, wild-eyed and anxious, with leaves caught in her hair. Her people stopped and stared at her as she stood in front of them, breathing hard, clutching her spear.

Raia set down her ax. She moved toward Kori. "What's wrong?" she asked. "Where's Werror?"

"I don't know where Werror is." Kori turned from Raia to the rest of the people. "Has he been here? Or Feroh?"

They glanced at each other. No one spoke.

"Werror was with you," Raia said. "Why should he be here? And Feroh—did you find him?"

"Yes." Kori tried to calm herself. She combed some of the leaves out of her hair. "Yes, we found Feroh, and Tithea was with him, and she has been returned to the White River Tribe. Raor went with her."

"Raor went with her?" Raia repeated the words as if

they made no sense. "Why didn't you take Tithea back to them yourself?"

Kori rubbed her face with her hands. Raia's question seemed sensible, but Kori couldn't answer it. "I've been—distressed," she said. "Over Feroh. This has been a difficult time." She realized suddenly, she was displaying weakness to the tribe that they never normally saw. If she wasn't careful, she would infect them with her anxieties, and they would lose their faith in her—and their confidence—and that would just make them more vulnerable—

Kori disciplined herself with a huge effort of will. She forced herself to stand straight and speak calmly. "If Werror comes here," she said, "please find me immediately. He disappeared during the night with Feroh. I don't know where, and I don't know why." She took a slow breath. "Now I must speak to Uroh. Where is Uroh? And Meiri?"

"Haven't seen them this morning," said Raia, shrugging her plump shoulders. She turned and looked at the other villagers, still standing around the felled tree. "Has anyone seen Uroh?"

Kori looked hopefully at their faces, but they stared back at her blankly.

"Must be still in your hut," said Raia. She winked at Kori. "Sleeping, probably."

Kori refused to show the new wave of fear that Raia's words stirred in her. "I'm sure you're right," she said. She forced a smile. "Thank you, Raia. I will come back in a little while and help you with your work here." She turned away from her people without another word and strode on through the forest till she emerged in front of the familiar hill where the village

stood. She hurried up the zigzag path, barely acknowledging the welcoming cry from the lookout. She ran
through the village, shouting a brief greeting to some
women who were working in the Meeting Place. Finally
she arrived at her hut.

She threw the door flap aside, ducked in—and
stood motionless. The hut was empty. Some furs lay
strewn across one of the beds. A dish woven from reeds
lay beside the bed, with remnants of a meal on it. There
was no fire burning, no sign of human life.

Once again Kori tried to calm herself. Probably,
Uroh and Meiri had gone out somewhere. They could
have taken one of the canoes. It was fine weather—

She shook her head. Uroh wouldn't do that. He
would want to be down in the forest, supervising the
villagers while they hacked the wood with their axes.
And Meiri wouldn't go off alone without him.

More and more, Kori sensed that her world had
changed. There were forces at work that she could not
see and could not name, but she felt them as clearly as
she could feel the wind. Someone, or something, had
chosen to disrupt everything that she relied upon and
believed in.

She turned to leave the hut—then stopped herself.
She looked again at the uneaten food beside the bed.
There were slices of bluefish, which Uroh often enjoyed
for dinner. So, he had eaten his dinner here, but he had
not taken the leftovers away. That was unusual. He was
lazy about cleaning the hut, but not that lazy.

Kori crept over to the remnants. Now that she
looked closely, she saw fragments of fish on the floor. It
almost looked as if someone had stepped on the wicker
plate, tipping it and spilling the food.

She studied the floor more closely. There were many footprints in the thin film of dirt over the stone. Nothing unusual in that; many people came to this hut. But some of the footprints were not clearly defined. They were smeared, as if moccasins had scraped across the floor.

Why should that be? She imagined a person being held from behind, struggling as he was dragged out of the room. Yes, the long smears were just the kind of marks that would be made by a man—or his daughter—struggling and kicking.

She looked at the bed. The furs had been tossed aside. Uroh never left them like that; he rolled them. Kori imagined someone else's hand throwing the furs where they lay.

Finally, near the door, she found the most telling detail. It was a thong, no longer than her hand, bleached white. At first that made no sense. No one would bleach a thong, because the bleaching would weaken it. Then she remembered one of Uroh's favorite robes, ornamented with a decorative fringe that he had made by cutting the deer skin into narrow strips—like thongs. Quickly she checked the place where he kept his clothes.

The robe was missing.

Kori clutched the strand of deer skin in her fist. Silently she made a vow: that she would find her husband, she would find her child—*both* her children—and she would not allow her happiness, her peace of mind, to be disrupted any further in this way.

Quickly, methodically, she gathered things that she might need: an extra spear, a warm but lightweight blanket made from rabbit pelts, and a spare set of fire sticks. She emptied her backpack, repacked it, and shouldered it. A part of her was still anxious, sensing that she was facing an unknown threat to her own life and the lives of those she loved. But pitting herself against it, or them, gave her a new feeling of purpose that overlaid her fear. She had always responded to any challenge. It was in her nature.

She stepped out of the hut into the daylight and paused for a moment. She wanted to set off immediately; but she knew she would be stronger if she fed herself first.

She walked back to the Meeting Place. Shoeni was there with half a dozen other women, smoking fish in little tents of deer skin wrapped around low wooden tripods. The women hailed Kori and she exchanged greetings, feeling good, as always, to be welcomed by those who cared for her and respected her. But behind their smiles she sensed their concern.

"Feroh is still missing," she told them, answering their unspoken question. "But we found Tithea, and she has been returned to the White River Tribe, and I hope that this will satisfy some of their demands, at least." She turned to Shoeni. "I must go out of the village for a day, perhaps two days. I ask you to make decisions for me in my absence. You are a good, wise person, Shoeni. Those who are here now are my witnesses, as I give you the authority to act in my absence."

The women stared at her. There was silence in the Meeting Place. Wisps of smoke drifted from the deer-skin tents, and wind murmured around the houses. Somewhere, a baby cried.

"This is very sudden," said Shoeni.

"Where is Uroh?" one of the other women asked.

"I am going to find Uroh," Kori said. "And Meiri. In the meantime, from tomorrow, I want everyone to stay inside the village. No one shall go back to the forest to work on the canoe. Is that clear?"

There was another long silence. "This is not clear at all," Shoeni said finally. "What do you mean, Uroh is missing? Where did he go? And where are Werror and his daughter?" She gave Kori a severe look. "You are not confiding in us, Kori. How can I make decisions in your absence when you don't even tell me what is happening?"

There was a murmur of agreement from the other women. Their welcoming smiles were gone.

Kori sighed. "There is much that I don't know myself," she said. "I don't know where Uroh is, or Meiri, or Feroh, or Werror. All of them are missing."

"But did they just walk away?" one of the women asked, looking incredulous.

Kori hesitated. "I think Uroh and Meiri may have been taken from us during the night."

The women looked even more shocked. "How do you know this?" Shoeni demanded.

"We should get together some of the men and do a proper search," said another of the women.

"This is terrible!" one of them exclaimed.

Kori imagined the time it would take to gather people together, and the problems she would have leading them across the land without causing noise and betraying their presence. She shook her head impatiently; she had already said more than was wise. "I must do this alone," she said. "I have decided, and it is so." She went to the food caches, pushed their stone lids aside, and scooped corn, dried fruit, pine nuts, and jerky into her food pouch.

"Kori, this is wrong." Shoeni no longer sounded severe. She sounded worried. "We must call everyone together and talk about these things."

"No," Kori said. "There isn't time. And I don't want to risk other people from our tribe. I want the tribe to stay safely here in this village. Make sure the lookouts are alert. Make sure every person has a spear. If the White River Tribe come here, talk to them and be friendly, but be firm: tell them we do not know where Feroh has gone." She paused. "Do you understand?"

Shoeni glanced at the other women. Many of them refused to meet her eyes, and Kori could see that they didn't approve. Well, there was nothing she could do about that.

Shoeni sighed. "You are our chieftain, Kori, but please, if you know more, or if you have other thoughts that you can share with us—"

"I have told you all I know," Kori said curtly. "That is why I must leave now. To find out more."

She nodded to the women, then strode out of the Meeting Place.

At first she headed toward the path that zigzagged down to the forest where the rest of her people were working. Then she stopped herself. If Meiri and Uroh had been stolen away by force, their captors wouldn't have taken them past the lookout.

Kori circled around to the north side of the village. Grimly she remembered walking here with Werror, mentioning that it would be hard for a large number of warriors to climb this slope without dislodging the loose rocks and making noise.

But what if there had been just two or three men?

Kori eyed the slope carefully. The stones were pale gray where they faced the sky—but she noticed one that was darker than the rest. It had been turned over, exposing its underside, which was dusted with soil.

Kori started down the slope. Now she saw blades of grass that had been broken, and another stone that had been dislodged. And then, as she neared the bottom of the hill, she found another bleached thong.

She picked it up. "Thank you, Uroh," she said, clenching it in her fist.

She eyed the landscape that lay ahead of her. The terrain was hilly, spotted with trees. To her left lay the ocean; to her right, the trees grew more densely and became a forest. Her instinct told her that Uroh and Meiri had not been taken that way. It would be difficult to march two spirited, rebellious captives among close-spaced trees and underbrush on a night when there had been no moon.

Kori opened her food pouch and ate handfuls of corn and pine nuts as she walked. She reached a narrow river that snaked down to the sea, and she kneeled to drink from it, lifting her cupped hands and taking care to watch the land in front of her. Then she wiped her palms, picked up her spear, settled her pack more comfortably, and moved on.

She found another pale thong. It was dangling from a blackberry bramble, swinging in the breeze like a rat's tail. She plucked it from the thorns with grim satisfaction. The men who had taken Uroh must have been careless to allow him to leave such an obvious trail. That thought gave her new confidence. Her enemy was not infallible. He could be conquered, just as she had beaten Werror at the game in the Meeting Place even though he was far bigger and stronger than she could ever be.

Kori moved more cautiously now, slipping as quietly as she could among the scattered trees. She imagined Uroh preceding her, perhaps with his hands tied behind him, but still able to pluck strands from the fringe at the back of his robe. Yes, there was another, directly ahead, on another bramble.

The men had taken a path that was parallel with the ocean. Perhaps, Kori thought to herself, this meant they were strangers in this area of the country. In the darkness, they'd had to follow the line of the coast.

But if they were strangers, did that mean they were warriors from Green Valley? The same men who had massacred Werror's people?

Then she wondered: had a massacre really taken place? She only had Werror's word for it, and she no longer trusted him. Even Jalin had said nothing about the massacre—because Jalin never said a word to anyone. But why should Werror have lied? And why would he have risked his life, and Jalin's life, out on a raft in the open sea?

Kori grimaced with frustration. She walked on— and now she noticed more traces of the men she was tracking. They had become less cautious as they moved farther from the village. She found a broken branch, and footprints in patches of sandy soil among the grass. Where the soil was moist, she could actually see the stitching of the moccasin pressed into it. She squatted and studied it for a moment. The style was different from any that she knew among tribes in this part of the world.

She stood and studied the land ahead of her. The

wind gusted, still blowing from the north—and she caught the scent of ashes.

She stiffened, glancing around warily. The fire must have burned out, otherwise she would have smelled smoke. Nevertheless, the warriors might still be close by.

She moved forward more cautiously now, stooping and running from tree to tree. She pulled out her second spear from under her pack, and held one in each hand. The smell of ashes grew stronger, and now she also smelled the remains of cooked meat. She remembered encountering Baryor in the forest, and being surprised by the lookout he had posted high in a tree. She paused and scanned the trees ahead of her, but none of them was big enough or strong enough to hide a man.

There was a thicket though, directly ahead. And another footprint in bare soil that seemed to lead directly toward it.

Kori hunkered down for a moment. She closed her eyes and listened intently. She heard the inevitable rush and roar of the ocean, and the whisper of the wind. She heard bird calls, then a sudden flurry of wings as a bird swooped past her. She heard the scrabble of tiny claws on tree bark as a squirrel leaped from branch to branch, then paused and made its angry little barking sound high above her.

But there were no human sounds, and no human scents.

Kori straightened up and opened her eyes. She slowly circled the thicket, holding her spears ready. Finally she found a vantage point where she could see into the area surrounded by the tangled vegetation. She glimpsed a patch of black ashes where the fire had been, and she saw some flattened grass. But the place was empty.

She moved quickly, pushing through the bushes. She went directly to the ashes and felt them with her palm. They were still hot, almost too hot to touch.

She glanced quickly around and saw five flattened patches of grass, and a sixth patch that was smaller than the rest. So, Uroh and Meiri had been here with four warriors. Kori clenched her spears in her fists. She had hoped for three warriors, not four. Perhaps Shoeni had been right; Kori should have brought others with her instead of coming here alone.

Just as quickly, though, she dismissed her doubts. She would have the advantage of surprise, and she had lost most of her respect for the men she was tracking.

She surveyed the campsite once more. She saw something lying in the grass beside a spot where a man had rested. She walked over, looked down—and found not one thong, but three. They had been carefully placed, forming an arrow. It pointed northeast, inland from the ocean.

She stared at it in wonder. The warriors must have felt so confident, they had talked among themselves, discussing their destination, so that Uroh had been able to leave this mark for her to find.

She straightened up and started away from the campsite, striking through the trees. They grew more densely here, providing more cover. On the other hand, there was no bare earth to reveal footprints. But then she spotted another pale thong dangling from a thorn bush, over to the left, and when she went there she saw where footsteps had scuffed the carpet of pine needles on the ground.

Now the trail became easy to follow again. She slipped through the forest, scuttling forward, then pausing and listening and sniffing the air, until finally she saw the forest ending ahead of her.

Kori dropped to her hands and knees. Slowly, with great caution, she crawled to some bushes at the edge of the forest. She wormed her way among them and peered ahead.

She found herself facing a circular dip in the land, with a small pond in the center. The forest enclosed the area on three sides; on the fourth side, opposite her, there was a bare rocky ridge.

Just to her left, no more than a hundred paces away, she saw six people.

Her pulse raced as she saw that one of them was Uroh and one of them was Meiri. Both of them were sitting in the grass, and both of them appeared to be unhurt. The four men with them were well armed, with two spears apiece. Their faces looked ugly and stupid, and their robes were ragged and shapeless. Their hair was dull with grime, and their moccasins were worn.

One of them was standing, leaning on his spear, facing the ridge that lay beyond the pond. Two others were sitting with their backs to Kori, and the fourth was lounging on his side in the grass.

Kori studied their positions, imprinting them in her mind. Then she turned her attention to Meiri and Uroh. Both of them had their wrists bound behind them, as she'd expected. But their ankles hadn't been hobbled.

Softly Kori made the sound of a bird call.

The warriors paid no attention, but Kori saw Uroh's

back stiffen, and he glanced at Meiri where she sat beside him.

Stealthily Kori wriggled back into the forest. She moved a little way around the pond, staying hidden amid the trees, till she judged she was as close as possible to the warriors and their prisoners. She dropped her pack, pulled her knives out of it, and tucked them in her belt. She gripped a spear in each hand, and then she stood for a long moment, summoning her strength.

Thirteen years ago, she had fought and killed in order to save herself and the person she loved. After that terrible time, she had vowed that there would be no more killing. Still, she had always known that if she or her loved ones or her tribe were sufficiently threatened, her vow might have to be broken.

She closed her eyes, preparing herself for what she had to do. She didn't doubt that she could fight those four men and conquer them. She was concerned, though, that Meiri or Uroh could be hurt. With their hands tied, they had no way to defend themselves. If one of the warriors thought of using Meiri as a hostage—

Kori shook her head. She would have to move so swiftly, the warriors would have no time to do that.

She moved forward, searching the ground till she found a rock the size of her fist. She transferred both her spears to her left hand, picked up the rock in her right hand, and hefted it. Then she found a place where she was still screened by foliage but had a clear view of the men in front of her.

The one lying on his side in the grass was her first target. She studied him, breathing deeply, steadying herself, knowing that she only had one chance to strike him down. His head was propped on his hand, with his elbow resting on the ground.

Kori swung her arm back, then hurled the rock with all her strength. It whirled through the air, making no sound. It hit the man on the crown of his head and he fell forward with a grunting, gasping sound.

Had she killed him? Had she stunned him? There was no time to check. The warrior who was standing, leaning on his spear, heard the sound made by his friend. He looked around, frowning, then took a step toward the man on the ground. He shouted the man's name.

Kori shifted a spear to her right hand and focused on the man walking to his wounded comrade. She steadied herself, hurled the spear, then threw herself after it, chasing the shaft before it had even reached its target. She saw the man look up with a startled expression as the spear struck him in his chest. He fell backward with a shout, clutching at the shaft. He screamed as he hit the ground, and he went on screaming.

Kori ran to the first man, still lying in the grass. He was pressing his hand to his head, cursing as blood flowed freely. Kori seized his spear where it lay beside him in the grass. She turned and hurled it at the warrior who had been sitting close to Uroh and was starting to his feet, his face contorted in surprise. Kori's spear struck him in the shoulder. She cursed her aim; the wound wasn't serious enough to stop him.

She still had to deal with the fourth man. He, too, was grabbing his spear, getting up, stepping forward—but he fell as Uroh kicked his ankle.

Kori ran to the fallen man, seized a knife from her belt, dropped down onto the man's chest and stabbed him in the side of his neck, once, twice, and a third time, till blood suddenly started gushing.

She felt a moment of revulsion as she saw the horror in his face and he screamed, clutching at the wound. Then she heard a warning cry from Meiri, and she looked up just in time to see the third man plucking Kori's spear from his shoulder and turning it, ready to cast it at her. At the same time, behind him, the man with the head wound had struggled onto his feet, and he, too, was holding a spear.

Kori herself had only one spear left. She threw it at the man with the wounded shoulder, since he seemed the most dangerous target. He ducked, and the spear flew wide.

"Kori!" Uroh shouted her name at the same moment that the warrior with the wounded shoulder cast his spear. Kori threw herself flat on the ground, and the shaft hissed harmlessly above her. She found herself close to Uroh, lying in the grass. He was pushing his wrists out toward her. She seized another knife from her belt and cut the thongs.

She turned back to the man with the wounded shoulder. He was bleeding, but not seriously. He was striding toward her, groping in his belt.

Kori jumped up and ran directly toward him.

He pulled out a knife, but still Kori didn't hesitate. She saw a flicker of uncertainty in his face as she bore down on him, but then he gathered his courage and yelled a war cry. He ran toward her holding his knife high.

She ignored the blade. All her attention was on his abdomen. She took two more paces, then screamed as she leaped with all her strength, thrusting her right leg out in front of her. She saw his eyes widen with surprise, then felt her heel thudding deep into his belly.

The knife flew out of his hand. The force of her blow literally knocked him off his feet. He landed hard on his back, clutched his stomach, and made coughing, choking sounds.

Kori dropped onto him and pressed a knife to his throat, barely hard enough to break the skin. "Lie still!" she shouted at him.

She glanced over her shoulder and saw Uroh calmly confronting the man with the head wound. The warrior was still holding his spear, but blood was pouring down his face, and he could barely stand. Uroh seemed almost apologetic as he sidestepped, turned, and effortlessly plucked the spear out of the warrior's hand.

The bleeding warrior stared at him for a moment, then started toward Uroh again, pulling out his knife. Uroh shook his head and warned the man softly; but still the warrior wouldn't stop. Uroh grunted with displeasure. He turned the man's spear so that the blunt end rested in the grass and the flint point faced the warrior. The man hesitated; Uroh reached out, seized the man by his hair, and jerked him forward.

The warrior lost his balance. He fell onto the spear and it plunged through him. He collapsed on the ground, coughing and moaning, impaled on the shaft. Uroh turned away, shaking the man's blood off his hand.

Kori's skin was so hot, she felt as if she was going to burst into flames. Her mouth was dry; her pulse was still hammering.

She saw Meiri struggling to her feet with her hands

still tied behind her. The girl ran over to Kori, shouting her name. Uroh, meanwhile, had gone to check on the first man Kori had speared. He was still lying in the grass, shouting in pain. Uroh bent over him briefly, and the shouting stopped.

Meiri fell to her knees beside Kori and the man she was holding at knifepoint. "Kill him!" she cried. "Mother, kill him!"

"No," said Kori. "I want him to speak." She felt a twist of sudden, unreasoning anger. "I want to know who they are. I want to know why they captured you."

"There is no time for that," said Uroh. He came striding across the grass. He wasn't smiling, as Kori had expected. His face was drawn with worry.

"What do you mean?" Kori called to him.

He bent down, seized Meiri's wrists, and cut her bonds. Then he gestured to the lake and the ridge beyond it. "Don't you see why they brought us here?"

Kori felt disconcerted. She had expected him to thank her, to praise her.

"This is a meeting place," he said.

Now, with dismay, she understood. The dip in the land was secluded, and the pond was a distinctive landmark. It was a perfect place to wait in safety, to meet—someone.

"Quickly," said Uroh.

Kori scrambled off the fallen warrior. She turned, ready to flee to safety with her husband and child—but at that moment, she saw something move from the corner of her eye. Figures were appearing along the rocky ridge, silhouetted against the sky. There were a dozen of them—perhaps more, all holding spears.

"If we run, they will kill us," Uroh said quietly.

"No!" Meiri cried out. She turned, ready to flee toward the forest.

Uroh seized her and held her by her shoulders, ignoring her wild struggles. "There are many of them," he said. "They can easily strike us down with their spears. Even if we manage to reach the forest, they can still come after us, and they can probably catch us. Listen to me, Meiri! It's better that they capture us alive."

Kori looked at Uroh, at Meiri, and then at the warriors massing along the ridge. She felt anguish, outrage, then disbelief that Uroh could be so calm. "Why?" she cried. "Who are these people? Why do they want us?"

"I don't know," said Uroh.

Kori looked again across the pond. Most of the warriors were still up on the ridge, holding their spears high, ready to hurl them. Meanwhile, three figures were walking down from the ridge, circling the pond, and coming closer.

Meiri started crying. Kori reached for her and held her, trying to comfort her. At the same time, Kori watched the three men as they came closer, and she felt herself trembling with anger and fear.

They stopped three paces away: close enough for Kori to see their faces, but not so close that they would risk being injured accidentally if the men up on the ridge cast their spears.

Two of the men were young with brutish faces, like the warriors whom Kori had just slain. Standing between them was a taller, older man wearing a hooded robe of black bear skin, concealing his features. But even before he reached up to push the hood back from his face, she knew what she would see.

He confronted her for a long moment, staring at her with his one good eye. Slowly, then, he smiled. "You are Kori," he said, in a voice as dry as sand.

"And you," she said, "are the man I saw on the beach."

His grin widened, exposing ruined teeth. "That was not the first time we met," he said. His grin turned sour, and his lips curled. Abruptly he spat onto the ground in front of her, then glared at her with such an expression of hatred, she felt it strike her like a weapon. "What, don't you recognize me?" he shouted at her. He slapped his palm against his chest. "I am Derneren!"

And now, finally, she understood.

PART 3

17

Kori stared at Uroh in confusion. "You told me he was dead," she said, as one warrior pinned her arms behind her and another tied her wrists. "I remember it, Uroh, so clearly, that night so long ago. I speared Yainar from my canoe. I went to fetch you from the shore, and you stepped over Derneren's body. You'd struck him down with a rock."

Another warrior was tying Uroh's wrists. "It's true that I struck him down," Uroh said. "But I never said that he was dead. I told you *perhaps* I had killed him."

The man behind Kori tightened the thongs and moved away from her. Another man moved in front of her—and she recognized him. He was the one she had hit in the shoulder with her spear. He gave her a murderous look and raised his fist, ready to hit her in the face.

"No." The word was spoken softly, but there was no mistaking its air of authority. Derneren stepped forward

212 ⫷⟡⫸ CHARLOTTE PRENTISS

and confronted the wounded man. "You will not strike her," he said.

The warrior slowly lowered his arm. "She killed two men," he protested. "She should suffer for it."

Derneren patted the man on his good shoulder. "She will suffer," he said. "But not yet."

"Time hasn't been kind to you, Derneren," Kori called out to him.

He turned toward her. The skin inside his empty eye socket was dark purple, like a bruise that had never healed. The skin of his face was mottled yellow, and so deeply scarred it looked as if it had been raked by huge claws. He had a rank odor that she could smell even from two paces away.

He stared at her, and emotions tugged at his face. "Time," he said, "has nothing to do with it." He bared his teeth. "I was burned by the fire that destroyed our tribe. Over the years, I have been wounded by hostile warriors." He turned his head and ran his fingers up to the side of his skull. He was almost totally bald, and Kori saw a deep dent in the skin. "I received this mark from your lover, here."

"Uroh is not my lover," Kori told him. "He is my husband." She felt an awful mixture of anger and fear, standing helplessly like this, tied and surrounded by Derneren's warriors. Still, no matter what happened, she wouldn't allow Derneren the satisfaction of intimidating her.

Once again he spat on the ground. "You betrayed your people," he said with disgust. "You ran away with a man whose tribe slaughtered your parents in their sleep. He can never be your husband; he is no better than an animal. Because of him you killed Yainar, and then you ran and hid yourselves like rats." He glowered at Uroh. "It has taken a long time, but now there will be justice." He turned his back to them. "Come!" he called to his men. "We will return to Green Valley."

Kori felt Meiri pressing against her. Kori looked down and saw the girl staring up at her fearfully. "Is this really the man who used to serve Yainar?" Meiri asked.

"This is the one," said Kori.

"What will he do to you?" Meiri asked, her voice rising in pitch. "And what will he do to Uroh?"

"He will want to kill me," said Uroh. "And he will try to humiliate your mother and strip away her pride, till she surrenders to him." Uroh shook his head. "But this is not the time to worry, Meiri. Not yet. Derneren will want to spend time proving that he has power over us. He is a stupid man, and an arrogant man. Your mother and I defeated him before, and we will do so again."

They marched through the afternoon. When they finally reached Green Valley the sun was almost setting, but Kori saw people still working in the fields. Then she came closer and realized that all of them were women, and their ankles were hobbled with heavy leather straps. A few guards moved among them, overseeing their work.

One woman stood up as she saw Derneren and his warriors approaching.

"You!" One of the guards strode over to her. "Get back to work!"

She turned on him. "It's late," she said. "Do you expect us to work in the dark?"

He grabbed a whip that hung at his hip. He uncoiled it with a flick of his wrist, swung it behind him, then brought it around, lashing the woman across her back. The heavy braided leather hit her hard enough to make her stagger. "You'll work all night if we tell you to," he shouted at her.

She dropped to her knees. Slowly, with a sick expression, she picked up the hoe that she had been using, and she resumed dragging it through the soil.

"They killed the men," Uroh said softly, "but they kept the women."

"You are the animal, Derneren," Kori shouted. He was walking ten paces in front of her with half a dozen of his men, while the rest of the warriors marched beside and behind Kori, her husband, and her child. "You are evil, just as Yainar was evil!" she screamed at him. "And you deserve to die as he did, because so long as you live, there will be fear and suffering across the land."

From the corner of her eye she saw the women in the fields giving her anxious looks. She ignored them, focusing all her attention on Derneren, staring at him as if somehow she could wound him with her eyes.

He stopped abruptly, and the warriors stopped around him. Derneren turned toward Kori, and his one good eye gleamed malevolently in the red light of the setting sun. Slowly he raised his arm and pointed at her. "It is my destiny," he said, "to bring you to justice and punish you for what you did. It is your destiny to learn to obey me." He turned and called out the names of some men. "Take her and put her in the empty food cellar," he told them. "She's not fit to enter our houses."

The warriors strode over to her and seized her by

the arms. Kori glanced back at Meiri and Uroh as she was hustled away. She saw Meiri looking at her in horror and Uroh standing silently, giving her a sad smile. It occurred to Kori that this might be the last time she would ever see him, and the thought wrenched at her stomach, making her want to cry. But just as quickly, her sadness turned to defiance. She would not yield, and he would not yield.

The warriors marched her toward six great square houses built from massive pine logs and sun-baked mud. Each house was big enough for thirty people or more. These were the homes where the Green Valley Tribe had lived before the massacre.

But the warriors took her away to one side, where a dozen stone cairns stood in a line. Each cairn was half as high as a man, with a crude wooden lid covering a hole in the center. The warriors hustled Kori to the fourth cairn and then held her for a moment while two other men climbed up, hauled heavy rocks off the lid, and dragged the lid aside.

"Up," one of the warriors told Kori. He jabbed her with his spear. "Get up there!"

It was hard for her to keep her balance with her hands tied behind her, but she managed to climb the low, rounded cairn, finding footholds among the stones. She reached the circular opening at the top, kneeled at its edge, and peered down. The stone dome covered a pit, but she couldn't tell how deep it was.

"In there!" a warrior shouted at her.

She considered resisting them—but she saw that it was pointless. If she refused to obey, they would simply seize her and throw her down. Quite likely, she would be injured; and that would make her less able to defend

herself and less useful to her husband and child, if they
ever had a chance to resist their captors.

She squirmed around and managed to fit her legs
through the circular opening. The air inside the cairn
felt cold.

"In there!" the warrior shouted again.

Kori slid forward and dropped down into the darkness. The pit was deeper than she'd expected. She fell
freely and cried in pain as her feet hit the floor and she
fell sideways, bruising her hip and shoulder.

She looked up in time to see the wooden lid being
dragged back across the circular opening. She heard
heavy stones being set back into place, and then, faintly,
she heard the warriors walking away.

After that, there was nothing but darkness and
silence. With no one to see her and no one to hear her,
she found her spirit weakening. She felt a great wave of
misery sweep over her, and she started crying. The floor
of the cellar was paved in stone, and her body throbbed
with pain where she had fallen against it. The thongs
were painful where they cut into her wrists, and she felt
exhausted. She sobbed, and her tears flowed down onto
the cold stone that pressed against her cheek.

After a while her misery was spent. Her body no
longer hurt so badly, and when she rolled onto her back
and pressed her feet against the wall of the cellar, she
found that neither of her ankles had been injured by her
fall. She reminded herself that Derneren would not
allow her to die in here. As Uroh had said, the man's
purpose was to weaken her, not kill her—at least, not
yet.

So, she would make the best of her situation. She
squirmed around the floor of the cellar, feeling her way

in the darkness. She reached its circular wall and found something that felt like soft gravel around its bottom edge. It was corn, she realized. This was a corn cellar, still containing some remnants.

She rolled onto her stomach, pressed her lips to the floor, and sucked some kernels into her mouth. The corn was hard and raw, but she ground it between her teeth and derived some value from it. Even though it might not be enough really to sustain her, she found pleasure in the knowledge that she was defying Derneren. He had placed her here to weaken her. Instead, she vowed, she would find new strength.

For a long time she lay in the darkness, chewing corn and trying to imagine what lay in store for her. Would people from her tribe follow her and try to rescue her? That seemed unlikely. She had told them to stay in the village, and in any case, as Werror had said, most of them were better suited to fishing than fighting.

Would Uroh be able to save her, and himself, and Meiri? She knew that his gentle manner was deceptive, and he could be cunning and brave—but there must be at least fifty warriors here. How could he possibly prevail against them? It had taken only four of them, after all, to seize him and Meiri and steal them away from the village.

In the end, Kori thought, she would have to depend upon herself. She wondered how she would manage if Derneren tortured her. The idea filled her with dread—but there was something much worse. If he inflicted pain on Meiri, Kori knew she wouldn't be able to endure that.

Well, there was nothing she could do now except wait; so she refused to think anymore about the punishments that Derneren might have in store. She dragged her knees up and covered herself with her robe. The floor was cold and hard, but she managed to lift her thoughts away from her body in this cruel prison. She forced herself to think back to all the things in her life that had given her pleasure: the time she had spent with Uroh building her home, their first attempts to travel out onto the ocean, the wanderers who had joined them, and the love she had received from her people.

In her mind she saw the bright blue of the sea and the rich colors of the land; the gray and white clouds and the golden sun. She told herself that even if she died tomorrow, she had lived a joyous life. And as this thought warmed her, she managed to fall asleep.

18

She woke with sudden light in her eyes. At first she couldn't understand where she was. Then she saw one of Derneren's warriors peering down at her through the hole in the roof of the cairn, and she remembered.

With knowledge came pain. Her knees protested as she tried to straighten her legs. Her shoulder and hips were badly bruised. Her neck was stiff where her head had rested at an angle on the stone floor.

Still, she forced herself to sit up, and then, with an even greater effort of will, she stood.

The warrior eyed her for a moment, then withdrew. Kori heard him saying something to another man, though the words were indistinct. There were rubbing, scraping sounds, and a tree branch was pushed down through the hole.

Instinctively she backed away.

"Stand still!" the warrior shouted. She saw his face

and hands as he thrust the branch toward her. "Der-neren wants you out."

She understood then. A smaller branch stuck out at an angle from the end of the larger one, and had been hacked short so that it was like a hook. The warrior struggled and cursed and finally managed to fit it under Kori's left arm.

Another warrior appeared, squinting down at her. He thrust a second branch down. It, too, terminated in a fork, and he pushed it under Kori's right arm.

Kori saw what they intended to do. She was afraid that it might not work, but how else could they get her out of her prison with her hands tied behind her?

The warriors braced themselves, then started pulling up on the two branches. Bit by bit, Kori was hoisted into the air. The tree limbs dug into her armpits, but she ignored the pain. Her only fear was that they would drop her, causing her to break a leg or crack her skull.

But the warriors were strong, and the branches were thick enough to take her weight. The men pulled her up, hand over hand, and she found herself being hoisted into bright sunlight. She lifted her legs out of the hole and managed to rest her moccasins on the stone rim.

The warriors threw their branches aside and grabbed her by the arms. They dragged her down to the ground, then marched her across a flat area of grass toward the nearest of the houses.

Kori glanced quickly around. She saw women working in the fields again, and guards walking among them. In the other direction, behind the houses, she saw warriors lounging in the sun, eating, talking, and practicing with their spears. A couple of them glanced in her direction, but the rest ignored her. Either they didn't know who she was, or they didn't care.

Kori was hustled through a doorway into the nearest big, square wooden house. She had visited the Green Valley Tribe several times over the years, but still the size of their buildings awed her. The middle of each house was a communal area, with a square stone hearth under a smoke hole in the center of the roof. Around the hearth were mats woven from reeds and grasses, so that people could kneel or sit comfortably while they cooked and ate. Around the walls of the house, curtains stitched from animal skins divided the space into separate sleeping quarters, and there were straw beds covered in thick furs.

When Kori had been here in the past, she'd found everything maintained with scrupulous care. The houses were a legacy from the forefathers of the Green Valley Tribe, and the people treated them with reverential respect.

That had changed. In dim light filtering through the smoke hole, Kori saw that the house had been thrown into disorder. Skins had been ripped down, bedding was strewn around, spears were scattered carelessly, and food had been trodden into the floor of hard-packed earth. She noticed a sour, rotten odor, and at first she thought it must be rotting meat. Then she saw big dark stains on the floor and she realized that the smell was of human blood.

She imagined warriors pouring into the house—at night, probably. She imagined them carrying flaming torches as they ran from one sleeping quarter to the next, thrusting wildly with their spears, killing every man and child. Although the house was empty and silent, Kori could imagine it resounding with battle cries, shouts of pain, and screams of women as they were separated from their slaughtered kinfolk and herded together as prisoners.

Her guards marched her across the great room and out through another doorway in the opposite wall. They took her across a short space where a path had been paved with stones. Then they pushed her ahead of them into the house that stood at the center of the village, where Baryor and his family had once lived.

The two guards stopped just inside the doorway of this building and held Kori between them. She peered into the dimness and saw that there were people in here: a dozen warriors with spears standing around the hearth in the center where some logs were burning. A chair had been crudely built from tree branches lashed together with thongs, and a man was sitting in that chair, dressed in a hooded robe of black bear skin.

There was a long moment of silence, and Kori sensed the black-robed man looking at her. She couldn't see his face, but there was no doubt that it was turned toward her. Finally he spoke. "Bring her here," he said in the same dry, rasping voice she had heard the previous day.

They hustled her forward. Once again she noticed bloodstains on the floor, but this house had been restored to a better state of order. Kori looked at the fine furs, the skins with ornamental zigzag patterns scored into them, big baskets of food around the hearth, and beautiful robes hanging from pegs in the wooden walls. It had taken generations for the Green Valley Tribe to create their fine homes. And now, because their leader had been an ineffectual, foolish man, and his people had forgotten how to defend themselves, everything had been stolen from them.

Kori was brought in front of Derneren where he lounged in his primitive chair, chewing on a piece of venison while his guards stood around him. More freshly cooked meat lay on a big square of bark beside the fire, and the smell tantalized her. Still, she forced herself to ignore it. She faced her captor and eyed him without humility, showing as much defiance as she could manage.

Derneren finished gnawing a bone and tossed it into the fire. It hissed briefly among the flames. He licked his fingers, then wiped them casually on his robe. Faintly, in the dimness, she saw his eye gleaming as he watched her.

"You slept well?" he asked.

Kori remembered him being one year younger than herself, yet his voice made him sound like an old man. She wondered what had happened to him. "I slept well enough," she said, trying to speak without any trace of emotion.

He poked his finger in his mouth and rubbed it around his gums. He grimaced, and she guessed that his discolored teeth must be causing him pain. He pulled out a fragment of venison and flicked it aside.

"I wasn't sure it was you," he said, "when I saw you on that beach that night." He grunted to himself. "But there's no doubt."

He shifted in his chair. Now that he was sitting, Kori saw what his loose robes had concealed the day before. His body was emaciated. Fourteen years ago he had been a big, powerful man.

"You should know," Derneren went on, "what I have endured, because of you."

Kori still said nothing. She had some interest in his story, but she was much more concerned about Meiri and Uroh.

"Fourteen years ago," Derneren went on, "you abandoned me." His lips pulled back from his teeth as he scowled at her. "You left me by the river with my head bleeding and my kinfolk dying. You left our homes devoured by fire, and our people punished by the Old Ones for *your* defiance and lack of respect." His thin chest heaved and his gnarled fingers clutched at the arms of his chair.

So many years had passed, Kori had almost forgotten the superstitions of her old tribe. "You still believe in the Old Ones," she said in wonder.

"How can I not believe?" He waved a skeletal hand. "The Old Ones spared my life, and they spoke to me." He pointed at her. "They told me to find you and punish you."

"And this is what has guided you?" Kori said. "For fourteen years? And this is how you excuse yourself for killing scores of innocent men, stealing their homes, and enslaving their women?" She gave a short, derisive laugh. "If you were not such an evil man—if your warriors had not killed so many innocent people—I would pity you, Derneren."

He pulled himself forward in his chair. Tendons stood out in his neck, and his jaw muscles clenched. "Quiet!" he snapped at her. "Quiet, or I tell my men to stuff your mouth with animal droppings. Do you understand?"

Kori said nothing. She repressed her anger as well as she could, and she waited.

Derneren slumped back in his chair and gave her a long look of brooding hatred. "My skin was burned," he said. "I suffered when I tried to save my kinfolk from the fire. And then, after I gave up and fled down the river, alone in a canoe—I almost died from hunger." He looked somber for a moment. Then he tilted his head up, gathering his pride. "But I found warriors, and we prospered." He nodded slowly. "The Old Ones have guided me well. And now that the time is right, they have brought me to you, as I knew they would."

Kori moved restlessly. "So why did you run from me when you found me on the beach?" she asked him. "If these Old Ones were guiding you and protecting you—"

"I already said, I wasn't sure it was you." He gave her a devious look. "And I had no spear, and I was walking alone. One thing I have learned is patience. Another thing I have learned is caution. So, first we conquered the weak, stupid people of the Green Valley Tribe, and then we questioned our prisoners. They knew your name, and they told me where you could be found. They told me about your daughter—and your son." He squirmed around in his chair and glanced back into the shadows. "Come forward."

Kori stiffened as she heard footsteps. She hadn't realized that anyone else was in the house. She saw a figure moving forward into the light, and she felt confusion—then outrage. She stared at the big man as he stood before her. "Werror," she muttered.

Derneren grinned, deriving satisfaction from the emotions he saw in Kori's face. "I had to be sure that you were the one I was seeking," he said in a voice that sounded as hoarse as the hiss of a bobcat. "Our prisoners said you were a formidable woman, a dangerous fighter, with your tribe in a place that would be difficult to attack. So I sent Werror, here, to win your trust." Derneren's smile broadened. "At night, he slipped out to meet me where I hid with some of my warriors in the forest. He said it was true that you are a dangerous fighter. But he said you have a weakness. You care for your husband and children. So, I decided to steal them and bring them here, to tempt you." His face twisted suddenly. "I was disappointed when Werror said that your son had already left the tribe. I wanted all your kinfolk. If I let your son live, he might try to take vengeance upon me."

Now, at last, Kori understood why Werror had volunteered to help find Feroh, and why he had stolen the boy away into the night. "You have Feroh here?" she asked.

"Of course," said Derneren, grinning at her.

Kori remembered sleeping on the table of rock, after Raor had left with Tithea, taking her back to the White River Tribe. That night Kori had woken and found Werror looming over her. He must have been thinking of seizing her and bringing her here with himself and Feroh. But he had seen that she was alert, with her spear beside her, and she would have posed a risk. He had known that Derneren's men were stealing her husband and daughter away that same night—and she would follow them soon enough, of her own free will.

There was still one thing, though, that Kori couldn't understand. She saw Werror standing tall and proud, so much more powerful than the crumpled figure in the chair. She turned her attention to him. "Why did you jeopardize your life, and the life of your daughter, casting yourself adrift on that raft, just to win our trust?" she asked.

Werror smiled. His teeth flashed in the dimness, and Kori felt humiliated as she remembered how she had been charmed by that smile only a few days ago. But she saw no kindness in him now. When he exposed his teeth he looked like a predatory beast.

Werror paused for a moment, choosing his words carefully. "You are a strong woman," he said. "But still, you are a woman. You don't understand the pleasure a man finds from risking death, deceiving his enemies, fighting them, and killing them."

"I have seen the pleasure that some men take," she said, "proving their strength and causing pain and death." She showed him her disgust in the way that she looked at him, though he seemed indifferent to it. "Still," she went on, "one thing makes no sense." She nodded toward the crumpled figure in the chair. "Why do you serve him?"

Werror shrugged as if the answer should have been obvious. "He hears the Old Ones," he said. "They guide him, and he guides us. And they speak truly. With their guidance, we have conquered and prospered."

Kori looked into his eyes. He stared back at her impassively, showing no hint of uncertainty—but she felt sure that he was lying to her, just as he had lied so often before. He had spoken too quickly. This was a speech he had prepared long ago. He was a shrewd, practical man; she didn't believe he had faith in the ravings of this withered figure in a hooded black robe.

But then Kori glanced at the other warriors standing by, and she saw in their simple faces that *they* believed in Derneren. Now it was clear: Werror would have seized power in a moment if the warriors hadn't been so loyal to Derneren's visions. So Werror was biding his time, waiting for Derneren to die—or name him as the one to inherit his power.

Once again Kori felt a wave of disgust. She turned away from Werror. Now that she saw his true nature, she had no further interest in him. She only cared about her people. "Where is Uroh, and where is Meiri?" she asked. "And where is Feroh?"

Derneren grimaced. He coughed suddenly, and his thin body shook. He leaned forward and coughed again, and it sounded like a death rattle in his withered throat. He spat on the floor, and took a shaky breath. Gradually he recovered himself. "Bring the boy," he whispered.

More footsteps sounded in the big house. Two warriors came forward out of the shadows, bringing a smaller figure between them.

They stopped in front of Kori, and she found herself confronted with her son, less than three paces away. He stood without fear, and Kori saw that although the warriors flanked him, they didn't touch him, and his wrists weren't bound. Then, with a feeling of despair, she saw that he had cast off his old robe. He was wearing a black bear skin, like Derneren's.

She looked back at the withered figure in his chair, and he was grinning at her with an expression of evil delight. "When your son was brought to me last night," Derneren said, "I saw something in his face that interested me. A resemblance that was very striking. Do you know what I'm speaking of?"

Kori felt a terrible sinking sensation. She said nothing.

Derneren chuckled. "I asked your son if he had ever heard of a man named Yainar. And yes, he knew the story." He glowered at Kori. "He knew how you and your lover killed the man." Derneren paused for a moment, calming himself. "He knew, too, that he had never felt—kinship, with your lover Uroh. There were other things, too—little things—that had spawned suspicions in his mind."

Kori felt herself swaying.

Derneren turned to Feroh. "Ask her," he said. "Go on. Ask her!"

Feroh paused a moment, gathering his strength. Kori saw his nostrils flare as he breathed deeply. "I want to know," he said, "the name of my father."

Time seemed to freeze around Kori in the big, dark house. She felt Feroh's eyes upon her, uneasy yet demanding, and she felt herself weakening as she realized there was no way now to keep the truth from her son.

Then a wild spasm of anger seized her. She glared at Derneren. "This is your doing!" she cried.

Derneren grinned. Her anger was a pleasure to him; it nourished him. "Just answer the boy," he said.

Kori looked at Feroh in anguish. "I kept this knowledge from you because it is so hurtful," she told him. "I thought you should never have to endure it." She drew a slow breath. "But now I think you already know the answer, and in any case, I cannot lie to you. Your father was Yainar, the man who raped me, the man who fought my husband—and the man I killed."

Feroh drew in a sharp breath. Even though he must have known what she would say, her words unleashed something inside him. He let out a strange sound, a little cry of anger and pain. And then, without warning, he threw himself forward.

The warriors on either side of him moved swiftly. One of them seized the boy by the neck of his robe and jerked him back. The other tried to grab Feroh's arms.

For a moment there was a fierce scuffle as Feroh turned against the men, flailing wildly with his fists. Then Werror grabbed Feroh's wrists and twisted the boy's arms behind him. "Not now," the big man said. "Listen to me, Feroh. *Listen to me!* This is not the time. But the time will come. Do you understand?"

Gradually Feroh's struggles subsided. He stood for a moment, panting. His face was flushed and his hair hung across his forehead.

There was an eerie, rasping sound from Derneren. Kori looked at him and saw him shaking in his chair—and she realized he was laughing.

"What is the purpose of this?" Kori screamed at him.

Derneren turned his mottled, ugly face toward Kori. "The purpose is justice," he said. "I already told you that."

Kori looked at him with righteous fury. "You dare to judge me? You dare to speak of justice?" She tugged futilely at the warriors holding her arms. "You have no right to punish me. You have no right even to live."

Derneren's one good eye glittered in the dimness. "Your words mean nothing," he hissed at her. "The Old Ones spared my life, and they guide me still. Theirs are the only words that mean anything to me." He gestured to her guards. "Take her out to the log."

19

The men marched Kori to the rear of the house. Conflicting emotions raged inside her. She felt shame at the way she had been deceived by Werror, she yearned for Uroh, and she agonized over Meiri's fate. She also felt sadness and regret over Feroh—but most of all she felt fury at Derneren.

She wondered if she should have tried to kill him while she faced him inside the house. She might have pulled free from the men holding her, and even though her wrists were tied behind her, she could have leaped at him. She imagined kicking out, slamming her moccasin into his hideous face. With luck, she could have broken his neck.

But of course, the guards would have slaughtered her. Once again she reminded herself what Uroh had said: that even though Derneren might want to kill her ultimately, he would want to prove his power over her first. She believed that Uroh was right; which meant she would have some time at least—perhaps several days—in which to free herself. Therefore, she should do whatever she could to prolong her survival.

She blinked as the guards dragged her into the sun. She found herself at the rear of the houses where she had seen warriors lounging around earlier. They were still here, thirty or forty of them. As they saw her, they rose slowly to their feet.

She felt a sucking sense of dread as she saw a look of anticipation in their eyes. She wondered how much they had been told about her. At the very least, some of them must know that she had killed two of their comrades and wounded a third.

She half expected them to converge upon her, but they stood and watched as her guards walked her forward among them. Their faces were battle-scarred; their robes were dirty and torn; their spears were crudely fashioned, and the shafts were stained dark with blood.

Then she saw a big dead log ahead of her, standing upright, embedded in the ground. Freshly turned earth around the log showed that it had been set here recently—perhaps that morning. Finally Kori understood what was to happen.

Her guards took her to the log and turned her back to it, so that she faced the houses. She felt fingers grasping the thongs binding her wrists, then there was the brief cold touch of a flint knife, and suddenly her hands were free.

For a moment she considered trying to break away. But the warriors were gathering around her, forming a human wall. No matter how much it humiliated her, she forced herself to remain passive. For the sake of her husband and her daughter, she must preserve her life and strength.

Several hands clutched each of her arms, raising them up. She closed her eyes, trying to find the strength she needed, as she felt her wrists being tied to a branch that stuck out of the log above her head.

Without warning, her clothes were cut and ripped away from her. She cried out involuntarily as she felt the cool air on her skin and realized she had been stripped bare in front of the men. She tensed herself, waiting for the punishment that she knew must come—but there was an eerie silence, and no one touched her.

Slowly, cautiously, she opened her eyes. The men were watching her, but none of them moved. Then she saw three figures emerge from the rear of the house where she had faced Derneren, and she saw that one of them was him, with Feroh on his left and Werror on his right.

They moved toward her slowly, so slowly Kori that felt like crying out, screaming for them to do whatever it was they were going to do. But they stopped a dozen paces away, and there was another long pause in which the only sound she heard was the singing of birds in trees and the rapid rhythm of her own heart.

Finally Derneren turned to Feroh. "She is yours now," he said. "I give her to you." He gestured at the warriors all around. "What would you have them do?"

"She shall be punished." There was a catch in Feroh's voice, and she saw emotion flickering in his face—excitement, anger, and anxiety. Somewhere inside him, he still had feelings for her, Kori realized. Still, he drew himself up and he forced himself to stare at her.

Derneren turned to his men. "Let everyone understand," he said, "this woman is a murderer. She killed this boy's father. She has admitted it. She killed your comrades, and she defied the Old Ones." He turned back to Feroh. "Now tell us what the punishment will be."

Feroh was breathing fast. "I want her pelted with stones," Feroh said in a voice that was high-pitched with tension. "Strike her, beat her, hurt her." He paused, and she thought she saw him trembling. This was not easy for him; it violated a taboo that was so deep, so fundamental, he must know in his soul that what he was doing was wrong. Still, once more he forced himself on. "She shall not die," he said. "And I do not want anyone to spill too much of her blood. Not yet."

Kori could remain silent no longer. "Feroh!" she cried. "Feroh, you are my son! I am your mother!"

"No!" His voice was a sudden shout. "You are not my mother!" He glared at her wildly. "You are a murderer!"

Derneren nodded. He laid a withered hand on the boy's shoulder. "It shall be as you say." He gestured to his men. "Begin."

Kori cried out in pain as she felt the impact of a dozen stones. Some of them struck her torso; two struck her arms; three hit her face. Pain blossomed like a terrible flower whose scent filled her body and mind.

Another fusillade of stones hit her, and she felt blood starting to trickle from the wounds. She closed her eyes, clenched her jaw, and tried to conceal her pain, because she felt sure that if she revealed it, she would spur the warriors to hurt her more.

A hand slapped her cheek. Another hand raked her belly. Someone tried to force dirt into her mouth. She smelled the acrid body odor of the warriors as they pressed around her, hitting her, spitting on her, kicking her, abusing her with casual cruelty. Someone beat her with a stick. A man elbowed her in the belly. Another man punched her hard in the face.

Despite herself, Kori started crying—not from pain, but from frustration. She imagined herself breaking loose, seizing a spear, and stabbing the men who were tormenting her. She imagined watching their blood flow and seeing them crumple to their knees before her. In her mind she crushed them into the mud.

But her imagination was impotent, and she was tormented all the more by knowing that this punishment was only slightly worse than the humiliation she had allowed her people to inflict on Feroh. But no; he had violated the taboos of his tribe. He had *deserved* to be punished. In her heart, Kori knew she had done nothing wrong. She had cared for Feroh as a baby; she had nurtured him and given him all the love she could find in herself. She had slain his father, but only when there was no other way to protect herself and Uroh, and only after Yainar had raped her and tried to enslave her.

The abuse went on and on, and she began to wonder if it would ever end. Finally, faintly, she heard a voice commanding the warriors to stop. They retreated from her, and she slumped in her bonds, shaking and gasping. Her body hurt horribly, and she felt herself bleeding from scores of wounds, but none of them was fatal. She would live. And if she lived, surely there was still some hope that in some way, somehow, she might take revenge.

She opened her eyes, blinked away her tears, and saw Feroh standing in front of her. His face twitched as he looked at her. Even now, a part of him was afraid of her. "Cut her down," Derneren said, standing further back. "Then clean her up and take her to Feroh's new sleeping quarters."

"Feroh!" Kori called out, as warriors moved to obey their master. "Feroh, this you must know. I am still your mother, no matter what you say. And I care for you, Feroh. I love you now as I have always loved you."

Her words enraged him. With his left fist he hit her face, causing her to cry out as his knuckles met her cheek bone. With his right fist he hit her in the belly.

He glared at her, shaking with emotion. Then he turned his back on her.

They took her to the broad river that ran through Green Valley, nourishing the fields where crops grew. Downstream, the river took away human wastes. Upstream, it supplied water for the tribe to drink. Midway, it provided a place for people to wash themselves.

Several warriors armed with spears stood guard while Kori stepped down into the water. The water was chillingly cold, but she welcomed it, for it helped to dull her pain.

She squatted in the river, shivering as she rinsed the blood and dirt from her skin. There were dozens of cuts all over her chest, abdomen, and legs, and she winced as she touched them. Tomorrow she would be covered in bruises.

When she struggled back out of the water, one of the men threw her a dirty robe of deer skin that was so old and thin, there were holes in it. It smelled bad and looked miserable, but still Kori arranged it carefully to cover herself. She was determined that no matter what they did to her, she wouldn't lose her pride.

When she had dressed herself, they took her to another of the big houses. There were many young men inside, and Kori realized it had become a barracks for the junior warriors. Some of them were in sleeping spaces around the edges of the room, lounging and dozing on their beds of furs. More of them had gathered around the hearth in the center where a couple of sad-eyed women were setting out wicker trays of fruit and baked corn beside a freshly roasted deer.

Kori's stomach groaned as she smelled the food, but her captors turned her away from it. They took her to a corner of the room and pushed her down on the straw bed there. They tied her wrists in front of her with a long, thick leather strap, then hobbled her with another strap and laid its free end out on the floor. Three more men brought a huge slab of stone that was so heavy, all of them together could barely lift it. They set it down on the strap, leaving less than an arm's length of it free. Finally someone came over with a stone dish of hot, soft resin, which he dripped onto the knots in the straps, sealing them. He blew on the resin till it cooled and solidified, leaving Kori no way to free herself.

The men abandoned her, and she slumped down on the bed and closed her eyes.

Dimly she heard people feeding themselves, talking and laughing. There were some shouts, and she heard men calling Feroh's name.

She opened her eyes and peered across the dim-lit room. The young warriors were gathering in two lines, with each man holding a strap, a length of hemp rope, or a bundle of thongs. Feroh had entered the house and was standing over at the far side, stripped naked to the waist, with Werror standing close by. The young warriors started chanting Feroh's name, and Kori saw Werror slap Feroh between his shoulders, urging him forward.

Feroh braced himself, then ran between the lines of men. They yelled and whooped and lashed him as he passed them. Then they seized him and turned him and made him run back again; and then they threw him down into the center of a golden-brown skin that looked as if it had come from a mountain lion.

The young warriors gathered around and lifted the skin by its edges, while Werror still stood to one side, watching over them. There were more whoops and cheers as they heaved on the skin, jerking it upward, hurling Feroh into the air.

They bounced him a dozen times, and finally they set the skin down and hauled him onto his feet. Kori glimpsed his face glistening with sweat and his body crisscrossed with pink welts. He was grinning, though— exulting in their attention.

Werror pushed through the crowd. He picked up the lion skin and draped it around Feroh's shoulders. "This man has come among us as a friend," the big man shouted out, turning to face the crowd. His voice boomed so loudly, it drowned their cries. "Our food shall be his food. Our house shall be his house." He turned to Feroh. "Honor us now. Pledge yourself to the Island Tribe."

The voices of the warriors died into silence as everyone stared at Feroh, waiting expectantly.

"I pledge myself to the Island Tribe." Kori heard his voice faintly but clearly. She groaned in anguish. The Island Tribe was where she had been born and nurtured, and they had been a peaceful people. It was an offense against her kin and forebears for Derneren to take that name and apply it here to this band of thugs.

Werror was speaking again. "Tell us now, Feroh," he said, "if you would join our tribe. Will you give your life to protect the lives of your comrades?"

Feroh's face was deadly serious. "I will give my own life to protect the lives of my comrades," he said, without hesitation.

"You will serve Derneren, and honor the will of the Old Ones," said Werror.

"Yes," Feroh answered him. "I will serve Derneren, and honor the will of the Old Ones."

"You will serve us as your only people, renouncing all others. And you will serve us from now until the day you die."

"Yes!" Feroh cried out.

Werror nodded solemnly. "Then you have joined us, Feroh, and we accept you. You are one of us from now until death."

The young warriors yelled their approval.

"Stand before me," Werror said.

Feroh faced the big man. Kori saw the flash of polished flint, and she heard Feroh give a muted cry as the knife slashed three times on the left and three times on the right, inflicting ritual chest wounds that Kori had seen on other warriors in the tribe.

"Your blood is our blood," Werror called out. "Share it with your comrades."

The young men clustered around and reached out

eagerly, rubbing their hands across the cuts that Werror had made. Kori saw many of the warriors licking Feroh's blood from their fingers.

"It is done," Werror said. "Let all men know, you are now Feroh of the Island Tribe. Your enemy is our enemy. Our strength is your strength. You shall serve us, and we shall protect you, from now until death."

"From now until death!" all the young hunters shouted in unison.

"Eat with us now," said Werror, "for you are reborn among us. You will live among us. You will die among us. And after your death, your spirit will be honored among the spirits of other warriors who have died before you."

There was another wave of cheering, so loud that it hurt Kori's ears. Feroh was pushed to a mat beside the fire. He dropped down onto his knees, and Kori saw that his chest was still bleeding freely where Werror had cut him. Instinctively, despite everything that had happened, Kori felt concerned. But then Werror scooped ashes from the edge of the fire and rubbed them into the wounds, staunching the bleeding. Feroh didn't flinch; his face was still glowing with the same expression of righteous satisfaction. His eyes were wide, his smile was broad, and he held himself proudly as his new comrades gathered around him.

Kori felt overwhelmed with sadness. She saw now that this was what her son had always wanted, and Werror had sensed it in him, and had known how to tempt him with it. Her kindness and love had meant nothing to Feroh, because he despised it. Her attempts to discipline him had enraged him, because she was a woman, and she showed him no respect. All he wanted was to be surrounded by men who would validate his desire to be strong.

As Feroh began to eat and the men cheered him yet again, Kori turned away, trying to deafen herself to their cries. She had never felt so estranged from her son, and so alone.

During that afternoon, after the feasting was done, all the young men left the house, and it became silent. Probably, Kori thought to herself, they wanted to compare their strength and skill against Feroh's, to see who was best at hunting and killing.

She checked her bonds to see if there was any way she could free herself, but the resin had set hard, and she saw no knives or spears anywhere in this house. And so, with weary fatalism, she lay on the bed, trying to find a position that would avoid causing too much pain from all her wounds.

Finally, after a long time, she slept.

She woke to find a wicker platter being thrust under her face. Remnants of baked corn were sticking to it, and there were a few scraps of meat. Kori found herself salivating, gripped by overwhelming hunger. She seized the platter in her two hands, which were still tied in front of her. Then she hesitated, peering up at the figure who was standing over her.

The light in the house had grown dimmer, but Kori could just see the outline of a young woman's face. "Jalin!" Kori exclaimed.

The girl eyed her for a moment without speaking. She averted her eyes.

Kori raised the platter and nibbled the remnants of

food from it. She felt humiliated to have to eat this way, but still she was determined to take any opportunity to maintain her strength.

"She is mine now," said a voice.

Kori turned and found Feroh squatting in the shadows, watching her. "What are you talking about?" Kori asked him. "Are you telling me that Werror has given his own daughter—"

"Jalin isn't his daughter." Feroh stood up and stepped forward. Casually he reached down and seized Kori's hair. "Get off my bed."

Kori grunted in pain as he dragged her aside, threw her onto the hard floor, and took her place on the furs. She looked up at him as he made himself comfortable, and she suddenly imagined herself rising up, throwing herself upon him, and closing her hands around his throat. Even with her wrists tied, she might be able to choke him if she took him by surprise. Then she could seize the knife from his belt and use it to free herself—

She cut off the train of thought. She heard voices and realized that other men were coming into the house. Even if she cut her bonds, she was still a prisoner here. And in any case, no matter what Feroh had done, she doubted she could take his life.

With an effort of will, she turned away and looked again at Jalin. "Is it true?" she asked. "Are you not Werror's daughter?"

Jalin looked questioningly at Feroh.

"She is not allowed to speak without my permission," Feroh said.

Kori stared at him. He looked so calm and confident reclining on his bed, with his body scarred with wounds that testified to the pledge of loyalty he had made. Even though he now had such power over her, she couldn't remain silent. "Why do you not allow her to speak?" she said. "Are you afraid she might say something that would humiliate you? Are you so weak, you fear the words of a mere woman?"

Feroh had been watching her impassively. As she spoke, though, he became enraged. He sprang to his feet and kicked Kori in the stomach. "Show respect!" he shouted at her.

Kori coughed and choked and struggled to breathe. Her chest heaved, and she was afraid she might vomit the dregs of food that she had just eaten.

Slowly Feroh regained his self-control. "Remember this," he said, as he sat back on the bed. "Derneren has told me I may punish you in any way I choose." A muscle tugged at his cheek as he glared at her. "You are my servant now. If you obey me, I will feed you. If you anger me, I will torment you."

Kori stared at his face and saw madness in him. Perhaps she would have seen it before, years ago, if he had not been her son. On the other hand, no one else in her tribe had ever sensed the real sickness in his spirit— except, perhaps, for Meiri.

"What did I do," Kori whispered, "to make you hate me so?"

Feroh's eyes flickered with emotion—but when he spoke, his voice was controlled. "You deceived me," he said.

Kori shook her head helplessly. "I tried to protect you from something too awful for a young boy to know."

"No." He sounded adamant. "You deceived me, and I always knew—"

"You couldn't have known!" Kori cried.

For a moment he was silent. He gave her a long, brooding look. Then he shrugged. "I never knew exactly what you were hiding. But I always knew there was something. I saw the guilty way you looked at me. You never looked at Meiri that way. And you never looked at me as kindly as you looked at her. You just wanted me to *obey* you." His chest heaved as once again, he wrestled with his emotions.

Kori saw his sullen resentment and realized that really he was still a child. But he was a child whose temper tantrums could kill her. He had gained more power than a child should ever have.

"There's no point in talking like this," Feroh said suddenly, sweeping his arm to push the words away. "I know the truth now, and that's all that matters. Derneren saw how I resembled my true father—"

"You do," Kori said bitterly. "You look like him, and you behave like him. You resemble him in more ways than you can ever know." Surely, she thought to herself, she couldn't be entirely to blame. Feroh had not turned out this way just because of the way she had treated him as a child. Somehow, the sickness in him must have been passed on in his father's seed.

She sighed, realizing that it was pointless to argue with him. "Tell me," she said, "about your sister. She is still your sister; both of you came from my womb. Where is she now? Is she being cared for?"

Feroh brooded for a moment, debating what to tell her. "She is alive," he said finally. "She will be kept with the other young girls of this tribe, till she comes of age. Then she will be given to a man for him to use as he sees fit."

Kori looked at him in dismay. "You talk as if she is just a piece of property, like a spear or a robe."

Feroh shrugged. "That is how women are in this tribe. They are owned by men, just as I own Jalin now."

Kori glanced at the girl and found her still sitting nearby on the floor, looking down, saying nothing. "You mean," Kori struggled to understand. "Jalin has been paired with you as your mate?"

Feroh shook his head dismissively. "Derneren does not allow pairings. He knows that when a woman is paired with a man, one way or another, she will try to steal some of his power. No; in this tribe, a man may have as many women as Derneren chooses to give him. And when a man grows tired of a woman, he gives her to any other man who will take her."

Kori suddenly felt like crying. She remembered all the times she had spoken patiently to Feroh, explaining that although women and men might seem different, they must be treated equally. She remembered teaching him to respect the women of her tribe and understand their wisdom. And everything she'd said had been cast aside now, as if she had never spoken at all.

"Must you hate *all* women," she asked him, "just because you hate me? Must you prove your power over them just because I wielded such power over you, as your mother and the chieftain of your tribe?" She looked at his face and felt sure that this was so. "Why," she cried out, feeling overwhelmed by his cruelty, "Jalin is just a young girl. She isn't yet of age!"

"She is," Feroh contradicted her. He turned to Jalin. "Tell her," he said.

Jalin shifted nervously. "I have bled twice," she said in a small voice.

Kori looked at the girl's face and realized she was speaking truly. "So once again, Werror lied," Kori said to herself. She turned back to Feroh. "But where did Jalin come from? If she is not Werror's daughter—"

"She is from the Green Valley Tribe." Feroh looked at Kori as if she were stupid. "Her father was killed. Her mother works in the fields."

Kori shook his head, still not understanding. "Then why did Werror—"

Feroh grunted with impatience. "Werror brought her to your tribe because he thought you would trust a man and his young daughter more readily than a man alone." He gave her a smug smile. "And Werror was correct."

Kori thought back. Yes, she realized bitterly, her protective instincts had been roused by the way Werror cared for the girl. At the same time, Werror had taken a risk, bringing the girl with him. If Jalin had spoken—but of course, she hadn't been allowed to speak. She had been terrified into silence. Werror had insisted on bringing her when they went on their journey to find Feroh, because he had wanted the girl under his control at all times.

"So," said Kori, feeling weary. "You must feel very important now, Feroh. You have been accepted by these men—these warriors. Derneren has bribed you with not just one woman to serve you, but two."

"This is so," Feroh agreed with her. If he heard the scorn in her voice, he didn't show it. "Derneren has honored me because he revered my father, who was a hero to his people." He paused, frowning. "Still," he said, "you should not think of yourself in the same way as Jalin. Jalin has not deceived me. She has committed no crimes against me, or my—my father." He clenched his fists reflexively as he spoke. "So she will not be punished as you will be punished." He drew a deep breath, pumping up his courage, driving himself to defy her. "Jalin will still be alive," he told Kori, "long after you are dead."

"Speak plainly," Kori said, although in her heart she already knew what he meant.

Feroh breathed deeply. "There will come a time," he told her, "when I have punished you as much as I wish to. At that time, I will return you to Derneren. And then—then, he will make you pay the ultimate price. For your crime against my father, and against the—the Old Ones." He drew another deep breath. "And when that time comes—then, it will be over for you. You will be executed."

20

At sunset, when the patch of sky visible through the smoke hole turned from blue to purple, the rest of the women were brought in from the fields. Kori watched them from her place on the floor by Feroh's bed. Some were in bondage like her, with their wrists bound in front of them and their legs hobbled. Others—mostly young ones, like Jalin—were unfettered. They were the ones who seemed most cowed and least likely to pose a threat to their masters.

Several women carried in fresh wood for the fire, and soon the flames were leaping high, casting giant shifting shadows upon the walls. Other women brought food in baskets and water in gourds, and Feroh left his bed, joining the men who sat and started eating while the women knelt respectfully behind them and waited in silence.

Kori looked at Jalin. "Are you hungry?" she whispered to the girl.

Jalin hesitated. She eyed Kori nervously for a moment, then nodded.

"I am too," said Kori. She felt cold and uncomfortable on the floor, and her stomach was a hollow pit of need. She was trying to be patient, trying to be philosophical, knowing that it would not help her to create any kind of disturbance; but her anger still simmered inside her, and the hunger just made it worse. "When will we be allowed to eat?" she asked.

Jalin parted her lips as if she wanted to speak—then seemed to think better of it. Finally, though, she found the courage. "After the men have finished, we will be given food," she whispered.

Kori felt she had achieved some kind of small victory, persuading the girl to talk. She reached out and touched Jalin on the shoulder.

Jalin flinched away.

"Feroh hasn't told me not to touch you," Kori whispered.

Jalin looked embarrassed. She forced herself to look at Kori, and she gave her a brief, awkward smile.

"It must have been so hard for you," Kori whispered. "You saw your father die, and then you were taken away by Werror. You must have thought you would die, too."

Jalin's mouth turned down at the corners. She fretted with the hem of her robe. "I was very scared," she murmured.

"But still," said Kori, "you concealed your fear. You were brave."

Jalin bit her lip. She looked as if she might cry. "It's not true," she said. "I am not brave. Not like you."

Kori patted the girl gently. "I'm not so courageous,"

she whispered. "Just reckless. And when I show my anger, it's because I've never learned how to contain it."

"Shh," Jalin said sharply.

Kori looked up and saw a figure approaching, silhouetted against the firelight. It was Feroh.

He stopped in front of Kori and Jalin and surveyed them with the same calm satisfaction that a man might show toward an animal that he had just trapped or speared. Then he dropped a basket on the floor in front of them and turned away without a word.

Jalin seized the basket eagerly. She grabbed a lump of venison from it—then stopped herself and turned to Kori, looking ashamed.

"You need the food more than I do," Kori said, eyeing Jalin's young, thin body. In any case, there was another piece of meat. It was undercooked and stringy, and Kori saw that the men had taken all the best parts. Still, it was more than she had hoped for. She picked it up between her tied hands, and she devoured it.

Over by the fire, men were abandoning the food that they hadn't eaten. The women didn't attempt to maintain their dignity. They moved forward and fed themselves ravenously from the leftovers.

Some of the men stood nearby, watching with idle amusement. Kori saw one hunter reach out and seize a piece of meat from a woman's hands. He taunted her with it, holding it just out of reach. He made her kneel before him, then dropped the meat on the floor and told her to eat it with her hands clasped behind her back. She bowed her head and ate the food like an animal, while several of the hunters laughed at her.

Kori turned her eyes away. She found herself shaking with anger, and she felt so sickened, she wasn't sure if she could finish her meal. Once again, though, she reminded herself that she needed to conserve her strength. There was powdery pemmican in the basket, and some chunks of boiled marrow fat. Kori choked them down quickly, just as Feroh returned.

He took the basket out of Kori's hands and tossed it aside. He stood over her for a moment, staring at her with an unreadable expression. Then he grimaced, and without warning he kicked her. His moccasin struck her knee where she had already been wounded by a stone while she was tied to the log outside. He kicked her again, and then a third time, as hard as he could.

Kori grunted with pain and tried to scramble away from him, but her tether snapped tight. "Why?" she gasped, as her eyes watered with pain.

"To remind you," said Feroh, "you are my property, and I can use you in any way I wish."

Once again Kori imagined assaulting him. She could grab his foot and jerk it toward her. He would fall backward, and he might crack his skull on the floor.

She closed her eyes, willing herself to swallow her anger. She heard other hunters all around, talking and laughing as they moved to their sleeping quarters. She heard cries of women being manhandled. If she struck out at Feroh now, there would be many men to share the pleasure of punishing her, and no one to defend her.

Kori heard Feroh settling himself on his bed of furs. "Here," he said.

For a moment Kori thought he was talking to her. She opened her eyes—and saw him beckoning to Jalin.

With a look of dread, the girl edged toward him.

"On the bed," he told her, pointing to the furs where he sat. His eyes were bright and his cheeks were flushed, and Kori had no doubt about his intentions.

Jalin crouched beside him, clutching her arms around herself.

Feroh reached out and ran his fingers along the line of her jaw, then down to her neck. "Put your arms by your sides," he told her. He gave the command casually, as if he felt entirely sure of himself, but Kori saw that he was nervous behind his mask of authority.

Reluctantly Jalin obeyed him.

Feroh tugged at the thongs that closed her robe. His fingers were impatient. He cursed and tore at the thongs, ripping them open. He seized the robe and pushed it down behind Jalin's shoulders, exposing her breasts.

For a moment he stared at her, breathing quickly through parted lips. Jalin closed her eyes and turned her face aside. Her lower lip quivered, and Kori saw that the girl was near tears.

Feroh reached out and grabbed her small, young breasts. His fingers dug into the tender skin, and Jalin let out a wail of distress.

Her cry released something in Feroh. He grabbed Jalin by the back of her neck and threw her facedown. He ripped her robe off and tossed it aside. Then he cast off his own robe and stood naked for a moment, panting heavily. He grabbed himself between the legs, and even though Kori felt she should look away, she couldn't bring herself to do so. She stared at Feroh's genitals—and saw, with surprise, that he was not tumescent, even though he seemed eager to throw himself on the girl.

His impotence made him furious. He turned and seized a bundle of thongs hanging on the wall, then swung his arm and lashed them across Jalin's back.

The girl cried out in surprise. She started to turn over.

"Lie still!" Feroh shouted at her. He raised his leg and stamped on Jalin's back, forcing her down. Then he wielded the thongs again, lashing her with all his strength, raising pink and red welts in her tender skin.

Now, finally, Feroh was aroused. He dropped the thongs, forced her legs apart, kneeled between them, and forced himself into her.

Jalin screamed. She started to struggle, but Feroh grabbed her by the back of her neck and held her easily. He reached higher, dug his fingers into her long hair, and twisted his hand. Jalin cried out in pain—and Feroh gasped. His hips jerked spasmodically as he reached his climax, and then he collapsed onto her, panting like a dog.

Kori felt overwhelmed with disgust. She turned away and found herself looking at a score of young warriors who had gathered to witness Feroh's act. Clearly, they knew that this was his first time. Kori saw their smiling faces, and then they started cheering him.

Feroh pulled himself off Jalin and turned around. He stared up at his comrades with wide eyes. Then he scrambled onto his feet, looking flustered but forcing an embarrassed grin. The men moved forward. They slapped his shoulders, congratulated him, and made crude comments.

It didn't last long. They turned away and returned to their own quarters, where their own women were waiting. Feroh was left standing on his own, groping for his robe to cover his strong young body and his genitals, which were smeared with Jalin's blood.

Feroh pulled the robe around him and stood for a moment, still looking dazed. He looked back at Jalin, lying on her stomach and weeping quietly. Then he glanced at Kori.

For a long moment they stared at each other. Feroh seemed suddenly unsure of himself. Kori gazed at him with loathing, making no attempt to hide her feelings, and Feroh blinked, disconcerted by her glare.

Then he lifted his jaw and his defiance returned. He straightened his robe, squared his shoulders. He said nothing, for nothing needed to be said. Kori watched him helplessly as he turned and walked away.

The big fire died down, and the house became shrouded in darkness. A few men still sat around the hearth, talking quietly, their faces lit red by glowing embers. Others coupled briefly with their women, and Kori heard the sounds of bodies moving and skin against skin.

Finally the house was quiet. The only sound Kori heard was of Feroh breathing deeply where he lay beside her. Even Jalin had fallen into a restless slumber.

Kori felt exhausted, but sleep was impossible. Again and again she remembered how her son had looked at times during the day when he took defiant pleasure in his cruelty. Savagely she told herself to erase Feroh from her mind. She must think only of her husband, her daughter, herself, and her tribe.

She felt a pang as she imagined her people in their village. She didn't believe, anymore, that Derneren's killers would be content to stay here. It was in their nature to desire new conquests.

Freeing Uroh, Meiri, and herself would not be enough. They would never be safe so long as Derneren lived and his men were loyal to him. He had pursued her for fourteen years; if she escaped from him now, he would be enraged, and he would make an even greater effort to punish and kill her.

Really, there was only one solution: to destroy Derneren and all the people who served him. It sickened her to contemplate such bloodshed, but it was inescapable.

How could it ever be done? She felt helpless confronted with such a task. But she reminded herself that she had achieved things already that most people would have considered impossible. If she was cunning enough and resourceful enough, surely she had at least a small chance of prevailing over her adversaries. Derneren seemed a shrewd, devious man—but was he, really? In her childhood he had seemed slow-witted, incapable of thinking for himself. She found it hard to believe that he had become wise, no matter how much time had passed. His men respected him, but that was because he convinced them that powerful spirits spoke through him.

Kori remembered her encounter with him at night, on the beach. He had been nervous. In fact, he had fled from her.

Then she remembered Werror arriving among her people, and everything he had done to win their trust. Kori felt certain now that Werror must have been the one to conceive of this plan to infiltrate her tribe, no matter what Derneren claimed. Werror was cunning— more cunning than any man she had ever known. And he was a strong, skillful warrior. So, he was the real threat. If she disposed of him, then Derneren would be much easier to deal with.

Kori shifted impatiently, then winced as her bruises pressed against the hard ground. There must be at least thirty women in the big house where she lay, and all of them had reason to hate their captors—but the spirited ones had been put in bondage, and the others, like Jalin, were too meek to resist. In any case, even if Kori could somehow rouse their courage, there wouldn't be much that they could do. Bulky figures of men were sleeping in front of the doorways out of the house, guarding them through the night. And it was no accident that weapons weren't kept here.

Kori felt a sudden, overwhelming need for Uroh. Then she felt a terrible sadness as she imagined Meiri imprisoned in one of the other houses, alone and scared.

With her sadness, anger returned. It was intolerable that her daughter should be trapped here forever by these terrible men. It was unthinkable that she should be given to one of them, who would mistreat her in any way he chose. For her daughter's sake, if nothing else, she must overcome the warriors of this tribe—if only she could find a way.

21

At dawn the house was filled with noise. Men were talking loudly, a fresh fire was crackling, and Kori found that someone had left another basket of food scraps in front of her. Feroh was missing from his bed, and she couldn't see him anywhere. An older woman came to the corner and gave Kori a vexed look. "He wants you out in the fields," she said. She glanced at Jalin. "You too."

Kori stuffed food into her mouth, fearing that the basket might be taken from her at any moment. "Who wants us in the fields?" Kori asked.

The woman didn't bother to answer. She looked at the heavy stone that tethered Kori, and she muttered something to herself as she turned and walked away.

"Who is that?" Kori asked Jalin.

"Her name is Magra." Jalin was sitting on the edge of the bed, looking weary and miserable. "The men decide what needs to be done. They tell Magra, and Magra gives orders to us."

The woman returned a moment later with four warriors. "This one has to work in the fields," Magra said, pointing to Kori. Her manner had been brusque before, but facing the warriors, she was humble and apologetic.

The men dragged the stone aside, and Kori felt a wave of relief. Even though her ankles were still hobbled, at least she could move around a little.

The men walked away, and Magra glared at Kori. "Come on," she snapped. She beckoned to Jalin. "You too."

They followed her out of the door at the side of the house. Most of the other women had already gathered there in a silent crowd. Kori looked at their faces in the fresh morning light. All of them seemed resigned to their fate. Well, Kori reminded herself, they were the wives and children of farmers, and their tribe had never taught women to use spears. It should be no surprise that the women were easily intimidated.

A dozen men came walking over. Kori saw that they were older than other warriors she'd seen, and they were not in good physical condition. One of them limped; another was missing several fingers from his right hand. Their bodies were thin and bent, and Kori guessed they had been selected to guard the women because they were no longer useful for any other task.

One of the men shouted a command, and Magra started moving among the women, dividing them into groups. "Pemmican," she told six women. "Seed grinding," she told four others.

She paused in front of Kori. "You're from the Ocean Tribe."

"I am the chieftain of the Ocean Tribe," Kori corrected her.

"Not anymore," said Magra. She eyed Kori without much interest. "So, you know about fishing, but nothing about planting and harvesting."

Kori opened her mouth to speak, but Jalin pushed forward. "I will teach her," the girl said.

Magra eyed her, considering the offer. "All right," she said, turning away.

Kori gave Jalin a curious look.

"She was going to give you the heaviest work," Jalin said, speaking so quietly, Kori could barely hear her. "I could see it in her eyes. She would have sent you to rebuild one of the cellars or cut and drag wood from the forest—the work that the men used to do."

"Thank you for speaking up for me," said Kori.

Jalin looked down shyly. "It was nothing."

The women started splitting into groups, each accompanied by a couple of guards. One group went over to some wide, flat stones beside one of the houses, where they would grind meat under other stones to create powdery pemmican. Another group went to make marrow butter by crushing bones and boiling them.

Four elders seated themselves on the ground beside some bulky leather sacks. These women moved with dignity, and their robes were finely ornamented, suggesting that they had enjoyed a high status in the tribe before the warriors attacked.

"Who are they?" Kori asked Jalin.

"They will choose corn seeds," Jalin answered. "It's the most important task, sorting the seeds to select the ones that will flourish. They used to be paired with elders of the tribe. They will pray to the Corn God and hope that he guides their hands wisely."

"I see," said Kori. "And what will we do?"

Jalin shrugged. "We will dig the fields."

"All right, get to work!" a male voice shouted.

Kori found herself in the center of a group of about twenty women, moving out into the fields that lay on either side of the river where it flowed south of the great houses. A guard moved ahead of them, another guard walked behind, and two more walked either side.

Kori found it difficult to walk fast enough. The strap binding her ankles kept snapping tight, forcing her to take tiny steps. She wondered if there was any way she could cut that strap. But even if she did, the guards were carrying whips and spears, and there was nowhere to hide in the flat land beside the river. The men would strike her down without hesitation; she had no doubt of that.

The women divided into groups of five and spread out in regular lines. Jalin stooped and picked up an L-shaped bone—the shoulder bone from an elk, lying on the ground where someone had been using it the previous day. Kori saw a similar bone in front of her, and she took hold of it, following Jalin's example. "Now what do we do?" Kori asked.

"We dig the earth." Jalin raised her bone and brought it down, cutting into the dry soil, extending a furrow that someone had dug the previous day. "Later," Jalin went on, "seeds will be planted here. Then we will turn the earth back over them, and we will fetch water in gourds from the river, and we will pray to the Sun God to nurture the seeds and give them life."

Kori swung her bone experimentally, holding it between her two hands tied in front of her. It struck the ground, sent a tremor up her arm, but didn't dig in.

"Not like that," said Jalin. "Let me show you." She demonstrated the right way to turn the bone so that it sliced into the soil, digging a groove that was not too shallow but not too deep.

Kori tried it again, and this time she got it right.

"Good," Jalin said encouragingly.

Kori looked at the girl's simple, well-meaning face. "And this is all we do?" she asked. "For the whole day?"

Jalin looked away in embarrassment. She turned her bone awkwardly in her hands. "It was—different, before the warriors came. The women would sing together, and we would feel happy, knowing that we were making new food to sustain our tribe. And the men would work close by, clearing weeds and bringing water from the river . . . "

Kori nodded to herself, remembering how she had felt each time her people built a new canoe or wove a new net. "Even dull tasks can be good when people work together," she said. But then she remembered where she was, and she knew that the men who had captured her could deprive her of that simple contentment, now and forever. She swung the elk bone viciously, imagining that instead of striking the earth, she was smashing a warrior's skull.

For a while she and Jalin worked in silence. All around them, the only sound was the rhythmic sound of bones striking soil.

"What do you think will happen to us here?" Jalin whispered to Kori after a while. "Do you think we will live to harvest the corn that will grow from these seeds?"

Kori paused for a moment. Already her arm was tired and the sun was hot on her head. She glanced around, making sure that none of the guards was close enough to hear her. "These warriors are not going to turn into farmers," she said. "They live to fight. They will want to fight again."

"They'll move away and leave us here?" Jalin's face showed sudden hope.

"No," said Kori. She wondered whether to share her fears. Jalin seemed so innocent, so naive, it seemed unfair to inflict the truth on her. But the truth should never be concealed. "If you want to know what I really believe," Kori said, "they will kill many women before they leave this place. They will make a game of it, but the game will end in death. Only a few young ones will be allowed to survive—and they will be taken away with the men. These are evil people, Jalin. Werror himself told me that they gain pleasure from hurting and killing others."

Jalin looked down at her hands. "I see," she said.

"I'm sorry," said Kori, "but it does no good to lie to ourselves."

"Of course." The girl looked away, and her face changed. Her features seemed to harden, and her posture straightened. "I'm glad you didn't try to lie to me, Kori," she said. "If what you say is true, we really have no choice."

Kori looked at her curiously. "What do you mean?"

"We must fight to free ourselves," said Jalin, as if it should have been obvious. "While Werror controlled me, I said nothing and didn't try to move against him, because I knew he would kill me. But if most of us will die anyway, we have nothing to lose."

Kori frowned at her. "You would be willing to fight?"

Jalin met her eyes. "I've seen how strong you are," she said. "I saw how you faced Werror in your village. They thought I was asleep, but I wasn't. That was an important moment for me, Kori. It showed me something that I thought was impossible. I saw you do something that I never thought a woman could do." She flexed her fingers where they held the elk bone, and Kori saw the muscles tense in the girl's arms. "Last night," said Jalin, "when Feroh forced himself on me— I realized then that I would rather die than endure that kind of humiliation."

"Are you sure?" Kori studied the girl's face, looking for uncertainty or weakness.

"I made myself a promise last night," Jalin said. "I want to be like you, Kori. I want to learn to fight, and defend myself, and free myself, and help my people." She blinked, looking self-conscious. "Perhaps you think this is foolish."

Kori wished she could reach out and embrace the girl. "Of course it's not foolish," she said. "You speak truly, Jalin, and—"

"Get back to work!" a voice shouted.

Kori bowed her head, avoiding looking at the guard who came wandering down the row of women. She and Jalin resumed wielding their elk bones as the man strolled past them.

When he was out of earshot again, Kori edged closer to Jalin. "Are there others like you?" she asked hopefully.

"I don't think so," Jalin said, "because they have not seen what I've seen, and they haven't experienced what

I have had to endure. In any case, it would be dangerous to ask them. Some, like Magra, would betray us to
the men. They still think that if they do what they are
told, they will please the men, and the men will be kind
to them or will even free them."

Kori laughed without humor. "The men have no
interest in freeing anyone. Why should they?"

"I see that now," said Jalin. She swung her bone
again, and it clinked against a stone. She bent down,
scooped the earth with her fingers, and pulled out a
small flint.

Quickly she hid it in the palm of her hand.

"Does it have a sharp edge?" Kori whispered.

"Sharp enough to cut your bonds," Jalin whispered
back. "But the men will search us before we go back to
the house."

Kori shrugged. "There are many ways for a woman
to hide such a small thing."

Jalin stared at her. "What do you mean?" Her eyes
widened. "Inside my body?"

Kori nodded.

Jalin grimaced. "I still hurt inside after the way
Feroh took me."

"Then give it to me," said Kori.

"No." Her air of determination returned. "I should
not be afraid of pain." She dug the soil in silence for a
while, glancing surreptitiously on either side till all four
of the guards were looking away. Quickly, then, she slid
her hand inside her robe and down between her thighs.
She winced, then forced a smile. "It is done."

"Perhaps you should have waited till the end of the
day," Kori said.

Jalin quickly shook her head. "No. Flints are hard

to find in these fields. Most were harvested long ago, to make knives and spears. In any case, the discomfort is good for me. It will help me to remember my pledge."

Kori studied the girl. "When I first saw you," she said, "I never guessed you could be so brave."

"I never needed to be brave before," said Jalin. "Then Werror took me with him—because I looked so young—and we drifted on the raft, where I truly believed I would die. After that, I realized that death is not such a terrible thing."

Kori noticed a movement over at the edge of the field. She tried to watch out of the corner of her eye as she continued hacking the earth. Two men were walking toward the stone cairns, the grain cellars where Kori had been imprisoned the previous night. "What are they doing?" she whispered.

The men stopped by one of the cairns. They climbed up, removed the rocks anchoring its wooden lid, and dragged the lid aside. One of them threw something down into the cairn, and then they replaced the lid and walked away.

"There must be a prisoner there," Jalin said, half to herself.

"Uroh?" Kori asked, feeling sudden hope.

"It must be," said Jalin. "All the male prisoners that they took when they invaded our houses were killed many days ago." She looked quickly at Kori. "Could your husband help us? He seems such a timid man—"

Kori shook her head impatiently. "He is the bravest man I know. But he can't help us so long as he is in that prison." She swung her elk bone, and once again she imagined that it was a weapon crushing her enemies. It tormented her to think that Uroh was suffering as she had suffered. "And where is my daughter?" she said. "Did Feroh speak the truth about her? Even if I free myself, I can't leave without her."

"I believe it's true that she is being kept with the other girls who are not yet of age," said Jalin. "In the third house. They are well guarded, because the men value them, just as they valued me, before I was—violated, by Feroh." She looked down, and suddenly her strength seemed to disappear, displaced by her shame.

"Jalin," Kori said sharply. "I too was taken by force, when I was young. I was raped by Feroh's father."

"Ah." Jalin stopped, staring straight ahead, as she assessed what Kori had said.

"There is no shame," Kori said, as forcefully as she could. "I killed the man who did it to me."

"You killed Feroh's father?" Jalin's eyes widened. "And Feroh knows this? Now I understand." She raised her elk bone and brought it down savagely, scattering a shower of powdered earth. "Feroh is an evil man," she said. "He should die as his father died."

"He is still my son," Kori reminded her.

"Ah," Jalin said again, and once again she paused, considering what Kori said.

"I have thought about it," Kori went on, "and even though he says he despises me, and he looks forward to my death, I cannot find it in myself to kill him."

"But if *I* turn against him?" Jalin asked.

Kori felt a terrible mixture of emotion. She was still full of wonder at the spirit she saw in Jalin, and she felt an immediate need to cultivate it and encourage the girl to strike out against the warriors. At the same time, Kori hesitated at the idea of encouraging Jalin to turn against Feroh.

Still, she told herself, there was a limit to her responsibility. "You must make your own decision," she told Jalin. "If you should ever turn a knife or a spear against my son—" She summoned the strength to say what must be said. "I wouldn't condemn you for it, because I saw how he treated you, and I know the evil in him." She rubbed her tied hands across her forehead, wiping away the film of dust and perspiration. At the same time, she took the opportunity to glance around. The guards were still keeping careful watch, and she guessed that they wouldn't cease their vigil.

"It's not a question of right and wrong," Kori said. "The question is how it can be done."

At noon Magra walked among the women, placing food and water in front of them. Kori sank down onto the ground and drank greedily from the gourd. Her throat was dry; her face was wet with sweat.

Then she turned to the meager amount of food on the plate of woven reeds. "What is this?" she asked, pointing to a small portion of yellow paste.

"Fermented corn," said Jalin. "When corn is mixed with yeast, and it is placed in the sun—"

"Yes, I know of this," said Kori. She remembered visiting the Green Valley Tribe one time at the winter solstice, when they celebrated the end of the old year and the beginning of the new. She had eaten something that made her giddy. Her face had become flushed, and she had spoken more freely than she intended to, though no harm was done, because everyone around her was equally intoxicated. Soon enough she had fallen asleep, drugged by the strange food.

"Do the men know of this?" she asked quickly.

Jalin shook her head. "The women who prepare the food give us just a small portion to ease the pain of working through the afternoon. It's a secret—"

From the corner of her eye, Kori saw a figure moving out into the fields from one of the houses. She stiffened, recognizing the way he walked, even though he was still far away. "Feroh," she whispered.

Jalin looked dismayed. "He's coming here?"

Kori nodded. "Probably he just wants to see that we are suffering sufficiently." She paused, thinking quickly. "Jalin, listen to me. Is there more of this fermented corn?"

"I think so. They keep it—"

"It doesn't matter where they keep it," Kori said. "There's no way we can find it and steal it for ourselves, is there?"

"No," Jalin said, without hesitation.

Kori thought some more. She saw Feroh coming closer, and clearly there was no time to waste. "Listen," she said again to Jalin. "When Feroh gets here, if he asks you a question, speak the truth, Jalin. This is important. We have a chance to save ourselves, but only if you do as I say."

Jalin looked anxious. "What do you—"

"Quiet," Kori told her.

Footsteps sounded on the freshly turned earth. A shadow reached across the ground.

"It's fortunate the men don't know of this," Kori said in a loud, clear voice, as she scooped the fermented corn with her fingers and thrust them into her mouth. Then Feroh stopped in front of her, and she looked up quickly.

For a long moment they stared at each other. Slowly Kori took her fingers from her mouth. She looked away from him, down at the platter in front of her.

"Are you enjoying your labor?" Feroh asked her.

"No," Kori said. She reached out to the platter, hesitated, then picked up a piece of roasted rabbit. She ate it quickly, still averting her eyes from Feroh.

"What is that?" he said, pointing to the corn paste.

Kori shrugged. "This food is as strange to me as it is to you."

He stooped, seized her hair, and tilted her face up toward him. "If you don't learn to speak with more respect, I will have you tied to the log again." He gave her a little shake. "Do you understand?"

Kori winced. She said nothing.

He slapped her, hard. "Do you understand?" he repeated.

"Yes," Kori said.

Feroh released her and straightened up. He stood for a moment, eyeing her with satisfaction. Then he turned to Jalin. "What is that?" He pointed to the corn paste on her plate.

"Fermented corn," Jalin said, looking down and speaking in a low voice. The plate trembled in her hands—then became steady.

"And what does that mean?" Feroh dabbed his finger in the paste and put it in his mouth. "It tastes bad. Why would anyone want to eat this?"

"Because—" Jalin hesitated. "It dulls pain and creates happiness."

Feroh grunted with disbelief. He seized Jalin's ear and twisted it. "You lie to me—"

"No!" Jalin cried. "Ask any of my people. What I say is true."

Feroh paused. He looked speculatively at Kori, then back at Jalin. Without another word, he walked away.

22

By evening, all the young warriors were shouting and laughing and singing in the house. Their faces were flushed and their eyes were bright. Some were lying on the floor; others were staggering with their arms around each other.

When the women entered the house, the men started cheering. The women tried to prepare the evening meal, but the men dragged them down and tore off their clothes. Soon there were naked bodies coupling everywhere.

Kori managed to slip among the warriors and seize some chunks of venison. It was cold, but it had been cooked the previous day, and in any case she wouldn't have cared if the meat had been raw. She stuffed some in her mouth, clutched more of it in her cupped hands, then ran to the corner where Jalin was waiting.

The two women gorged themselves on the food. They had barely finished when Feroh appeared in front of them. He was holding a platter heaped high with fermented corn, and he was barely able to stand.

He faced Kori for a long moment, looking at her belligerently. With elaborate care, he set the platter aside. "Don't ever try to deceive me," he told her, slurring his words.

She watched him warily. It was hard enough for her to predict his behavior when he was sober. Now that he was drunk, she had no idea what he might do. He looked too clumsy to be dangerous—but with her ankles hobbled and her wrists tied, she was in no position to defend herself.

He grabbed the bundle of thongs that he had used to beat Jalin the previous night. He swung his arm and the thongs smacked Kori's cheek. "Don't deceive me!" he shouted at her.

She edged away from him. "I didn't deceive you, Feroh."

"Liar." He lashed her again. This time the thongs hit her shoulder. She barely felt the blow through her robe, but still she cried out, feigning pain, since she knew that was what he wanted.

"You wanted to keep it secret," he said, pausing and trying to steady himself. "You have no secrets from me. None. Never." He stepped toward her, scything his arm. The thongs lashed her from the left and from the right. She brought up her hands to protect her face and winced as the thongs cut into her palms.

Feroh seemed to tire quickly. He stopped lashing her, lowered his arm, and turned away, breathing heavily. He grabbed the platter and scooped up some more of the paste.

Four warriors came over to him. "Share it!" one of them shouted.

"You found it, but you don't keep it," another said.

They started jostling Feroh, playfully at first. He laughed and pushed them away. They pushed back, and suddenly fists started swinging. One man received a blow to the nose, and Kori saw him snorting heavy droplets of bright red blood. Feroh was hit on the mouth; he stumbled, fell, and sat on the floor looking surprised. He touched his lip, looked at his hand, and found it smeared with red. He let out a shout of anger, jumped up, and seized his attacker by the neck. The two of them blundered away, turning around each other in circles. Meanwhile, someone else took the platter of corn paste and carried it back to the other men gathered around the hearth.

"Are you hurt?" Jalin asked, looking at Kori.

"No." Kori touched her cheek. There were little ridges in the skin where the lash had bitten her, and her cheek felt hot and tender, but it was trivial compared with the punishment she'd received when she had been tied to the log the previous day.

"The men are dangerous like this," Jalin said.

Kori nodded slowly. She saw that some of the women were being beaten, and she realized she was responsible for it. But most of the violence was among the men themselves. "They are more dangerous to each other than to anyone else," Kori murmured. "I just hope the noise doesn't attract the older men from the other houses."

Jalin shook her head. "The junior warriors always sing and shout in the evening."

"Still," said Kori, "this is a gamble."

"Yes," said Jalin, "but I think it is a wise one."

*   *   *

A while later, the revelry was over. A few men were still crawling around, but the others had fallen unconscious. The women, of course, were unaffected; none of them had been allowed to share the corn paste. Kori lay with Jalin on the furs, watching silently. The women had retreated to the quarters where they normally spent the night, and they were lying down to sleep.

Feroh was over by the hearth somewhere. Kori had lost track of him, but she assumed he had fallen into a stupor like the other men whose bodies littered the floor. She felt restless anticipation surging inside her, and it was almost unbearable to sit and wait. She found herself imagining all the bad things that could possibly happen. If she and Jalin tried to leave the house, and one of the warriors was still sober enough to shout an alarm—or if she were caught outside in the night, and turned over to Derneren for punishment—or if she tripped over one of the sleeping men, and he turned out to be Feroh, and he rose up in fury—

She forced herself to stop thinking such thoughts. "Soon now," she whispered to Jalin.

The girl laid her hand on Kori's arm. "Werror still hasn't checked the house."

Kori looked at her sharply.

Jalin hesitated. "Surely, you saw him last night? He comes here every night."

Kori experienced a terrible sinking feeling. She shook her head helplessly. "I closed my eyes because I had seen Feroh abuse you, and I couldn't bear to see any more. I had no idea—"

"Shh," Jalin warned her.

A footstep sounded on the stone-paved path outside the house. The door flaps were pushed aside, and a tall, muscular figure stepped in.

Kori held herself motionless on the furs, lying as if she were sleeping. She watched through half-closed eyes as Werror looked around the house, and she sensed his puzzlement. He sniffed the air. Then he went to the nearest unconscious warrior, stooped down, grabbed the neck of his robe, and shook him.

The man mumbled something. He tried to push Werror away.

Werror grunted with annoyance. He dropped the man, went to another, and tried to rouse him, without success.

Kori felt anxiety gnawing at her. She felt angry with Jalin for not thinking to warn her that this was going to happen. Then she realized that Jalin had trusted her to know what was best, and Kori turned her anger against herself for not planning more carefully. But there had been no time. She had had to seize her opportunity.

Perhaps, she thought, Werror was wondering if the men had been poisoned. Even if he thought the men were just sleeping soundly, he might still call for help. Naturally, he would want the house to be properly guarded.

She watched Werror as he paused and sniffed the air again. Then he walked slowly to the center of the house, where the fire was still burning. He picked something up, and Kori saw it was the platter of corn paste. He lifted it to his face and nodded to himself. He knew what it was, she realized. While traveling from tribe to tribe as a young man, he must have met other people who knew the secret of fermenting corn. She saw his arm move as he scraped some remnants from the platter, into his mouth.

He tossed the platter aside and started walking slowly around the edges of the room, checking each of the sleeping quarters. Kori closed her eyes and tried to slow her breathing. The tail end of the strap hobbling her ankles was dangling freely, since none of the men had wedged it back under the heavy stone. She had draped it behind the stone, hoping that if anyone looked at it, it would seem to be tethering her. Still, Werror was a smart man, and a suspicious man. She dreaded the sound of his slow, measured steps as he came closer to her.

The footsteps approached—and stopped. There was a long, agonizing moment of silence.

Kori cried out as he shook her roughly. She opened her eyes and found him staring at her in the dimness. "Get on the floor," he told her softly. His teeth flashed in a predatory grin. "If Feroh finds you on his bed, he will punish you. Do you want to be tied to that log outside and stoned again, eh?"

Kori moved to obey him. She slid onto the floor— and as she did so, the strap attached to her ankles shifted slightly.

She sensed Werror still studying her. He stepped over her, bent down, and seized the loose strap. Then he looked at her with new interest.

"The men were celebrating," Kori whispered. "They didn't bother to tie me."

Werror paused a moment, assessing the stone. Kori waited, trying to conceal her anguish. Surely, he would fetch other men to help him. Surely—

Werror squatted down, facing the stone. He

reached out with both hands, breathed deeply, then pulled with all his strength. The stone shifted, scraping across the floor toward him, till it nudged the toes of his moccasins. Werror pulled harder, and he tilted it up.

"Drop the strap under it," he told Kori.

Quickly she obeyed him. Werror braced himself and started to lower the stone—and something strange happened. A shadow seemed to move in the dimness behind him, like a great black bird.

Without warning, Werror dropped the stone. The massive weight thudded onto the floor. At the same instant he turned to face the shadow that still hovered behind him.

The shadow moved again in the dimly lit room. There was a thud as something hard hit human flesh.

Werror swore. He fell down onto one knee, clutching the side of his head.

"Jalin!" Kori gasped, glimpsing the girl's face. Kori saw that while Werror's attention had been focused on her, Jalin had run to the hearth and seized a stone between her hands. Now she swung her arms, wielding the rock for a third time, striking Werror in the center of his forehead.

The great warrior fell backward. His body hit the floor, and he lay still.

Jalin stepped forward, moving hesitantly, taking quick, panicky breaths. She bent over the big man, then fell down onto his chest, still with the stone between her hands. In a wild frenzy, she started hammering his head with it.

"Enough!" Kori hissed at her.

Jalin paused. She pulled back from the warrior and tried to stand, but she was trembling so much, she almost fell. "I had to," she whispered. "He would have fetched other men. I know he would. With the young warriors so drunk, none of them are fit to guard the house. And Werror would never leave it unguarded."

"Yes," Kori said. She reached out, gripped the girl's hand, and squeezed it tightly. "But hush, now." She paused, looking around the room. Many of the women must be still awake. Even in the dim lighting, some of them would have seen Jalin running to the hearth, running back again, and striking Werror with the stone. They would have heard Werror grunting in pain, and then they would have heard Jalin beating his head.

Kori realized what had to be done, and she steeled herself to do it. She stood up. "Hear me," she said, pitching her voice loud enough to reach every corner of the house, but not so loud that she would be heard outside. She looked slowly around. "I am Kori, of the Ocean Tribe. You have heard of me. You know I am a hunter and a fighter. You know I have killed many men."

She waited. There was no reply—but she was sure the women were listening.

"Hear me now," she said. "If you saw what happened in this room just now, you will not speak of it. If any of you makes a sound, I will silence you. If I have to, I will kill you. For your own sake, lie quietly. If you are awake, pretend to be asleep. What happened here does not concern you. You will not be punished for it, so long as you say you saw nothing. Be silent, and be still."

She waited again, feeling far more anxious than she had made herself sound. She listened; but none of the women spoke or moved.

She turned to Jalin. "Quickly," she whispered. "Give me the flint."

Jalin groped inside her robe. She pressed the sharp stone into Kori's hand. "Did I do the right thing?" she whispered anxiously.

"Yes," Kori said. She started sawing at the strap binding her ankles. "Yes, Jalin. I think you saved us. Yes, you did a fine, brave, wonderful thing. This man deserved to die." Kori grunted with satisfaction as the tough hide finally yielded to the edge of the flint. She started sawing at the remaining length of leather that tethered her to the stone, and a moment later she was free. Her wrists were still bound, but she could deal with them later. Escaping from this house was her first concern.

"Quickly," she whispered to Jalin.

Together they ran lightly through the darkness. All around them, men were snoring. Some were sleeping in their own vomit. Kori stepped carefully over the slumbering forms. One of them must be Feroh—but there was no time to search for him. She didn't trust the women in the house to stay silent for long.

She went to the far doorway, pulled the flap back, and peered outside. She allowed herself a smile of satisfaction. She had estimated that the moon would not be up yet, and she was right.

"Guards are on duty," Jalin whispered from behind her. "Only the junior hunters ate the corn paste."

"I understand," said Kori. "But the duty of guards is to watch for intruders. They'll be posted at the perimeter, facing out, not in." She hesitated, then turned back to face Jalin. "You know, you can still stay here. You don't have to risk your life with me."

Jalin's eyes flashed in the darkness. It was the first time Kori had seen the girl show anger. "You think I'm not brave enough?"

"Hush." Kori squeezed Jalin's shoulder. "You are braver than any woman I've known."

Slowly Jalin relaxed. "Of course I'm coming with you," she whispered. "Here. Your hands are still tied. Let me free you."

Kori gave Jalin the flint, and the girl quickly sliced the thongs.

"All right," said Kori, "walk calmly beside me now. If anyone sees us, we should not look furtive. That would just rouse their suspicion. In the darkness, they won't be able to tell who we are. They shouldn't even be able to see that we are women."

"But how are we going to get away?" Jalin whispered.

"First we must free Uroh," said Kori. She didn't confess the truth: that she had no idea how to escape safely. She only hoped Uroh would know what to do.

With Jalin beside her, Kori walked boldly through the night. Patches of stars showed among low, ragged clouds, shedding just enough light so that Kori could avoid blundering into objects in the darkness. She walked around the next house, and then, straining her eyes, she could just make out the cairns.

She paused, counting till she was sure she had the fourth one. She climbed it, trying to move silently up the mound of stones. Her pulse was still running fast, but she no longer felt fear. She had such a sense of purpose, it eclipsed everything else.

"Here," she whispered, lifting a stone from the

wooden lid of the cairn and passing it back to Jalin. "Place it quietly."

One by one, she passed the rest of the stones to the girl, till the lid was unencumbered. "Up here, now," Kori whispered.

Jalin scrambled up beside her.

"Are you all right?" Kori whispered, reaching out.

"I told you," Jalin said, "nothing can scare me after what I endured with Werror on that raft."

"Good." Kori stooped down. "Help me lift this."

Together they shifted it.

Kori dropped down onto her knees, then onto her stomach. She peered into the open mouth of the cairn. "Uroh," she whispered.

There was no reply.

Kori felt coldness spreading inside her. She was sure this was the right cairn. She was certain of it.

"Uroh!" she hissed again. But still there was no reply.

She told herself that he had to be alive. Even if they had starved him and given him no water, surely he could not have died.

In desperation, she turned to Jalin. "Give me the flint," she whispered.

Jalin handed it to her, and Kori threw it down into the cellar. There was a tiny sound as it struck something. Finally Kori heard a movement.

"Uroh!" she hissed again.

"Kori? Is that you?"

Even though the voice was a whisper, she recognized it instantly. Warmth spread through her, erasing the chill. She gripped the mouth of the cairn. "Why didn't you answer me?"

"I was sleeping."

Kori almost laughed. Of course he had been sleeping; nothing could ever stop him from sleeping. "The stone I threw down is a flint," she whispered. "Cut the thongs tying your wrists."

She heard the rustle of his robe and the sound of his palms as he moved around the cellar, searching for the flint with his outstretched hands. There was a faint sound of flint on leather, and he grunted with satisfaction.

"I'm reaching up," he whispered.

Kori leaned forward as far as she dared. She swung her hands around in the darkness. Was the cellar too deep? Would they ever be able to touch each other? Suddenly, blessedly, her fingers met his. She clasped his hand. "Help me," she called to Jalin.

Jalin lay down beside her, reached down, and grabbed Uroh's other hand. Together they tried to lift him.

It was far harder than Kori had expected. She had to lever her elbows against the sides of the hole in the cairn, and the stone bit into her painfully. But when Uroh was high enough to reach the edge of the hole himself, he took hold of it, releasing his grip on Kori and Jalin. Then he hauled his body up and wriggled out.

Kori seized him and embraced him. The warmth of him, the strength of him, had never felt better. She was overwhelmed by feelings. For a moment she couldn't speak.

"Thank you," Uroh whispered.

Suddenly Kori felt a terrible pang of guilt. "I'm sorry," she blurted out. "Uroh, I'm sorry—"

"For what?"

"For—for what I did. For hurting you. For—
Werror. He betrayed me. He serves Derneren, or he did.
Jalin struck him down—"

"Jalin?" He turned in the darkness. "Is that her?"

"Yes," said Kori.

Uroh reached out. He touched the girl. "Thank
you," he whispered. Then he turned back to Kori.
"What now?"

Kori hesitated. She still wanted to assuage her guilt,
to apologize and hear him forgive her. "I'm sorry," she
blurted out again.

"It doesn't concern us now," he said. "I have no
interest in Werror. You came for me, and we must
escape. That is all that matters. Now, what do we do?"

Kori hesitated. "Meiri is still being held—"

"Where?"

"She's with the other girl-children," said Jalin. "In
one of the houses."

"Are there guards?" Uroh asked.

"Of course."

"Do we have weapons?"

"No," said Kori.

Uroh grunted. "Then we will have to save ourselves
and return later."

"You mean abandon her here?" Kori seized his arm.
"We can't do that. They may kill her."

"No," said Uroh. "She will be valuable to them as a
hostage. They will understand that."

Slowly Kori realized that he was right. After all, that
was why Derneren had taken Meiri originally.

"Where is Feroh?" Uroh asked.

"Feroh—serves Derneren now," Kori told him.

Uroh was silent for a moment. "I see," he said. He paused, peering into the night. "All right, let's go to the river, unless you have another plan."

"The river?" Jalin said.

"It will carry us away," said Uroh.

Jalin was silent for a moment. "But it will be so cold," she said. "It's still early in the year—"

"You can't swim," said Kori. "Is that it?" She remembered seeing how desperately Jalin had clung to the raft in the ocean.

The girl didn't answer.

"We will carry you," Kori whispered. "Trust us, Jalin. Uroh is right. The river is the safest way for us to avoid the lookouts."

"All right," Jalin said.

"Quickly," said Uroh. "Show us the way."

Jalin started forward—then froze. Distant voices suddenly sounded from one of the houses. Then a woman shouted something, and a man replied. The words were indistinct—then they sounded clearly. "Awake! Warriors, awake! Come quickly!"

Kori felt a stab of anguish. To have come this far, and now face capture—it was intolerable.

"Behind the houses," Uroh whispered. "They'll expect us to go the other way, to the south. Run!"

Jalin ran, and Kori and Uroh followed. Kori felt as if she had never run so fast in her life. Her feet flew through the grass, around behind the first house, past the log where she had been tied and stoned. To her right she heard more shouts. Men started pouring out of the first house, milling around uncertainly in the night. Someone shouted that a woman had killed a man in the junior warriors' house. Men ran in that direction through the darkness, never seeing the three fugitives less than fifty paces away.

Yellow light suddenly flashed among the houses. Kori glimpsed someone holding a flaming torch, but he was heading south, into the fields, as Uroh had expected. "Search the land!" a voice shouted. "Two women are loose!"

Now there was a cacophony of voices. More men came running out of another house—but Kori saw the river just ahead, a wide, sinuous shape that was even darker than the night around it. Jalin was leading them to the bathing place where Kori had washed her wounds.

"Down on your hands and knees!" Uroh hissed to her. "Crawl slowly into the water. Don't hurry. Make no sound."

They fell to the ground. Kori felt an almost unbearable need to leap forward and dive into the water, but she restrained herself, knowing that Uroh was right. More torches started flaring among the houses, and the branches of nearby trees were suddenly etched in yellow. But she and Uroh and Jalin were hidden now among the tall grass that grew by the river. There was a faint rippling sound as Jalin slid into the water, and then Kori herself slid forward, gasping as the frigid river closed around her arms and legs and flowed under her robe, seizing her body.

"Help me!" Jalin gasped, as she moved into deeper water.

Kori moved alongside and held her left arm, high under her armpit. Uroh took her right arm. "Lie back," Uroh told the girl. "The water will carry you. Tilt your head up. You will be able to breathe. Just lie back."

Jalin tried to obey. She took quick, panicky breaths. "Be calm," Kori whispered to her. "We have you, Jalin. You will not drown. I promise you."

Meanwhile, Kori found herself shivering. She was exhausted, and she had eaten only meager meals during the past days. She wondered if Uroh had made a mistake, leading them into the river. They would have little resistance to the cold in their weakened state. Worse still, the river flowed south. It was going to take them between the fields where the warriors were searching for them.

Kori heard men running through the grass up on the riverbank, calling to each other as they spread out. Well, Kori thought to herself, she would have been in far greater danger if she had stayed up on the land. Almost certainly, the men would have found her.

Kori kicked her legs, trying to move faster than the current.

"Be patient," Uroh whispered to her. "If we swim, it will make noise. These men are land dwellers. They won't look for us here."

Kori told herself to trust him. It was terrifying, though, to hear the hunters prowling so close by. A figure suddenly appeared right at the river's edge, holding his torch high. Kori ducked her head under the surface. She held her breath as long as she could, until finally she had to raise her face and gulp air. She looked up anxiously, but the man had gone.

The two of them clung to Jalin. They drifted with the current, and gradually she started to believe they would be safe. Even though she was shivering uncontrollably, and she felt Jalin shivering with her, she saw that they could survive.

The river carried them beyond the fields and farther south, into forested country. Trees loomed on either side, sheltering them from view.

"How much longer?" Jalin gasped.

"We will stay in the water as long as we can bear it," Uroh answered. "And then we will stay in a little longer. After that we will go to the shore and wring the water out of our clothes. Then we will run, and we will keep on running, through the whole night." He paused, and Kori sensed him smiling. "After that," Uroh said, "we will be free."

23

It was noon the next day when the three of them finally emerged from the forest in front of the hill where the village stood. All of them were exhausted and ravenously hungry, yet Kori felt such joy and relief as she saw the home of her people, she could almost forget the weariness dragging at her mind and body.

She stood with her arms around Jalin and Uroh, and she hugged both of them to her. "I would not be here without your help," she said. She turned to Jalin. "If you hadn't had the courage to attack Werror, we would never have escaped from that house. The men would be punishing us—"

She broke off, hearing a faint rustling sound in the forest behind them. For a moment she forgot that none of them had weapons. Her hunger conjured up a vision of a bobcat or a fox, and she saw herself spearing it, then gorging herself on its meat. She stared at the foliage, looking for the creature.

To her astonishment, the forest itself seemed to be moving. Bushes and underbrush rose up from the earth. A moment later arms came into view, carrying spears. Faces peered out from among the leaves. A party of men had tied branches to themselves, and had been lying in wait.

She stared at the faces—and recognized none of them. She stepped back in fear, but Uroh restrained her. "They would have killed us already," he murmured, "if they wished to do so."

Kori saw that he was right; still, she felt horribly vulnerable, standing with no weapon, as the men started toward her from their hiding places. There were at least a score of them, and their eyes were not friendly. For a moment she wondered if Derneren's warriors had outrun her somehow during the night, and had placed themselves here to wait for her. But then the leader of the men stepped into a shaft of sun, and even though his face was painted with broad stripes of brown and black, Kori recognized him. "Biffrar," she said. Finally she understood.

Jalin clutched at Kori's arm. "You know this man? Is he a friend or an enemy?"

"He has been our friend," Kori answered cautiously. "He is the chieftain of the White River Tribe."

"Ah," Jalin said. Now she, too, understood.

Kori was still dressed in the tattered robe that she had been given at Green Valley. Her hair was disheveled, and her arms and face were crisscrossed with bramble scratches. Still, she tried to stand proudly. Biffrar stopped four paces away from her, and for a long moment they eyed each other in silence.

"We have come," Biffrar said, "for Feroh."

Kori inclined her head respectfully. "If he was with us," she said, "I would surrender him to you—because my own son has turned against me." She spread her arms, turning her palms upward in the sign of peace that the White River Tribe understood. "He is not with us, Biffrar. He has joined the warriors who have conquered the Green Valley Tribe. He serves them now."

Biffrar eyed her for a long moment. Slowly he folded his arms around his spear. Kori relaxed slightly, seeing this sign that he didn't intend to use his weapon. "So it is true that the Green Valley Tribe has been conquered," Biffrar said, narrowing his eyes. "Pettrar told us of this."

"Yes," said Kori. She gestured to Jalin. "This girl's father was one of the men in Green Valley who lost their lives." Kori still felt desperately tired. All she wanted was to climb the hill, rejoin her tribe, satisfy her hunger, and rest. Still, she saw she had an obligation here that must be satisfied. And more than that: she sensed an opportunity.

As briefly as she could, she told Biffrar her own story.

When she was done, the chieftain no longer looked at her with such suspicion. There was respect in his eyes. "Pettrar told us that Feroh had turned against you," he said. "I found it hard to believe. But now I understand." He gestured suddenly. "Come. We have food. We will feed you."

Kori glanced at Uroh, then at Jalin. "We should rejoin our people," she told Biffrar. "You would be welcome to join us as our guests."

"No." He spoke the word flatly, leaving no room for compromise.

"Why would you reject our hospitality?" Kori asked.

Biffrar glanced quickly around. "It is still possible that Feroh will come here. This was his home. And if what you say is true, he may seek revenge. So, if he comes here, we must be ready."

"It seems unlikely—" Kori said.

"But not impossible." He turned to his men. "Go back to your hiding places. I will give food and water to this woman and her two companions."

The hunters edged backward and hunkered down, concealing themselves. Biffrar beckoned. "Come," he said, walking deeper into the forest.

They followed him into a tiny clearing where skins full of cooked meat and dried fruits had been stacked under more concealing branches. "Sit," said Biffrar, pointing to the ground.

They sat cross-legged, facing him. He placed a gourd of water in front of them, and he handed them heavy pieces of meat on plantain leaves. He stood, waiting for them to eat. Kori knew that, according to the rigid customs of his tribe, he himself could never eat, or even allow himself to sit, until his guests had satisfied their hunger.

"Tell me," she asked, as she bit into the food, "was your daughter Tithea returned to you safely?"

Biffrar nodded.

"And the boy, Raor—"

"He is with our tribe. He will be returned to you when we have Feroh."

Kori felt unsurprised but guilty, knowing that she had consented to Raor escorting the girl back to the White River Tribe. "I hope Raor has not been harmed," she said.

Biffrar looked offended. "You think we would injure an innocent boy who has not even come of age?"

"Of course not," said Kori. "But I know you are a man of pride and honor, and since your daughter was stolen—"

Biffrar waved his hand. "All that concerns me is that Feroh must be punished."

"Even though your daughter wasn't violated by Feroh?"

Biffrar grunted. "If she had been, we would not be talking now. Our tribes would be at war. There would be no way to satisfy our honor except by killing all of Feroh's kin, as well as Feroh himself."

Kori saw him looking at her fiercely, and she realized she had antagonized him. Over the years, she had always had difficulty talking to Biffrar. He had such strong male pride and such severe ideas of right and wrong, and she was a woman who tended to speak without the elaborate politeness that his people expected.

Kori glanced at Uroh, hoping he would know what to say.

"We admire your fairness and we thank you for your restraint," Uroh said, nodding to Biffrar. "Feroh committed a shocking crime when he accepted your hospitality and then betrayed you as he did. We thank you for speaking to us as our friend and our equal, and we will accept whatever punishment you feel is appropriate for Feroh. More than that: we pledge to help you achieve this justice."

Kori felt a qualm as she heard those words, but she saw that Uroh was right. Biffrar relaxed visibly. "What you say is good," he said. But then he turned back to

Kori. "You are still the chieftain of the Ocean Tribe. Does your husband speak for you? Are his words your words?"

"Yes," said Kori. She felt a heavy weight of responsibility as she spoke—yet she felt relief. There was no question now that she had abandoned Feroh to his fate. There was no point in agonizing over it any further. The deed was done.

She looked at Biffrar frankly. "I should tell you more about my son," she said. Quickly she explained how Yainar had raped her, fourteen years ago, and how she had slain him.

When she finished talking, Biffrar looked deeply shocked. "By our code," he said, "Feroh is not your son at all. If a man forces himself on a woman who has not been paired with him, their child is an abomination and should be cast out."

Kori felt a moment's irritation. It didn't please her to deal with this man, with his simple, brutal code of honor and justice. Really, there was not so much difference between him and a man like Werror—but no, she corrected herself, the two of them were a world apart. Biffrar could be ruthless, and he would kill without remorse, but he had no interest in wanton cruelty. So long as his code was not violated, he would never attack another man. That was how the Ocean Tribe and the White River Tribe had managed to live in peace for so long. He had made his code clear to Kori, and she had always respected it. Biffrar was wise enough, also, to see that trading with the Ocean Tribe would give his people far greater benefits than he could achieve by conquest.

"I am a woman," Kori said, feeling a need to explain herself. "It is not in my nature to cast out my own child,

no matter how he was conceived. This is why I protected him, and tried to redeem him—until now."

Biffrar considered that. Then he shrugged. "The
past is not important," he said, "and it is not important
if you and your people have a code that is different from
ours. Only two things matter to us now. First, I must
have Feroh—but you have already agreed to that.
Second, these warriors in Green Valley who have
accepted Feroh among them are clearly a threat to all
other tribes, if what you say is true, as I believe it is.
Therefore, together, we should try to overcome them. In
this way we can ensure our security against a common
threat."

"This is true," said Kori, feeling gladdened by his
words. "And your assistance would be of great value
to us."

Biffrar saw that his three guests had finished eating.
He squatted down and extended his hands, palms up.
"So, let us make a pledge," he said.

Kori hesitated. "I must still know one thing. If you
find Feroh, and you take him away—I should know
what his punishment will be."

Biffrar eyed her frankly. "The elders of my tribe dis-
cussed this. We will offer him a choice. Death by his
own hand, or castration."

Kori found herself flinching from the words.

"There is no alternative if our tribes are to be allies,"
Biffrar said, watching her carefully. "Everyone must see
the penalty a man suffers if he deceives me and steals
my eldest daughter."

Kori nodded reluctantly. "Very well."

Biffrar grunted. "You agree, then? Your husband
and your friend, here, are witnesses."

Kori breathed deeply. "I agree," she said. "It is severe, but—there is no choice."

"So, we will pledge," said Biffrar.

Kori extended her hands, palms up. She placed them over Biffrar's hands. Uroh added his hands.

"And you," Biffrar said to Jalin. "You shall represent the survivors of the Green Valley Tribe, who are still living as prisoners in their own houses."

Diffidently Jalin leaned forward and added her hands.

Biffrar looked down. His face was solemn. "Together we will seek vengeance against the warriors in Green Valley," he said. "All of them, and all those who are allied with them, shall be slaughtered. We will fight them as one people. The people of my tribe will defend your tribe as we would defend our own, and you shall defend us in return. This I say, and it is so."

"It is so," said Kori.

"It is so," said Uroh and Jalin in unison.

Biffrar remained kneeling for a moment, considering what he had said. "Good," he said finally. He stood up.

"But what shall our strategy be?" Kori asked him. "Should I gather my people now? Will we march to Green Valley?"

Biffrar shook his head. "You should rest. There is no urgency. You have suffered much. You will be stronger tomorrow than you are today. Eat and sleep and restore yourselves, and tomorrow we can discuss our plans."

Kori saw the sense of what he said, although it was against her nature to wait passively instead of taking immediate action.

"Will you join us?" she asked Biffrar. "Our village shall be your village, and together we will be stronger—"

"Thank you, no." Biffrar inclined his head respectfully. "We will remain here, because as I said before, there is still a chance that Feroh will come here, and if he does, we must be ready for him."

As Kori reached the top of the winding path, the scene was eerily familiar. The people of the Ocean Tribe flocked around her, just as they had when she returned after surviving the storm. They shouted their greetings and showed their love, and they assaulted her with a score of questions.

This time, though, she was with Uroh and Jalin instead of Meiri and Feroh, and she found she had far more explaining to do. The tribe followed her into the Meeting Place and gathered around her. Wearily she told her story as quickly as she could. The food that Biffrar had given her had begun acting like a sedative, making her lethargic and desperate for sleep. Still, she had to explain the pact that she had just made with the White River Tribe, and all the events that had led up to it.

She had hoped that the pact would make her people feel more secure; but instead, they seemed filled with new doubts and fears. They had never felt comfortable dealing with Biffrar and his people, and they were shocked by the idea of pledging death against all the warriors in Green Valley. Even now, after everything, they still clung to the fantasy that they need not get involved. Surely, the situation in Green Valley could not be as bad as Kori made it seem. Surely, there was some good in all men, even the warriors she spoke of. Could there be some kind of peace agreement?

In the end, Kori exhausted her strength and patience. "I must sleep now," she told her people. "You should talk about this more among yourselves. And tomorrow morning, we can discuss it again. But for now, remember this: the men in Green Valley have killed the father of Jalin, here. They would have killed me, and they would have killed Uroh." She eyed them sternly. "At the very least, you must be ready to defend yourselves. I want a dozen lookouts on duty tonight, and a dozen more to take their place halfway through the night. This is not something that I will discuss with you. This must be done. I say it, and it is so."

She turned away without waiting for anyone to reply. "Come," she said to Uroh. "And you too," she said to Jalin. "Since Meiri is not here—" Kori had to pause for a moment to suppress the stab of sadness that the words roused in her. "Jalin, you can sleep on her bed." Kori embraced her, cutting off her protests. "You saved my life last night, when you attacked Werror. My house is your house, and it will always be yours, even if we free your people and you return to Green Valley."

Jalin said nothing, which puzzled Kori for a moment. She pulled back, looked at the girl's face, and found that she was crying. "Hush," Kori said, trying to comfort her. "There is nothing to be sad about now."

Jalin shook her head. "I'm not sad," she said, smiling through her tears. "Kori, your praise means so much to me. You have made me happy."

*　　*　　*

Even though the sun was still high and evening was far away, Kori fell asleep immediately. She lay on her bed with Uroh, clutching him against her. He exclaimed with alarm when he saw the small wounds and bruises covering her body, but she refused to talk anymore about what had happened. More than anything, she needed rest. And so, together they rested.

For a long time she enjoyed a dreamless sleep. She woke once around sunset, roused by her hunger again. Some kind person had placed delicacies beside her bed: roasted crab meat and bluefish. She ate ravenously, roused Uroh and Jalin and shared the food with them, then fell back asleep again with Uroh still beside her. She relished the warmth of his body and the freedom she felt from fear.

The next time she woke she was refreshed, even though she could see from the blackness outside the door flap that it was still the middle of the night. Her limbs were stiff, her body ached, but her strength was restored.

She lay for a while, listening to Uroh breathing quietly beside her. Jalin whimpered softly where she slept at the other end of the hunt, and she stirred restlessly, tormented by a dream. Kori stood and went to the girl, just as she had gone so often to Meiri and Feroh when they were infants. She laid her hand gently on Jalin's forehead and stroked her hair. "Hush," she whispered.

Jalin half opened her eyes and recognized Kori bending over her. She rolled onto her back. "I dreamed," Jalin whispered. "There were evil men—"

"You are safe here," Kori said. "I'm sure you will

have many dreams, Jalin, because of everything you've endured. But they are only dreams, and you are with us now."

Jalin reached up and squeezed Kori's hand. "Thank you," she whispered.

Kori waited for a while, watching as Jalin fell back asleep. But Kori herself no longer felt tired. She took one of her robes and slipped into it. Then she picked up a spear and went to the door.

Outside, the moon had finally risen. It was a thin yellow crescent, low in the eastern sky. Kori paused for a moment, breathing the night air. Everything around her was reassuringly familiar, from the distant sound of surf to the little stone-walled, wood-roofed huts silhouetted against the moonlit sky. She could almost pretend that nothing had happened, and life was the same here as it had always been.

But her life had been threatened, her son had turned against her, and her daughter had been taken from her. There was no way she could forget those terrible facts, and no way she could rest until Meiri was back again.

Kori walked out along the cliff edge, thinking that this would be a good time to check her lookouts. She gave a soft animal cry as she reached the top of the path that led down the cliffs to the beach, and she heard the cry returned. As she came closer she recognized the man sitting there, huddled in a fur robe. "Greetings, Kireah," she called out.

"Greetings, Kori."

Kori stopped beside him and placed her hand on his arm. "Thank you," she said, "for helping to protect our tribe."

"My duty and my honor," he told her. "I'm glad that you're back."

She nodded to him and moved on, following the same path she'd taken when she was showing Werror around the village. That thought filled her with a mixture of shame and outrage, so she tried to thrust it out of her mind. She reached the northern edge of the village and paused there for a moment, looking down the rock-strewn slope to the forest below. A thin cloud passed briefly in front of the moon, shrouding the land in darkness. Then the cloud moved on, and Kori drew in her breath sharply. In the distance, down at the bottom of the slope, there were shadows upon the land— dark shapes that she didn't recognize. And while she watched, the shadows moved.

She stared for a moment, not wanting to believe what her eyes revealed to her. Perhaps, she thought, there was a pack of wolves; or perhaps it was some trick of the shifting light. Her strength, so newly restored, wavered as she contemplated the thought that the half-seen shapes might really be warriors who had come to attack her tribe. She had gone through so much, she didn't know if she could rouse herself to face another threat.

Then she heard a distant scream. The sound made her flinch, and she felt a shudder pass through her. *No more,* she thought. More than anything, she wanted no more killing and dying. She felt a deep urge to turn and run back to her hut, and hide there with her husband; but just as quickly, she felt ashamed of the impulse. She forced herself to peer into the darkness. Had one of the shadows fallen?

There was another shout of surprise and pain, and

three more, following in quick succession. Then Kori saw points of light flaring beyond the foot of the hill. There was a terrible wailing sound, the sound of many men shouting together, yelling their intention to kill their adversaries.

The points of light spread out. Each was a torch carried by a running man.

"Biffrar," Kori murmured to herself. She tightened her grip on her own spear, then whirled around, facing the homes of her tribe. "People!" she shouted. "People of the Ocean Tribe! Come quickly! Come to the northern side!"

She started hurrying down the steep slope, holding her spear ready in one hand while reaching behind her with her other hand, steadying herself against the slope as she slipped and stumbled over the dew-soaked, rock-strewn grass. By the time she was halfway down the hill she saw that a massacre was taking place. The hunters of the White River Tribe were hurling their spears, attacking the shadow-figures from behind. The warriors were staggering, screaming, dazzled by the sudden flaring torches and panicked by the sudden attack.

Kori was close enough to cast her own spear. She raised it, taking aim at a warrior who had climbed farther than the rest. But he fell before she could kill him.

Then she realized her danger. In the darkness, the White River hunters might easily mistake her for one of their enemies. "Biffrar!" she shouted out. "This is Kori!"

She heard an answering shout. Still, she saw she would be foolish to venture any farther. And in any case, there was no need for it: the White River Tribe was moving with ruthless speed, felling every one of their enemies.

Tall men festooned with camouflaging foliage came striding forward, holding their torches high as they moved from one prostrate figure to the next, bending over them and methodically butchering them. For a moment Kori felt sickened—yet deeply thankful that she had made her pact with Biffrar.

She saw him then, moving up toward her. "Kori!" he shouted out.

"I'll come down to you," she shouted back. Cautiously she descended toward him.

At the same time, she heard confused shouts from behind her as the people of her tribe gathered at the top of the hill, trying to understand what had happened. She paused and turned toward them. "People!" she cried. "There was danger, but it is ended. Biffrar's hunters have killed the warriors who came to attack us. Don't cast your spears. Hear me! Do not cast your spears!"

She looked back at Biffrar, just a dozen paces away. His face was starkly lit by the flickering torch that he held in his left hand. His features were etched in shadow. "Come," he said. "You must see these men." He gestured at the bodies strewn across the hillside. "Tell me if you recognize them—and tell me if any of them is Feroh."

Kori felt a moment of dread. Clearly, though, this was a responsibility that she couldn't avoid. She picked her way across the grassy slope. "Thank you," she said to Biffrar, "for your vigilance."

He grunted dismissively. "These men are little more than boys. They were stupid and reckless. We slaughtered them as easily as lame deer."

Kori stopped near the first body and turned his face

with her foot. She recognized him: he had been among the warriors who stoned her. "He is from Green Valley," she said.

She moved on to the next man, and the next. Most of them were young, as Biffrar said, and she knew them from the house where she had been a prisoner. The last time she had seen them, they had been drunk on the fermented wine.

"They sent only their fledglings," said Biffrar. He looked slowly around. "This bothers me."

"These are the ones who allowed me to escape with Jalin," Kori explained. "It was their responsibility. I'm not surprised they were sent to bring me back."

"I see." Biffrar nodded slowly. "But still, I see no elder warrior to command them."

"Derneren is a cautious man," Kori said. "He would keep his strongest warriors around him, to protect him." As she spoke, though, she felt just a moment of doubt. Her feeling of warm security, which she had enjoyed in her hut such as short time ago, was gone.

"I wonder if there are other men still hiding in the forest," said Biffrar, turning and scanning the darkened land. "Derneren himself may be here."

Kori thought for a moment. "Derneren is not a strong man. He could never make the journey here from Green Valley so quickly. In fact, a few days ago, when he sent four men to steal Meiri and Uroh, he met them halfway."

Biffrar considered that. "So," he said, "perhaps you are right. Of course, Derneren has no idea that my tribe is allied with yours now. He must have thought these youngsters would be more than enough to seize you from your people."

"I believe so," said Kori. "I'm worried, though, that he sent them at all. He still holds my daughter hostage; he has no need to attack."

Biffrar shook his head. "You insulted the honor of these young men. You are a woman, and you made them look like fools."

"True," said Kori, taking some satisfaction from that.

Biffrar's hunters had been stepping among the bodies, retrieving their spears. They stood now with their torches blazing, waiting for their chieftain's command.

"We will go back into hiding," Biffrar told them. "I think it's unlikely that other warriors will attack. But it does no harm to be vigilant."

"Good," said Kori. "Thank you."

Biffrar shook his head. "Wait till we have rescued your daughter and killed all the men who hold her among them. Then you may thank me."

Kori watched him as he started back down the hill. One by one, his hunters extinguished their torches. They disappeared into the night with a rustle of leaves.

Kori turned and looked toward the summit of the hill. Her people were still waiting there, crowding together, talking excitedly. Well, Kori thought to herself, the attack tonight would have one useful consequence: it might make them more willing to believe her, and to fight.

She started up the grassy slope, turning her back on the young warriors, leaving them lying in their own blood under the dim light of the moon.

24

A little later, after she made her explanations, her people returned to their houses. Their faces looked anxious in the moonlight, but Kori told them that Biffrar and his hunters were still on guard, and she saw that this provided some reassurance.

Uroh and Jalin went to their hut, and Kori joined them—but she knew as soon as she sat down on the edge of her bed that she was too restless to go back to sleep. In truth, even though she despised the young warriors who had kept her captive in Green Valley, she was distressed by the carnage she had just seen. No matter what their crimes were, surely there should be a solution that stopped short of death.

She left Uroh and stepped outside again. The moon was higher in the sky now, but there was still no sign of dawn. Kori wandered silently among the houses of her tribe, weighing her spear in her hand and contemplating a dilemma that had often preoccupied her over the years. If a tribe abhorred killing and wanted just to live in peace, how could it be secure? How could people protect themselves without becoming as ruthless and murderous as other tribes that threatened them?

She imagined an island somewhere—not on a river, as the island of her childhood tribe had been, but out in the ocean, completely isolated from all other people. Surely, this would allow them to live without any fear of war. But what should they do if they found a boy such as Feroh among them? If they killed him, they would turn away from their intention to be peaceful. If they let him live, he would be a danger to them.

Kori's steps brought her back to her own house, just as her thoughts brought her back to her starting point. She paused for a moment, leaning against the stone wall. She looked up and saw clouds moving across the sky, reaching out toward the moon. There was a serene beauty in the silence of the night, and she found herself remembering the gull she had seen when she had been lying in the bottom of the canoe, before the storm struck and almost killed her with her children. She imagined the pleasure of soaring up and away from her enemies, drifting high among the clouds—

She heard a faint sound.

She blinked, returning sharply to the reality of her world. She scanned the narrow path among the houses, but saw nothing. Perhaps a lookout was returning to his home early, although that seemed unlikely. Perhaps one of her people was restless, like her, and had ventured outside—but in that case, why didn't she hear footsteps now?

Kori stepped into the moonlight. She strained her eyes, scanning the shadows.

Another tiny sound—or were her ears deceiving her? She was nervous, and her senses could be playing tricks. An owl could be out there, or some small animal—maybe just a hare or a field mouse, although it was unusual for those creatures to be out so late.

Feeling irritated by her own anxiety, Kori tried to discipline her mind. Her instincts told her to search harder, but really there was not enough light to show her anything meaningful. And so, standing beside her house, she closed her eyes.

She used her ears to build an image of the world around her, just as she had done so often in her games with Meiri. She saw herself standing, holding her spear, breathing gently through parted lips. She sensed currents of air moving around her. She saw the ocean far below, restlessly caressing the shore. She saw her tribe's houses, a dense mosaic of stone atop the hill.

She heard something—and she recognized it beyond doubt. It was a footstep; she visualized the moccasin that had made it, about twenty paces from her. She caught the faint rustle of a robe—a heavy fur. And as she listened intently she heard a man breathing. She was sure it was a man; his breaths were too deep to be those of a woman.

Kori heard a quick succession of sounds: the man's robe rustling again as he raised his arm, his breath as he drew it in and held it, and the tiny noise his moccasin made as he shifted his weight—

With dismay and disbelief, she realized that he was about to hurl a spear. Kori shook herself out of her state of contemplation. She threw herself down onto the ground. At the same instant she heard the faint whisper of a shaft as it flew through the air barely a hand's breadth above her. There was a sharp, startling noise of flint against stone as the spear struck the wall of her home, and then a clatter of wood as the shaft landed close beside her.

Kori sprang to her feet. "Wake!" she cried. "There's an attacker among us!" She saw his shadow move as he turned and ran, a big man with heavy footsteps, dodging from one shadow to the next. She glimpsed more spears slung under straps across his back—but then he bumped into one of the little buildings, and the extra spears fell to the ground behind him, leaving him unarmed.

Kori pursued him. "Wake!" she shouted again as she ran. Now she saw other shadows darting from one hut to the next, and her breath caught in her throat. Her skin crawled with the sudden understanding that the young warriors on the northern hillside had been a decoy—or at least, a force that could be sacrificed if necessary. If they had succeeded in penetrating the village, they would have served their purpose. But they had served a lesser purpose just by distracting the tribe's attention. The lookout on the south side must have abandoned his post to see why Kori had been shouting. The south side of the village had been unprotected, and other warriors had seized their opportunity, creeping in and hiding among the buildings, waiting for the villagers to return to their beds, complacent in the belief that their attackers had all been killed.

"Wake!" Kori cried a third time as she flew through the night, pursing the shadow of the man who had cast his spear at her. Behind her she heard people stirring, calling out in confusion, and venturing from their homes. Then there were more shouts—of surprise, recognition, anger, and pain.

Perhaps she should turn around and help her tribe; but no, she could not. She had to pursue the man in front of her, not just because he had tried to kill her, but because she knew, with terrible certainty, who he was. And so long as he lived, she and her people could never be safe.

He sprinted across a patch of moonlight, out of the village, under some trees. His hands were still empty; he had lost his first spear when he cast it at her, and the others were scattered back where they had fallen. She ran after him with new confidence, between the big rocks where the southern lookout should be—and he was there now, shouting a challenge.

"Get into the village!" Kori yelled at him. "They need you there. Quickly!"

She ran past him, not waiting for his reply. She found herself in a secluded open space: the space where she had played so often with Meiri, and where she had coupled so shamefully with Werror.

The glade was empty. Or was it? Once again, she stopped herself, closed her eyes, and listened. She was gasping for breath, which made it hard for her to use her ears; and there was a rising cacophony of noise from the village behind her. But now she heard the man moving, unable to suppress his own heavy breathing. He was out among the tall grass, crawling on his belly. Why? If he really wanted to escape from her, he would take refuge among the trees at the edge of the clearing.

She realized what the answer must be. He was a cautious man, and he had left some extra weapons here, just in case.

"I know it's you, Werror!" Kori shouted into the darkness. It had to be him. Why else would he have taken the risk of casting his spear when the rest of his men had been moving silently, preparing to burst into the houses and murder people in their beds? He had seen her standing in the moonlight. He had recognized her, and his lust for revenge had overcome his caution.

Well, he would pay for that now, and so would his men. She had discovered their attack before it had been launched, and she had discovered Werror himself.

Kori raised her hand and held it diagonally across her mouth as she stepped silently around the edge of the glade. "I'm going to kill you, Werror," she said. She changed the angle of her hand. "I will finish what Jalin started. I swear it, Werror."

He made no sound in response. She imagined him in the tall grass, lying flat, clutching the spear he had hidden there. He would be peering through the grass, trying to see her as she moved among the shadows between the trees—

The light suddenly faded. Kori looked up quickly and saw that the clouds were masking the moon. Darkness swept across the land, and she smiled to herself, knowing that she had the advantage now.

Her skin was tingling, and each breath felt tight in her chest. Her pulse was tapping fast, and her body felt light, as if her feet were barely touching the earth. She paused for a moment, groped in front of her, and plucked a dandelion. Slowly, taking her time, she folded it and crushed it in her fist. Then, with infinite caution, she began moving toward the center of the glade.

In all the times she had played here with Meiri, she had never imagined that she might stake her life on the outcome. Strangely, she felt no more fear than when she had faced Werror in the Meeting Place, playing the game with the stick and basket. Of course, she reminded herself, she had been a little too confident that time. He had tricked her, and he had almost won.

She paused and listened. Was he really in the center of the glade, where she assumed he was? Suddenly she doubted herself. She strained her ears—and heard nothing. Then she heard a muffled gasping sound, and she realized he had been holding his breath. Even now, he was muffling his breathing somehow. She guessed he was pressing the fur of his robe across his mouth.

She heard another sound, away to her left. She turned quickly toward it, thinking that she had been mistaken, and he wasn't in the center of the glade at all.

Then there was a faint rustling noise, sounding from yet another location. Kori felt sudden fear. Were two men here?

With difficulty, she disciplined herself. She forced herself to close her eyes again. She stood, and she listened. Now she heard a tiny sound of his moccasin pressing down into the earth—and it was close to where she'd imagined him originally. He must have thrown a small stone, deceiving her just as she had deceived Meiri in the past. She chided herself for being so easily fooled.

She visualized the clearing, and herself standing in it, and the grass waving in the faint night breeze. Now she saw him clearly, from the tiny sounds he made. He was standing less than fifteen paces away from her in the darkness. He was waiting and listening, as she was.

Kori crept forward, slowly, slowly, with infinite care.

His robe rustled. He had heard her, despite her caution. She sensed him raising his spear; it was the same arm motion that she'd heard when he was hiding in the village. He was being more careful this time, though, making certain of his target before he risked throwing the spear.

Kori glanced up. She saw a shifting patch of stars, and she realized that the cloud covering the moon was moving on across the sky. In just a moment, moonlight would shine again, and she would be revealed, facing a man of twice her strength.

Simultaneously she heard him tense, preparing to cast his spear. She realized with dismay that she had made a tiny sound as she tilted her head upward. Should she dive for cover now, as she had before? No, that would make so much noise, he would know exactly where to find her, and she wouldn't be able to use her spear against him if she was lying flat on the ground.

With a flick of her wrist, Kori tossed the crushed dandelion. She threw it so it landed just one pace to her left.

He heard the tiny sound. She sensed him turning slightly, refining his aim. He hurled his spear—

She cast her spear at the same instant. His shaft grazed her arm; she felt the point rip her robe and cut her skin. But her aim was true. Werror shouted in the night, and she heard his body fall.

Kori turned and ran after the spear he had thrown at her. It wasn't likely that her spear had killed him outright, and it was even less likely that she could retrieve her own spear from him and stab him again. But how could she find his spear amid the grass? He had thrown it powerfully; it could have traveled far.

Behind her, she heard him grunting with pain. She imagined him wrestling with her spear, dragging it out of his shoulder or his thigh, wherever it had struck him. Then the world suddenly brightened around her as the moon showed its face. Kori fell to her knees—and saw Werror's spear slanting out of the grass, with its point buried in the earth.

She seized the shaft and turned to face him. He was rising up onto his knees, clutching the side of his chest with his left hand while he held her spear in his right hand. His face was contorted with pain, and with fury. His head was mottled with dry blood, and Kori saw the wounds that Jalin had inflicted when she'd hit him with the stone. The stone had not been heavy enough, and Jalin had not been strong enough. Kori cursed herself for not lingering a moment longer in the junior warriors' house to make sure that Werror had been dead. Still, there was no point now in thinking of the past. She stood facing her adversary, and she raised her arm, ready to cast his spear back at him, just as he raised his arm, ready to cast her spear at her.

He glowered at her. His face was a predatory mask, and his eyes were as wild as the eyes of a mountain cat. He stook a step toward her, looking confident in the knowledge of his greater power, despite the wound she had inflicted. The wound was serious— already, she could see blood glistening in the black fur of his robe. But he could ignore it for a while at least, while he took his revenge upon her.

From the direction of the village, Kori still heard distant shouts. Even if she screamed for help, no one would hear her. The villagers were fighting their own battles. And if she ran, she had no doubt Werror would spear her in the back with casual ease.

So she faced him, with her mind working desperately, trying to decide what to do. If she cast her spear first, and struck him but failed to kill him, she would die. There was no question of that. If he dodged her spear, her situation was even worse. If she waited for him to strike first, and his spear struck her, she wasn't sure if she would still be able to fight him. She had never been badly wounded; she didn't know how she would respond. Even if she managed to duck his spear, she still wasn't sure if she could deal with him. She would need precious moments to regain her footing and take aim at him—and during those moments he could fall upon her, crushing her and stabbing her with the knife that she was sure he had in his belt.

She found herself trembling. She was starting to feel helpless, as if he had already beaten her. And he sensed it. His smile broadened as he weighed the shaft in his hand.

Kori shook herself. How could she allow this to happen? It was wrong, it was unthinkable, that she could tolerate such weakness in herself. Her anger rose up, erasing her moment of fear. She remembered facing Werror in the Meeting Place. He was strong, but he was not invincible. She was fast, she was lithe, she was clever; and there was one other thing that she should never forget: she was a woman, and he was a man.

She started circling around him, moving quickly, skipping through the grass. So long as she moved like this, she couldn't take careful aim at him—but he would have equal difficulty striking at her.

"Is your head painful, Werror?" she said, as she

danced around him. "Is your chest bleeding freely? How does it feel, to be such a big man, wounded by women?"

She saw him narrow his eyes, watching her carefully, ignoring her words and waiting to strike at her.

Kori paused for an instant, just long enough to allow him to take aim. Then she sprang to one side. She'd hoped he would be tempted to cast his spear—but no, he had seen the trap. Still, she saw his chest heaving. He was in pain, and he was angry.

"Remember, Werror, when we coupled here?" Kori said, still circling around him.

He said nothing.

The knowledge that she had allowed him to have her filled her again with shame—but she forced herself on. "You excited me," she said, though the words were painful in her throat. "You had me here," Kori said, pointing to the grass with her free hand. "You were like a bear. Do you remember, Werror?"

He made a growling sound in the back of his throat. "Your words mean nothing," he said. "Say what you will, woman. You will die here."

She paused, forcing herself to stand still in front of him. She looked up into his face. "You would really kill me?"

For a moment he looked disconcerted. She was presenting herself as a target that he couldn't possibly miss, and he saw that she no longer seemed afraid.

"Can I distract you with my words?" she said. "What if I tell you that there's a bear behind you, eh? Or what if I say the moon has turned green, wouldn't you want to take a look to make sure?"

His face contorted into a terrible scowl, and she

knew with utter certainty that he was remembering how she had humiliated him in their game in the Meeting Place. He raised his arm, ready to hurl his spear.

She laughed, watching his eyes. "How about if I tell you that my robe is hanging open?" And as she spoke, with a wild gesture, she tore at the thongs and threw her robe wide, exposing herself shamelessly to him.

She saw his eyes move. He was distracted for only a moment—but a moment was all she needed. She hurled herself forward, racing across the grass. He had not expected this; he'd assumed that if she attacked him at all, she would cast her spear. She stooped as she ran, and he took a quick step back and tried to bring his spear around to strike at her. But he was too late. Kori fell to her knees in front of him. She clenched her left fist and summoned all her strength, punching upward into his genitals. She felt the soft flesh yield to her fist, and she knew her aim had been true.

Werror's mouth opened in a silent scream. He staggered. For a moment she thought he wouldn't fall; but then he lost his footing and he crashed down into the grass, clutching himself between the legs.

She scrambled onto her feet, leaped up, and brought her heel down with all her strength on the wrist of his right hand. His fingers opened, and she kicked his spear aside.

He was grunting, struggling to breathe. At the same time, he was groping in his belt. She glimpsed a knife and saw him raise his arm to hurl it at her.

Kori screamed. All her anger, all her fear, her lust, her shame, and her hatred for Werror were in that scream. She saw him flinch from the sound of it, and he hesitated as he held his knife.

She took her spear in both hands, raised it above her head, and leaped up again, still screaming. She slammed the spear down into the center of Werror's chest, forcing it into his heart. Her weight bore down on the shaft, thrusting it through him, deep into the soil beneath his back.

Still he hurled his knife, but it went spinning past her. Kori dropped down astride him with her robe still hanging open. She watched as he tugged helplessly at the spear that pinned him to the ground. He growled and shouted with pain and fury. Blood gushed out of him, and he thrashed under her, kicking wildly.

Kori felt herself trembling, overwhelmed with emotions she couldn't name. Werror's blood splashed over her, hot and wet, but she didn't even notice. She was watching his face, seeing how it tormented him to know that after all his bravery, all his battles, he was dying at the hands of a woman whom he had seduced and ravished, here in this very spot.

He reached up for her with hands like claws, as if he wanted to rip at her nakedness. But then his head tilted back and he groaned in agony. His arms fell away from her, and she saw him digging his fingers into the earth, gouging furrows as he arched his back and his whole body became rigid.

He slumped under her. His chest heaved once, and was still. His head slowly turned to one side and rested there, with his cheek against the grass. His jaw hung slack. His eyes stared without sight.

Clumsily Kori managed to stand up. She stood for a long moment, gasping for breath, leaning on the spear that still impaled Werror. She glared down at him. "You forced me to do this thing," she told him. "You and your pride, Werror. Your stupid, ugly pride." She shuddered. "I didn't want to kill you. You gave me no choice."

She let go of the spear and turned her back on him. She searched around, found her own spear in the grass where she had kicked it out of his hand, and picked it up. She closed her robe, covering her nakedness.

Then she walked out of the glade, back to the people of her tribe.

25

Kori entered the village as streaks of cloud were touched with the first rose-colored light of dawn. Torches were burning, and figures were running to and fro. Women were wailing. Men were shouting. Kori saw a warrior lying dead in front of her, his blood pooling around his black robes. Farther on, she saw an old man propped against one of the houses, clutching his shoulder while a woman bent over him, binding his wound. He was Taran, Kori realized, and the woman was Shoeni.

Kori felt shaken and drained, but still she roused herself to do what needed to be done. "Shoeni!" she called out. "Is there still danger? Are any warriors still alive?"

Shoeni turned to look at her. "I don't know, Kori," she said, with a fearful look that Kori had never seen before. She stared at Kori's robe, so drenched with Werror's blood that it looked as if it had been painted entirely red. "What happened? Are you all right?"

Kori nodded. She turned and strode to the Meeting Place. More warriors were lying dead here, and two more of her people were badly wounded. She found Biffrar and a couple of his men walking among the houses, holding their spears ready.

"Is the village safe?" Kori called to him.

"At least twenty of Derneren's warriors have been killed," he said.

"But what of my people?" she asked him.

"I have seen three dead, six or seven wounded."

Kori found some reassurance in his words, although it maddened her to know that Werror had deceived both Biffrar and herself, slipping into the south side of the village with his warriors.

"Where have you been?" Biffrar asked, giving her an odd look.

"I didn't abandon my people," she said, answering his unspoken question. "I raised the alarm when I was attacked by the man I mentioned to you before—the man named Werror. I knew that none of us would be safe if I let him live, so I pursued him, and I killed him."

Biffrar looked unconvinced. "You killed this man?"

"His body lies in the grass just south of the village." She gestured. "You can go and see for yourself."

"Kori!" The voice came from behind her.

She turned and found Uroh standing with his robe almost as deeply drenched in blood as hers. "Are you all right?" she called to him.

"Of course." He sounded puzzled, as if the idea of him being injured was absurd. "Bring your healer's pouch," he said. "Raia has a bad wound. I cannot stop the bleeding."

Kori followed him. She found Raia lying in her hut, where a warrior had attacked her while she slept. The big woman tried to force a smile as Kori hurried in, but the smile turned to a grimace of pain. She had been badly cut in her side, and Kori was soon working to bind the wound. After that, as the day brightened, she found herself hurrying among other wounded villagers, trying to calm hysterical children and offer reassurance to terrified women.

Jalin joined her, quietly providing assistance without question or complaint, even though the girl had been wounded herself. There was a long, shallow cut on her leg, inflicted by a stray spear. She ignored it as she helped Kori.

Finally, by the middle of the morning, the village was quiet. Biffrar had been wrong in his estimate of the number wounded; more than a dozen people from the Ocean Tribe had been hurt. In most cases, though, the wounds weren't life-threatening. The invaders had been forced to act in haste after Kori's shout had roused the village. Spears had been thrown carelessly. Warriors who had hoped to slip from house to house, murdering people in their sleep, had found themselves forced to turn and run.

Now all the villagers were gathering in the Meeting Place. Even the people who had been severely wounded were struggling in. Kori had toured the village with Biffrar, looking at each of the Green Valley warriors in case Feroh should be among them; but he was not. Biffrar seemed unsurprised, and his face remained impassive as he stood with Kori now, with Uroh on her other side, facing her people.

She waited till everyone was present. Biffrar's hunters stood in a group at the edge of the Meeting Place, looking grim and fierce in their war paint. Then two more of them arrived, dragging a Green Valley warrior between them.

"This is the last we can find," one of them shouted to Biffrar.

Biffrar nodded. He gestured to the prisoner. "Bring him here." He pointed to the ground in front of him.

Biffrar's men dragged the warrior forward and forced him to kneel. The man looked up at Biffrar, then at Kori—and his face changed as he recognized her. He had been one of her guards when she was working out in the fields.

"Don't take his life," she said quickly, as she saw Biffrar tightening his grip on his spear.

He gave her a quick, stern look.

She realized she should not have given him a direct order. "Forgive me for speaking sharply," she corrected herself. "But it might be wise to send this man back to Green Valley, to convey a message."

Biffrar relaxed his grip. He nodded slowly. "What should that message be?"

"I'm still concerned about my daughter," Kori said. "And you still want my son."

Biffrar's eyes narrowed. "Perhaps we should tell Derneren that if he surrenders your children to us, we will spare his life."

Instinctively Kori opened her mouth to object. But she felt Uroh touching her arm, and when she glanced at him, his eyes warned her to be silent.

She turned back to Biffrar—and he, too, was looking at her in a way that told her she should agree with what he proposed.

Kori's spirit impelled her to refuse. It was unthinkable to allow Derneren to go free—but Uroh knew that as well as she did. And both of the men were calmer and more calculating than she was. She sensed an ulterior motive that couldn't be stated while the warrior kneeled in front of them. "All right," Kori said. "If Derneren frees Meiri and returns Feroh to us, he shall go free."

Biffrar turned to the warrior and jabbed him with his spear. "Do you hear?" he demanded. "This woman is Kori, chieftain of the Ocean Tribe. Take her words to your leader, and we will wait here for his response."

The warrior nodded quickly. He had expected to be killed, and now he saw that he was being allowed to live. "I will do as you say," he told Kori.

"Go!" Biffrar shouted at him.

The man scrambled up. His face was mottled with grime, streaked with blood, and spotted with bruises where the White River Tribe had beaten him after they captured him. He bowed to Kori and bowed to Biffrar, even though he obviously didn't understand who Biffrar was, or why he was there. Then he turned and ran out of the Meeting Place.

Kori waited a moment, giving the man enough time to reach the path down to the valley. She turned to Biffrar. "Why did you want me to make that bargain with Derneren?" she demanded.

Biffrar shrugged. "He will be easier to kill if he believes we want to negotiate peacefully."

Kori saw the truth in that, and she was glad to know that Biffrar was still determined to fight their common enemy. Still, the deception bothered her. "It is not honorable," she said, "to make a pledge that we intend to break."

Biffrar grunted dismissively. "The man we are dealing with has no honor. He attacked innocent people in
this tribe without provocation or mercy."

Kori shook her head. "If we lie and cheat, surely we
are no better than the man we deceive."

Once again Uroh laid his hand on Kori's arm. "In
your games with Meiri," he said quietly, "I have seen you
using deception to win."

"Well, this is true," Kori admitted reluctantly. Still,
somehow, she felt it was different; but perhaps it was
foolish to have this argument.

"Good," said Biffrar. "We agree, then, that we should
attack Derneren as quickly as possible, while he is un-
prepared."

"I must speak." The voice came from the villagers
gathered around. Kori turned and saw Taran standing
up, resting his hands on the shoulders of the people sitting either side of him. Despite his wound, he looked as
contentious as ever. "It is not right for this man to speak
for our tribe," he said, looking at Biffrar. "And it is not
our way to attack other tribes."

For a moment Kori found herself thinking that if
some of her people had had to die, it was a pity that
Taran had not been among them. But she suppressed
the thought. Even though he irritated her, he served a
purpose: he voiced complaints that other villagers
might be thinking, even though they remained silent.
And if she could answer him, she knew she would satisfy everyone.

"You have seen that Derneren is determined to kill
us," Kori said. "Surely, to protect ourselves, we have to
attack him."

"But this man Derneren has nothing to do with

me," said Taran. He turned slowly, looking at the villagers around him. "He has no grudge against any of us here." Finally he turned back to Kori. "You and your husband are the only people he is concerned with."

Kori stared at him for a moment, feeling shocked, then outraged. "What would you have me do?" she cried. "Should I surrender myself? Should I go with Uroh and leave this tribe, never to return?"

There was a murmur of dismay from the villagers. Quickly it turned into shouts of protest.

"Wait!" Taran called, holding up his hands. "I suggested no such thing. I just say that if this is a private matter between Derneren and Kori and Uroh, they should resolve it between them, without involving the rest of us."

Kori found herself finally losing her temper with the old man. "I have protected you," she said. "All of you—"

"No," Uroh murmured to her. "Let me speak."

Kori stopped herself. He was right, she realized; she would not do any good by shouting at her people.

"Speak," she said to Uroh.

Uroh nodded. He eyed Taran frankly. "You have never been a hunter or a fighter," Uroh said. "There is no shame in this, but it is a fact. Therefore, you cannot judge the mind of a man like Derneren, who believes he has a right to oppress and kill other people, and takes pleasure from it. I think there were many people like you, Taran, in the Green Valley Tribe. Like you, they had no quarrel with Derneren. They had never even seen him before." Uroh shrugged. "They are dead now, every one."

Taran glanced around and saw the villagers moved

by Uroh's words. The old man's jaw worked silently for a moment, and he quivered with anger. "You are a young man!" he cried, pointing a shaking finger at Uroh. "Do you claim to be wiser than I am?"

"In this matter," Uroh said softly, "I have more experience than you."

Taran took a step back, shocked by Uroh's lack of respect.

"Now," Uroh went on, "no one expects you to come with us, Taran. Naturally, anyone who wishes to stay in this village may do so. Am I right?"

"Yes," Kori said emphatically. "We are all free in this tribe to follow our own paths."

"But we will not be safe so long as this man Derneren lives," said Uroh. "I am a peaceable man, as you all know. Still, I say Derneren must die."

"We are not fighters," someone complained.

Biffrar held up his hand. "I will speak," he said.

Kori nodded. "You have helped to defend our people tonight. You have saved many lives. We are indebted to you."

"More than fifty of Derneren's warriors have been killed here," Biffrar said. "On the north slope, and here in the village. He is weakened. When the man that we released tells him about this massacre, he will be scared." He gestured casually. "My men are fierce fighters. I think we could kill him on our own. But it will be easier if you join us, because the more numerous we are, the more we will scare this man, and when a man is scared enough, he can be killed more easily."

A woman stood up. It was Geren, Kori realized. She turned to Taran, who was still standing. "You have had your say," she told him bluntly.

Taran glared at her. "Perhaps I haven't finished," he said.

"Please," said Kori, "let us listen to Geren now."

Taran clamped his mouth shut. Proudly, defiantly, he sat down, folded his arms, and stared straight ahead.

"Thank you," Geren said. She turned to Kori. "Most of us were wanderers before we came here," she said. "None of us were fighters. You have trained us, Kori, and Uroh, as well as you can. But we pledged ourselves to this tribe because we hoped to live here in peace. If there is to be war—some of us might prefer to become wanderers again."

There was a reluctant murmur of agreement.

Kori stared at her people in dismay. "You would not fight for your homes and families?" she cried out.

"We would defend ourselves," said Geren, "if we had to. But if we can simply move away—" She shrugged.

"But many of us here are courageous," Kori blurted out. "Kireah, and Jebal, and Onor—" She gestured to some of the younger men, who prided themselves on their hunting skills.

"They are strong and brave," Geren agreed. "But they are few."

Kori felt hurt. She felt betrayed. And she realized that for fourteen years, she had deluded herself, imagining that her people's love implied such a bond of loyalty, they would always rally in defense of her and the tribe.

Some of the faces in the crowd looked unhappy with Geren's words. Some men, in particular, looked ready to fight. But many others avoided Kori's eyes, and she saw clearly that she couldn't count on them.

"May I speak?"

The voice was small, young, and female. Kori searched the crowd and saw Jalin near the back, holding up her arm.

"Yes, speak!" Kori cried, knowing how brave the girl could be.

Geren sat down while Jalin got to her feet. "I am Jalin, of the Green Valley Tribe," she said, turning slowly to look at the faces around her. "As you know, Werror brought me among you. I think everyone understands now that I was not his daughter, but his prisoner. My people were massacred by his warriors." She paused a moment, choosing her words carefully. "I used to be like you," she went on. "I would rather walk away than face an adversary. But with Kori's help, I've learned that I have more courage than I ever realized. I saved her life, and she has saved mine. And I see now that no matter where you go, no matter how far you walk, you can never be truly safe. Sooner or later you will have to take the responsibility to defend yourself. This is the price you must pay to live in peace."

Some people around her shouted out their approval for what she said. Others, though, still looked discontented and afraid, and they started voicing their objections.

"Hear me!" It was Kireah, rising to his feet. He stood patiently, as he had stood so often on duty as a lookout. He waited till the noise died down. "Listen," he said. "I know how some of you feel. You fear that if you follow these people," he gestured toward Biffrar and his hunters, "you will be risking your lives in a place where many of you have never ventured before, and you may never return."

There were murmurs of agreement.

"So this is what I suggest," Kireah went on. "We can travel along the shore, taking our canoes. The wind is still blowing from the north, but we can tow the boats through shallow water near the beach, and the cliffs will hide us from anyone on the land. Green Valley is not so far from the ocean. We can leave the boats safely on the sand as we move inland, and then, if there is some mistake, or our enemies turn out to be stronger than we expect, we can retreat back to the beach. We are the only tribe that can travel across the water. So as long as we have our canoes, we will always be able to retreat safely."

He sat down, leaving a long moment of silence as the villagers considered what he had said.

Kori glanced at Biffrar. "What do you think?" Kori asked softly.

"It would be good to attack from the ocean," Biffrar said, "in case Derneren has left any men watching the usual paths between here and his tribe." He eyed the villagers coldly. "If you wish to follow this plan, I have no objection."

Kori turned to Uroh. She found him smiling faintly. "This amuses you?" she asked.

"It saddens me," he said, "to see so little spirit in our people. But our boats have always been a source of strength, so maybe they will be of some help."

Kori nodded. "Very well. I say again, anyone who wishes to remain in this village may still do so—though I think you will feel ashamed when we return two days from now, having crushed our enemies and defended our tribe." She paused, looking from face to face. "Jebal," she said, seeing him leaning forward, watching her eagerly. "Will you join us?"

The youngster sprang up without hesitation. "I will," he said, shouting out the words.

"Onor," Kori said. "Will you?"

He stood, holding his head up with pride. "I will."

"How many others?" Kori asked, sweeping her hand around.

One man stood, and then another—and suddenly more than half the people in the tribe were rising to their feet. A few men, and many of the women, started edging away, retreating to their homes. The rest, though, stood firm. And finally even Geren joined them.

Kori turned to Biffrar. "When should we leave?" she asked.

"Immediately," he said. "The canoes will make our journey slower, and the beach is not the most direct route. It will take a day and a night to get there. Near the end of the night, just before dawn, we should be able to attack."

Kori hesitated. "You think it's best to leave right away? Shouldn't we prepare—"

Biffrar shook his head dismissively. He turned to Kori and lowered his voice. "If we wait, many of these people will change their minds. You and your friend Jalin have given them courage, but it is like this war paint on my face." He licked his thumb and wiped it across his cheek. "It is on the outside, not the inside. As soon as they remember their fear, it will wash their courage away."

26

They trekked along the beach throughout the day, taking turns to walk through the shallow water and haul the canoes behind them. The day was bright and the ocean was peaceful, shimmering in the sun. It was a day that seemed no different from any day when Kori and her people might be out riding the waves, reaping their harvest from the sea. She found it hard to believe that she was marching with a war party that would soon be launching an attack against her enemies, to spill their blood.

For a while she walked beside Biffrar. Even though it was difficult for her to deal with his pride and his need for respect, she needed to maintain his friendship and cooperation.

"I fear I misjudged my people," she confided in him as they strode along the unbroken sand. "For years I warned them not to take their security for granted. With my husband Uroh, I trained them—"

"But you imagined they would share your spirit," Biffrar said. "Surely, you see that you are an unusual woman."

"Yes, I am unusual," she agreed. "But is it so strange for any person, male or female, to want to defend her tribe? In any case, even though I may be an unusual woman, my husband—"

"Your husband is a shrewd man," said Biffrar. "When I heard the sounds of fighting in your village just before dawn, and I ran up there among the little houses, I saw your husband take spears from three men, even though he was unarmed. Then he turned their weapons against them. He could be a fine warrior—if he chose to be." Biffrar shook his head. "But he takes no satisfaction in it. He, too, lacks your fighting spirit."

Kori felt momentarily confused. Yes, she could see she was more combative than Uroh. Yet—she would never want him to change. She would never trust a man who took pleasure from fighting and killing. "It seems to me," she said, "it is good for a man to be decent and kind, but fierce when his life is threatened. Why should that be so rare? And why should so many of my people be unwilling even to defend themselves?"

"Let me tell you how it is in my tribe," said Biffrar. "A boy begins learning the discipline of a hunter when he is three years old. If he is a coward or flinches from pain, he knows he will be ridiculed and rejected by the men. He will be left to work with the women for the rest of his life, and he will not be allowed to take a mate. So, every boy tries to prove himself. And when they come of age, they endure beatings and other punishments that last for two days and two nights." He held up his hand. "You see I lack my little finger?"

Kori nodded. She had noticed it the first time she met Biffrar, years ago; but it had seemed unwise to mention it.

"Each boy must make a sacrifice before he can become a man," Biffrar told her. "This was my sacrifice. Many of my hunters did the same." He dropped his hand back by his side. "Now, if you want your people to fight without hesitation, and without fear, this is how you must train them. This mixture you see in your husband, of gentleness in everyday life and fierceness in times of danger, is so rare, you should never expect to find it in another man."

"But why should that be so?" Kori protested. "Why must I inflict pain on children to give them courage? I suffered no pain when I was a girl. I didn't even learn to use a spear till I was in my twentieth year. But I have courage, isn't that so?"

Biffrar gestured irritably. He seemed to be getting impatient with her. "Of course you have courage. You suggested I should look at the man you killed this morning, so I did. If you truly faced him alone, you are fierce and brave indeed."

"No one helped me to kill that man," Kori said.

"And you expect others to be like you?" Biffrar gave her a stiff, grim smile. "You lead your people well, Kori, but I fear you don't understand human nature. Forgive me for saying this, but—you are naive."

At sunset, they reached a place where Kori judged they could leave the canoes. While her people dragged the boats high up onto the beach, she stood alone for a moment, staring out to sea. Half a dozen orcas were frolicking within sight of the shore, their black bodies glistening as they leaped among the waves. She heard a hissing sound and saw plumes of spray as they vented fountains from their blowholes, and she had the eerie sense that they weren't there just by coincidence. They almost seemed to be watching over her people on the shore. Maybe, Kori thought, it was a good omen, even though she didn't believe in omens. She found herself envying the great sea creatures their freedom, just as she envied the gulls that wheeled overhead.

"Are you nervous?" said a voice.

Kori turned and found Jalin beside her. "No," said Kori.

"I felt brave when we were escaping from Green Valley," said Jalin. "I had courage then. Yet—now we're returning there, I have to confess, I feel afraid."

"Your mother is a prisoner," Kori reminded her. "You'll be able to free her."

"Of course," said Jalin. Yet her face showed no joy.

"We will prevail," Kori said. "I have no doubt of that."

Jalin forced a strained smile. "I'm sure we will." Quickly she hugged Kori. Then she turned away.

Kori wondered if she should go after Jalin and question her further. No, she had other obligations. Her people had finished beaching the canoes, and they were waiting, looking apprehensive.

Kori went over to them, striding purposefully to demonstrate her confidence. "People of the Ocean Tribe," she said, speaking loudly so that her voice carried above the sound of the sea. "This will be over soon enough. We will walk through the forest, following Biffrar and his men. Since they are such great hunters and fighters, I will yield to Biffrar's judgment from this moment on. And so will you." She stared hard at each person in turn, especially the younger men who might feel a need to prove themselves. "You will listen to Biffrar and do exactly what he says, because he has the experience as a fighter that we lack."

She waited for any objections, but there were none.

"Remember," Kori went on, "our enemy is scared and he doesn't know that we plan to attack him. He is a weak man, and a stupid man. Werror served him, and I believe it was Werror who devised the attack against us today. But I killed Werror with my own hand this morning, and the messenger that we sent back to Green Valley will give that news to Derneren. This is another reason why he will be afraid."

One of the men stepped forward. "When we attack," he asked, "should we kill any man we see? Are any farmers who used to live in Green Valley still alive?"

Kori looked inquiringly at Jalin.

"All the menfolk were slain," she said. "The only men in Green Valley are the warriors who massacred my people." Her face became grim. "You should kill them all," she said.

"Except for Feroh," said a man's voice.

Kori turned and saw Biffrar moving toward her. She nodded reluctantly. "Feroh shall be given to you. I have agreed that this shall be so."

"Good," said Biffrar. He assessed the people facing him. About thirty men and ten women had chosen to come on this journey. They looked nervous, and they stood close together for mutual support. Most of their faces showed neither pride nor confidence, and the weapons that they held had been made for hunting bobcats, deer, and squirrels. Many of the men were small-boned, and some of the women were heavy around their waists. They looked vulnerable compared with Biffrar's tall, proud hunters.

Biffrar turned away from them. "If you are ready," he said to Kori, "we should start into the forest. I have a scout who knows this land well, but we will have to move slowly, because there will be no moon in the first half of the night, and we must be careful not to lose our way." He frowned at a tall, thin woman who stood at the edge of the crowd of villagers. "You there," he called to her. "What is your name?"

She glanced to either side of her, hoping that Biffrar was addressing someone else. Finally she answered him. "I am Dispi," she said in a low voice.

"How would it be," Biffrar said, "if I asked you to stay behind here and watch the canoes?"

The woman glanced furtively at the other villagers. "I should do my part in Green Valley," she said.

"You will do your duty by staying here," Biffrar told her. "Hide in the bushes up on the ridge, and if you see any strangers, anything that makes you suspicious, run to us immediately."

"All right," the girl bobbed her head. "But how will I follow you—"

"My men will cut notches on the trees as we travel inland," said Biffrar. He turned away from Dispi and strode to the front of the party where his men were waiting. He surveyed them in silence for a moment, eyeing them critically. Then he gave a curt nod. "We will find our enemies," he said, "and we will kill them." He turned and started into the forest.

With varying amounts of reluctance, the villagers went after him.

Kori saw Uroh lagging behind, and she went to him. He was looking out to sea—watching the whales, she realized. They were still romping in the same location as before.

"They know we are here," Uroh said. "And you know, I think they envy us."

"But I was envying them," Kori said in surprise.

Uroh shook his head. "They see that we can walk on the land, and build homes and canoes, and make clothes and fishing nets—while they are trapped in the water, and they can build nothing. You know, when a whale dies, often it comes to the beach and rests here during its last day. I think it wants to understand the mystery of people, and how we manage to dwell beyond the sea."

Kori turned back toward the forest. She saw that most of her people had already disappeared under the trees. "We must leave your whale friends and do our duty," she said. "Our daughter is waiting."

Uroh threw his head back. Facing toward the ocean, he shouted a sound without words.

"Are you speaking to them?" Kori asked. "Do they understand you?"

"Perhaps they do," said Uroh. "Who can say?" He gave Kori one of his self-effacing smiles. "Perhaps they think I'm just a weak creature who can't swim properly, and I'm making a foolish noise."

Kori put her arm around him. "I will never really understand you, Uroh," she said. "But there will never be anyone who can replace you."

"Not even Werror?"

He spoke carelessly—yet she saw that the words were not really careless at all. She stopped, realizing that she must respond to him in some way. It wasn't the best time; still, she felt it was necessary. After all, they were going to face an adversary, and no matter how confident Biffrar sounded, there was always the possibility of death. Kori would never be able to forgive herself if Uroh died without understanding how she felt.

"I will always be ashamed," she said, "by my foolishness in being charmed by Werror. He planned from the start to deceive me and learn as much about me as he could, so that it would be easier to fight us and kill us all."

Uroh looked at her thoughtfully. "Did you couple with him?" he asked.

"You know I can't lie to you," she said, feeling a pain in her chest at the knowledge of what she had to say. "I have to admit, Uroh, that I lay with him once." She shook her head, feeling torn by the emotions inside her. "You must understand, though, how lonely I was. I missed your company. As the years have gone by, you've looked at me less and less. I felt as if I had become too old to be of interest to you. And Werror sensed this. He used it against me."

Uroh's face changed. He looked at her in surprise. "You were lonely?" He reached out and touched her face, as if he needed to prove to himself that she was the one who had spoken. "But I felt there was no place for me near you," he told her. "You are so strong, and your people love you, and you know how to guide them. I had no function. I was like your spear, or—your moccasins, something useful, but only when you need it."

She looked back at him in shock. She seized him

quickly and hugged him to her. "Nothing, no one, could be more important to me than you," she told him. "I revere you, Uroh. I admire you more than any man I have ever known."

He stood in her arms, saying nothing.

"Don't you believe me?" she said, releasing him and staring into his eyes.

"I suppose I do." His face was deeply serious; and then, unexpectedly, he laughed. "I am happy to know this. It makes me very happy."

"We are the same people now as we were fourteen years ago," she told him. "And you know how strong we were then."

He looked away, remembering. "We were very passionate," he said. "And reckless. And brave."

"Good," she said. "So we will be that way tonight." She put her arm around him, and together they moved deeper into the forest, pursuing the people who had almost disappeared into the dimness ahead. "We will rescue our daughter and confront Derneren and his warriors," Kori went on. "And then, afterward, perhaps you can forgive me for what I did."

He shrugged. "I understand it now, which is always the first step. And you rescued me from Green Valley. And then you slew Werror with your own hand. And now you say I am the only man you care for."

"This is true," said Kori.

"Then I think that is enough, don't you?"

27

The moon was high and the night was old by the time they reached Green Valley. On a hilltop overlooking the big houses, Biffrar told the people of the Ocean Tribe to wait and be still while two of his scouts crept down into the valley.

Kori could see that many of her people were tired and unhappy after the long, slow journey through the forest. She went among them, thanking them for their loyalty and praising them for their courage. The villagers shared a quick meal as they lay in tall grass at the edge of the forest, and they waited uneasily in the silence of the night.

For a long time, nothing happened. A cool wind sighed through the trees and thin clouds smeared the moon, casting a shifting light across the land. Kori looked down at the house where she had been held captive, and without knowing why, she started to share Jalin's feeling of apprehension. Derneren's warriors had taken this peaceful, fertile valley and transformed it into a place of pain and cruelty. There was evil here, and she felt a deep instinctive desire to separate herself from it, especially since she had reconciled her differences with Uroh. Yet, of course, her daughter was here.

Away in the distance, an owl cried—once, and then again. It sounded so lifelike Kori almost thought it might be real, but she saw Biffrar lean forward intently as he squatted in the tall grass, watching the valley.

There was another long wait. Kori felt time dragging around her, and the delay was almost unbearable. Then another owl-sound came from a different direction, near the rear of the buildings.

Biffrar stood up. "It is safe," he said.

Kori peered at him. "How can you be sure?"

"If my scouts believed there was danger, they would have come back to us here—or they would have remained silent, because they would be dead by now."

"But there must be lookouts posted," Kori protested.

"I doubt there are lookouts. If there were, my scouts would have come back to warn us." Biffrar turned to his men. "We will attack from the rear." He glanced back at Kori. "Divide your people into three groups, and have them lie in wait on either side of the houses, and in the front area, so that they can kill any people who try to flee."

Kori hesitated. "I want to be among your men when you attack," she said. "And I want Uroh with me."

Biffrar shook his head. "It will be safer to stay with your people."

Kori turned and found Uroh close by her. He nodded to her, and she turned back to Biffrar. "Our conflict

with Derneren is a personal matter, and he holds my
daughter hostage. I must be among your men when
they find him, and my husband must be there too."

"Yes," said Uroh. He said nothing more; he didn't
need to.

"Very well," said Biffrar. "We can certainly use your
fighting skills. But who will supervise your villagers
while they lie in wait around the houses?"

Kori scanned the pale shapes of her people's faces
till she saw Jalin. She beckoned to her. "She is young,
but she has proved herself," Kori said. "And she knows
the terrain."

Biffrar looked at the girl skeptically, then shrugged.
"Hide yourself with the people of the Ocean Tribe
around the houses till you hear us call," he told her.
"One owl-cry means danger; be ready to strike down
anyone who runs out. Two cries, and there is no danger;
you may leave your hiding places. Three, and we are
outnumbered by our enemies, and you must come
quickly to help us kill them." He fixed her with his
fierce eyes. "You will stay hidden, and you will do nothing, till you hear one of those signals."

"I understand," she said. She looked quickly at
Kori, then back at Biffrar. Her eyes seemed nervous in
the moonlight, but she held her spear fiercely.

"Go, then," said Biffrar. "Move swiftly, so you will
be ready when we strike."

Jalin turned without another word. She strode
among the villagers, gathering them around her. Many
seemed shocked to be following her instead of Kori, but
she told them she was the only one who knew the land
well enough to find hiding places around the houses,
and they accepted this.

Kori and Uroh waited with Biffrar while Jalin set off with the villagers following behind her, running silently between bushes scattered across the hillside. From a distance the moving figures were barely visible in the night, and the soft sound of their moccasins was lost in the wind.

"Which house is Derneren in?" Biffrar asked Kori.

"The center house," she told him.

"Then that is where we will begin." He turned and called softly to his men. Then he started down the hill.

Kori followed close behind him, running doubled forward, dancing from each piece of cover to the next, with Uroh beside her. The wind touched her face and the grass brushed her legs, and she felt good to be moving at last, although there was still an ugly feeling of apprehension gnawing inside her, the knowledge of evil around her as she neared the massive, dark, silent houses.

Biffrar stopped at the edge of the clear area at the rear, and Kori saw the log where she had been tied and stoned. Her instinct shouted even louder than before, warning her to flee this place and seek a sanctuary elsewhere. But Uroh was near her, and his presence helped to calm her. And Biffrar stood tall and confident, turning his head from side to side, peering into the night and sniffing the air as his men gathered behind him.

A figure loomed in the darkness, silent and terrifying—but he exchanged a tiny animal sound with Biffrar, and Kori realized he was one of the scouts. Then the other scout appeared like a drifting shadow, and Biffrar listened as they whispered to him.

He turned and called softly to one of his men, who moved forward carrying a bundle of straight, well-trimmed tree branches, each as long as a man's arm. He slung the bundle down, fell to his knees, and pulled fire sticks from a pouch. Kori and Uroh joined the hunters as they gathered around and squatted in a tight circle. Everyone receive one of the tree branches, and Kori smelled animal fat daubed around its tip. Meanwhile, the man with the fire sticks was working busily, spinning the drill between his palms. The tip glowed red in the darkness, then the tinder flared, the hunter added pieces of dry grass and twigs, and suddenly flames were dancing.

"Light your torches," Biffrar said.

Kori, Uroh, and the hunters thrust their branches toward the fire. There were sizzling, popping sounds, and the night became alive with yellow light. Biffrar checked quickly that every man's torch was burning. Then he turned and pointed at the center house. Without a word he charged forward, holding his spear high and running so fast that Kori could barely keep up with him.

The house loomed in front of her. Its wooden beams were picked out in sharp relief in the flickering torchlight—and finally Kori understood her feelings of dread. She was not so much afraid of the men inside these houses; she was more chilled by the men around her. Surely, what they were doing was not so different from the way it must have been when Derneren's warriors attacked the innocent farmers of the Green Valley Tribe. She was reenacting something that felt terrible in its premeditated viciousness. It was the only way to ensure the security of her own people—yet this wild rush toward the houses didn't feel like self-defense. She had joined a gang of men whose purpose was to destroy anyone who lay in their path.

Biffrar plunged through the doorway. Kori and Uroh followed him with the rest of the hunters on their heels. Their breathing and footsteps were loud in the great house, but they made no other sound as they ran quickly around its edges, thrusting their torches into each of the sleeping quarters, seizing bedding and hurling it onto the floor, jabbing their spears into every possible hiding place, and moving on—till they realized, finally, the house was completely empty.

Kori stood for a moment, breathing hard, still glancing around as if she expected an attacker to come lunging at her. She saw Derneren's makeshift chair beside the fireplace, and baskets of food still ranged around the hearth. Biffrar strode forward and touched the ashes. "They were here," he said in a voice that was low-pitched but angry. "And it was not so long ago." He seized his spear in both his hands, and Kori saw the muscles in his arms flex as he gripped it fiercely. Still, he controlled his anger when he turned to his men, quickly dividing them into two groups, one to enter the house on the left, the other to enter the house on the right.

"You think Derneren has fled?" Kori asked.

"I think he is hiding," Biffrar answered. "Come!" He ran to the side door.

Kori and Uroh followed him. "The next house belongs to the junior warriors," Kori called to the chieftain.

She couldn't tell if he heard her. He charged forward, and Kori followed him despite her fear. With Uroh and a score of Biffrar's hunters she ran into the house, spreading throughout it—and they stopped as they saw women in all the sleeping quarters, huddling on their beds, gaping at them in wide-eyed terror.

Biffrar held up his hand, turning slowly, studying every detail of the house. "Why are all these women awake?" he said.

"They must have heard us in the other house," said one of his men.

Biffrar shook his head. "If that was so, and they woke just moments ago, they would still be touched by sleep. They would not be like this, alert, with their eyes staring wide." He turned to the woman on the bed nearest to him. He seized her by the hair and pressed the point of his spear to her throat. "Where are the men?" he demanded.

She quivered with fear. She shook her head helplessly.

"I will kill you," he warned her.

She gave a helpless cry and raised her arm, pointing upward.

At the same instant, one of Biffrar's men let out a shout of pain—and then another, and another. Suddenly the hunters were falling all around with spears in their chests, while a terrible chorus of war cries filled the house.

Kori looked up. "In the roof!" she cried.

Figures were perched among the great wooden beams. She saw one of them raise his arm, and she threw herself to one side as the spear hissed through the air. It made a sharp cracking sound and its shaft thrummed as the flint head embedded itself in the wall behind her.

All the women were screaming. Biffrar and his surviving hunters ran for cover in the corners of the room. They started casting their own spears at the men hiding above, and Kori saw one of them fall, spraying blood as his body turned and smacked onto the dirt floor.

Uroh hustled Kori to one of the posts supporting the beams. The post was not wide enough to shield them completely, but it made them a more difficult target. Kori glanced around quickly, fearing that this was just one part of a trap, and other warriors would come pouring into the house. She saw the door flaps ripped aside—but the men who entered were the rest of Biffrar's hunters, attracted by the commotion.

"Go!" he called to them, shouting above the wailing of the women. "Enter all the other houses. There must be more men hiding there. Less than a dozen are here." He gestured to the beams overhead.

His men obeyed him. Kori clutched the wooden post in front of her as if she hoped to draw strength from it. She still felt terribly vulnerable, and she was horrified to see how many of Biffrar's men had been felled. She counted eight of them lying on the floor. Still, that left another twelve, plus herself and Uroh and Biffrar himself. All of them were shielding themselves now from the attackers under the roof. Six more spears rained down, but none struck a target.

Kori tried to steady herself. She tried to think. Now that the warriors had revealed themselves, they were trapped up on the beams with no way to escape. How could they hope to survive?

Suddenly one of them launched himself from his perch, yelling defiantly as he fell onto one of Biffrar's men and dragged him down to the floor. He drew his knife and stabbed the man once, twice, and a third time. But Biffrar and three other hunters cast their spears, and Derneren's young warrior made a terrible throttled sound as he fell onto his back with four shafts embedded in his chest. He clawed at them, thrashed briefly, then lay still.

Suddenly all of the warriors hurled themselves from their refuge. Their desperation was terrible to see, and Kori felt terrified as she realized that they had planned from the start to sacrifice their own lives just for the glory and honor of killing their enemies. She saw a figure drop like a hawk, his black robe flapping as he seized another man from the White River Tribe just three paces away. Instinctively Kori raised her spear. She hurled it into the attacker's back, striking him before he had a chance to kill his prey. He reared up, reaching behind him, yelling in shock as he tried to touch the shaft buried between his shoulders. Then he slumped to his knees as another of Biffrar's men speared him in the chest.

The house was filled with men grappling with each other. The women started screaming again, adding to the din. But the fight was ending almost as soon as it had begun. Derneren's men fought fiercely, but the White River men who still survived were killing the warriors one by one. All around, men were screaming and dying.

"Kori!"

It was Uroh's voice. She turned—and saw one of the last of Derneren's warriors rushing at her with his spear held high. Kori had cast her own spear, and she had been too dazed, too dismayed, to rearm herself. In sudden desperation she groped behind her for one of the other spears that she had placed under her pack, but she was clumsy in her fear; and then she froze as she recognized the young man before her.

"Feroh!" she screamed.

For a moment, in the midst of the battle, he stared at her, and his aim faltered.

In his eyes, Kori saw how he burned with hate for her—still, there was something else, an instinct or a desire that was almost equally powerful.

She brought her hand away from her spear. Instead, slowly, she held it out to him. "Give me your weapon," she called to him. She took a step forward, staring into his eyes. "Give it to me, Feroh." She took another step, bringing her just a couple of paces away from him. The sight of her seemed to stun him. He stared back at her, panting, trembling, unable to move.

"Give it to me!" she screamed.

He woke suddenly from his trance. His eyes widened, and his face contorted. He screamed wildly, drew back his arm, and Kori realized that she had misjudged him.

Before he could cast his spear, though, he staggered backward with a shaft embedded in his left shoulder. His spear dropped from his hand and clattered onto the floor.

Feroh fell on his back. He grabbed the spear that had lodged in him, and he worked it savagely, trying to free it. But the pain was too intense. His face twisted in agony.

Kori felt a presence beside her and found Uroh there. "I'm sorry," he said, stepping forward till he stood in front of Feroh, staring down at him. "I could not let you kill my wife."

The bedlam in the room was diminishing. All of

Derneren's warriors had fallen, and Biffrar's men were turning away from them, going to help their comrades who had been hurt. Kori was barely aware of these things; she only saw Feroh lying in front of her with blood staining his robe.

Kori shook with emotion. She kneeled beside Feroh and reached out to him.

"No!" he cried. Once again he wrenched at the spear in his shoulder—and this time he pulled it free.

Kori looked into his face, fearing him; but the killing lust had been erased by his own pain, and there was nothing there now but confusion and misery. He took the spear between his two hands and turned it to face his own chest. For a moment he lay gathering his courage while blood pulsed from his shoulder wound. Then he let out a terrible wail, like a trapped animal facing its tormentor. Still staring at Kori, he plunged his spear into his own heart.

"Feroh!" she screamed. She seized the shaft, but she was already too late. As his blood gushed across her hands, he moaned and closed his eyes. His body shook in terrible spasms—until gradually, the spasms died away. Breath rushed out of his lungs, his muscles went limp, and he was still.

For a long time Kori stared at his lifeless face. Her strength drained out of her, leaving her so weak she was afraid she might collapse on the floor. She was overwhelmed with grief and pity—and yet, as she looked at his face, she saw that this was ultimately the only way he could escape the demons that had raged inside him. Death was easier for him than life. The anguish that he had felt, which she had tried to understand and cope with for so many years, was finally over.

Kori looked up and saw Biffrar joining Uroh. The chieftain's cheek had been cut, smearing his face and neck with blood, but he stood calmly, folding his arms around his spear. Behind him, his hunters were making sure that all of Derneren's warriors were dead.

"Your son planned to sacrifice his life here," Biffrar said. "So did all of them." He scowled as he looked around the room. "In their bravery, or their stupidity, they took ten of my men with them."

"But how?" Kori said, as she struggled onto her feet. "How did they know we were coming here? They must have been warned, otherwise they wouldn't have had time to position themselves up in the roof."

One of Biffrar's hunters appeared in the doorway. "We searched all the other houses," he shouted. "All of them are empty."

"Is there no one?" Kori cried. "Not even my daughter?"

"No one," the hunter told her. He turned to Biffrar. "Shall we bring out the people of the Ocean Tribe to help us search the land?"

Biffrar didn't answer. For the first time, he seemed unsure.

Then a faint cry sounded from outside. It was a woman calling Kori's name.

Biffrar grunted in anger. "I told your villagers to wait for my signal," he said.

"No," said Kori. "That's Dispi's voice." She seized a torch that was still alight where it had been dropped on the floor. Quickly she strode into the night. "Dispi!" she cried. She peered into the darkness. "I'm here. Come here!"

The woman came into the light, gasping for breath,

looking pale from exhaustion and fear. "Derneren and his men are at the beach!" she shouted. "They came out of the forest after you'd gone. Twenty of them. I didn't know what to do. I came here as fast as I could—"

Suddenly Biffrar was beside Kori, his eyes flashing with anger. "They must have had a lookout posted up on the cliffs," he said. "And the lookout came here in time to warn them." He threw his head back and made an owl-cry—once, and a second time. Then, as the people of the Ocean Tribe emerged from their hiding places, he turned to Kori. "Choose six of your people to stay here and care for my wounded men," he told her. "The rest will come with us."

"Back to the ocean?" Kori asked.

"Of course!" He glared at her, and she saw that his rigid self-control had finally failed in the face of his mounting rage. His men had been ambushed, ten had been killed, and more had been wounded. It maddened him beyond reason to know that he had been outwitted, and his ultimate enemy was still free.

"I tell you now," he said, "this man Derneren will die. I cannot return to my tribe so long as he lives." He swept past Kori and threw his torch aside into the night. "Come!" he shouted, as the light sputtered out. "Follow me. To the beach!"

28

The journey back to the ocean took half the time they had spent traveling inland, because there was no need for caution and silence now, and they could follow the clear path that they had trampled through the forest. Biffrar strode ahead, forcing his way through foliage, slashing at low branches with his spear, and his men followed him, hurrying to keep up.

"Is this wise?" Kori said to Uroh, as they went after the hunters with the villagers following behind them.

"It's never wise to act like this," said Uroh, "in anger and haste. But maybe, this time, it doesn't matter."

"What do you mean?" she asked, as she struggled through the darkness, dragging her robe free from brambles and underbrush.

"I mean that Derneren will not be there," Uroh said. "If he wanted to face us, he would have stayed in Green Valley."

Kori saw the truth in what he said. "You mean, he's afraid of us now."

"Afraid, or cautious," said Uroh. "So many of his warriors were killed when they attacked our village—and the messenger we sent back to him must have warned him that we are aided now by the White River Tribe. We were foolish to think that Derneren would negotiate. He knows we have a superior force, and he is a weak man. He is ruled by his own fear."

"But he still has Meiri!" Kori cried.

"Yes," Uroh said flatly, without emotion. "This is so."

Kori's thoughts were in turmoil. In her anguish over Feroh, her confusion over Werror, and her anxiety about saving her daughter, she had trusted other people's judgment instead of her own. Biffrar was the one who had sent the messenger back to Green Valley. Kireah had suggested traveling north along the beach, so that the tribe could bring their canoes with them.

"We should have made our own decisions," she said to Uroh, "instead of following others."

"I see that now," he agreed with her. "But there is no point in looking backward. It is the future that concerns us."

As he spoke, Kori heard the ocean ahead. The forest began thinning around them, and she saw dark gray sky beyond the leaves above. Dawn had broken while they were hurrying among the trees.

She heard a cry from up ahead, and she felt alarmed in case Derneren had placed another ambush, leaving more warriors lying in wait to kill anyone who pursued them to the beach. But then Kori realized that the cry was not a war cry, it was a cry of rage and frustration from one of Biffrar's men.

Kori and Uroh burst out of the forest onto the ridge that overlooked the sand. The hunters of the White River Tribe were dark shapes in the grayness, running down the beach toward the ocean.

"See there," Uroh said softly, as the villagers emerged around him.

Far in the distance, black specks floated upon the gray waves. At first Kori couldn't make sense of what she saw. Then, in sudden comprehension, she turned and stared at the sand where her people had left their canoes.

There was nothing there but footprints and ruts where the canoes had been dragged back to the ocean.

The villagers saw what she saw, and they let out a terrible wail. They ran toward the water, following Biffrar and his hunters as if they imagined they could somehow continue running across the waves. They shouted in rage and grief, knowing that they had lost not only their chance of killing their enemy, but the precious possessions that enabled them to feed themselves from the sea.

"How is this possible?"

Kori heard the voice from beside her. She turned and found Jalin standing there, staring at the distant specks. "Your tribe is the only one that knows how to ride the ocean," Jalin went on. "How could Derneren—"

"Werror rode a raft," Kori said impatiently. "You rode it with him, didn't you? Desperate men can do desperate things."

"But the wind has dropped," Uroh said softly. "Did you notice that?"

She turned to him in irritation. "What are you talking about?" she snapped. "What does it matter whether there's any wind?"

Uroh smiled. "Without wind, they will find it hard to move far. Last night, when we left the canoes—I felt concerned, abandoning them on the beach. It wasn't something I could explain, so I said nothing. I just felt that our possessions shouldn't be so vulnerable. I took the paddles and hid them in the forest, just in case."

Kori stared at him. She felt suddenly ashamed for being short-tempered, and chagrined that Uroh had thought for himself while she had blindly trusted Biffrar.

"Still," said Jalin, "there's been enough breeze to take Derneren and his men far from the shore. They can paddle with their hands if they have to. I know you are at home in the water, Uroh, but even you can't swim after our enemies."

Uroh didn't answer. Down by the water, the villagers and the White River Tribe were waving their spears and shouting empty threats at the distant warriors. Uroh calmly walked across the sand, first joining the line of people, then moving past them into the water. Their shouts died down and they stared at him as he waded forward till he was forty paces from the beach with the sea surging around his chest.

He stopped there, cupped his hands around his mouth, and gave the cry that Kori had heard him use before. He repeated it, then gave it a third time.

Kori squinted into the dawn light. Behind her, the sun was rising, touching every ripple on the ocean with a trace of gold. Then she saw what Uroh had seen. "The whales," she said. "They're still there." She turned to

Jalin. "Look! See, they were playing in the ocean when we were here last night. Six of them—no, more—not far from the shore."

"But what's he doing?" Jalin cried.

"Come with me," Kori said, taking Jalin's hand. "I think perhaps we should believe in Uroh. Perhaps I should have believed in him more myself, long ago." She led Jalin down the beach. "Come," Kori called to her people. "Follow." And she strode into the ocean.

Her people stared at her, then looked doubtfully at each other. Some of them took a couple of tentative steps. They shouted questions to Kori, but she ignored them.

Uroh was voicing his cry again to the orcas.

"Can he really speak to them?" Jalin asked.

"I don't know," Kori said. "But they're coming closer."

The great sea creatures had ceased frolicking with each other and had turned toward the shore. The massive oblong shapes of their heads reared briefly above the waves, and their tails kicked up spray.

"But you know I can't swim!" Jalin protested, as Kori waded deeper.

Kori tightened her grip on Jalin's hand. "We protected you in the river," she said, "and we will protect you here. I won't let you drown." She glanced back and saw that many of the villagers were starting to venture cautiously after her—while Biffrar and his hunters remained at the edge of the water, staring at Kori and Uroh as if they were insane. "See," she said to Jalin, "you're already more courageous than the White River Tribe. They daren't even venture into the shallows."

"Perhaps they're right," said Jalin. "This makes no sense to me."

"Let us see what happens before we try to judge," Kori answered. "For years, Jalin, I refused to believe anything unless I saw it or touched it. My way was always different from my husband's way, and because I didn't understand his way, I had no faith in it. But now I'm wondering if I was wrong to be so quick to judge."

She came up beside Uroh. The ocean was terribly cold—at least as cold as the river had been. But they had endured that well enough, so she forced her mind away from the chill that gripped her.

Again Uroh made his cry; and now the orcas were so close, Kori found herself wanting instinctively to run from them. Still, she reminded herself that a whale had saved her from the storm. In all the sea stories she had ever heard, no one had ever claimed that an orca attacked a human being.

Kori looked back again at her people. They shared her reverence for the whales, and they were all moving into the ocean as the orcas came steadily closer. "We must trust my husband," Kori called out to the villagers. "And we must trust the orcas. We have no other choice. Is it not so?"

The water surged around her, and when she turned around she found the black body of a whale rising up from the ocean so close to her and Uroh, he could almost touch it.

Uroh turned to Kori. "See," he said, "they can't come nearer to the shore than this. The water isn't deep enough. We must go to them now."

Even though Kori felt intimidated by the size of the creature, she found herself following Uroh, stepping toward it in a state of awe.

"What about me?" Jalin cried.

"Hold me from behind," Kori told her. "Ride my back. The water will carry us both."

She waited while Jalin wrapped her arms around Kori's neck. Together they approached the whale's glistening bulk. Forcing herself to be bold, Kori kicked herself into deeper water. She reached out and touched the whale's skin. The surface was textured like well-worn leather, and there were fine grooves in it. She realized with a start that the orca's eye was no more than an arm's length away, and it was watching her.

Meanwhile, other whales were arraying themselves on either side, all of them facing the men and women venturing toward them.

"Do you really think they understand us?" Kori called to Uroh.

"They have watched us for many years now," he said. "And they have seen me often. The flipper there, at the side of the body—you should take hold of it."

Kori felt a sudden suspicion. "Have you done this before?"

"Sometimes," he said, "I have played with the orcas in the ocean."

Kori felt Jalin's breath against her neck in short, sharp gasps. "Hold tight," Kori called back to the girl, then kicked her legs and swam through the gentle swell, following the curve of the orca's body till she reached the side flipper. She went around behind it and took hold of it—gently at first, then tightly, as she realized how strong it was.

The whale started edging backward. Kori gave a cry of alarm, and Jalin seized her so fiercely, Kori feared the girl would strangle her.

"Be calm," Uroh called to them from the other side

of the whale's bulk. "I have the other flipper. I'm with you, and this creature won't harm us. That I know."

Water surged and flowed around Kori, and she felt the huge power of the whale as it turned. She saw many of the villagers watching her, shouting with excitement. Their excitement overwhelmed their fear; they went to the other whales that were waiting for them.

Meanwhile, Biffrar and his men were still on the beach. They had fallen silent, and were staring in awe. "They are people of the land," Kori murmured to herself. "I believe the ocean is the only thing they are truly scared of."

Without warning, the whale lashed its great tail. It pushed forward toward the open sea, launching itself so violently that Kori almost lost her grip. She gasped as the whale writhed, forcing its way through the water. Her arms felt as if they would wrench free from her shoulders. Jalin cried out—but not in fear, Kori realized. She found herself shouting too, with the sheer thrill of being lifted and hurled across the ocean.

When Kori looked over her shoulder she saw the sun's disk creeping above the forest, and the sky lightening to a delicate blue. Ahead of her the ocean shimmered, mysterious yet welcoming, and Kori exulted in the feeling as water rushed around her and under her belly and legs. Spray stung her face, and her body was buffeted by wave crests as the whale plowed wildly toward the horizon.

In moments when Kori could make out the view ahead, she saw the black silhouettes of the canoes coming closer. Uroh had been right; the great creature understood. It recognized him. It knew that he and his friends could only journey on the water in their wooden shells, and it had seen the shells being stolen from them.

The whale hit a high wave and water smashed against Kori's face. For a moment she could neither see nor breathe; but then the whale reared up and she found herself being lifted right above the waves as the orca gave a joyous leap.

Suddenly the canoes were so close, Kori could see the men in them. They were jumping to their feet, pointing and shouting.

The shore was now so far away, Kori feared she might not be strong enough to swim back if she were abandoned out here. But she felt no fear; she trusted the great whale.

She feared the men ahead of her, though. She eyed them anxiously as they loomed closer, and she wondered how she could possibly fight them. Then she recognized Meiri in one of the canoes—and the hunched form of Derneren with her. Kori let out a cry of dismay.

The whale suddenly plunged down. Kori was dragged beneath the surface, and she felt Jalin clutching her in panic. Water roared in her ears, the sky was a blurred, rippling circle of light above her—and then the whale twisted upward. Kori glimpsed a dark shape against the sky. It was one of the canoes, she realized. The whale struck it with its massive head, throwing it out of the water.

Suddenly Kori was back in the sunlight, blinking and gasping for air. She glimpsed warriors hurtling through the air, splashing into the water like carelessly tossed stones. Meanwhile, the whale ceased its wild forward motion and slumped down, floating beside the canoe, which lay empty on the waves.

Kori released her grip on the whale's flipper. She started swimming desperately toward the canoe, still with Jalin clinging behind her—and when she was able to see among the wave crests, she saw Uroh approaching from the other side.

"Climb into it!" Kori called to Jalin as they reached the canoe. Kori seized it between her hands and felt Jalin scrambling, almost losing her balance, flailing, finally sprawling in the canoe. Quickly Kori hoisted herself up and followed her.

The canoe rocked under them as Uroh joined them. Kori kneeled in the little vessel, steadying herself as it pitched and rolled in the swell. She gasped for breath, dizzy and dazed from her incredible journey.

"Jalin, take hold of the mast."

It was Uroh's voice. Kori turned and saw Jalin crawling forward, reaching out, and wrapping her arms around the mast. The girl's face looked fearful, but still determined.

Meanwhile, the whale that had brought them here was lingering close by, and its companions were approaching, bringing their human passengers with them. All around, warriors in the other canoes were shouting in panic. One man stood and cast his spear at the nearest whale. The flint tip struck the whale's head and lodged there for a moment, but was knocked free an instant later as the great creature plunged under the surface. A moment later the warrior screamed as the whale threw the canoe into the air, scattering men into the ocean.

The other whales did the same. Suddenly all the canoes were empty, and all the warriors were floundering with such desperation, Kori realized that most of them were unable to swim. Meanwhile, Kori's people were swimming directly to the canoes, boarding them, and yelling in triumph as they looked down on their enemies.

"People!" Uroh called out. "People, hear me! Hear me!" He paused, waiting for the villagers to turn toward him. "The whales will not kill," he shouted out. "That is for us to do."

Kori saw a man in the water almost within reach of the canoe where she was kneeling. She looked quickly around and saw a bundle of spears that the warriors had left in her canoe, lashed against its shell. She dragged one out, then stood up, hefting the weapon in her hand.

The man in the ocean saw her looming over him. He groped inside his robe, reaching for a knife. A moment later he pulled his arm out from under the water and shouted in defiance as he drew back his hand.

"Stop!" she warned him, raising his spear high.

The man paid no attention. His face contorted with desperation and fear as he hurled the knife at Kori.

As she ducked the blade, she saw that death was the only thing this man would ever really understand. She cast her spear and it plunged into the water, embedding itself in the warrior's chest. He screamed and started struggling futilely, choking as his face sank among the waves.

All around, Kori heard other men scream as her people attacked them. All the canoes had weapons stowed in them. The villagers shouted their defiance as they rained death upon their enemies. Meanwhile, as blood spread across the surface, the whales retreated, forming a wide circle, watching and perhaps trying to understand.

"Meiri," Kori shouted, as she turned away from the warrior she had slain. "Where is Meiri?"

Uroh didn't answer. He was standing at the prow, searching the ocean all around.

"Meiri!" Kori screamed, suddenly fearing that the girl might have been slain simply because she had been tossed into the ocean among the warriors.

Then she heard an answering cry. "There!" Jalin shouted. She pointed where Meiri was briefly visible among the waves, stretching out her hand toward Kori, even though she was a dozen paces away.

At first Kori couldn't understand. Meiri was a strong swimmer; there was no reason she should be helpless here. Then she realized that the girl was not alone. A man had grabbed her from behind and was holding her as a shield.

"Don't cast your spears!" Kori screamed to a canoe that was nearby. "My daughter is there!" She turned to Uroh. "Paddle us closer!" she cried. Yet as soon as she spoke, she remembered: the paddles were hidden on the shore.

Kori raised her own spear, looking for an opportunity to cast it at the man holding her daughter. "Fight him!" she shouted to Meiri. The warrior had only one arm around the girl. Meiri knew a dozen ways to break such a simple hold; Kori had taught them to her. At the very least, Meiri could swing her elbow into the man's face. But she seemed paralyzed with fear. She reached out futilely and Kori heard the girl's plaintive cry: "Help me!"

Kori's canoe rocked suddenly as Jalin stood up,

dragging her flint knife out of her belt. Jalin lifted her foot, rested it on the edge of the canoe, and then, before Kori could stop her, the girl threw herself into the water.

"No, Jalin!" Kori shouted.

The girl paid no attention. Even though she didn't know how to swim, she floundered and kicked herself through the waves, performing a clumsy imitation of the movements she had seen Kori make.

Kori started stripping off her own sodden robe, ready to dive in herself. "Wait," Uroh called. "This is something that Jalin needs to do."

Kori hesitated, holding her spear ready. She saw Jalin approaching Meiri, with the warrior still holding her as a shield. Jalin didn't hesitate; she swung her knife and stabbed it into the back of the warrior's hand.

He flinched, but still he held his hostage.

Jalin swung her arm again, this time jabbing her blade into the man's elbow, paralyzing his arm with pain. He yelled and released his grip, and now Meiri was free. She turned and swam wildly toward Kori, staring up at her as if she feared that Kori would somehow disappear in front of her eyes.

"Leave the man!" Kori shouted to Jalin.

Jalin glanced back—and she understood. She brought up her knees and kicked out, striking the warrior in the chest, pushing him away. Kori hurled her spear, and its point struck the man in his face. He gave a terrible gargling cry and blood splashed around him.

Meanwhile, Meiri was dragging herself onto the canoe. She threw herself forward, clutched Kori, and almost knocked her over. Kori seized the mast to steady herself, and she hugged her daughter, feeling tears of relief pricking her eyes—but she was still watching

Jalin. "Let go," Kori cried to Meiri. "I must save Jalin."

Meiri didn't hear—or chose not to. She clung to Kori with furious intensity.

Kori gave a little cry of frustration. She saw Jalin trying to swim back to the canoe, but her face was pale and she was gasping for breath. In desperation, Kori seized another spear, turned it around, and reached out with the blunt end of the shaft.

Jalin was exhausting herself. Her eyes showed renewed fear as she realized the limits to her strength. She made one last desperate effort, kicked herself forward, reached out—and seized the spear. Kori shouted with relief as she dragged the girl toward the canoe. She took the spear between both her hands and with all her strength, she hoisted Jalin up.

Jalin struggled and managed to hook her elbow over the side of the canoe, and then her leg. She dragged herself in over the side, shivering and gasping, with water pouring out of her robe. She fell down into the bottom of the canoe, smiling with relief, still holding her knife in her hand.

"Thank you," Kori called to her, feeling so moved by emotion, she could hardly speak.

Jalin held up her hand. "Derneren," she gasped.

At first Kori didn't really hear her. But Jalin shouted the word again, and a third time, and finally Kori understood. She glanced down at Meiri. "Let me go!" she told the girl again.

"No." Meiri was still clinging to her. "I'm scared!"

"There he is," said Uroh, pointing to the east.

Kori squinted into the rising sun. One canoe had drifted apart from the others and was edging toward the orcas who still lay close by. The canoe looked as if it was empty; but Kori saw an arm moving furtively, reaching over the side, dipping into the water. Derneren had saved himself, she realized. He was lying in the canoe, quietly paddling it away.

In a spasm of anger, Kori seized Meiri's hands and pried them off her. She glanced around and saw her people in their canoes. She saw their faces change as they realized that Derneren was trying to evade them.

"Leave him!" she shouted. "This concerns me, and me only." She reached down, pulled off her moccasins, and thrust one into Meiri's hand. "Paddle with this!" Kori cried.

Meiri looked frightened and uncomprehending.

"Just lean over the side and paddle with it," Kori told her, trying to speak more gently.

Reluctantly Meiri moved to obey.

"Let me help," Jalin said, trying to sit up.

"No," said Kori. "You've already done too much." She turned to Uroh and held out the other moccasin.

He shook his head. "Give me the spear," he said.

Kori gave him a fierce look—then laughed grimly. "You had your chance to kill him fourteen years ago," she said. "Now it's my turn."

Uroh returned her stare—and then, slowly, he smiled. He stepped down from the prow of the canoe and made his way over to her. "So," he said, "you don't acknowledge my authority on the ocean anymore."

"Just this one time." She thrust the moccasin into his hand, stepped around him, and moved forward.

The other canoe wasn't far away. With Meiri and Uroh both paddling, Kori saw the gap steadily narrowing. She spread her legs to steady herself, and she raised her spear. She found herself thinking of everything that had happened in the past days—all the fear, the pain, the cruelty, and the lives that had been lost. She felt her anger rising, fueling her resolve, her absolute determination that this man should never have the power to cause such suffering again.

Ahead of her, her target came into view as it crested a wave, then sank down out of sight, then came back into view again. Kori waited impatiently. She glanced down and realized that there were no more spears after this one was gone. Very well, she thought to herself: she would fell him with one stroke.

She looked forward. Now the other canoe was only a dozen paces away. "Derneren!" she shouted.

For a long moment there was no response. Then a thin, bent figure struggled slowly to his knees, holding the mast to keep himself from falling. He saw Kori standing proud, with her spear held high; and he saw the rest of her people behind her in their canoes, watching and waiting. Finally he saw blood on the water and knew that the last of his warriors had died.

"Have mercy!" he shouted.

Kori stared at him, remembering how he had ordered his men to abuse her, and how he had vowed that she would die. She remembered how he had held her daughter hostage, and how her own son had died serving him.

"Mercy!" Derneren shouted again, as she came closer. His face was as pallid as ocean foam in the morning light. He was shivering in his waterlogged robe. He was a pathetic figure; a broken, scared old man.

"The Old Ones have deserted you, Derneren," Kori shouted at him. She prepared herself to strike him down—and then, as she found herself yearning

to see his blood, she hesitated. She despised the pleasure that men took in killing. She had seen people
moved by a need for vengeance, and she always
doubted the wisdom of it. Derneren had caused so
many deaths, but would the victims be brought back
to life if Derneren's own life was taken? If she killed
him like this, coldly and without mercy, wouldn't that
mean she was no better, really, than he? If she was
going to be true to her principles, shouldn't she take
him prisoner?

She lowered her spear a fraction—and he saw her
hesitate. His lips pulled back from his ruined teeth and
his one good eye widened. Her canoe had drifted so
close to his, they were only five paces apart. Kori saw
the tendons in his neck pull tight under his withered
skin, and she realized that while he was holding the
mast with his left hand, his right hand had been hidden
in the folds of his robe. His piteous expression turned
into a look of wild hatred as he brought his right hand
into view, holding a spear that he had been concealing
behind his back.

Kori's anger rose up. It was so intense, she could
barely stand. With a wild shout she flung her spear, so
quickly that Derneren never had the chance even to lift
his up.

If Kori had moved more carefully, her aim would
have been true. As it was, her spear flew wide. It struck
Derneren in his left arm—the arm holding the mast of
his canoe.

He yelled in pain. Instinctively he let go of the mast,
dropped his spear, and clutched his wound with his
right hand. The canoe pitched under him as a wave
passed by, and he stumbled. He threw out his hands to

steady himself—too late. His knees hit the side of his canoe and he tumbled into the water.

Kori was as angry with herself now as she was with him. She turned, searching the canoe again for another spear, but there was none. Meanwhile, she heard Derneren floundering.

Uroh rose calmly to his feet. He cupped his hands around his mouth and gave his whale-cry.

Kori looked and saw that an orca was close by. It twitched its tail and edged forward, trying to understand Uroh's message.

Uroh pointed at the figure struggling in the water. He spread his own hands wide, to show they were empty. He opened his mouth wide in a silent scream, then closed it, clicking his teeth together.

The orca came closer with a renewed sense of purpose. It nudged Derneren with its great blunt snout, as if it were sniffing him. Derneren saw the huge creature looming over him, and he yelled in terror.

"Yes!" Kori cried.

Again, Uroh cupped his hands and gave his whale-cry.

Slowly the orca opened its jaws. Its mouth was so wide, it could have swallowed an entire canoe. Derneren thrashed in the water, trying desperately to distance himself from the orca. He saw the huge row of conical teeth and the gaping throat beyond them.

Uroh opened his mouth as he had before—then snapped it shut.

The whale lowered its head. Water poured into its mouth, sweeping Derneren with it. The man flailed helplessly as the great jaws closed on him, and his scream was extinguished. Suddenly he was gone as if he had never been—except for a telltale spurt of red that leaked from one side of the orca's mouth and trickled down its glossy black skin into the ocean.

Uroh gave the call one last time. He held up both arms and waved them.

The orca sank lower in the sea. It vented a geyser of spray from its blowhole. Then it turned and plunged under the waves, and a moment later Kori saw its great tail churning the water as it swam away, turning toward the open sea, leading the rest of the whales behind it.

29

Later—much later—when all the celebrations were over, and the people of the Ocean Tribe had feasted in the Meeting Place till the middle of the night, and Kori had been honored and praised and honored again, she retreated to her hut with her husband, her daughter, and Jalin.

Meiri was still panicky and insecure despite all Kori's efforts to calm her. The girl had not been physically harmed while she was Derneren's prisoner, yet the experience had taken its toll. Even now, in the familiar little hut where she had lived her entire life, she trembled and looked fearfully at the door as if she expected more warriors to come bursting in at any moment.

Meanwhile, Jalin moved with new pride and confidence, having faced her greatest fears and overcome them. When she asked shyly if she could spend that night in Kori's hut, Kori was quick to agree, because even though Jalin and Meiri were almost the same age,

Jalin now seemed ten years older. Since she had freed Meiri from the warrior who'd held her in the ocean, Meiri trusted her. It would comfort Meiri if the two girls shared the same bed.

Kori placed a bear skin over them, kissed Meiri on the cheek and stroked her hair, then turned and joined Uroh where he lay waiting for her. At first she felt there were a thousand things that she wanted to say, to assuage her guilt again and reaffirm the trust and respect and need that she felt with such painful intensity. She wasn't sure how these things could be said with Meiri and Jalin not yet asleep, lying so close by—but then she saw the look in Uroh's eyes, and she realized that she didn't really need to say very much at all. He looked at her with such love and pleasure, there was no doubt that he forgave her for turning away from him.

"Thank you," Kori whispered as she lay next to him and he embraced her. "I need you, Uroh, and I have always needed you."

He tightened his grip for a moment, then relaxed. "We each need the other person's special talents," he said.

She nodded silently.

They lay in silence for a while. Kori was so tired, her body felt immensely heavy and her muscles seemed powerless. At the other end of the hut she heard Jalin whispering some reassurance to Meiri, and after that their breathing gradually quietened as they fell asleep, because they, too, were exhausted.

Finally Kori sensed Uroh relaxing, drifting off beside her, and she knew that if she had any sense she would join him. Somehow, though, her mind refused to allow it, at least for a little while. How could she rest while there was still so much to relive, contemplate, and understand?

It was painfully clear to her now, she had been too fierce toward her husband and children. Uroh had retreated into solitude because he felt he had no role to play in her life. Feroh had felt trapped, overwhelmed by her, desperate to prove himself as a man in the face of her female power. Of course, he had been haunted by his own strange madness—but her relentless strength had made it worse.

Meiri also had been a victim. Kori had always assumed that the girl would be eager to inherit the role of chieftain of the Ocean Tribe. In fact, it seemed so natural, she had never actually asked Meiri whether she wanted it. Instead, Kori had spent endless days teaching Meiri to be strong—because otherwise, how could Meiri possibly lead the tribe?

Well, it was clear now that Meiri had no desire to take care of her people; she wanted her people to take care of her.

Kori felt shaken and lonely as she recognized the great gulf between herself and her daughter, and she felt melancholy with the knowledge that because she was sterile, she would never have another chance to have a daughter who shared her bold spirit.

On the other hand, there was Jalin. During the feast, Jalin had taken Kori aside and made a strange confession, claiming that she never wanted to return to Green Valley. She begged, instead, to join the Ocean Tribe.

"Anyone can live among us," Kori told the girl. "I have told you already, my house will always be your house. But why would you want to abandon your own people?"

"Because there's so much I need to learn," Jalin said. "I want to know how to cast a spear, and how to defend myself the way you do, with your hands and feet, if you have no weapon. I want to know how to hunt—and of course," she smiled with embarrassment, "I must learn to swim."

"You want me to teach you these things," Kori said, with a feeling of wonder.

Jalin nodded. Despite the bravery she had shown when she saved Meiri, she was still shy when she faced Kori.

"Well, of course I can teach you," Kori said, thinking of all the times when she had wanted to teach Meiri, and Meiri had endured it reluctantly, without pleasure. "Still," Kori went on, "there's your mother to think about. Won't you want to be with her?"

Jalin's expression changed, becoming somber as she contemplated something that seemed almost too difficult for her to say. "I haven't told you who my mother is," she said.

"You mean, I know her?" Kori asked.

Jalin nodded. "She is not a good woman. She was the one who disciplined the other women while Derneren's warriors ruled the valley."

Kori felt shocked. "You mean, Magra?"

"Yes, Magra." Jalin shrugged, forcing herself to be strong. "I don't want to go back to her, now or ever."

Kori needed time to consider the idea of Jalin turning to her in this way. But now that the feasting was done, and everyone was at peace, with Jalin and Meiri both sleeping close by, it didn't seem so strange to Kori after all. She had lost a son—and she had gained a new daughter, even though the girl was still a stranger to her in many ways.

Well, Kori told herself, she had never been afraid to live her life differently from other people, so it shouldn't worry her to think about adopting Jalin. Maybe, one day, Jalin could even inherit the leadership of the tribe if she proved herself to the people.

The thought gave Kori a feeling of hope—yet she was wary of her own optimism, because she also saw that Biffrar had been right when he told her that she was naive. Her blindness had allowed her to think that her people would be as brave and eager to defend their tribe as she was. The reality had turned out to be crushingly different: her people were weak and fearful.

Were they any different now? Had they been changed by their great adventure, riding the orcas out into the ocean? Kori didn't think so. They had followed her and Uroh. Even now, most of them lacked the courage to act alone.

Could she ever change them? Could she be a leader like Biffrar, imposing discipline and cruelties on boy-children so that they would grow up to be fierce hunters and fighters?

Kori shuddered as she thought of it. The idea was repugnant. She never wanted to see this aggressive spirit dominating the menfolk of her tribe.

She remembered how the White River Tribe had helped her, lying in wait and killing the young warriors who had started up the northern hillside. How wonderful it would be if there was a tribe like that, willing to shoulder the burden of guarding her people. But Biffrar was back among his own people now; he had come to her aid only so long as their tribes were both threatened by a common enemy. He would have no reason to defend her in the future.

Or would he? Kori reminded herself of the strengths of her people. Their skill as mariners enabled them to catch far more food than they could eat, and many of them were fine craftsmen, weaving beautiful baskets and creating finely ornamented robes. The White River Tribe, like other peoples who dwelled nearby, were always eager to trade with the Ocean Tribe because the Ocean Tribe had so much to offer.

Kori saw something that had never occurred to her before. Trade could mean more than simply exchanging objects. Her people could trade their foods and handicrafts for something very different: security. Why should her people try to learn the art of war when it was not something they were good at, and another tribe already possessed that skill? Her people should concentrate on the things they could do best, and then use their foods and clothes to pay Biffrar's people to defend them.

The idea was exciting, and it seemed as if it should work. Biffrar had always been willing to trade; he certainly saw the sense of offering something and receiving something else in return. Surely, he would be flattered if she told him that even though her people possessed a strange, powerful magic enabling them to swim with orcas, they still needed his help.

Here, then, was a way for the Ocean Tribe to be secure without turning its people away from their generous, gentle traditions. Perhaps it was another of Kori's naive ideas, but maybe her naive nature didn't have to be such a disadvantage after all. It meant that she could act without fear of failure, because she wasn't as cautious as other people. She could even achieve goals that seemed unattainable, because she felt free to tackle any task in a new way.

This was something she shared with Uroh, this willingness to follow a strange path no matter what other people might think.

Kori nestled closer to him in the silence of their little hut. She felt calmer now, although she did still feel remorse over the way she had allowed her personality to dominate the people around her. If she had been less demanding, less forceful, would fate have protected her from adversity?

It seemed to work that way for Uroh. Yet if Kori had been any less fierce, any less courageous, she would have remained a slave in Green Valley—or she would have been killed by Werror when she faced him.

Now she understood. Her strength was a wonderful, indispensable tool—when she used it for herself. It caused trouble only when she tried to force other people to change themselves to be like her. So, suddenly it was clear to her: it was a fine thing, this strength of hers. It had helped to build the Ocean Tribe. She should maintain it without shame or regret—so long as she was wise enough to allow other people to follow their own paths, no matter what those paths might be.

Kori remembered what Uroh himself had said just before he fell asleep beside her: that each of them needed the other's special talents. The thought gave her a new sense of security—and a growing feeling of contentment as she lay with him in their little home, listening to sound of the distant surf, and knowing that they were safe from harm.